WONDERLAND II

WONDERLAND II

FEAST OR FAMINE

ACT ONE

J. M. Alexia

Cover design by Podium Publishing

ISBN: 978-1-0394-2989-5

Published in 2023 by Podium Publishing, ULC
www.podiumaudio.com

Thanks to my friends, readers, and patrons
who have helped me get through the year.
I couldn't do this without you.

WONDERLAND II

PART ONE

MAD TEA PARTY (REDUX)

OR, "NEW FRIENDS, NEW FACES, AND THE NEIGHBORHOOD POTLUCK

Then they all crowded round her once more, while the Dodo solemnly presented the thimble, saying 'We beg your acceptance of this elegant thimble'; and, when it had finished with this short speech, they all cheered.

Alice thought the whole thing very absurd, but they all looked so grave that she did not dare to laugh; and, as she could not think of anything to say, she simply bowed, and took the thimble, looking as solemn as she could.

—*Alice in Wonderland*, Lewis Carroll

I

Twice upon a time, I find myself haunted by glass in a strange and danger-ous wonderland.

Once, I ruined the life of a girl who thought she could trust me; now, I dream my past self's machinations through that ruined girl's eyes. Once, I plucked a needle of glass and wove it into a blood-red blade; now, that blade returns to my hands dormant but awakening. Once and now again, I feel the shadow of a Glass Tower and a Crawling Chaos. I have felt the touch of a dark and terrible Demiurge, and I wonder how far back her influence stretches.

I drift to wakefulness in a sea of confusion and curiosity, mind whirling with fragments of memory. I am Reska Ines Zelic, sick with jealousy and long-ing. I am Homura Annatar Bloodfallen, twisting the truth to get my way.

I am Maven Alice, lying in bed with a cat curled in my arms.

I groan, head still spinning, and find myself wishing that just once I'd be able to wake up in this fantasy otherworld without having to process entirely new revelations about the nature of my presence here. I mean, I get that mysti-cally important dreams are a staple of the fantasy genre, but *every night*? Hells, I even had one of these vision-dreams while knocked out from a fae sleep spell.

I feel Cheshire stir in my arms, the changeling seeming to wake at my noise of discontent. I open my eyes and see the white-furred cat stretch her limbs and yawn, which of course gets me yawning too. The cat steps out of my arms and hops to the floor below, and I keenly feel the absence of her warmth, though I still have too much pride to ask her to return.

I roll from my side onto my back and stare up at the plain beige ceiling. "We don't *have* to get up," I grumble-mumble, unwilling to part with my bed quite so soon. It's not the comfiest bed I've ever slept in, sure, and there are still bloodstains from the two times that I've slept in it while covered in my own blood—that is to say, the two times that I've slept in it—but . . . eh, a bed's a bed, and I'm used to sleeping on the floor.

I hear Cheshire's rich laughter, and then her pale face is looming over mine, once more in her human form—or rather, human-adjacent, as those cat ears remind me. Her mismatched blue-and-yellow eyes gleam with mirth, and when she smiles I see hints of her cute little fangs.

"You know," she says, "we *are* on a timetable, but far be it from me to say no to more cat-cuddles."

I grimace, but of course she's right, so I reluctantly kick the covers off and rise from the bed, Cheshire taking a step back to give me space. Then I stop and blink a few times at Cheshire, because her appearance has changed. "You look different."

Cheshire gives a little twirl and shows off her new outfit. "You like?" She's traded her skimpy JRPG outfit for something relatively more modest: a baggy sweater with thumb-hole sleeves, faded jeans, and scuffed sneakers. "New dynamic, new threads. This is what I'm more used to wearing anyway."

Were those other outfits just another vector of manipulation, then? Did she pick those to throw me off, knowing I would be made uncomfortable by how they accentuated her attractiveness? Did she—

I blink hard and try to banish my paranoid ideation. *We agreed to give her a chance. Trust is a risk, but risk is the creed we've sworn to live by.*

I force a smile and tell her honestly, "You look great. It suits you a lot better."

Cheshire preens and gives a little wiggle, smiling, but then she pauses and claps her hands together. "Oh! One more detail: I can't make my ears disappear, because they're part of my changeling tell, but I *can* hide them under a hat. That's what I used to do when I was mortal, and it might be useful if we want to keep anyone else from figuring me out like Bashe did."

She lifts her hands and materializes a knit beanie cap with two raised parts made to look like cat ears. She slides it over her own cat ears, fitting perfectly, and once it's snugly in place she looks like an ordinary human girl, albeit one with heterochromia and white hair. "Ta-dah!" She grins.

"Cute." Then I frown, the implication registering that at some point as a mortal she felt the *need* to hide her ears. A reminder that, if her story is to be believed—and again, that's the choice I've made—then Cheshire has spent a great deal of her life as an outsider for her changeling nature. And that, inevitably, draws me to my dreams.

I remember Reska: aberrant, monster, demon. I remember her shame and fear, cursed with magic that made her a pariah in her own home. And I remember Homura, lovely lying Homura, with her words sweet like poison. From one outcast to another, it's so easy to pull the heartstrings. *But which of us is really in control?*

Perhaps neither of us. A wave of revulsion passes over me and I shiver at the memory of Nyarlathotep's violating touch. Whether I'm taking advantage of Cheshire or she's taking advantage of me, we're both just puppets on the Soul-Sculptor's strings.

Cheshire sees my shiver and tilts her head, expression curious. "What's up?"

I grimace. "Just . . . processing implications." I wave a hand dismissively. "We can talk about it later. Breakfast?"

"Sure! You'll have to make me physical again, though."

I don't remember unsummoning her, but I can see the charm bracelet lying on the bed where Cheshire had previously curled. "Ah." *So she can unsummon herself. That . . . probably shouldn't surprise me, it only makes sense.*

I grab the bracelet and hold it out, beginning to concentrate on the summoning ritual. I take in Cheshire's new form and try to burn it into my mind like the way my dreams have been seared into memory. I say the words, calling upon my authority as a demon and the inherent properties of the anchor object I've chosen for her.

"Let the stuff of dreams become your body, and may you ever take the form you please. Rise, Cheshire, O geist of mine, and walk with me along this winding path."

Physicality fills Cheshire's form, and once again she moves with mass and solidity. She stretches her newly physical limbs and again I am struck with a keen difference in detail: the first time I gave her a body, she stretched to tease me; this time, there's no artifice or showmanship to her casual motions. She's just stretching.

I wonder . . . is it just to put me at ease, or has she really accepted taking the long road to a relationship? Is this a fresh start, or just a new mode of attack? I tense, struggling to halt all the suspicious thoughts running through my mind. Paranoia is my default state, but I refuse to let it control me.

Cheshire looks at me and I see uncertainty in her eyes, in the corners of her lips, in all the little micro expressions of her face. I can taste the faintest whiff of fear, with that strange demonic sense of mine, and I know that she is afraid of what I might think of her. She told me that she was scared, in that dark hollow in the heart of my soul, and I believed her. I still do.

"Thank you," I say softly. "I . . . I don't want you to think I'm ungrateful, whatever else I may feel. I couldn't have gotten this far without you. And . . . I don't just mean power. Thank you for being there for me when I needed comfort, and there to challenge me when I needed perspective. Thank you for . . . for understanding me. I know I'm not the easiest person to deal with, and I know it wasn't really your choice, but . . . I appreciate you. Thank you, Cheshire."

Her expression softens, and her eyes are wet with held-back tears. "Thank you for letting me in, when it mattered most. I hope I can continue to earn your trust, Alice. I . . ." She hesitates, lets out a ragged breath, and looks away from me. "I think I'll go get something ready for breakfast."

"Thanks. I, um, I'll be out in a minute." I watch her leave the room, closing the door behind her, and when she's gone I let out a deep breath of my own.

Okay. Let's utilize a classic healthy coping strategy and bundle up all our complicated feelings about Cheshire to deal with literally never. Instead, we can play with our shiny new sword!

I curl my fingers around the swept hilt of my recently acquired war rapier. I lift the weapon from where I had left it leaning against the bedside, and I am mesmerized by its crimson blade and the memories that it evokes. I remember Homura holding this sword, naming it as her sorcerer Crest: Vorpal, the Blood-stained Blade. And dimly, in less detail and less clarity, I remember the months of effort that went into forging this blade.

I remember the night horrors we carved through to retrieve the bloodstone ore. I remember teaching myself—I remember Reska teaching Homura—how to attune to her affinity, how to shape it and externalize it. I remember the needle of red glass you—I, Homura, dammit—produced as if by miracle.

Somehow, this artifact was made by *me*. A younger me, parted by time and space, full of rage and hate with a silver tongue, but still me in ways I can't ignore. I made this sword, named it my Vorpal Blade, a weapon fit for an Alice. And now that I have returned to my forgotten wonderland, Vorpal has returned to me. That cannot possibly be coincidence, and I am more convinced than ever that the Homura of my dreams is somehow my past self. It feels right, narratively.

I take a few swings with the blade, finding it perfectly fitted to my palm and so easy to maneuver. I have so, so many questions, but I think my very first question has to be purely practical: can I store this sword inside my soul, or will I have to carry it with me wherever I go? I take a final test swing, then picture one of the many rooms of my soul's castle and send Vorpal away.

At the very start of my very first vision of Reska's tragic story, the Shadow-born princess trapped a sentry artifact inside an extradimensional space: her second shadow, which she identified as a manifestation of her soul's pleroma. She said, "No artifact would allow itself to be imprisoned for even an hour's length."

However, I've held several artifacts in my own extradimensional space for far longer than an hour; my bug-summoning artifact [Swarmheart] has spent most of a day—or more—inside my throne world, while my more recent acquisition [Hunter's Marker] has been there for at least half a day. Neither of them have given any indication of fighting back against that storage, so will Vorpal also go without a fight?

Alright, let's keep an eye on that while we grab breakfast, see if there's any reaction. With the artifact blade secured in my throne world I finally step out of the bedroom and into the apartment proper.

It's weird having this whole place basically to myself. It's not a penthouse or anything, but it's still a very nice and very modern apartment . . . in another world full of magic and monsters, where rent as a concept doesn't exist because this is a city maintained by simulacra of humans with hollow souls being puppeted by a terrifying eldritch horror convinced that she's made "paradise."

Okay, so maybe the nice apartment isn't the weirdest part, but it makes for some very surreal contrast.

I join Cheshire in the kitchen, where she is snacking on some of those coconut rice cakes that Bashe brought with the rest of his grocery run. I probably wasn't going to eat those, ever, because I don't like coconut, so I'm glad to see Cheshire enjoying them. I rifle through the pantry and fridge but Bashe didn't actually get us any proper breakfast food, and a quick check of my throne world's kitchen reveals that I *also* neglected to acquire any item of food more suitable for before noon than after it.

Ah well, it won't be the first time I've eaten like a scavenging possum. I grab one entire hunk of blue cheese from my throne world and wash a tomato from the apartment fridge, and then I chow down while contemplating the question of my new artifact.

Vorpal hasn't sprung out of me yet, and I don't feel any strain on my soul that might indicate it *trying* to break free. I have to assume the artifact that Reska captured was less metaphysically important than a full-blown sorcerer Crest, so why isn't Vorpal fighting me?

It could be that artifacts of the "new" system—which I can now confirm to be new after a comment from Cheshire—are more placid and easier to seal away . . . or perhaps the key distinction is that I'm not "imprisoning" them because they're metaphysically tagged as mine to hoard, or maybe it's some quality of my throne world that allows for such storage. If affinity magic pre-dates the existence of Thrones and Truths, maybe sorcerers like Reska didn't have throne worlds at all.

From my limited time in Pandaemonium, I've learned of two parts to the soul: the pleroma, which Bashe called the soul's "outer body" and named essential to casting spells and storing mana; and the core, which contains one's fundamental qualities—with the animus at its very center, the animating principle of the self. Perhaps my throne world is more core than pleroma, and that's what allows it to hold artifacts.

It certainly seems to be holding. I'll keep checking in on it, of course, but for now it would appear that Homura's Crest has no issue staying inside my throne world.

. . . Which spares me to think of the other pertinent details from my latest vision: the presence of the Crawling Chaos, the mention of a tower made of glass, and the reveal that my presumed-younger self chose the name "Homura Annatar Bloodfallen."

I almost laugh, and having polished off both cheese and tomato I quickly grab a peach and a plum to keep my mouth distracted so I don't give the game away to Cheshire. Homura Annatar Bloodfallen. What an absurd name. The first and last are characters from anime, and that middle name . . . I know it from somewhere, but where? It seems very fantasy, and I'm pretty sure it's from a book, but I can't quite put my finger on *which* book. That's going to bug the shit out of me until I figure it out.

"You know, you really are cute when you're lost in your own head, Allie. How was the meal?"

I blush as I realize I've been staring off into nowhere while Cheshire's right there next to me, leaning against a kitchen counter and watching me think. There's an empty box of rice cakes next to her, and I've consumed the remainder of the food I grabbed. "Sorry, lots to think about. Uh, good. Blue cheese is divine ambrosia. We should probably grab actual breakfast food at some point, though."

The catgirl laughs lightly. "Yeah, probably. But I'm actually a little more interested in the meal you had last night: the one that came with meat." Her gaze sharpens, and I get the distinct feeling that we're back in geist-and-demon mode.

"Right. Yeah. The woman I killed and ate. Probably worth talking about." I dump the fruit pits and pour a glass of lemonade from my throne world. I take a few big gulps, then set the glass down, lean against the fridge, and close my eyes.

I breathe deep and let my senses rove at random over my body. I felt something when I ate Mahiri, just like I felt something when I ate the hunter in the hall of doors, and when I bit into the werewolf, and into Lena. Each successive act of hunger and consumption brought something new into me: the blood of a husk, the blood of a beast, the blood of a kill, and the blood of a soul.

I flex my fingers, and I feel strength in my hands. I breathe, and my breath is clear and easy. I roll my shoulders, and I feel coiled potential in my spine. I run my tongue along my teeth, and I hunger to sink my fangs into someone just to prove I can. I could, too; I could have any meal I wanted, with just a bit of effort and will.

"I feel . . . powerful. Confident, mentally and physically. I feel an energy, contained but present, crackling and full of potential. Like reified volition." I open my eyes and stare straight into Cheshire's. "I feel indomitable. I feel hungry for more."

Cheshire watches me with those clever eyes, taking it all in. "Do you still feel that way when you think of facing Averrich?"

Like a layer of frost settling over my skin, that feeling of power and strength dampens. Averrich, the man with a soul like old stories and moonlit nights. Averrich, the elven huntsman with a cabal of hunters and beasts arrayed around him. "I think I could take any of his followers at this point: the hunters, the goblins, the imp and the lycan, even the owlbear. But even just from that short interaction, I could feel something of the difference in power between his followers and the fae himself."

And he's coming for me, soon. I pull [Hunter's Marker] from my soul, the artifact dagger that I made in Averrich's throne room from the residue of half a dozen tracking spells. The dagger is still keyed to Averrich, and a tickling in the back of my mind gives me the sense that he's far from me, but he's on the move . . . and I bet I know why.

"I think he's already moving against his rivals," I tell Cheshire. "Maneuvering himself and his forces in position to strike against the other candidates as soon as the Nobles call for their Game of Glass."

"Which includes us," she says grimly, "if we're to believe his guess at Eirdryd acting on someone else's orders."

Eirdryd Llewellyn, who bought my name for a magic compass, and who may be working for another of this Labyrinth's Noble rulers. I'm still disturbed by the idea that our chance encounter in the forest may have been premeditated, but that's a problem for later. "Even if Averrich is wrong about that, it won't change his actions; he has plenty of reason to hunt us down."

Cheshire nods. "So what's the plan?"

I crack my knuckles and grin. "Simple: we murk his ass before he can murk ours. Which means finding whatever [Find the Path] thinks will help us win that fight." I call the wheel of flame to my hand, its burning arrow currently pointing toward the door of my apartment.

My geist smiles back at me. "Sounds good. Shall we?"

"Absolutely. But first, I should *probably* change out of these bloody rags and take a shower."

My clothes keep getting ruined by people stabbing me, which is incredibly rude of them, to be honest. It would be nice to find an outfit that regenerates on its own, but barring that, maybe I could grow some extra layers of bone plating for modesty? Since my body has doll anatomy and porcelain skin, I could go around wearing just a cloak, like Ryūko in that one episode of *Kill La Kill*, but that still might be more fanservice than I'm comfortable with.

Ooo, what if I could get one of those cool magic cloaks that are like, made of shadows and cosmos and whatever, and they're always as long as they need to be for any given scene, so I could wrap it around myself and also let it flutter dramatically in the nonexistent wind? Yeah, that sounds rad, kinda wanna find something like that. Or make something like that, since I do have an artificer superpower.

If the sky's the limit, maybe I could get a symbiote suit like Gwenom. Actually that one might be feasible—maybe it's close enough to *Creepy Crawlies* that I could leverage my Truths to get a spell? Wait, Truths, could I make an outfit out of my own blood? Or could I clothe myself in my own shadow like Darquesse?

Man, now that I think about it, there are a lot of fictional characters that have weird relationships with clothing.

I step out of the shower, dry off, and consider what to wear. I dumped my damaged vampire magician outfit in my throne world, and I've got a few choices to replace it with. I could pull out the witch's ensemble I put together during our trip to the mega-mall, but it's a bit more femme than I'm feeling right now and it doesn't seem appropriate for my character now that my build has switched from "blood-draining fragile-as-glass summoner" to "rapier-swinging soul-eating juggernaut." I mean, I'm not invincible—yet—but if I can get my hands on someone I can basically guarantee that they'll die long before I do, and that leads to a very specific set of battle tactics.

I could be lazy and just wears jeans and a graphic tee, but the semiotic logic of this world's magic system would penalize my spellcasting as a consequence. So, okay, let's try to work through that semiotic meaning. I conjure and dismiss articles of clothing in sequence and examine each one of them, trying to interpret what meaning they would broadcast and how that might tie into my Truths as a demon.

My three Truths are Blood, Gluttony, and Fear, and the animus I have chosen to live by is Feast or Famine: the principle of ultimate risk or sacrifice in exchange for ultimate reward. My Truth of Blood contains the concepts of risk and sacrifice, but also bonds, both mutual and parasitic. My Truth of Gluttony is a hunger for power and knowledge, and is associated with consuming flame and the ravenous Abyss. My Truth of Fear contains fear of death, rule through fear, and fear of abandonment—the last of which could be reframed as a desire for attention if we wanted something more active and positive.

The desire for attention could be read two ways when applied to fashion: something distinctive and flashy, like this gothic lolita dress, or something skimpy and revealing, like this backless red dress. The skimpy reading would actually synergize with risk, since baring skin is inviting the point of a sword, and it would synergize with bonds, if you consider the natural endpoint of that kind of attention to be intimate interaction.

The flashy gothic lolita outfit might align with other elements of Fear if I added details like bird skulls and other bits of macabre imagery, but I'm not sure about my other Truths. Maybe if I took the witch's hat and swapped the funeral veil for a pair of glasses, I could channel the "nerdy sorceress" aesthetic and splice in Gluttony's concepts.

. . . Hmm. It does occur to me now that there is a very obvious intersection point between "nerdy sorceress" and "skimpy outfit." Fuck, have I accidentally logicked myself into dressing like a sexy anime witch?

No no, we can reason our way out of this one. Whatever aesthetic we settle on, it still has to feel like us, right? So anything sexy is definitely out of the picture.

Okay, counterpoint: Cheshire would definitely say that's us being self-loathing and possibly gender dysphoric. She would also, in all likelihood, be correct about that.

Bleh. Nope, not engaging with that one.

I pick the skater dress with the black-and-white tentacle pattern, the black-and-white stripey leggings, the lace-up thigh-high boots, and the oversized witch hat. For maximum spell-boosting I should really keep thinking about the optimal aesthetic choice, but for now I just want to get moving and figure it all out later.

Cheshire beams at me as I emerge back into the living room. "Oh, nice, that dress was my favorite. You know, with round shades and some kind of shawl you could get a real hipster goth vibe."

I pause, envisioning that, and find the image actually quite appealing. "Okay, remind me to do that when we get a chance. If we get a chance. I have no idea where this spell will lead us."

I summon the burning compass and we follow it out of the apartment complex and into the city of Sanctuary 7. To my surprise, it's still nighttime outside, but then it was still bright out when I crashed in bed after making it back to the apartment, so I guess that makes sense.

The starry sky glitters above, and lampposts line streets devoid of cars. A sprawl of stone and metal greets me, the city of grand architecture and neon signs that is both paradise and prison to its free-willed inhabitants.

A stone amphitheater dominates the skyline in one direction, a vast structure that I know to be the domain of the Beast of Lamentation and Euphoria. My compass points away from it and toward the other major structure visible from here: the massive techno-pyramid that contains several malls' worth of "shops." Because this is a Sanctuary in the Labyrinth, and money doesn't exist here, I still maintain that "shops" is a misnomer.

We start walking toward the Pyraplex, the streets relatively clear except for a few early risers. A quick scan with my soul sight shows none of the people milling about to be actual people, just figments, and [Hunter's Marker] doesn't show Averrich getting any closer, so we seem to be in the clear. For now.

Cheshire actually walks alongside me, hands in her pockets and humming to herself, rather than vanishing into my shadow or turning into an animal. She seems pensive about something.

"What's on your mind?" I ask.

The geist bites her lip and looks up at the stars. "Thinking about the Game of Glass. I'm . . . nervous."

I raise an eyebrow. "What, don't like our chances against the competition? We don't even know who most of them are going to be yet, beyond guesses."

Cheshire laughs. "No, not that. I'm confident we'll overcome whoever stands in our way. No, what I'm really worried about is what comes *after.*"

Ah. "You mean the shard." The corporeal animus of the Beast of Lamentation and Euphoria, which grants its wielder godlike power at the cost of stagnation. The glass shard that the Beast offered me when it plucked me from the Reveler's maze just in time to escape the hunter on my tail.

"Yeah. It's irrational of me; you rejected the shard when it was offered, after all, and that was when the Beast was just going to *give it* to you. But . . . I get nervous. What if, after fighting off all the other contenders, you change your mind?" She's still looking away from me, toward the sky, but I can clearly see the lines of worry on her face.

"I won't," I say with conviction. "I made the choice to trust you, to shape a new animus, and I'm sticking with it. We are in this together." That doesn't stop me from having my own doubts and fears, but I have a lot of practice managing paranoia. "And hey, even if I start to feel some sunk cost from whatever goes down in the Game, it won't outweigh the less fallacious sunk cost of whatever advancements I make in my demonic abilities. I promise you, Cheshire: I have no intention of claiming the Beast's shard unless I can do so in a way that preserves my demonhood and my connection to you."

She looks away from the stars to meet my gaze, visibly relieved, and she smiles. "Thanks. I needed to hear that. So . . . what *is* the plan?"

I shrug and fold my hands behind my head. "Kill a bunch of powerful assholes before they kill us, eat their souls, then kick the Beast's ass and turn her shard into a paperweight? Throw it off the side of the island? Backtrack to the abandoned schoolhouse and dump it in the Abyss?"

Cheshire shivers. "Let's not do that last idea. No one deserves to be trapped in the Abyss for all eternity."

"Oh, hey, you still need to finish telling me that creation myth at some point. But yeah, fair, we'll find some other way of dealing with the Beast. Got any suggestions?"

"Maybe. I think we should start, at least, by defining our goals. If our objective in the Game isn't going to be attaining the shard, we could instead define our objective as preventing our enemies from attaining the shard. Averrich is one of those enemies, obviously, and I think it's very likely that Vaylin Kirinal will be another."

I nod. "Yeah, the few things I've heard about Vaylin suggest she's going to be a problem for us sooner or later." Part of me is almost looking forward to matching wits with a rival demon, but the more intelligent parts of me are concerned about fighting a demon with years of experience on me and a whole pack of minions at her beck and call.

"Conversely," Cheshire continues, "we've met with Esha of the Myriad and right now she *isn't* our enemy. The Machinist was mentioned as another major power in this city, and one that the Myriad have at least a neutral relationship with."

I chew my lip and consider that. "I don't think we have enough data to make any decisions about the Machinist, but Esha . . . she seemed positively inclined toward me, when we had our little talk. And she is, so far, one of the only people I've met in this city who wants to treat figments like people, which is a pretty big point in her favor."

"So the question: are we okay with Esha being the one to claim the shard, if that's what it comes down to?" Cheshire watches me intently.

I mull it over, but it's not really a difficult decision. "I think that there are much worse options, and it would piss off the bastard that set Eirdryd on me, so I'm giving that a tentative yes. If I can find a way to claim the shard without losing my demonhood, I will, but otherwise the plan is to put it in Esha's hands and stay on her good side."

The compass spell leads us inside the grand shopping center, which is fully open despite the early hour as yet another sign of this city's unnatural nature. There are fewer figments here than last time but still a fair number, and the whole interior is awash in the glow of neon circuitry and touchscreen kiosks.

[Find the Path] leads us to the center of one of the mega-mall's two distinct food courts, and there it does something I haven't seen happen before: the lines of the flaming arrow reorient to overlap, both pointing to the top of the circle, and then that single line of flame starts inching slowly to the right, like the minute hand of a clock ticking down.

"Huh," I say.

"Huh," Cheshire repeats.

"Have you seen anything like this before?"

"Nope. Granted, I've not seen much of this spell at all, but I definitely didn't know it could do *that*. It looks like a clock, right?"

"Yeah, I see it too. So, what, it's counting down to when the target will be in this location?" I take a few steps back from where I was standing, but the clock remains. I circle the entire food court and there's no change in the structure of the burning circle, just the very slow movement of the clock hand. "If it's telling me my target isn't here yet, why isn't it just pointing me to where the target is right now?"

Cheshire leans over my shoulder and peers at the spell, brow furrowed, and then she snaps her fingers and brightens. "Ah, I think I've got it! [Find the Path] is supposed to be the ultimate pathfinding spell, one of the aces of the Summer Court, but it can't show you a path to something that's genuinely unreachable. You asked for 'that beyond the maze which would be most helpful in defeating Averrich,' and I think that, somehow, the spell identified something that isn't here *yet* but is going to be soon. Something beyond the Labyrinth, or beyond the part of the Labyrinth we can access with our means, but which is in transit toward this destination even as we speak."

I whistle appreciatively. "Damn. That is a powerful spell effect. Almost makes it seem worth the trade for my name, if not for the incredibly limited number of uses."

"And whatever Eirdryd's plotting to do with that name," Cheshire adds.

I sigh. "Yeah, still far from an equal exchange, but it was my only real option. Let's just hope whatever's on its way has enough value to justify burning the last charge. But, uh, it seems like we've got some time to kill before it arrives, so . . . breakfast?"

Cheshire's expression is wry as she says, "Didn't we just have breakfast?"

"That was first breakfast." I grin. "Now it's time for second breakfast."

The Pyraplex has an actual full-service breakfast restaurant on one of its floors, because of course it does. I dig into French toast piled high with butter and syrup, the objectively superior counterpart to waffles and pancakes. Because I am a bottomless pit and I'm not sure my body is actually capable of eating "too much" anymore, I also order stuffed hash browns with sour cream and cheese, and an omelet with tomato and spinach.

I consume all of them, and second helpings of the French toast, and when every scrap has been devoured I find myself *still* hungry for more—not hungry in a hollow stomach way where I *need* more, but hungry in the sense that I could eat more and I know I would enjoy it. I sip my orange juice while I contemplate that.

Cheshire, seated across from me, ordered a much more modest breakfast of bacon, sausage, and cheesy eggs, with a glass of water for her drink. She also eats at a more reasonable rate, whereas I practically inhaled each portion of my meal.

"Is it a demon thing," I ask, "that I'm still kind of hungry after eating all of that?"

Cheshire swallows a bite of sausage and nods. "Absolutely. Hunger is an essential part of the Throne of Shadow, for one, but you also have to remember that this stuff isn't really your food anymore; souls are your food—and to a lesser extent, mana, which in your case mostly means drinking blood."

I frown. "Okay, but I just ate two big souls less than twelve hours ago. That's the kind of feast that should leave me feeling sated for a while, isn't it? Hells, some vampires in fiction can go weeks without feeding after a particularly good meal."

"Ah," she says, pointing a fork with some egg on it at me, "but you're not just any demon. You, my dear Allie, are a demon with one third of your soul dedicated to the Truth of *Gluttony*. You're right that the average demon probably wouldn't be hungry the day after winning a throne duel and chowing down on a nice, juicy soul, but your Truths make you a special case. I don't predict you'll *ever* remain sated for very long, even after feeding in the ways you're meant to. And food like this?" She makes a sweeping gesture at what remains of her breakfast. "No matter how tasty it is, it'll be a trickle of sustenance at best."

It seems obvious, in hindsight. I feed on mana and souls, and *feeding* like this only provides trace amounts of mana. And, yes, I've tied one third of my essence to the very principle of disordered and excessive consumption: the sin of Gluttony. "Strangely enough, I don't think that actually bothers me. It feels . . . right."

Cheshire grins. "Toldja you'd make a great demon."

She finishes up and we hit the shops, checking [Find the Path] periodically to make sure we don't miss the big arrival. I grab two new anchors for Cheshire—a ceramic cat figurine and a manticore wargaming model—though I honestly doubt I'll be manifesting her that way very often when I could go werewolf or put her on [Feast or Famine] duty instead.

I find replacements for all the parts of my vampiric regalia that were damaged during the maze run, and I also pick out the round shades and black shawl that Cheshire suggested I add to my current ensemble. I have to admit: with my black hair, slender frame, and dark red lips, I look pretty damn good in this outfit.

We return to the food court as the minute hand ticks down, watching the line of flame slowly return to its zenith. Then, through the glass ceiling of the food court, I see night become day as clear blue replaces starry swirls. The minute hand strikes twelve and the burning circle vanishes, and I feel the spell at last vanish completely from my awareness.

In the center of the food court, the air begins to splinter and warp. Tables and chairs turn to glass and then shatter, and the shards fly through the air to that crack in reality. A few seated figments are caught by it too, their bodies twisting and contorting, but they show no sign of pain or fear as their forms are torn apart and reshaped. The figments smile placidly as they are transmuted to sculpted glass, and then that glass shatters and is drawn inexorably to the growing mass in the center of the room.

The shards whirl around each other, orbiting at different velocities, and then all stop at once before starting again in perfect sync. The shards come together and form a single pane of reflective glass: a mirror, tall and wide, with no frame and no foundation, anchored in the warped air.

The mirror ripples and a man comes tumbling through, his clothes disheveled and a sheathed sword at his belt. Then, rushing from the mirror as a unit, three monsters leap after him—and as soon as all three are clear of the mirror, it melts to glass slag behind them, its purpose spent.

I I

The moment I see the monsters, I'm ready to fight. I'm not afraid, I'm not hesitant, I'm not even fazed. Whatever these things are, they can't be worse than what I've already faced.

These creatures actually remind me of the very second type of monster I faced on my arrival in the Labyrinth: the spiderlike not-dogs that chased me through the woods outside the abandoned schoolhouse. If I were to give these things a name, it would be not-cats: the bodies of big hairless sphynx cats but stretched out unnaturally, eyeless, and with large scorpion tails.

"Cheshire—"

"Already on it!" My companion slips behind me, expression focused as she concentrates on priming castings of my signature spell. She's already anticipated what I need, so the rest is up to me.

"[Carrion Swarm]," I call out, arm extended and fingers outstretched in the direction of the new arrivals. The spell diagram flashes in my mind's eye, full of arcane symbols I've yet to decipher, and then it's gone as I unleash the spell and send white ravens flying from my hand, their feathery bodies emerging from my porcelain skin.

The birds soar for the beasts and I run after them. The not-cats are chasing after the man who fell through the portal, the man my seeking spell led me to, as he races away from them through the emptied food court. One of the not-cats is larger than the others, and it sprints ahead of them on elongated limbs.

My birds reach the two smaller beasts, and as each raven lays a claw or a wing on the flesh of a not-cat, the raven is wreathed in noxious black mist that clings like muck.

A splintering pain wracks my body as [Feast or Famine] takes a bite out of my soul to fuel each casting. My thoughts are scattered like viscera before the claws of a great beast, and every nerve feels electrified with fresh and horrid sensation. I stumble in my stride and have to catch myself, still unused to the intensity of the spell, and then its second half hits.

The black mist spreads from birds to beasts and consumes the essence of the Labyrinth's latest horrors. The catlike monsters wither into husks, skin stretching taut against frames that lose mass until they're just bone, and as they fall I drink in their life force, their very souls, and the resonance-rich mana tied to such consumption. It is a soothing balm after the torment of the initial casting, and I revel in it, but there's still something disorienting about rapidly shifting between pain and pleasure like that.

The few ravens that went for the third beast take longer to reach it, and as they approach they are swatted from the sky by the lightning-quick motion of the not-cat's scorpion-like tail. The tail's barb pierces each bird in succession, tearing through them. For an instant the black mist is there, rising from the ravens and clinging to the tail, but the birds scatter to shadow too quickly and the creature's tail shrivels not quite to uselessness. Again I experience the cycle of soul-rending agony and hungry satisfaction, but it's muted compared to the other burst of sensation.

I hiss and call out to my other minions, "Surround the big one!"

The white ravens flap their wings and rise from the dehydrated-looking husks of the lesser not-cats, but as they do they begin to fall apart. Feathers and flesh alike slough from fragile bone, and then it all melts into shadow.

The last monster takes advantage of the opening to pounce, lunging for the fleeing man as he looks back at my shout and nearly trips. His momentary stumble is enough for the beast, which knocks him to the ground and pins him there.

He looks up at it with fear in his eyes, and I peer closer at the object in his hands: an ornate sheath of blue and gold, with a sword hilt poking out of it. He raises the sheath and manages to wedge it in the creature's toothy maw, blocking it from biting him, but its claws rake into him freely.

Shit. I can't rely on summons for this, I'll have to do it myself. I close the distance with the beast now that it's stationary, and as I move in I conjure Vorpal, the hilt appearing in my hand with ease. I lunge for the creature, movements purposeful and fluid, the killing instrument seeming almost eager to guide my strike.

With my first movement I slash at the beast's tail, the rapier's edge cutting through with only the barest of resistance. The top half of the tail falls to the ground, stinger rendered useless to the monster, and clear water bleeds from the point of severance.

The mutant sphynx cat turns its eyeless face toward me, at last recognizing the real threat in the room, but that ornate sheath is still wedged in its mouth and it can't move away from the man it's pinning fast enough to avoid my second strike. The point of my blade pierces its skull and Vorpal runs clean through to the other side.

Black mist erupts from the blade and consumes the monster, and again I am wracked with pain and joyous voracity. My soul splinters and is forged anew, fractures of essence sealed with an influx of stolen soulstuff. I arch my back and clench my other hand, nails digging into skin hard enough to draw blood, but each puncture seals just as quick as it's made thanks to the vital force flowing from the beast to me.

I tear Vorpal from its skull and it dies, and I flick droplets of water from the blood-red blade.

When the high fades and my breathing steadies, I turn to the man who fell and finally take him in: tousled blonde hair, big brown eyes, sun-tanned skin, and an altogether unremarkable build and face. His white shirt is torn and rapidly staining with blood from the wounds that monster gouged in him. Belatedly, I realize that's a serious problem and one I don't have any immediate way to solve.

I grimace and extend a hand down to help him up. "Hey, guy: get up and we can try to . . . find a . . . healer."

Before my eyes, the bloody gashes in his chest knit together and seal up like the skin was never broken. There's no mark on his body, no indication he's still in pain, nothing. The only sign there was ever a wound is the blood still staining his shirt and visible on his chest through the holes in that shirt.

He regenerated. He regenerated his wounds, which *isn't how this magic system fucking works*, because the only kind of magic that can heal a wound that quickly is transfusion magic. I didn't see him leech that life essence from any-where, and I certainly didn't give up any of mine, so where the hells did he get it from?

I stare at him, speechless, as he takes my hand and rises to his feet. He scratches his head, looking sheepish.

"Thanks for the assist," he says awkwardly. "I'm Dante. That was, uh, that was really cool with the sword. Sorry I didn't do much with mine; I got it, like, today, and I really don't know how to use it."

I'm barely paying attention to what he's saying, because I've just noticed what he's wearing: he's in a navy-blue blazer over a white button-up shirt, with bland gray trousers, a gray necktie, and black dress shoes. It looks like a school uniform.

Arriving in another world wearing a school uniform and chased by monsters, gifted an item on entry and powers that defy the conventional laws of magic. Just like me. He has to be. He has to be, there's no way he isn't.

No, no, I refuse. This can't be happening. And that's my fucking power! That's the cheat ability I asked for, and the God of Death laughed at me.

One way to confirm, not that it isn't blindingly obvious what's going on.

I flicker on my soul sight, shifting my vision from the false corporeal to the true meaning lying beneath the skin of the world. The mall around us becomes ink on paper, sketch lines and vague impressions of physicality. When I look at most people with my sight, I see a mask of bone and a form that tells me something about them. The only exception is Cheshire, who, like me, is a witch that can foil sixth senses.

The only exception until now, I should correct, because when I look at Dante all I see is a blue storm of swirling, random, meaningless nothing. When I peer closer, straining my sight, I can just barely make out a glimmering star beneath, dim yet oddly hopeful, but that's it.

His soul looks nothing like Averrich's, which showed me the infection of madness coursing through him, and it's nothing like the souls of figments, held up by strings that lead back to the tower of black glass. There's nothing to prod at here, no meaning I can discern, no clues I can draw. He's obscured to my senses, just like my soul has been obscured to everyone who's tried to peer at it.

He's a witch, just like me and just like Cheshire; someone specially chosen by Nyarlathotep herself to be granted special powers and privileges outside the bounds of the normal magic system.

In isekai terms, he has a cheat ability. And it's not *proof* that he's from Earth, just like that outfit isn't proof and being chased by monsters certainly isn't proof, but when you put that all together and compare it to my own arrival in this world . . . the parallels are disturbing, and this does not seem like a universe where coincidences are just coincidences.

It's a sick joke, and I bet I know who to blame: Katoptris and Nyarlathotep, my two tormentors.

I flicker off soul sight and see the kid—Dante, he said his name was Dante—waving at me nervously. He says, "Uh, hey there, weird magic woman. You've been staring at me kind of intently. Do you, like, have a name?"

"Oh. Right." *Okay, gotta look cool, gotta look cool to impress the new kid so I can get him on my side in dealing with Averrich because* apparently *my magic compass thinks he's the key to that particular showdown. I need a title, cool people have titles, why don't I have a title? I need a badass moniker to show how badass and awesome and powerful I am. Argh, fuck it, let's just steal something from anime and hope he's not a weeb.* I straighten up, pose with my rapier, and proudly announce, "My name is Maven Alice of the Crimson Moon, the True Ancestor vampire princess."

He looks at me with befuddled confusion. "Isn't that from *Tsukihime*?"

"Dammit," I swear, clenching my fist in frustration. *Well now we know he's definitely from Earth.* Why is he here? Is he meant to be the hero to my Demon King of Tyranny? "Who the hell knows *Tsukihime* in 2022?" I ask instead, stalling for time while I try to figure out how the fuck I'm supposed to respond to meeting someone else from the Zero Sphere.

"There was a remake last year, and a new *Melty Blood.*"

"Oh, yeah. Okay, never mind that, I need you to tell me everything about how you—"

I'm cut off by a flash of prismatic light, and then the air is filled with an ominous hum as shards of fractal glass flicker into existence all around me. Each node expands, contracts, expands, and they all resonate with that awful tone. The fractal shards become fractal panes of stained glass that grow to encircle both myself and Dante.

My gaze meets Cheshire's in the instant before the rainbow glass can encase me entirely, and she reaches out. Our hands intertwine for a single moment and then she's melting into my shadow, charm bracelet around my wrist, as the cocoon completes itself and the prismatic glass swallows me whole.

When I blink my eyes, I am standing within the swirling rainbow-colored maelstrom I've seen twice before: it's the Corridor of Reflections, the Labyrinth's world between worlds that contains within it the mirror-paths connecting all reflective surfaces within the Labyrinth.

The kaleidoscope effect is as dizzying as ever, and instinctively my gaze flits to the tower of black glass that pierces the sky. The storm of prismatic color bleeds from that tower, from each point where jagged glass cuts into the skin of the cosmos.

The last time I was here, I fell from one mirror into another with barely a glimpse of the Corridor. The first time, I walked across panes of glass from mirror-portal to mirror-portal. This time, I appear to be standing on a circular stone platform suspended in midair.

Below me and in front of me I see a much larger stone platform, circular like the one I'm standing on but missing a chunk, like a cookie with a bite taken out of it. Six thrones are arrayed in a half circle on the side of the platform not missing a piece, and six figures sit upon those thrones.

I take in their visages scattershot, attention flitting rapidly between figures: a man with golden skin and a haughty air reclining on a throne of glittering jewels; a woman dressed like a flapper from the 1920s slumped against a throne of velvet, sipping from a glass of wine; someone dark-skinned and gray-haired, gender uncertain, resting listlessly on a throne of unadorned stone; a jackal-headed woman with an exposed glass heart, her throne black jet but painted with red hearts; a misshapen amalgamation of animal parts in mismatching fashion, hunched upon the ruins of a many-colored throne; and a woman split down the middle, half corpse and half beauty, on a throne of grasping hands.

These, I immediately intuit, must be the Nobles.

Six more platforms, smaller like mine, are arrayed around the bitten half of the central platform, opposite the thrones. I see Dante on one, two figures I don't recognize on their own, and the three people I expected to see here: Averrich the Goblin King, Esha of the Myriad, and Vaylin Kirinal. Beyond them, seated in amphitheater rows, I see hundreds of silhouettes, figures cast in total darkness.

Before I have time to take in any more information, a resounding thunderclap fills the air and my attention is drawn back to the central stage. Shards of glass materialize and flow together into the form of an eerie, unclothed woman. Her skin, her hair, her eyes, all glass, just slightly discolored from each other to create the illusion of definition. She's not wearing my face this time, but I know she must be the Beast of Lamentation and Euphoria. Who else could accomplish this feat?

The Beast clasps her hands together and smiles up at me, then at the rest of the audience. I try to call out to her, to snarl at her, to say anything, but no sound leaves my lips. The Beast's smile grows wicked, and then she spreads her hands and begins to speak with joyous, manic fervor.

"Welcome, one and all, to a wonderful, horrible spectacle. I'm sure some of you are feeling very confused right now, or at least very surprised, though at least two of you know exactly what is going on." The Beast chuckles, voice echoing across the vast open space. "The festivities will begin shortly, but first, please, allow me a brief preamble. This city, my gift to all of you, has grown from a humble seed, nourished by dreams, into a magnificent garden overflowing with potential. I speak, of course, of Sanctuary 7."

The glass woman sighs heavily, and when she speaks again her tone is despondent. "But alas, a maze can have but one minotaur, a crown but one head to rest upon. I wish dearly that I could provide paradise for all of you equally, but we have seen time and again that it is human nature to create evils where none reside."

The Beast laughs and bares glass teeth. "You kill each other like *animals*. Presented with a banquet, you would rather feast upon the flesh of your brothers and sisters than partake of that which is without cost or caveat. You will lie and cheat and murder over something so worthless as *power*. You truly have no shame."

"All of what is to come could have been prevented," she mourns. "There was no need for this violence, no need for this miserable hardship. But the hard road has been chosen, and that choice must be respected. So you shall kill each other until one remains, and then that greatest of murderers shall claim a shard of glass and an empty throne, and she shall call herself a Red Queen."

The Beast of Lamentation and Euphoria spreads her hands wide, expression serene, caught in something approaching rapture. "Welcome, my beautiful fools, to the seventh Game of Glass."

I grimace at her several pointed comments. *Yes, yes, we're a garden of sinners and this is somehow all my fault for not taking the obvious bait when you dangled it in front of me. But "Red Queen," is that an* Alice in Wonderland *reference? She displayed knowledge of my past, just like Cheshire, so it could easily be that . . . and maybe it's a reference to the evolutionary principle and the realpolitik theory of warring states. The endless unmoving race that can only be broken with the emergence of an apex predator or a regional hegemon.*

Me.

The Beast brings her hands back together and announces, "Now, with that out of the way, let's introduce our lucky contestants. Our first candidate is a demon who arrived here only a few days ago, but she's taken to bloodshed like a corpse to a grave. Maven Alice, please step forward."

The platform beneath me starts to shift, and it lowers down to perfectly fill the hole in the circle where the Beast is waiting. I bare my fangs at the glass woman and flex my fingers, wanting nothing more than to rip that head off her shoulders . . . but I know better than to think that would work.

The Beast reaches out and grabs my left hand, lifts it up, and then traces a swooping design on the back of my hand that lights up and glows for a moment before vanishing. "Your key fragment has been implanted," she tells me with a smile.

I sprout claws from the ends of my fingers, and with my other hand I reach over and scrape those claws across the glass skin of her forearm. The sound it makes is ear-bleedingly awful, but her smile doesn't falter and neither does my snarl.

The Beast gently extricates her arm, and then she turns her back to me and gestures to one of the seated figures. "Maven's sponsor is the Noble of Grandeur and Shame, Lord Invernus. As the newest Noble of the six, he's got a lot to prove with this nomination."

I follow her gesture and see the man with golden skin, reclining with a posture of arrogant contempt on his throne of precious metals and glittering gemstones. He's completely hairless, not even eyebrows, and his eyes shimmer with rainbow color. He wears a rainbow-colored trench coat and no shirt, which reveals his literally chiseled chest, and his only other articles of clothing are a pair of pristine white trousers and white dress shoes.

Invernus. So you're the bastard who set me up. I'll enjoy wiping that smug look from your face.

My platform lifts away from the center as the Beast announces, "Our next candidate is an elf old enough to have seen the fall of his world, making him a real powerhouse in this competition. He truly embodies the spirit of euphoric celebration, and his revelry would make the Wolf Queen proud. Averrich, you splendid rogue, get over here."

Averrich's platform drifts down and he receives his key fragment with an exaggerated bow, the flamboyant fae seemingly entirely unperturbed and unsurprised by everything transpiring. He's still bedazzled in sapphires and emeralds, with a crown nesting in his glam rock mop of hair, and I idly fantasize about ripping those gems out and tossing them into a gutter somewhere.

"Averrich's sponsor is the Noble of Relief and Regret, Lord Kasumi. Her love of entertainment is legendary, so perhaps she's hoping Averrich will prove an excellent thrower of parties as the seventh Noble."

Again the Beast turns and gestures, and I see the woman sipping wine with a bored expression on her face. Kasumi has dead eyes like polished stones, bright red lips, and completely unkempt black hair. She's dressed in a black-and-gold flapper dress, the kind with sequins and beads and feathers, and she lets it hang lazily off one shoulder. Her throne is black stone carved with carnal images and upholstered with plush velvet, and upon one throne arm sit three bottles of wine, two of them empty.

Kasumi, who gave Averrich advanced warning of the Game's approach. She and Invernus both interfered to set up their candidates, so I wonder if any of the others did the same. And those titles they have, it matches the construction of the Beast's title. Will whoever wins this game become the Noble of Lamentation and Euphoria?

Vaylin is next to be brought before the Beast. The azure-skinned demon looks mostly the same as the projection that Esha showed me—two pairs of upward-curving horns, all-black eyes with white-dot pupils, and a black-lipped smile—but she's discarded the tank top and leather pants for a strawberry-patterned pink dress, though she's still adorned in golden jewelry and red body-stitching.

"This demon is the biggest reason this city has devolved into so much infighting and urban warfare," the Beast crows, "and if she gets her way I'm sure every soul in the Sanctuary will be turned into a puppet on her strings. It's a pleasure to have you in the running, Vaylin Kirinal."

Vaylin receives her key fragment and examines her hand with clear interest, waving it around and poking at the skin where the glowing design briefly appeared.

The Beast continues, "Vaylin has been sponsored by the Noble of Enthrallment and Apathy, Lord Krendagrel. I'm sure it would watch her performance with great interest if it hadn't already found a new fixation to occupy itself with."

Krendagrel is a creature with elongated limbs covered in a messy mix of feathers, fur, and scales. One of its hands ends in three digits, while the other ends in nine, and it has one leg ending in a cloven hoof and one leg ending in a birdlike talon. It has a wide mouth full of shark's teeth; big, round, entirely white eyes; no nose or hair upon the head; and a set of tall, pointed ears that curl at the tips and sprout chitinous growths.

The amalgamation of parts has an equally eclectic taste in clothing: it wears a red-and-yellow scarf over a green-and-blue shawl over a brown cloak, a purple sash over bare chest, and a checkerboard skirt, but nothing else. Its scattered patches of uncovered skin are muddy teal in color and possess an odd, warped texture. It crouches on the ruins of a throne that looks to have been sliced apart in two places, and the fragments are splashed with paint of all colors.

The Noble of Enthrallment and Apathy, true to its name and the words of the Beast, is completely ignoring the proceedings to instead pick at a puzzle. Its long digits toy with one of those mechanical puzzles that require you to disassemble interlocking pieces, though the puzzle in its hands is more complex than any I've seen in stores.

Vaylin's platform drifts back, and one of the figures I don't recognize drifts in to take her place.

"Introducing our next candidate, Valentina Vasquez! She's a wizard who has, until now, attempted to stay out of the fighting between factions. Sucks to be you, Vasquez, but welcome to the brawl!"

The woman brought before the Beast looks to be in the peak of physical fitness, and her expression remains serene and unbothered despite the Beast's comments. Vasquez has a healthy glow to her skin, short-trimmed brown hair, and wears blue-and-red sleeveless robes patterned with designs of flying fish and fire flowers. She receives her key fragment without ceremony.

"This candidate's sponsor is Lord Juno, the Noble of Love and Hate. I think she might have a desire for Ms. Valentina, or perhaps she wants to see her murdered horribly by a demon."

Juno is the jackal-headed woman, with clawed hands and an exposed heart of unbeating red glass. She wears red suspenders, a white button-up shirt, and black trousers, and she snacks on candied meats from a dripping pile atop one of the arms of her throne of black jet and carved red hearts. Juno doesn't look up when the Beast calls out her name, as she's too busy baring her teeth at the split-body woman, a hungry look in her eyes.

The wizard is dismissed and the other unfamiliar figure takes her place. This guy looks exactly like the archetypal necromancer, which in this setting means he probably is one and is playing into that appearance to enhance his spellcasting. He's got the sickly pallor, dark hair and eyes, hooded robes, and even a skull pendant around his neck. He also has a permanent scowl etched into his face, which might be more of a personality issue than anything magic-related.

"Introducing Hubert Ulchen, a necromancer who would have preferred to remain hidden in order to continue his silly little experiments. Too bad! Hubert has been sponsored by Lord Urna, the Noble of Desire and Disgust, who before her ascension to the ranks of Nobility was once a necromancer like him."

Urna is the woman of two very different halves, the corpse and the beauty. One half is that of a shapely bombshell with very pale skin, an ice-blue eye, full lips, and very long platinum blonde hair styled in a side cut. The other half is that of a skeletal corpse, exposed bone and dripping gore, bloody teeth, and cold blue light in the depths of a skeletal eye socket. She wears a fluffy fur mantle over her shoulders, and a dress made of sheer black-and-white fabric that leaves nothing to the imagination, conforming tightly to her buxom living half and hanging loose against the skeletal frame of her corpse half. She sits with regal airs upon a throne of grasping hands carved in marble.

Like most of the Nobles, she seems to barely notice the Beast, though in Urna's case that seems to be because of her fixation on Juno. As Juno bares her teeth at Urna, Urna curls her lip with a look of revulsion, but when Juno looks away to eat another candied meat, that look becomes lustful and vulgar.

"Perhaps she feels a sense of kinship, or perhaps she finds his experiments as revolting as any sane person would and wants to put a target on his back. Either way, I don't think he'll last long now that he's been exposed to the other candidates."

The Beast chuckles and sends the necromancer back to float with the rest of us. I find his situation curious, and that of the wizard. The way the Beast talked about both of them framed them as almost less important than Averrich, Vaylin, or I, and that makes me think of how Cheshire talked about figments: as extras in a stage play. The Beast has established Vasquez and Ulchen as obstacles to be overcome rather than true contenders for the grand prize. They're not the main characters of this story.

Esha is next to drift down, and there's only one Noble remaining to be her backer. The priestess is dressed in those same plain white robes I saw her in last, carrying her shepherd's crook staff and wearing a blindfold over her eyes.

"Our sixth candidate is the priestess bonded to my city's precious eidolon. Esha leads the Myriad and strives to be a voice of reason and compassion amid the chaos and conflict that rises around her. It is a shame that she has failed, and will fail, against the tide of human nature."

I can't see Esha's face from this angle, but I see her hand tighten around her staff. How must it feel to be told by a godlike existence that your purpose in life is doomed to failure?

"Ah, but I digress. Esha's sponsor is an individual of few words most days, but their reasoning for the choice of Esha is obvious: Lord Naryatska is the Noble of Isolation and Gregariousness, and Esha is one of the few people in this city that might be bearable to talk to after being granted the incredible power of my shard."

The last of the Nobles, Naryatska, is dark-skinned and gray-haired with silver eyes and a withdrawn, listless aura. Their clothing is plain compared to some of their contemporaries, just a full-body gray jumpsuit complete with black gloves and black jacket. Their throne is unadorned gray stone, and as they are addressed by the Beast they ignore her words to continue staring down at an open locket cupped in both hands.

Esha is sent away, and the Beast's smile grows wider, glass cracking at the edges of her mouth. "Historically," the Beast says, "my kind have taken a rather neutral role in the moderation of these contests. However, we do reserve the right to select a candidate of our own to vie for the grand prize of the glass shard. I have chosen to exercise this right, in this very special Game of Glass. Come forth, my champion: Dante Reyes."

Dante, looking surprised and confused, is brought down to the central platform and given a key fragment. I watch, seething internally, my suspicions confirmed beyond a shadow of a doubt: Dante was brought here by the Beast to be my foil, my opponent in this Game of Glass to force my hand . . . and presumably, Nyarlathotep found that funny enough to grant him the witch power *I* wanted.

The Beast doesn't dwell on it, though, once Dante's been given his piece of the key. She sends him back, and then she cracks her knuckles and spreads her arms wide once more.

"You've received your key fragments, but not all of you understand what that means. Allow me to explain the rules of our little game. The terms are simple: each of you possesses one-seventh of a key that can, once fully formed, open the door to my colosseum in the heart of the city. A key fragment can be given willingly to another, or it can be extracted from the corpse of the holder. While these fragments start in the hands of these specific seven, anyone who is capable of defeating a holder may take the fragment from their corpse, and any holder may give away their fragment to any person.

"Once the door is opened, a challenger may approach me within my lair, and there I shall judge whether or not they are worthy of taking up my shard. If I judge them unworthy, they may still attempt to take the shard by force, if they think they have what it takes.

"The shard, for those unaware, is the animus of my being and the incarnation of all my powers as a fragment of Katoptris, she who is the origin of this throne world. Possession of the shard means mastery over that throne world, or at least one region of it. You will be immortal and omnipotent within the bounds of your Sanctuary, and still very powerful beyond. You will be able to reshape this city to your will, expand it, destroy it, whatever is your whim. Each figment will answer to you, and you will have the capacity to create new figments, and to change the laws that govern those figments beholden to you. You will be like unto a god or an archdemon, an existence approaching Royalty."

But never reaching it, like a mathematical function approaching infinity in smaller and smaller increments the closer it gets. Forever tantalizingly out of reach. Glass does not grow. That was the downside that the Beast revealed to me, when she tempted me with the shard. I could have security, comfort, and a playground to rule over, but I would never escape the Labyrinth and I would never usurp the Divine Architect of Pandaemonium.

An unacceptable compromise.

"Now, before I let you loose to decide amongst yourselves who gets my shard . . . there is one other detail that will be different about this Game of Glass. You see, I'm afraid that two of you are *dirty rotten cheaters*." I tense, knowing exactly what she's talking about. "Invernus and Kasumi both acted to *interfere* with the conditions of this competition. They primed their candidates and nudged them into position to have actionable advantages over their rivals."

The others are looking at me, I can feel their gazes on my flesh, those judging, curious eyes. Vaylin, Esha, Valentina, Hubert, and Dante, all learning for the first time that my place in this Game of Glass is not normal, not unalloyed.

"And so," the Beast continues, "I have chosen to implement a measure to even the playing field once again. With the approval of those Nobles who did *not* attempt to cheat, I have decided to call for a one-day grace period in which no hostile action may be enacted by any keyholder, subordinate, or ally against any other person or property of those categories."

Invernus smirks, maintaining his haughty air of superiority, but I see his hand clench the bejeweled arm of his throne so tightly that it warps the metal and leaves an impression. Kasumi, for her part, simply rolls her eyes, downs the rest of her glass, and refills it, spilling wine in the process. The rest of the Nobles seem untroubled by this declaration, which makes sense if they were in on it from the start.

Outmaneuvered by the Beast herself. I must admit I'm pleased by that, even if I was one of the two benefiting from advanced warning. This'll hurt Averrich more than it hurts me, that's for sure.

"Take this time to prepare yourselves, my beloved candidates. Strike alliances, plot betrayals, and scope out the territory you'll be fighting in. But if you attempt to break my peace . . . I'll put you down myself. Have fun!"

In an instant, the world of color and stone vanishes, and both Dante and I are back in the mall.

This changes things. With a day of peace, we could do exactly as she suggested: strikes alliances and survey the terrain. If I could find where my enemies are located, that would be a huge boon. And if I could get Esha on my side, I'd have all the resources of the Myriad at my disposal.

Ah, but first . . . the kid.

Dante is looking worried and overwhelmed, so I clap a hand on his shoulder and give him a big grin.

"Hey, kid: ever wanted to win a death game?"

III

Dante blinks at me a few times, bewildered. "What?"

"Y'know, a death game: random bunch of people get their knives out and murder each other for cash, survival, and/or ultimate dominion over the cosmos, depending on the genre."

"No, I mean, I got that part, I watched *Squid Game* like everyone else. But—"

"Really?" I interrupt with exasperation, throwing my hands in the air. "You go to *Squid Game* before *Mirai Nikki* or, hells, even *Fate?*"

"Lady," he says in a pleading tone, "I feel like we've got way bigger issues than my taste in shows. This is kind of a lot to take in at once, and I would appreciate it if you helped me understand what's going on. I don't know where I am, and I don't really know who you are, either. You're a vampire, or maybe a demon, but you're also somehow from Earth like me? I'm so lost."

"Right. Yeah." I fidget with a strand of hair and try to stifle my embarrassment. Was I really about to launch into a tirade over stupid weeb shit that doesn't matter? "Sorry, I'm easily distracted. You probably have a bunch of questions, and I'll do my best to answer them. It's the least I can do for another Earthling. But that's also quite a lot of questions, so, do you want to get something to eat while I give you the rundown?"

I could go for a bite myself, actually—wait, no, I've already had two breakfasts and we're barely past the crack of dawn. Maybe just something to drink. I take a quick glance around and realize that the food court has magically repaired itself after my fight with the not-cats; not a trace of debris remains, and every table is back in place.

"Now that you mention it, I am pretty hungry. But is Earth money good here?" He looks down at his clothing and winces. "Scratch that, I don't have any money to begin with."

I grin and pat Dante on the back. "See, that brings me to my favorite part of this setting, which is that everything's free! Just pick a place that looks yummy and tell them what you want. Let's eat."

I let him loose on the food court's many options and pull up a seat a good distance away from where he's busy looking at teriyaki. I resummon Cheshire while Dante gets distracted by decision paralysis, and my companion emerges from my shadow anchored to the charm bracelet.

Cheshire gives Dante a critical look and tells me flatly, "This complicates things."

"Mhm. And not gonna lie," I say in a low voice, "there's a part of me whispering that we should kill him now before this all goes horribly wrong. But I'm pretty sure that's the Dark Lord part of me, and I know exactly what happens when the Dark Lord tries to murder the hero in act one of the adventure: it doesn't work, and half the time it's the inciting reason for the hero to overthrow the Dark Lord and foil all their plans."

"You think this is bigger than Averrich and the Game of Glass." It's not a question.

I blow a puff of air and fold my hands behind my head. "Is there really any doubt? Katoptris brought him from Earth, the Beast made him a contender, and Nyara gave him *my godsdamned superpower.* They're trying as hard as they can to broadcast that this guy is my counterpart in whatever fucked-up isekai story we're a part of. So: when you get sent to another world as the Dark Lord, and the goddess who sent you there shows you the hero that's destined to kill you, what's the smartest move?"

"You make friends," Cheshire guesses.

"You make friends."

Dante returns to us with a bag of food and sits down, pulling out a burger and fries. Then he pauses and takes in the new arrival. He points at the changeling and asks, "Wait, you were here before, weren't you? Right before we got taken to the place with all the colors, but then you were gone when we came back, and now you're here again. What's up with that?"

She waves. "Hi! I'm Cheshire. I'm pretty good at disappearing tricks."

He blinks a few times, glances over at me, and asks, "Remind me, what was your name?"

"Alice. Maven Alice. Yes, that's not a coincidence, but it's probably nowhere near the top of the list of questions you should be asking right now."

"Huh." He pops a fry into his mouth, chews it, swallows, and asks, "So, what's your deal? I've obviously got a lot of questions about this world and everything that just went down, but I'm still stuck on the vampire demon weeb. Were you just messing with me when you called yourself a vampire, or are vampires also demons in this world?"

"Well, first of all, I think it's very rude to call me a weeb."

Dante gives me a very skeptical look. So does Cheshire.

"Not inaccurate, mind, but still rude. To answer your question, I am indeed both a demon and a vampire, but what this world calls 'demons' aren't really much like what you'd typically picture, and to my knowledge there weren't any vampires in this world before I started calling myself one. I am, practically speaking, just a human with a few magic tricks and some unusual eating habits. Oh, speaking of which: Cheshire, can you fetch me a smoothie?"

"Sure thing. I know what you like." The changeling gets up and wanders off in search of that while I settle in for a nice, long stretch of exposition.

"A blood smoothie?" Dante asks with a raised eyebrow.

"Fruit, actually. I do drink blood, for the record, but I can still eat and drink normal stuff too."

"That's good to know. Alright, I guess . . . start wherever you think feels best." He starts eating the rest of his fries and watches me intently.

I crack my knuckles. "Big picture stuff first: physics is fake, chemistry isn't real, and the laws of reality as you know them are polite suggestions that the universe entertains only up until the point that someone with a bit of oomph behind them breaks those laws over their knee. I'm one of the people that can do that, and so are all of the other contenders in the Game of Glass. Magic is real, and it's everywhere.

"Speaking of magic," I add, "you should be warned that this isn't your typical nuts and bolts RPG-lite magic system. You might see someone throw a fireball or talk about spending mana, but the underlying framework isn't really about energy, it's about *meaning;* the spells you have access to, how you gather fuel for those spells, how you make your spells stronger and get more of them, that all comes from a place of meaning that's specific to each magic user's circumstance."

Dante swallows another fry and admits, "I don't really know what to make of that. Like, okay, magic is a thing and it's weird. Where are we? What else is different about this world compared to Earth? And why's the food free?"

"Practical concerns, fair." I lean forward and steeple my fingers. "Broadly speaking, we're in a universe called Pandaemonium that runs on meaning and is run by an all-powerful entity called the Demiurge. To my understanding, Pandaemonium is divided between the Spheres of Firmament, which are worlds where mundane physical laws apply unless violated, and throne worlds, which are made of soulstuff and have their own internal rules.

"Right now, we're inside one of those throne worlds, the Labyrinth, which happens to be the manifested soul of Katoptris, who that glass woman is a fragment of. It's called 'the Labyrinth' because it is an inescapable maze prowled by horrible monsters, like the beasties that tried to take a bite out of you. There are pockets of relative safety within the Labyrinth, and this city is one of them: the Sanctuaries. Life inside a Sanctuary is near-idyllic thanks to a post-scarcity economy where everyone's needs are provided for by the friendly and accommodating natives of the Labyrinth, so you don't have to pay for food, lodging, clothing, or entertainment. There's work if you want to feel productive, but nobody'll stop you if you want to laze around and play video games all day for the rest of your natural life."

Cheshire returns with a pomegranate smoothie *and* two Belgian sugar waffles, because she is a wonderful person who cares about me deeply. Cheshire also got a milkshake for herself, because even wonderful people can have bad taste.

Dante finishes the last of his fries and says, "So that's what the glass lady meant when she called this place a paradise. But if you can't leave . . ."

"Then it's really more of a gilded cage." I inhale my waffles greedily and keep talking through bites of sugary goodness. "And, of course, when you lock animals in a cage, even if you feed them well, eventually they're going to start nipping at each other and trying to prove who's top dog."

Dante snaps his fingers excitedly. "Like the wolf thing, right? The old alpha wolf myth, the one they debunked as only happening in captivity as a response to the conditions of captivity."

I preen, delighted to have someone else who knows that little factoid. "Yes, precisely. Here's the situation: the Labyrinth draws in people who have magic, or people who want magic, and it gives them a city full of people without magic who exist to please. The only consequences for your actions here are the consequences that other people with magic choose to inflict on you, and none of you can leave, so it quickly devolves into the law of whoever has the biggest gang or the most personal power. When that's not a certain thing, you get all kinds of tensions that build and build until *boom*, there goes the neighborhood."

I take a big gulp of heavenly pulverized fruit, the rapturous taste of pomegranate, before continuing, "Now, the bottle's uncorked and all the murderers and warlords are spilling out, and every last one of them wants to get their hands on us to forge the key that'll give them their grand prize. We're targets now, and, no offense, but if you couldn't handle three of the Labyrinth's weakest monsters, then I have my doubts about your chances against the likes of Averrich and Vaylin. So, we wrap back around to my original question: do you want to win a death game with me?"

His expression turns grim, and he contemplates my question while digging into his burger. After a few moments he says, "I . . . don't want to kill anyone. I know a lot of guys fantasize about this kind of thing, about getting dropped into a life-or-death situation and having to badass their way out of it, but . . . that's not me. And this game . . . do we really have to participate? I don't know how you feel about it, but what's stopping me from just giving away my piece of the key? That woman said it was possible."

I lean back and take another long sip of my drink, then raise two fingers. "There are two major problems with that plan. The first complication comes down to verification: how are you going to prove that you don't have the key fragment anymore? Looking at you right now, I don't see any sign of your fragment, but I know you must still have it in you. You might give your fragment to one pursuer only to have the next kill you to try and take it from your corpse. No one will take you at your word that you don't have your fragment."

"Ah. I didn't think of that."

"The second issue," I continue, "is what will happen if any of those bastards actually win. The prize for winning this game is godhood, or something like it, and the people most likely to win a game of killing are the *killers*, Dante. Every soul with a talent for murder and more sense than ambition is going to want that finished key, and if one of them gets it then they have a dangerously good shot at becoming the absolute ruler of this city. You might survive the death game, but you and all the other innocents in the city definitely won't survive the reign of terror that follows."

Dante eats in silence, his face still showing grim contemplation. I could wait for him to gather his thoughts, give him a chance to process and come to some kind of conclusion, but I feel like pushing my luck.

"The thing is, I'm stronger than most of those losers, and I don't need the Beast's handouts. I don't need the grand prize and I don't want it; I just want to stop the worst of those bastards from claiming it for themselves. You don't want to fight? That's fair, I get that, but don't just run away; stick with me, stick close to me, and when they come for your key fragment, I'll do the fighting and the killing until every warlord is dead. And then, once we have all the pieces of the key, we can give it to someone who might actually do some good with it."

Something in his gaze sharpens, and he quickly swallows his food and asks, "Do you have someone in mind?"

I share a quick glance with Cheshire, who nods approvingly. I turn back to Dante and tell him, "I do, actually. You saw her at the announcement: Esha of the Myriad. She's one of the few people in this city to hold on to her morals, and she maintains a community of like-minded folks that try to restore some sense of normalcy to this crazy place. She's got a proven track record of actually caring about the people here, which I think is a pretty essential quality of any would-be monarch. I was actually planning to talk with her about forming an alliance before you fell out of the sky."

Dante takes a deep breath and closes his eyes, and when he opens them again I see blazing resolve. He nods firmly and says, "Okay. I won't lie, everything you've told me sounds pretty daunting, but . . . I'm certain of it now: this is where I'm meant to be. This is why the Goddess chose me. This is what She asked me to do for Her."

Fuck. Fuck. Fuck. Fuck. "The Goddess?" Does he mean Katoptris? Nyara? Azathoth? Some entirely new variable to mess up the fucking equation? I fight the urge to freak out and keep my outer demeanor calm. I smile thinly and ask, "Which goddess would that be? There are quite a few entities in this setting that you could throw that label at. You're not talking about some religious shit from the old world, right?"

Dante shivers, and I no longer have any doubts about who and what he encountered. "She . . . She was fathomless, but so terrifyingly human. It was like staring into infinity. When She spoke, every word burned in my mind. I wasn't really religious before today, but . . . there was no denying that. That was a capital-G God."

"Sounds like you've had one hell of a morning. You wanna walk me through it? We might be able to shed some light on the situation."

He nods. "Yeah. Yeah, okay. So, this morning, I woke up early. Like, real early, and there was this itch in the back of my head keeping me from falling asleep again, so I decided to take a walk. And then . . . gone. No portal to another world, no delivery truck slamming into me, just one second I'm walking through the cold morning air, the next second I'm standing in this endless hall with checkerboard floors, massive pillars of pulsing red crystal, and darkness in all directions.

"I thought I was dreaming, or maybe hallucinating, so I tried to keep my cool, but it felt too real, as impossible as that seemed. I wandered until I saw a glimmer of brightness, and I followed that glimmer until the black-and-white tile crumbled into an ocean of swirling starlight. At the edge, just before it all plunged away, there was . . . it was a throne, but it didn't really look like a throne, just a well-made wooden chair, high-backed and ornate.

"Sitting there, slumped and too small for the chair, sized somewhere between a toddler and a preteen, was a doll in a puffy dress. Its throat had been cut and its chest stabbed, both wounds leaking this odd, pale, almost milky blood. It creaked to life as I approached, and its eyes bled black ichor, and then it spoke with the voice of the Goddess."

Breathe steady, keep calm, do not freak out, do not scream. This is fine. This is fine, we're fine, we're not fine, but we have to keep our cool anyway.

The doll. The *fucking* doll, which I obsessed over in the schoolhouse, the doll with the pink backpack and the pretty dress and the *red crystal* hairpin that just so happened to be the symbol of motherfucking *Azathoth*, the embodiment of the entire universe, who is inextricably bound up with Nyarlathotep, the Lucid Demiurge, in ways I still don't fully understand.

The doll was Nyara, or at least a vessel body of Nyara, and she is *mocking me* with that fact.

"What did she say?" I choke out, almost whispering, barely able to contain the storm of emotion rising within me.

Dante spares me a single worried glance, but then he continues his story. "She told me that I had been summoned from my world against my will by 'the Lady of Shards,' and that this broke some kind of rule, so She was going to balance the scales. She offered to send me home, to undo the summoning like it had never happened . . . but then She asked me to stay instead, and indulge a 'selfish request.' She . . ." He hesitates, words stuck in his mouth, before saying, "She asked me to save Her daughter, and said I was the only one who could."

"Eh?" I blink repeatedly, completely blindsided by this one. I turn to Cheshire for answers, but she's looking as confused as I am. "Daughter?"

Cheshire rubs her temples. "She never told me . . . there are no stories . . . there's never been *any* indication that she has a *daughter*. I don't even know who could—" Cheshire's face goes pale, and then she slumps against the table and clutches her head. "Oh, oh no. No, no no no. *Fuck.*"

"Cheshire? Cheshire, who are you thinking of?" I can feel my anxiety rising higher and higher.

She looks up at me, expression desolate. "Think about it: who do we know that doesn't quite fit anywhere in the cosmology? Neither Leviathan nor Titan, not Royalty, but with a throne world so vast and powerful that none can escape from it . . . and she's the only being besides Nyara and Azathoth capable of reaching into the Zero Sphere. It all finally makes sense."

My eyes go wide as it clicks like a grenade. "Katoptris. It's Katoptris. Ha. Hahaha. Hahahahaha." I can't help but laugh, the anxious energy exploding out of me in bursts and bubbles. Katoptris, the Nightmare Queen, the Lady of Shards, the minotaur at the heart of the maze, the undisputed master of the Labyrinth that's got us all trapped . . . is Nyarlathotep's daughter.

And Cheshire and I are trying to kill her. Hahahahaha.

It's funny. It's so fucking funny that I'm going to die laughing, because Katoptris is the Demiurge's daughter and we're trying to murder her. I try to imagine the look on Bashe's face if I told him that now, or if he had somehow known when I told him that I was here in the Labyrinth to kill Katoptris. He probably would have pushed me off the bridge right then and there, just to get away from the crazy girl who wanted to kill God's daughter. Ha. Hahaha.

Dante looks between me and Cheshire with confusion clear on his face. "Uh, can someone loop me in?"

I try to stifle my manic laughter, but I can't, so it's Cheshire who speaks up. "We think we know who your target is, Dante. We have reason to believe that 'the Goddess' was talking about Katoptris, who the inhabitants of the Labyrinth also call Nightmare Queen or Lady of Shards. She's the one keeping everyone trapped in the Labyrinth, and the glass woman you saw on that stage is a piece of her, which means so is the shard everyone's fighting over."

His face falls. "Oh."

I wave at him with lazy airs and finally manage to recover control of my voice. "Keep going. Tell me what happened next."

Dante purses his lips, pensive. "The Goddess told me that, if I accepted Her request, then the summoning would be completed and I'd be brought to another world, but with special powers to help me accomplish my task. Once I arrived, the first step would be to 'ensure the right key reaches the right hands.' But help me understand something: why me? If She could grant me powers, then why not just do it Herself? And what did She mean when She said that rules had been broken?"

Cheshire sighs. "I can answer those. The entity that you call Goddess is one that we call Demiurge, and she has a truly infinite well of power to draw on. She is, in fact, so powerful that nothing could challenge her if she applied her full strength. So, to keep things interesting, she's tied her own hands and agreed to abide by a set of restrictions. She has rules for when she can act, and rules for how other beings can act. When Katoptris summoned you and Alice, that broke one of the rules that the Demiurge cares about: the ban on interfering with Earth or its inhabitants. As a consequence, the Demiurge allowed herself to expend a certain amount of energy counteracting the violation."

I frown. "But this raises an obvious question: what is Katoptris after? Why summon me, and then why summon Dante?"

Cheshire taps her chin thoughtfully. "It may be that Katoptris herself wasn't responsible, but rather her fragment: the Beast presiding over the Game of Glass. She made you an offer, after all, and Dante wasn't summoned until after you rejected that offer."

"What offer?" Dante asks.

I grimace. "The shard. She offered me the shard that this death game is being fought over. The terms were . . . unacceptable. It was an obvious trap, so I said no."

Dante furrows his brow. "But I don't want that thing any more than you do."

Cheshire bites her lip and grins. "I think that's exactly the point. In both cases, the Demiurge used her allotted interference to push the two of you *away* from wanting to claim the Beast's shard. Subtly with Alice, giving her the strength to not need the shard, and more directly with you, Dante: telling you to give the key to someone else so that you wouldn't seek the shard for yourself. If the shard is what you're meant to save, perhaps that's part of it."

My grimace deepens as I realize that this means I might be playing right into Nyara's hands, but I quickly replace it with a neutral expression. I can't let Dante know too much of what I'm feeling about all this, not when I'm still planning to work with him.

Dante slowly nods. "I think that makes sense. All of that, really. Thank you."

"It explains the healing factor," I muse. "A superpower that helps you live through the death game but doesn't necessarily help you kill, because killing isn't why you're involved. But if that's the case, then what's with the sword? Did she tell you if it does anything special?"

He coughs and says quietly, "She, uh, said that it'll grant me three wishes."

I swallow hard. "Ah. One moment please." I stand up, walk over to a nearby table, and slam my fists down onto it as I scream as loud as I can.

The table snaps in half, shattered by the force of my blow, and I stare down at hands that a few days ago struggled to take the lids off pickle jars. These hands that I have infused with demonic strength, these hands that have taken lives, these hands that I have covered in blood to claim every scrap of power I have because all I was given in this world was one healing potion and a shitty artificer superpower that only works half the time.

And she gave him three wishes. She gave me scraps, and she gave him three wishes, because God hates me and she wants me to suffer. She's laughing at me, I can feel her laughing at me like a prickling in my spine and all along my skin.

Are you watching, Nyara? Do I entertain you, Toymaker? Are you fucking pleased with yourself?

I fix my hair and my hat, wipe the dust from my hands, and force a smile on my face. I turn around and stroll back to the table where Dante and Cheshire are still sitting. "My apologies. Please, continue."

Dante looks at me with wide eyes. "They, um, the wishes have conditions. A lot of conditions. But, yeah, that's what I have: I can heal from most injuries, and I have a sword that lets me make three conditional wishes. Are you okay?"

I laugh. "Oh, not at all, but that's not really your fault. I'm probably giving a terrible first impression right now, and a part of me is very sorry for that, but you would not *believe* the week I've had. In the past few days I have nearly died a dozen times. I have been chased by monsters, bargained with fae and fiends, tore out a third of my soul, became a demon, killed a man for the first time, and was hunted like an animal by the bloodthirsty minions of an entirely different fae from the one I sold my name to. I have been *tormented* by this world, and then you come along with the superpower I wanted and a sword that can grant three fucking wishes. I am absolutely *furious* right now . . . but it's not your fault, and you're not the one I'm mad at."

I'm going to kill you, Demiurge. I promise.

Dante says, "That sounds like a lot. I'm really sorry you had to go through that. And I'm sorry that I'm making it worse, for whatever that's worth."

I sigh. "Yeah, well, done's done. Look, why don't we take a quick break so we both have time to process things? I'm sure you need it more than I do."

He scratches his head and winces. "I like to think I'm a quick learner, but, yeah, there's a lot. Watching a few isekai shows has not at all prepared me for the real deal."

I fetch a notebook from my throne world and quickly write something out, then rip out the page and hand it to him. "Here, these are the most essential pieces of information you should try to internalize before interacting with anyone else. Memorize them if you can, refer to the page if you can't. The tl;dr is this: you can't tell people you're from Earth, and your healing factor is something called a Gift that marks you as a witch to anyone with the right awareness, so keep both those things hidden as much as you can. You're an abnormality in this world, and nails that stick out get hammered down."

He doesn't look like he entirely understands, but he nods anyway. "Got it."

"Take a walk, explore the mall, and grab whatever you want. Like I said, there's no money here, and the people are extremely nice. Video games, comic books, whatever takes your fancy. And, hey, you might want to get a new outfit, since that one's torn and I'm guessing not your real clothes anyway."

He pokes at the hole in his shirt and chuckles. "Yeah, that seems like a good idea. Uh, meet back here in an hour? Two hours?"

"However long it takes. I'll be here, and if I'm not, I won't be far."

Dante wanders off deeper into the mall, and the second he's out of sight I break another table.

"Fuck! Fuck damn shit ass piss fuck. Goddamn it!" I'm breathing heavy, which is stupid because I don't even need to breathe anymore, it's just an automatic response, a lingering piece of my old humanity. I breathe out and force my lungs to still, force my body to halt its reflex to breathe in new air. I clench my fingers and hold my whole body still and stiff like the porcelain I've reforged it in.

Claws at my fingertips. Fangs and a hinged jaw. Red eyes like pools of blood. Porcelain skin, smooth and without sexual characteristics, without pores or hairs or openings. This inhuman body is *mine,* I made it, I guided its evolution toward perfection. I am yet imperfect, but I am closer, and that's more than he can say, more than most anyone can say, but it's not *enough.*

She gave him three wishes. She denied me three wishes. She knows that I want *everything*, and she taunts me with my lack thereof.

I laugh, dark and hungry and hateful. "This is war. If it wasn't before, it certainly is now."

I can taste Cheshire's fear and I can see it in her eyes, but she swallows her hesitation and nods. "I'm with you. Wherever our path leads, I'm with you."

I let myself breathe again, and I slump into a chair at the nearest unbroken table, tilted to face away from it. "Well. We've got an hour to kill, or more. Let's make it productive."

Cheshire settles in next to me. "What did you have in mind?"

I conjure [Swarmheart], [Hunter's Marker], and Vorpal, and place them on the table. My fourth artifact, [My Heart], I keep safe around my neck. "The way I see it, I've got two advantages in this contest: my ultimate spell, [Feast or Famine]; and my witch ability, the Gift of Artifice." I don't know if that's its "official" name, but it's what I'm going with. "I should be working to get maximum value out of both, in whatever way I can."

The most obvious idea would be to pump castings of [Feast or Famine] into an amplifier artifact, but I already tried that and it didn't work. Back in the Reveler's maze, after killing the boss monster, I tried to capture the resonances from our fight, hoping that the single casting of [Carrion Swarm] wouldn't be enough to disrupt the purity of the resulting artifact. It didn't matter, though, because the object I used melted like my birds and vanished into black mist. The Abyss, it would seem, does not appreciate being caged inside an artifact.

"I can't directly empower [Feast or Famine] with artifacts, so we'll have to come at it from a different angle. Since I can cast that spell through the creatures I summon with [Carrion Swarm], it might be worthwhile to invest some energy in upgrading [Swarmheart]."

Cheshire hums and taps the chunk of amber. "I think we should be cautious with altering successful artifacts. We don't know what kind of effect it will have, and it could cause anything from diminishing returns to complete destabilization. With how limited your library of spells currently is, I think it might be wiser to focus on versatility and expanding your toolkit."

"I'm open to suggestions."

"Something to do with bats, maybe? They *are* associated with vampires, so you'll get that little boost."

I snort-laugh. "Have I really not used bats at all so far? Man, that is such a missed opportunity. Yeah, okay, let's do that. But . . . not just that. I have some ideas I want to try out."

I banish Vorpal and [Hunter's Marker] but keep [Swarmheart] handy, and then I quickly dart over to the nearest store with goth-adjacent jewelry and snatch up everything remotely bat-themed.

"When it comes to using my Gift, the biggest bottleneck right now is my inability to separate out resonances from each other. That makes any live combat situation practically useless in terms of artifact creation, and that's only gotten worse now that one of the two spells in my kit is anathema to any artifact."

I explain my process to Cheshire as I start casting instances of [Carrion Swarm]. The first casting summons a group of centipedes that immediately start eating each other. The second casting summons a group of bats that screech at the surviving centipede, and then I repeat both castings.

"To get stronger as an artificer, I need to learn how to divide resonances, and I think it's possible—no, I know that it's possible. The Beast said as much, and it makes sense. I just have to learn how to do it. So consider this a bit of essential practice."

I flicker on my soul sight, painting the world in paper and ink, and then I reach deeper within myself, seizing upon the spark of my Gift, and my vision changes again. The world around me, already cast in bare sketches, disappears entirely. The tables and shops, the figments and their strings, they all dim and fade.

Cheshire remains, her soul appearing identical to her physical form. The chunk of amber in my hand also remains, though with two key differences: first, the amber glows brightly and the centipede within wriggles and squirms; and second, the object vibrates with magic that I can hear and understand.

I hear the name that I gave it, and I hear the raw freshness of its existence, so young and so fragile. I could crush this with a thought and scatter the dust. I hear gnashing teeth and carrion cries, a pit of crawling, biting nightmares. It tells me that its primary purpose is to evolve many lesser bugs into a single greater bug, and that its secondary purpose is to amplify the creation of lesser bugs to be used as meat.

I turn my attention from [Swarmheart], and in front of me I see and hear writhing strands of lingering magic. The strands interfere with each other, digging into each other like parasites, and they intermix in ways that make it difficult to identify distinct threads.

I see birds eating bats eating bugs, all of it wreathed in black mist and shot through with black lines like a strange circulatory system. It's chaos, and every time I blink the pattern changes, the balance shifts, and what's eating what cycles from one to another. The sound of it is like nails on a chalkboard and a dozen untuned instruments struggling for dominance.

I know there are four spells creating this mess: my repeated use of [Feast or Famine] to slay the not-cats is undoubtedly responsible for the black mist creeping into everything, while the various resonances of animalistic consumption were born of the three different variations of [Carrion Swarm] that I've unleashed.

I scowl at the cacophony. *How the hell am I going to untangle this?* I try to focus on one strand at a time and let everything else fall away, but it's all too muddled, too contradictory. The second I bring one into focus, another surges in front of it and steals my attention.

I wade into the maelstrom, having to avoid tables and chairs by sense of touch—ow, ow, my ankle—and once I'm close enough I reach out and grab hold of one strand: a solitary bat, flapping its wings, mouth open wide.

The vibrations of the bat expand and surround me, flowing through me, thrumming in my bones. Sound. Proliferation. Focus.

I release the bat and grab one of the crawling bugs, and when its resonances fill me I immediately note the similarities to [Swarmheart]. These resonances are untamed, they lack purpose, but they still have that core of consumptive, adaptive hunger.

Still, though I can isolate a single resonance with my sight by grasping it, it's not a perfect solution. I try to pull an individual resonance into an artifact, but the surrounding resonances come with it, tangled and blending into each other. My first attempt melts as soon as I give it a name. I try again immediately, and my second attempt fails like the first, but that seems to clear up the Abyssal resonances in the area, which should make future attempts easier.

My third attempt explodes, which I really should have predicted. I recast [Carrion Swarm] a few times and try again, still going by brute force and speed, which results in another exploding artifact I have to toss away. On my fifth attempt I try another tactic: I unsheathe my claws and try to picture them as a severing force, pushing my will into the blades on the ends of my fingers. I slash through the resonances in the air with the intent to separate the bugs and bats, and after a few tries and a spot of mindfulness meditation I'm finally successful; my physical motion is echoed in the metaphysical world, cutting a clean line through the strand I was targeting.

This, too, is not a perfect solution; the line is clean, but the two halves are not pristine, as each possesses a few trace remnants of the other portion. Even with such brief contact between spell echoes, contamination is rapid and extensive. The resulting artifact doesn't explode, which is a relief, but from peering at it with my sight and listening to its whispers I come away with the understanding that it would eventually degrade from growing instability if I used it regularly.

Hmm. This does raise an interesting question: if I can create artifacts, can I destroy them? Could I reclaim this object's resonances and repurpose them?

Willing it to dissolve or return to its source doesn't work, nor do any of the command phrases I try on it. *So that's not part of my Gift, damn. But, maybe if I treat it like a resonance when making a new artifact?*

For my sixth attempt I slash more lines in the mass of resonances, cutting the threads into smaller and smaller segments until I can isolate a few pure strands that I bring together into the next artifact. At the same time, I clutch the previous artifact with all my strength and will the resonances within it to travel into the new artifact.

The impure creation crumbles to dust in my hand, and its resonances are drawn into the new object. I try to cut away the unwanted elements of that batch, but I'm not fully successful, and the result is still impure and thus doomed to degradation.

I sigh and crush this artifact, too, to release its resonances. I repeat the painstaking process of severing resonances, and this time I only use those which I can verify as truly pure.

The seventh artifact is at last my first success, but it's not a complete success: [Echoshriek] has the right passive property, which amplifies the quantity of bats that I produce when I summon them as part of [Carrion Swarm], but its active property is a form of echolocation that I just do not need when I have Cheshire pulling recon duty with her weird geist senses.

"This is a slightly bigger problem," I admit aloud. "I'm making headway when it comes to separating out resonances, but I don't even know where to start with *altering* resonances, and it looks like having the bats focus all their noises on a single target still gives off echolocation rather than 'sonic stun attack.' Ideas?"

Cheshire circles me and looks around at all of my summons. "Maybe the centipede is a bad target? I know their antennae can sense vibrations, but I'm not sure that's enough to disorient one, and I doubt it would give much sign of it even if you did stun one with sound." She stops in front of me, pulls off her beanie cap, and says, "You should cast it on me instead. I'm hypersensitive to certain noises like you are, and I can give you the right responses to sell the move."

I hesitate. "Are you sure? You don't have to."

She smiles at me. "It's fine, really. Go ahead."

"Okay."

Cheshire takes a few steps back, and I do quick cleanup: I unsummon the critters that hadn't already faded away, make a final volatile artifact and toss it to clear the lingering resonances, and then I cast [Carrion Swarm] half a dozen times in quick succession—making use of [Echoshriek] to pump their numbers—to make a truly impressive cloud of bats, all with orders to give their best debilitating shriek at Cheshire when I snap my fingers.

I give the command, and all the bats scream at Cheshire in unison. I wince at the sound, but it's much worse for Cheshire. The catgirl clutches at her ears and doubles over, face tight, teeth gritted. The image makes me uncomfortable, but I try to focus on crafting the artifact.

I steady myself, breathe, and imagine all the resonances in the area pouring it into a new artifact: "[Shriekwave]."

A focused blast of sound surges out of the bat-winged brooch that I used as a base for the artifact, and it slams directly into Cheshire. The catgirl cries out and wobbles, and if she was acting before she definitely isn't now.

"Cheshire!" I call out, and make to move toward her, but she holds up a hand and shakes her head.

"Keep going. You wanted to test if you can make artifacts stronger, right? Here's your chance."

"I . . . I did, yes. If you're okay." I hesitate only a moment before summoning more bats. They fill the air and once again blast Cheshire with sound. I seize those new resonances, gather them, and pour them into [Shriekwave], naming it aloud for a second time.

To my soul sight, the artifact looks like a living bat with an oversized mouth and four wings. As the second set of resonances is drawn into the artifact, the bat starts to glow brighter and brighter, and for a moment I'm worried about it exploding, but then the glow settles.

The whispering tells me that the artifact has the same properties as before, but now both properties have been strengthened and amplified. The test is a success.

Cheshire is still reeling from the second blast, eyes wide and blinking, ears flat against her head, but she gives me a thumbs up when she sees the concern on my face. "One more," she half-shouts.

I swallow my objections and nod, trusting her to know her own limits. I repeat the process a final time, and as soon as I tell Cheshire that the artifact is stable she stumbles over to me and melts back into my shadow, charm bracelet falling into my hand.

"Are you okay?" I ask Cheshire, concern in my voice.

"I will be," she murmurs, invisible and intangible but her words spoken directly into my ear. "I just need some time without a body, I think." She chuckles. "I can at least confirm that thing packs a real punch. Oh, you should probably drink somebody, after spending all that mana."

"Good idea," I murmur back. I spare her one more moment of concern, then get to hunting.

Finding a figment to feed on is never difficult, but I have to consider all the resonant implications of the act. As annoying as it was to realize, I have to accept that I'll get more mana from a woman than a man, and more mana from a woman I find physically appealing than not.

If I feed to kill, I'll get multiple times as much mana, but I'd rather not do that on someone who isn't trying to kill me. If someone threatens my life and my agency, I'll do the same to them without hesitation, but someone who treats me with kindness, even as a result of their programming, deserves the same level of consideration.

I know it's still hardly a moral act, but at least I'm abiding by some kind of principle.

I feed on four willing women, careful to control my hunger and take only a safe portion from each. The fresh mana floods into my system and invigorates me, makes me hungry for more, but I fight the urge to go on a feeding spree by thinking about magic instead.

I've made progress with my Gift, but my solution to the problem of mixed resonances has in turn created two new problems: it takes a lot of time and effort to divide mixed resonances into usable material, and the process is inefficient and wastes much of the source. Neither of those are obstacles when dealing with any resonance that I can reliably and repeatedly generate, but they'll severely hamper my efforts to make use of resonances produced by enemies.

Oh, and the severing technique I've learned also requires physical manipulation of the resonances in question, which is not otherwise a limitation of my artificing. So in three ways this technique is a step back from my normal process, even if it allows me to overcome a prior obstacle.

It works for now, but I need to practice differentiating resonances without relying on physical separation. I don't want to become overly accustomed to a slower, more demanding technique. If I can master purely mental manipulation of resonances, then I'll gain an incredible level of adaptability in combat against foes that rely on spells more than their innate abilities.

I return to the food court and lean against a wall, contemplating next steps. Cheshire emerges from my shadow, still incorporeal but looking better.

I give her a nod and a wave and ask, "Want me to manifest you? We can grab more food, if you're hungry, or you can turn into something fuzzy and I can give you lots of skritches."

She looks like she's about to object, but then admits, "That actually sounds great, yeah. Just the pets, thanks, I'm not that hungry."

I find a bench to settle into and chant the incantation to make Cheshire corporeal again. She immediately transforms into a fuzzy white cat and curls up on my lap, and I scratch her behind the ears and stroke her fur rhythmically.

After a few minutes of that, Cheshire speaks up. "While we have the time to set it up, I have a few ideas on how we can improve your spell utilization."

"Hit me."

"Now that you've won your first throne duel, you're able to take advantage of more of your scion powers. One of your unique privileges as a scion is the ability to create new spells, but the other half of that privilege is the ability to create spell *presets*. You can, in essence, set a spell into a particular configuration and then give that configuration its own name that you can cast directly. When you activate one of those preconfigured spells, it'll skip the priming stage and move directly to unleashing. That will improve your cast time, and it will also make it easier to rapidly switch between different versions of the same spell."

I lick my lips. "I like it."

Cheshire purrs and leans into my hand. "There's more: when we make a preset, I can link it to an artifact and have it activate that artifact as part of the casting. You won't be able to cast that preset without the artifact in hand, but that shouldn't be a problem. I've taken the liberty of making one such preset, [Carrion Heart], which is set to summon a large quantity of beetles, boosted by [Swarmheart], and as part of the casting it will activate [Swarmheart] to turn that swarm of beetles into a single giant beetle."

"Very efficient. Good choice, too, with the beetles; no offense to Mr. Wiggles or Sergeant Slicer, but I confess that Madame Hornsby was my favorite."

Cheshire giggles. "I thought you'd approve."

I continue my affections as I ask, "Any other presets?"

"Yes, one, and this one is a more sizable alteration: [Shadowbat Swarm] is not keyed to an artifact, though it will benefit from your [Shriekwave], but it represents a significant divergence from the baseline [Carrion Swarm] spell. These bats are digging deeper into your demonic connection to the Throne of Shadow in order to partially bypass the limitation we introduced to the spell to make it work with [Feast or Famine]: unlike your regular summons, these bats can fly outside of your max tethering range, which is otherwise a fair bit smaller than this food court."

It's a decent-sized food court, but even if that range completely encompassed the food court I'd find the limitation glaring. "Is there a catch?"

"Several. The less serious catch is that these bats will be insubstantial and frail, incapable of causing physical damage and easily degrading in response to physical trauma; however, as their primary purpose is to deliver a spell that, as we saw with the ravens, destroys the delivering host anyways, I consider that flaw largely moot. The more severe condition is that as beings of Shadow they will be particularly vulnerable to fire or very bright light."

"Hmm. Still worth it. Thank you, Cheshire."

We stay like that for a while, the Cheshire cat purring in my lap, and inevitably my thoughts return to the would-be hero with the sword.

Three wishes. Those are, in all likelihood, what the compass was leading me to. So, one wish to beat Averrich, two to spare. Do we try to leverage those other two wishes to gain some advantage, or do we want Dante to waste them so that he can't use them against us if we come to blows?

It would be nice to not have to kill that boy.

Aloud, I lament, "What has my life become, that a magical compass leads me to a wish-granting sword when I ask for help killing a mad faerie king?"

"An adventure," the cat says wryly.

I laugh quietly, and together we wait for Dante's return.

IV

Alright, I'm bored of waiting," I say half a minute later.

I pull a book from the shelf of my inner world's library and set it atop Cheshire, who shifts and meows but doesn't object or stop me. Where last we left off in *The Machinations of the Ashen Warlock,* the impoverished heroine had been thrust into the deadly Trials that all aspiring sorcerers must undergo to earn an apprenticeship. Her strong will and studious nature had carried her through the first few stages, but now she's up against the villainess, a twin-tailed prodigy from one of the most powerful sorcerer families in their society, and the difference in depth of formal education in sorcery is made stark.

There is, of course, a great deal of sexual tension between the two that I'm at least mostly certain is intentional on the part of the writer. When the villainess humiliates the heroine in magical combat and then lifts the heroine's chin and sneers down at her, I mean, come on, that's hella gay.

The story is just as engaging as it was when I started it in the bookshop, but I'm having trouble focusing on it now. This should be exactly my jam, but my reading keeps getting interrupted by spikes of anxiety about the Game of Glass and the kid with the wishing blade.

I grimace, shut the book, and wave over a passing figment. "Hey," I ask, "can you tell me the status of Dante Reyes?"

The figment smiles and politely shakes its head. "Apologies, Ms. Alice, but we're not at liberty to disclose information like that. If you'd like, we can pass along a message or a request to Mr. Reyes."

Yeah, figures that wasn't going to work. Would make surveillance too easy. "Mm . . . maybe. He doesn't know about figments yet, though I should really tell him before his ignorance makes someone think he's a lethe drinker. Ah, for now, could you have a figment frame it naturally, as a message passed along by hand?"

The figment nods. "Of course. We wouldn't want to break the illusion for any guest to whom that illusion is comforting."

I give a very flat look at that, but there's really no point picking fights with something that isn't really a person. "Please ask Dante Reyes how he's faring, then relay his response."

"Acknowledged." There's a brief pause, and then the figment speaks again. "Mr. Reyes is enjoying the Pyraplex's many shops, but will try to finish his browsing with reasonable haste."

I sigh. "Can't really hold that against him. Hey, Cheshire, I'm going to get up and go grab some food, fair warning."

Cheshire stretches, then hops off my lap and shifts back into her human form, complete with a beanie to hide the cat ears. I banish the book I was reading and meander back into the maze of culinary delights.

One vegetarian burrito later—beans, rice, salsa, guac, cheese, and sour cream—I drum my fingers along the table we're sitting at and complain to Cheshire, "I need more prep work to do. More ways to even the playing field between me and the other contenders."

Cheshire gives me a sympathetic look, but says, "It might do you some good to take some downtime, actually, while grace is in effect. You've already got an edge over most of the competition, at least the small fry, and the gulf between you and the heavy hitters like Averrich isn't something that can be closed in a day of artificing items and tweaking spells. You should try to destress while you have the chance."

I slump against the table and grumble, "I hate destressing. Relaxation is so unrelaxing."

She pats my shoulder. "Think of it like this: you know how, when you're stressing over an obstacle in a video game, or a bit of writer's block, or a hard math problem, sometimes the best thing to do is to get some rest and come back to it with fresh eyes? I think you can apply that principle to what we're doing here. You might be sharper after a bit of R&R than if you were to keep focused and on edge all the way from now to the Game's start tomorrow."

I find her logic annoyingly compelling. "Alright, fine. But we're not being completely unproductive; I'll think of something to do that'll be relaxing but also give us a chance to interrogate Dante further."

Cheshire chuckles. "I'd expect nothing less from you, Allie."

It isn't much longer before Dante returns from his shopping. He's traded the tattered uniform from before for an aggressively bland V-neck and jeans outfit, and he's added a belt for his sword and a messenger bag for whatever random garbage he picked out from the mall's plethora of options. He also has at least three shopping bags of miscellaneous goods hanging from one arm.

I rise from where I was sitting and walk over to meet him by the edge of the food court. "So, how was it?"

He grins and raises the shopping bags. "Pretty great. This place is awesome. If it weren't for the whole 'terrible death game' thing, this would actually be a pretty chill vacation."

"That is the rub, isn't it?" I breathe deep, roll my shoulders, and make my pitch. "So. I know we talked about it earlier, but, now that you've had time to process and maybe think it over, I wanted to check that you're still interested in working with me. It's a simple accord: I'll keep you safe, you'll make use of those wishes, and together we'll make sure this death game ends with the key in Esha's hands and both of us still alive. I know we've only just met, and you don't really have any compelling reason to trust me—"

Dante shakes his head. "No, I trust you. I'm in."

"Wait, what? Really? You trust me that easily?" I tilt my head at the strange man, baffled at the ease with which he said that.

He shrugs. "I like to think I have a good read for people, and you don't strike me as a bad person."

I burst out laughing. "I—I'm literally a demon. I'm a vampire. I turned myself into a demon vampire. I'm an actual real life nightmare fuel monster girl. I—have you seen what I can do with my mouth?" I unhinge my jaw and make my teeth razor-sharp, and then I flick a too-long too-pointy tongue through the air. "Are you seeing this?"

He actually does blink a few times at the display, but then he just shrugs again. "I mean, I think a lot of people would say that's pretty cool, even some people who aren't furries or monsterfuckers." Dante quirks an eyebrow at me. "Do you *not* want me to trust you?"

I flounder, the wind taken from my sails. "I mean . . . I guess I was expecting at least a *little* skepticism." *Why are you complaining about this!? Just take the win!* "Like, I was going to slowly defuse the undercurrent of tension by reminiscing about life back on Earth. Are you sure you have a good sense for people? I'm kind of awful. I may genuinely have been the worst person I knew back on Earth, and I only lose that contest here in the Labyrinth because I'm up against literal serial killers and insane conquerors."

He does not look like he believes me. "You say that, sure. The thing is, and maybe I'm generalizing, but most of the people I've known who talked about themselves like that? It was somebody else who made them feel that way." He actually looks at me with sympathy, the arrogant prick, and I have to suppress the urge to wipe that look off his stupid smug face.

"Yeah, well, shut up. We're going on a walk. To a park, or something. I want fresher air. I can't stand being cooped up in this mall for another minute. I can, like, show you the city, or whatever. Also give me your shopping bags, I have a magic inventory pocket dimension I can stick them in."

I teleport his bags, then stomp off and grab directions from the nearest figment, Cheshire and Dante trailing behind. We set off to finally leave the Pyraplex, and I stew in my own stupid emotions.

Argh, why is this kid so nice!? And he's not even dumb nice in a way I could infantilize and dismiss. He's got, like, empathy and shit! I hate it. Who in their right mind would trust me? What does he think I am?

I think he's judging us. He's already pegged us as crazy, you know he has. The table-breaking? The callous disregard for danger? We spaced out and he thought to himself, "Wow, what a fucking space cadet. I better be careful with this wild animal lest it fucking bite me." He's not ignorant of our nature as a monster, he's just acting nice and acting like he trusts us because he's scared of what we'll do otherwise.

He is nice! He's probably genuinely nice! If he were acting this way out of fear, we'd be able to taste that in the air. Can we not trust anyone? Am I not allowed to reciprocate a single goddess-damned ounce *of empathy?*

Since when have you had empathy? Since when do you care about having empathy? This is all so absurd. You should just kill the brat and be done with it. Take that Vorpal Blade and snicker-snack on his juicy innards. And hey, with that regeneration, how many meals do you think you could get out of him before he'd finally drop dead? How much mana? That's a feast begging to be eaten.

I grind my teeth and dig my nails into my palms. I am not going to lose control in front of both of them.

Oh, is that what this is about? Is it—

I dig my nails deeper, and then I remember I can make them *clawed,* so I do that, and the pain that follows is a joyous balm. I have to suppress the pleased sigh that threatens to bubble out of my throat. Control. I am in control.

I am not a child, I chastise my treasonous thoughts. *I am not a child, and I can control my emotions, and I'm not getting dragged down into this infuriating bullshit over something so stupid and minor. I—I don't even know why I'm reacting like this. Nothing he said really merits such an extreme response.*

Your disorder is defined by such extreme responses, the more rational part of me interjects. *Dante's casual assertion of trust was a shock, especially after you've spent the last few days obsessing over the difficulty and danger of trusting Cheshire. You lack faith in others, and so it unsettles you when someone has faith in you. And, of course, it's clear that his implication of victimhood struck a nerve. How will you handle that?*

I hum, mood shifted, and I conjure the ruined blouse from my vampire outfit. I wipe my hands on the blouse, cleaning off the droplets of blood drawn by my claws, and then I send the blouse back to my throne world. *Yeah. It's all cognitive dissonance, right? The self, the image of the self, and the world reflecting the self. I just have to reframe things and play the right part. This is nothing new for me, there's no great difficulty here. Just play the game and follow the rules.*

"Dante!" I suddenly say aloud. "Let's play a game."

"Hmm?"

I twirl around and clap my hands together, walking backwards as we stroll through the streets of the Sanctuary toward our destination. "I cannot possibly wade through a river of blood alongside you if I don't know at least a few details about you—your hopes, your fears, your waifus—and I'm sure you'd appreciate learning a few things about the creature that is to be your bodyguard and escort in the vicious, brutal Game to come." I show a toothy grin. "So let's get to know each other. You ask a question, I answer, you answer, then I ask a question, you answer, I answer, repeat until we're both bored of it. Sound fun?"

He sticks his hands in his pockets and gives me an easy, "Sure, why not."

"Great!" I twirl back around and slow my pace just enough to be walking between Dante and Cheshire. "Question the first: how do you answer to the trolley problem, the prisoner's dilemma, the ship of Theseus, and the ultimate question of free will?"

His face goes blank. "What?"

Cheshire snickers beside me. "Really going for the throat, huh? Those should really all count as different questions, you know. They're literally essay material."

"Bah! Bah, I say. But yeah, no, fair. Better first question: what's one piece of media that you get made fun of for liking but will defend to the death? The thing you can't say you like without sounding at least a little defensive about liking it, because you always have to argue against people telling you you're wrong or that it's shit." I peer at him expectantly, hands clasped behind my back and leaning in.

"Interesting question. I don't know that I have very controversial taste in most things." Dante hums and chews his lip, thinking about it, and then he winces and laughs. "Yeah, that's the one. Okay, uh. Hoo boy. How do I say this?"

"Off to an excellent start," I say gleefully.

"Okay, so, there's this game that my friend bought me as a joke. It's a puzzle game, one of those matching games where you have to move the tiles together. And it was actually a pretty engaging game! Like, the gameplay is solid, it's got a surprising amount of depth for what's essentially just a time-wasting mobile game. But it, uh, also happens to have a lot of . . . let's call it 'fanservice.'"

"Wait, are you talking about *HuniePop*?"

He winces again. "Ah, so you're familiar."

I laugh at him. "That's actually hilarious. I was not expecting you to pick the shitty match-3 softcore porn game, but that's incredibly funny. I mean, hey, no judgment, I played it too. Audrey best girl."

He protests, "I didn't play it for—wait, isn't that the really bitchy mean girl?"

"Mhm!" I grin. "She's the one who says, 'did I hurt your whore feelings?' which has since permanently entered into my lexicon. A truly delightful creature. Who was your favorite?"

"Definitely not telling. Your turn: what are your controversial takes?"

"Vriska did nothing wrong," I immediately respond.

"Who?"

I glare at the baffled man. "How do you *not* know *Homestuck*? Whatever, fine. Infect was one of the most interesting mechanics ever added to Magic: The Gathering and everyone who complains about it is a whiny baby because it's not even a competitive deck in any of the formats that it's legal in, so how the hell can you call it too fast when it's literally too slow for Modern!? Absurd."

"I do not play Magic, so I have no idea what most of that meant."

"Okay, fine, here's a different one: *The Last Jedi* was the best Stars Wars movie, fuck you fight me." When that fails to get a strong reaction out of him, I immediately follow up with, "Fourth edition was the single greatest edition of Dungeons & Dragons, objectively, and I will literally kill anyone who disagrees. It fixed the martial-caster imbalance, it added minions and healing surges and tags, and it fucking *worked!* And then a bunch of loser grognards couldn't handle that their precious game was different and actually functional, so they threw a tantrum and ruined everything."

He gives me an odd look and then chuckles. "You know, I actually have a friend who says nearly the same thing about that last one. You kinda remind me of him. My turn to ask a question?"

"Yeah, go for it."

He nods, picks his words, and starts to ask something, but then pauses and glances over at Cheshire. "Is she not going to take part in this, by the way?"

Cheshire waves at him and says, "Don't worry about me. You should just think of me as Alice's shadow; where she goes, I go, and what she decides, I support her in. I'm perfectly comfortable staying in the background."

He shrugs. "Alright. My question, then: let's say you had one week to do whatever you wanted. You'd have whatever resources you needed, no other concerns to manage, just one week to spend however you like. What would you do?"

I blow out air and lace my hands behind my head. "Man, that's a hard one. What would I do . . ." *Well I can't say "rule the world" or anything like that. Mm, what would I do, if I did have all the resources I wanted, godhood included?* "I would . . . attempt to make those resources permanently available to me even after the week has ended."

Dante rolls his eyes. "Come on, that's such a cop-out answer. That's like saying you'd wish for three more wishes."

"I mean, I totally would, but that's fair, you're right. I would . . ." *Seriously, what the hell would I do with a week like that?*

If I'm not pursuing more power, what's worth doing? What do I intend on doing once I have all the power I need? What am I going to do when I get the things I want? Can I not conceive of such a thing? Do I not have a vision of what comes next? Whatever, we need to answer something more normal anyway.

"I think that I would try to make something. I'd spend a week working on a book, or maybe a video game."

He looks at me skeptically. "Could you make either of those in a week?"

I shrug. "I'm interpreting 'resources' pretty broadly. Either way, I guess I'd just try to be productive."

"Wild." He shakes his head in disbelief. "Are you one of those workaholics who get anxious at the very thought of taking a vacation?"

I snort. "Hardly. I'm like sloth incarnate most days, that's why I'd use that week to get something done. I take it you'd go on some kind of big vacation, then?"

"Oh yeah, hundred percent. I'd get my friends together and we'd all go on a trip around Europe, hitting up all the major landmarks. Do you know how much food culture is spread throughout just a dozen countries? I once spent a whole day mapping out the best route to hit all the best eateries in a single trip, just on the off chance I'll be able to afford it someday."

"You've clearly put a lot more thought into this than I have. Alright, let me think of another question."

We reach the park as I ponder, and for a second I'm disoriented by the sudden shifting of our surroundings. One moment we're walking through the incredibly urban streets, stone and steel all around us, and then an idyllic scene of cultivated nature stretches out before us and behind us, the city skyline only visible in the distance thanks to the towering size of the central amphitheater.

The park is lush, full of green meadows and winding trails, tall trees, a pond with ducks, and people walking their dogs or settling in for picnics. It's a shockingly human scene, even more than anything I've seen in the mall or at that nightclub I nearly died at. There are just people here, enjoying life, even if most or all of them can't really enjoy anything.

Dante is way more disoriented than I am, and he whirls around and stares back the way we came, a bit of panic creeping into his eyes and into the tone of his voice. "What happened? Where did the city go? Did we get teleported or something?"

"Nah, that's just how this place is," I say casually, stretching and enjoying the fresh air and the scents of the natural world. "Cheshire, you explain it."

Cheshire smirks at me, but complies. "You both come from a world that obeys entirely physical laws, but the Labyrinth is a conceptual world and obeys conceptual laws. Some laws appear the same, like gravity, but others will be jarringly different. Distance in the Labyrinth is conceptual, and that manifests in a few ways. You've seen a bit of that, with the mirror portals, and now you're seeing another aspect. The Labyrinth is a fragmentary world, composed of many smaller sub-worlds. They're not truly different worlds, but their connections are conceptual, not physical. It would be inaccurate to say that you're a few feet away now from where you were a moment ago, and it would also be inaccurate to say that you're a mile away, despite appearances to suggest either. You're in the park, which is a separate district of the Sanctuary from the area surrounding the mall. You'll see that shift again when we leave, and likely more times over the course of the next few days."

"That is freaky," Dante mutters.

"That is not even close to the freakiest thing about this setting." I laugh. "Alright, I've got my next question: do you prefer solitary, social, or competitive hobbies?"

We start walking along one of the park trails as Dante thinks up his answer. "That's an interesting one, I've never thought of them that way. My main interests are cooking and fighting games, which I guess you could say are solitary and competitive hobbies, respectively, though I think there's a social aspect to both. I also make time to play in a D&D game twice a month with some of my friends."

I clap my hands excitedly. "Ooo, nice! What edition? And what's your character build?"

"We play fifth edition, and I've never played any of the others. As far as build, uh, I don't really think about that stuff all that much." He scratches his head sheepishly. "My first character was a dwarf cleric, entirely because I saw it in a webcomic that my friend kept trying to get me to read, and he helped me build the character. He was more into the wargaming aspect than me, though, and the character was more complex than I felt comfortable playing, so they let me switch to a human barbarian. I don't really think a lot about stuff like character build, I just roll dice and hit things with a big stick."

"Perfectly valid way to play. I am the kind of degenerate that can't help but minmax and optimize everything, so I'd probably start twitching if I saw your character sheet, but I can respect the mentality behind it."

"Ha. Yeah, you really sound like that guy sometimes. Anyway, how about you?"

I have an answer for this one prepped and ready, so I launch into it. "My main hobby back home was playing Magic. It's a card game with complex rules and an emphasis on interaction between game pieces and between player and opponent. To truly master the game, you have to understand not only the individual game pieces and how they fit together but also the environment you're building a deck for and how your opponents are likely to act. I enjoy sinking my teeth into a particular format of the game and steadily improving my skills at both deckbuilding and moment-to-moment decision-making. I do it for the satisfaction of feeling clever but also because, in all honesty, I just really enjoy winning. It's absolutely a competitive hobby for me."

I'm also something of a sadist and specifically gravitate toward archetypes that will cause my opponent as much pain as possible, but let's leave that part out. There's a fine line between enjoying healthy competition and seeking a socially acceptable outlet for sadistic impulses, and I'd prefer he thinks I lie on the former end.

"That aside, I believe the next question is yours."

"Hmm, yeah." He points over at the duck pond and says, "Let's go say hi to the ducks."

"Sure."

We head over that way, breaking from the path to cross the crisp grass, and Dante asks his next question: "Before all this stuff with magic and monsters and other worlds, what did you want to do in life? What did you want to be? Did you have any driving ambition?"

A god. I wanted to be a god. I still want to be a god. Nothing else could possibly matter. I clear my throat and say, "I, uh, I wanted to be a writer when I was younger, but I eventually gave up on that when I realized it was never going to happen."

He tilts his head curiously. "Why not?"

"Ah, well . . . it's hard. Writing isn't really about talent, is the thing. I had talent, lots of it, but talent is worthless if you don't have a good work ethic. Or, more charitably, if you've got a disorder or two sabotaging your ability to develop a good work ethic."

"Oh, like ADHD?"

"Something like that, yeah." *Try autism and borderline with a smattering of symptoms from the rest of Cluster B, but sure, let's go with that one. Better optics.* "It's not a big deal, though. I got over it a long time ago, and now I have magic. What's your ambition?"

"Oh, that's easy: I want to be a chef. I love cooking for people, I love food, I love learning about food from different parts of the world. I'm even taking some culinary arts courses online."

"Huh, neat." I sit down by the edge of the pond and skip a rock across, aiming away from where the birds are. "What do you enjoy about cooking?"

Dante sits down next to me, and Cheshire sits on my other side. He says, "There's a lot to like about it. You get to make something, you get to see people appreciate your hard work, and it tastes good too. Plus, hey, it's real popular with the opposite sex."

I snort-laugh. "I suppose that's one reason. Plenty of guys wouldn't know how to fry an egg if you showed them a manual. Next question: what's your favorite video game? You said you were into fighting games, right?"

He nods. "Yeah, that's most of what I play. Actually, that's basically all I really play, nowadays. I've played a bunch. I like *Guilty Gear* and *Melty Blood*, but my main game is *Smash Ultimate*. I like any fighting game that has a big enough roster to get some real variance in movesets."

"No memory problems? That's one of the things that kept me out of *Dota*, though I hear the competitive players don't really struggle with it despite the hundred-some heroes."

He wiggles a hand. "Kinda. It's not usually a problem, especially for the pros, but *Ultimate* is getting to that point."

"Mm. *Smash* is the only fighting game I've played, for the record. I mean I've played like, a teensy amount of *BlazBlue*, but I hated it. Liked *Smash*, though. I mained Meta Knight in *Brawl*."

Dante laughs. "Did you know he was banned from tournament play? He warped the competitive scene so much that he ended up being the first and only character to be banned in *Smash*'s entire history."

"Damn. That probably explains why I liked him so much."

He grins. "That competitive side of you, eh? Alright, what's your favorite video game?"

"I was massively into *World of Warcraft* for probably over a decade. I raided with a guild for a while, got into PvP for a time, but I spent most of my time solo leveling and collecting rare items. It was a game that I really felt like I understood, something I could genuinely get good at with the right time and effort. It's also way more intricate and engaging than people who don't play it give it credit for."

"*WoW*, huh? I actually got sucked into that for about a year before I realized how much of my time it was eating and I quit cold turkey. I played during, what was it, mists of something?"

I wriggle and grin. "*Mists of Pandaria*! The best expansion. It was great, it had some of the best world design, solid class design, awesome questing . . ."

I proceed to ramble about *World of Warcraft* for an unknown length of time, getting completely lost in infodumping about my special interest, until I am interrupted by a tap on the shoulder and a familiar voice.

"Hey," says Lena with a smile. "I was hoping I'd find you again."

Immediately my infodump slams to a stop and I'm thrown back to the last time I saw Lena, when she was stumbling away from me with a big hole in her neck. This was the girl—the figment—that I fed on in the nightclub. My first meal. The girl I almost killed.

I have no idea how to feel about that, so I quickly say, "Hey, uh, Dante, wait right here, I'll be back," and stand up to move away from where he and Cheshire are sitting.

Lena leads me to a nearby tree big enough that we can both stand behind it and be mostly obscured from the two by the pond. I follow her and I watch her closely, noting the faint scar on her neck and the same outfit as before and the way that she's *not dead*.

I wasn't really certain, after the condition I left her in, if she was going to make it. I drank a lot of blood, after all, and our departure was violent, even if she was immediately escorted away by her friends. But here she is, in the flesh, still alive.

Lena smiles at me, again. "Hey."

"Hey," I respond awkwardly. "You're not dead."

She laughs. "Are you surprised?"

"Kinda, yeah."

She tilts her head. "Are you disappointed?"

"What? No, of course not. I didn't mean to kill you. I wasn't trying to . . . I didn't want to take too much, I just got so lost in the moment. I'm sorry." And I actually kind of am, as weird as that feeling is. "I'm glad you lived."

Lena rubs her neck and says, "I am too. Well, not really, obviously, because I'm not a real person and I can't feel glad about anything, but you know what I mean." She keeps smiling as she reminds me what she really is, and I shiver.

The figments of the city unnerve me in fascinating ways. I want to keep talking to them. I want to get to know them. I want to dissect them. I stare at Lena and I remember the way she acted shy and sweet and flirty when she first approached me, and I remember the way she so casually admitted that she wasn't a real person. She's just a fake.

I raise two fingers to the mark on her throat and feel the warmth of her pale skin and the pulse of the blood flowing through her tall, lithe body. She is alive in the sense of meat, but she tells me that she cannot think or feel and that all evidence to the contrary is just part of the illusion. She is no more a person than any of the monsters I shaped inside my throne world.

But she can lie so very convincingly, and does truth really deserve to be given more weight than a lie? When I unsheathe my claws and the sharpened tips dig into the skin of her throat and her breath catches, eyes wide, lips parted, should that masterpiece of acting be discarded and ignored simply because it is only *acting*?

I retract my claws and brush my hand through her soft platinum hair, attention still locked on the micro expressions of her face. The removal of danger stimulus should prompt relief, but instead I see disappointment in the fall of her eyelids and lips and the deep exhalation of her breath. The story she's telling me is her character is motivated by attraction to danger, and the risk to her life is the very thing that drew her back to me.

Softly, I say, "When we met, you told me your purpose was to make people happy. Is that really your purpose? Is that the only reason you found me again?"

In the lair of the Beast, when it tried to force its shard on me, it used Lena to make a point. I saw her there only for a moment, like a phantom image, but it shook me. And now that I understand the connections between figment, throne world, and guiding will, I have to wonder: is Lena really acting on autopilot, just another attendant feeding lotus flowers to all who enter the paradise garden?

Or is she the Labyrinth's response to Cheshire?

Lena takes my hand in hers, intertwined between strands of hair. "A girl can have lots of reasons for doing something, can't she? My purpose is to make you happy. My motivation is allure. And if that happens to give you more options to consider . . . isn't that for the best?"

I hear a growl from behind me, and then Cheshire is at my side, glaring at Lena with murder in her eyes. I gently extricate my hand from Lena's and watch the two of them, intrigued by this about-face; last time they were in the same room together, Cheshire was encouraging me to flirt with Lena.

Lena beams beatifically at the changeling. "It's nice to see you again, Cheshire. You were a wonderful help, that night in the club."

"You were supposed to die," Cheshire hisses. "You were supposed to be food. If those hunters hadn't been there, you'd be a corpse right now."

Ah. It clicks: Cheshire was so willing to put me in the arms of another woman because she was expecting me to overfeed and kill that woman. Lena was meant to be a sacrificial lamb for the sake of my mana, but she lived.

Lena acts wounded by Cheshire's words. "Now, now, there's no need for that. Do we really have to fight over Maven's affections? Don't you think she'd be happier with *two* girlfriends?"

I wonder: would I enjoy seeing Cheshire kill Lena, or would I be horrified? I've always loved the yandere trope in fiction, the lovesick crazy girl willing to murder her rivals to be the sole recipient of her love interest's affections . . . but reality and fiction have different contexts, and now I'm not so certain if that's what I want most. Would Cheshire killing Lena prove her love for me, or would it just be another sign of a manipulator trying to isolate me? Of course, I've promised to trust Cheshire, and I've made no such promise toward Lena.

Cheshire laughs and says scornfully, "You're not even a person. You wouldn't be her girlfriend, you'd be a toy for her to play with until it breaks. A *thing* to be pulled apart piece by piece."

Lena bites her lip and hugs herself. "And doesn't that sound *wonderful*? To be known beneath the knife? To be put in such perilous danger for nothing more than another's pleasure? You should know that, Cheshire. You've lived it."

Cheshire's nails bite into her palms. "I was made for Alice. Made perfect for her, made to be exactly what she wants. I know her more intimately than you ever will. I can help her. I can support her. You're weak, but I'm strong, and with me at her side she will devour gods and archdemons until she stands before the throne of the Demiurge and eats her too."

"Ah, but are you really what she wants? Or just what she thinks she wants? You feed her hungers, but she can never be in *control* around you, with you, of you, because of the very nature of your being and how you were remade. Face it, Cheshire: you weren't made to be perfect, you were made to be *flawed*."

Cheshire's face flashes with emotion—rage, hate, fear—and she takes a step forward, tension coiling in every muscle, but when I reach out and squeeze her shoulder she stops.

"I have a proposal," I interject. "Let's settle this another time. I don't know if you've heard, but there's a big scary death game that I have to deal with for the next however many days, and I'm going to be a little too busy trying to survive to think about girlfriends or dating or anything like that. But! You both make some interesting points, and I do wish to pursue this thread further, so how about this: after I've won the Game of Glass, let's all go on a date—you, you, and me—and then we can sort all this out. Does that work for everyone?"

"I'm fine with that," Lena answers immediately.

Cheshire, having no choice but to agree or lose ground, reluctantly nods. "If that's what you want."

"Then it's settled! I look forward to a nice day with you both. Now, Cheshire, I think we should get back to Dante before he starts to get concerned. It was lovely to see you again, Lena."

"Likewise, Maven." She curtsies, gives me a wink, and walks off, Cheshire glaring at her as she goes.

"So," I say to Cheshire. "That went interesting. Oh, don't sulk; I'm taking you on a date once this is over! That's a step in the right direction, isn't it?"

The changeling swallows, nods, and finally replaces her angry expression with a smile. "Yes. Yes, that's right. I'm very grateful for that opportunity, thank you."

"I'm sure it'll be fun for everyone. Now let's head back to Dante."

I round the tree and start heading in his direction, but slow as I see another person talking to him, what looks like a man in plain garb. Another figment? Soul sight confirms it.

Dante waves as we approach. "Hey, Alice. There's a message for you. It's from that woman, Esha."

I quicken my pace. "A message?"

The figment smiles at my arrival. "An invitation, to be precise. You, along with several other key individuals in the city, have been invited by the Myriad to attend a summit being hosted at the community center. Esha wishes to discuss the Game of Glass while a truce is still in effect. She believes that a nonviolent solution is still possible, or, failing that, the establishment of terms of conduct that may prevent this conflict from bringing ruin to the city and its inhabitants. Are you interested in joining?"

"Yes, absolutely." My plan was to ally with Esha even before the Game was announced, and now it's a key part of my strategy for keeping Dante friendly. "We'll head there right away. Please let Esha know we're coming."

The figment bows. "Of course. I'll go at once."

He leaves, and I look to Dante and Cheshire. "Well, this is convenient."

Cheshire raises an eyebrow. "Do you think this summit will actually work?"

I laugh. "Oh, not a chance. But it'll give us a good view of the competition, and it's an excellent excuse to establish contact with Esha and discuss forming an alliance."

Dante frowns. "I think we should still try for a nonviolent option if we can."

"I'm not opposed to it, I just don't think Averrich or Vaylin will go for it in a million years. But, hey, we'll give it our best shot. I'm certainly not going to try and sabotage Esha's plans when I'm hoping to join her team."

He nods. "Alright then. Shall we get going?"

"Let's."

And with that, we set off for the Myriad's temple.

V

On our way to the Myriad, I give Dante a primer on the city's major factions. "The Myriad are the guys we're heading to now, led by Esha, and it probably wouldn't be inaccurate to call them religious, but I think spiritual might give you a better picture. Spirits are a thing in this setting, and they can embody different culturally held concepts. In this case, the Myriad are closely tied to the spirit of the city itself, which is distinctly different from the Beast, to my knowledge."

I glance to Cheshire for confirmation and she nods, saying, "Spirits are inherently tied to groups of people, and this spirit represents the people of this city. It's a separate existence from the Beast that created this city, and it likely opposes the death game that the Beast has called, since that disrupts the harmony of the city."

Dante considers that. "So, how religious are they, actually? Are we walking into a convent or a monastery or something?"

I wiggle a hand. "They call it a community center, but it definitely looks like a temple, and their leader is a priestess, but their organization is explicitly open to the irreligious. It's an odd thing."

"Huh. Alright. What about the others?"

I crack my knuckles and grin. "Well, the group that we're most likely to butt heads with is going to be King's Carnival. They're a bunch of hunters led by a crazy asshole fae, our fellow keyholder Averrich. You may have seen him during the announcements, and noticed that his patron was one of the cheaters. He was given forewarning so he could try and kill as many of the competitors as possible on day one."

"Right, yeah, I forgot about that." Dante pauses. "Wait, wasn't the other 'cheater' the one who chose you?"

I grimace. "Yes, and that's a long story, but the short of it is that I've never met that fucker and I hope I never do. He did *not* give me forewarning, just used a pawn of his to push me into the path of Averrich. I'm lucky to have survived my encounter with that man."

Dante looks uneasy. "You really have had a rough go of it."

I wave a hand dismissively. "Irrelevant. There are two more factions to be aware of: the Voidhearts and the Guild. The latter hasn't come up much yet, so all I know about them is that they specialize in making magic items. The former group is responsible for a great deal of strife in this city. The Voidhearts are led by Vaylin, a demon, and her hunger for power is what pushed the rest of the city into a cycle of escalating conflict."

"How so?" he asks.

I hum to myself. I could give him a simple answer, but that's really not my style. "Are you familiar with the Red Queen's race?"

He shakes his head. "Doesn't ring a bell."

"It's from *Through the Looking-Glass,* the sequel to *Alice in Wonderland.* In that book, little Alice meets the Red Queen and runs with her. She runs as fast as she can, but it takes all her speed just to stay stuck in the very same place. She's running and running and going nowhere."

And, I suddenly remember, *her goal in that book is to cross the chessboard and become queen. Fuck me running, is* that *why the Beast made that reference?*

Dante frowns. "So . . . it's pointless?"

I set possible revelations aside and give Dante a grin. "Ah, but see, if she stopped running, then she wouldn't be able to keep up with the Red Queen. And *that* is why people love to use it as an example. Take evolution: in a given ecosystem, organisms are constantly adapting to become better at both eating and not being eaten, and so every evolutionary advantage in one species is matched by an adaptation in another, and the overall fitness of the system remains at a stable level. Constant adaptation, but no permanent progress. They're running and running and going nowhere, but if they stop running they'll starve or get eaten.

"If you take that logic and apply it to international politics, you get something called the security dilemma. Every state is motivated to increase its own security, but doing so represents a potential threat to all other states, prompting them to increase their own security. When the power to the east starts equipping its soldiers with newer, better guns, you cough up the funds to purchase your own such firearms, even if those funds have to come from conquering a weaker state. The states that don't play the game, that refuse to take part in the arms race, become those easy targets. So everybody has to run, and keep running, even though nobody is getting any safer."

Dante absorbs all that and takes a moment to chew on it, brow furrowed in thought. "Okay, I think I maybe understand what you're talking about. So, how does this tie to the demon you mentioned?"

"As it was told to me," I say, "Vaylin swept into town, rounded up every little gang or group, and gave each of them a choice: serve or die. She never stopped recruiting, never stopped growing her faction, and that's forced the other factions to step up their own recruitment efforts lest they become easy prey for Vaylin."

"Why don't they just work together? Isn't that what we're trying to do?"

I shrug. "In theory, yeah. But it's not that easy in practice. How many concessions are you really willing to make to a supposed ally when you could just take what you want instead? That answer's going to be different for different groups and different leaders. In this situation . . . it would seem that Averrich and the Machinist—that's the Guild's leader—chose to prioritize their own survival over the alliance they once held with Esha and the Myriad."

"And that's why you think this summit won't work," Dante guesses.

"Among other reasons."

We finally arrive at the wide-open square that houses the Myriad's headquarters. This is Dante's first time seeing it, so he looks pretty impressed, and I have to admit the structure is impressive. Esha insists that her stronghold should be framed as a community center, not a temple, but I think that Bashe was right to call it a shrine.

The temple is a vast structure of ornate architecture and decorative statuary all carved from marble and basalt. The building itself is a work of art, but it pales before the massive tree growing out of it. The trunk is tall and thick, and its branches spread to create a great canopy that casts the whole area in shadow—or what passes for shadow in the Labyrinth. The leaves of the tree are a strange mix of vibrant summer greens and crisp autumn reds, like the tree exists in both seasons at once.

Standing out front are two familiar faces: the jackal-headed guards who were wary of me when I showed up unannounced asking for medical attention. This time they give me a nod, clearly recognizing and expecting me, and they usher us inside with a calm, "The priestess is waiting inside."

Okay, showtime. Let's try not to fuck this up.

The last time I was here, I shaped a persona around artificial Truths: curiosity, gratitude, and fear. I see no reason to abandon that groundwork, so I focus on how I can interpret my current feelings along those lines.

I am curious about the Game of Glass, but I am fearful of my competitors. I am curious about the shard, but I am fearful of what it would do to me, and I would be grateful to pass it to someone who can do good with it. I am curious what Esha would do with the shard. I am afraid of the Beast of Lamentation and Euphoria, and anything her hands have touched.

And hey, most of that isn't even a lie.

Dante marvels at the shrine's interior while I plot and scheme, and soon after entering we are approached by an attendant who offers to take us directly to Esha. We accept, of course, and are led through the halls.

I was expecting to be led to that central chamber with the glowing pool beneath roots, the room with all the murals, but instead we're led away, deeper into the temple. The attendant takes us to an open-air courtyard that has a nice garden quality to it, the kind of thing you'd see inside a monastery. There are flowers and vegetables in little patches, a tree in each corner, a few benches along the edges, and a fountain in the center. Clean flagstones line the space between patches of rich soil, and the great tree above casts its not-quite-shadow over the whole space.

Esha stands by the fountain, looking the same as ever, and she's accompanied by her bodyguard, Achaia, who's still wearing that outlandish power armor. There's one other figure with them, a person I wasn't expecting to see and am quite nervous to see: Bashekehi, the imp of Indulgence that I spent my first two days in the Labyrinth bickering with.

They make a fascinatingly mismatched trio: Esha in her plain robes and water globe staff looking perfectly at home in a classical fantasy setting, Achaia in power armor straight out of science fiction, and Bashe in a fancy blue coat but marked by ram's horns and a barbed tail as someone of fiendish nature.

I freeze for a moment when I see them. Bashe and I didn't leave on the best of terms to begin with, and that was before I sold him out to save my own skin. At least King's Carnival didn't track him down, I guess? If that's the case, he probably doesn't even know what I did.

He still won't be happy to see me, and I can hardly blame him, given what fresh hell our two days together were. Except, actually, I can totally blame him, because I saved his ass from eternal imprisonment inside a rock tomb.

The incubus and the priestess are having a friendly conversation when we walk in, but they both pause as I arrive with Dante and Cheshire at my side. Bashe's expression turns carefully neutral when he sees me, which I return with a quiet nod. Then his gaze flits over Cheshire, becoming briefly annoyed, and over Dante, and after a second of confusion his eyes widen in recognition.

Esha is first to speak, cheerful in that annoyingly peaceful way of hers. "Ah, Maven, it's so good to see you. I am most grateful that you accepted my invitation."

I give a friendly wave and a nervous laugh. "Ha, well, how could I say no? I was actually thinking of visiting anyway so we could talk things out and come to some kind of understanding that didn't evolve trying to kill each other. But, ah, we can get to that later. Did anyone else agree to come?"

Esha nods. "Yes, to my relief. Both Averrich and the Machinist have agreed to send representatives while grace is still in effect. They should be along some time in the next few hours, and then we can—wait, is that the seventh candidate?" Esha turns toward Dante in disbelief, finally registering what Bashe picked up on; the clothing may be different, but that's definitely the face of the final keyholder.

Dante waves awkwardly. "Hello, Dante here. I, uh, I'm really just following Alice's lead here. It's nice to meet you though!"

Esha, still baffled, manages to get out a quick, "Ah, yes, the pleasure is mine," before turning back to me. "How did you—I mean, it's not even been half a day, how could you possible have found him in that time *and* convinced him to come here? He's the Beast's own selection, Maven."

"That's actually not as long a story as you might think. I was in the right place at the right time, and after that it was just a matter of polite discussion."

Bashe raises an eyebrow at me and I resist the urge to stick my tongue out. *We must be polite in front of the priestess and the boy with the wish-granting sword.*

"Anyway," I continue, "what's important is that Mr. Reyes here is very willing to join this summit of yours, Esha, and I think he could be a valuable asset in making sure that certain entities like Averrich and Vaylin don't get their hands on the grand prize. We're in agreement that the shard cannot go to someone who would misuse it, and those two certainly qualify."

Dante nods. "I'm still really new here, so apologies in advance if I seem clueless about anything, but I know this 'Game of Glass' is important. I don't know the people of this city, but I know that nobody deserves to be oppressed by a cruel tyrant. Alice tells me that you're not like that, and I believe her. So, count me in."

Both Esha and Achaia are giving me surprised, almost impressed looks. Bashe's expression is still closer to disbelief and skepticism, like he can't believe I actually won this guy over with my personality alone. Screw you, buddy, I can be perfectly charming when I put my back into it.

Still, we should loop Bashe in before he puts the pieces together on his own. It's annoying that he knows our origin, but that means we have to extend a level of trust to him. Better he learns from us than figures it out independently and acts on that.

"I have a lot I wanted to talk about with you, Esha, but could I pull Bashe aside for a moment before we have that conversation?"

Esha nods. "Of course."

Bashe folds his arms, but slowly nods. "What is this about?"

I take him aside and lower my voice. "Hey, uh, we can talk after this, because I'm sure there's stuff we should catch up about, but I need a favor. It's about the kid."

Bashe is immediately suspicious. "Who is he, really?"

"You're not gonna like this," I warn.

"I absolutely believe. Who is he, and how did you win his trust in, what, two hours? Three?"

I take a deep breath, preparing myself for his reaction, and then I say in an even softer tone, "Dante Reyes . . . is from the Zero Sphere. He is also a witch. Like me."

I can almost *feel* the pain radiating from Bashekehi right now. A choked noise escapes his throat, but he says nothing.

I barrel on before he can find his voice and interject. "So, listen: I need you to keep him out of trouble, at least until I've filled in Esha on everything that's happened in the past day. This is important, and you and Cheshire are the only ones I can trust to keep Dante from sounding crazy to everyone else."

He groans and puts his forehead in his hands, obviously still distressed. He wipes his hands down his face, sighs deeply, and says, "You are *such* a pain in my ass. Do you know that? Do you understand the pain you cause me?"

"I am extremely aware. But for once, this isn't about me; Dante's a good man, and I don't want him to go through the experience that I had when I was adjusting to this strange new world. Please, Bashe: help him. It's the right thing to do."

Hopefully that's not pushing it too hard. I'm trying to play on Bashe's precious morals, those rules his past self etched into his soul before he was transformed from human to imp. Manipulating his more hedonistic desires as an incubus has proven largely ineffective, but his conscience is something that he struggles to deny.

And, as predicted, he takes the bait. I see it play out on his face for a few moments before resignation settles in. He sighs again, but nods. "Fine, I'll do what I can."

"Thank you. Seriously."

We return to Dante and I quickly fill him in. "Dante, meet Bashekehi the Ever-Gleaming, an acquaintance of mine. He can help get you up to speed on life here in the Labyrinth and Sanctuary 7 in particular. Cheshire, do you want to go with them?"

Cheshire opens her mouth to answer, but Bashe interrupts before she can. "No, veto, the geist can stay with you." Cheshire glares at him, and Dante looks between the two of them with confusion and uncertainty.

I bite back my annoyance. *Really gonna be like that, huh? Argh. I do not trust you alone with him. I mean, I fully believe you'll give him some useful information about the Labyrinth, but I also think you'll tell him about changelings or warn him away from me, which I do not want. Damn it.*

The issue is that I have things I need to talk to Esha about that I don't want to talk about in front of Dante, even if it might be inevitable that he hears about them. It would also genuinely be more efficient to have him get some of his orientation to the Labyrinth from Bashe instead of me, and if Dante makes a good impression on Bashe then he might be able to advocate for me to the incubus.

Bah, whatever. Dante has no reason to believe Bashe over me, and Bashe has no reason to sabotage me if he thinks there's a chance I'm being genuine about my desire to work with Esha. I'm not lying about my intent, either, so if he does act against me he'll just come off as paranoid. He probably can't ruin my plans. Probably.

"Fine. Have fun."

The incubus leads Dante off and away, leaving me in the courtyard with Esha, her bodyguard, and my geist.

"So," I begin. "You probably have questions."

"A few." Esha is quiet for a moment, leaning on her staff with a pensive expression. "You have proven surprisingly central to recent events, Maven Alice. I admit, when I first heard about you and saw you with my own eyes, I took you for a wayward soul and little more. But . . . that's not the whole story, is it? Please, tell me honestly: did you know the Game of Glass was imminent when we first spoke?"

I shake my head emphatically. "Not at all. I *did* know about it before most of the candidates, but only by about half a day. I learned about the Game of Glass thanks to an encounter with Averrich and his people."

The priestess frowns. "This was a different encounter from the one that first brought you to us, then."

"That's correct." I relay the broad strokes of my run in with Kado and the owlbear, the sleep spell, waking up in the Carnival's lair, and being brought before the Goblin King himself. "He questioned me about the scent of a second fae on me, and I was forced to tell him about my encounter with another Rider on my first day here in the Labyrinth. Averrich seemed to think that the fae I met then was acting on orders from one of the Nobles, and in musing the implications of that he revealed that he was in contact with another of the Nobles."

"Invernus and Kasumi," Esha murmurs.

I nod. "Averrich's guess, which we can probably take for truth now, was that I was being scouted by Invernus as a pick for the Game of Glass. He'd clearly been warned about the event by Kasumi, and he was preparing to take measures against prospective opponents. I have a tracking spell active on him, and this morning before the announcement I saw him moving through the city."

Esha's face turns grim, but it's Achaia who speaks up, equally tense. "Of late, Averrich only leaves his sanctum when he's *hunting*. If that's what you say, then you're right; he wanted to start the killing as soon as the bell was rung."

"Given the nature of the contest, I don't think it was in his interest to kill me then and there inside his stronghold; he wouldn't get my key fragment that way. So he used me to cull some of his own followers, sending the stupid and the ambitious to chase me through a maze full of Celebrants. He sent one trusted lieutenant to secure the kill if I proved too weak to escape, but it's possible even she was just a sacrifice to strengthen me into worthy prey for his hunt today."

Achaia's lip curls. "I see the bastard has only grown more distasteful with time."

Cheshire laughs lightly. "Are fae ever tasteful? He was rotten from the Fall."

Esha gives me a sympathetic expression. "I'm glad you made it out alive. I have heard tales of Averrich's pet maze, and you were lucky to survive."

I shake my head. "Luck had nothing to do with it, beginning to end. I used [Find the Path] to find my way out, and I bargained that spell from the fae that Averrich suspected of working for Invernus. I asked it to lead me to something that would be useful in defeating Averrich, and the spell showed me a path out of the maze and toward Dante."

Achaia whistles. "Potent spell."

Esha says, "So it led you to the seventh candidate . . . most intriguing. But if that's what you asked for, does that mean you intend to face Averrich directly?"

"If I can." I breathe out, remembering the sense of power I felt from him. "If I have to, which I think I will. If not for grace, he'd already be hunting me down. His plan was to slaughter as many competitors as he could before any of the rest of us had gotten our bearings, and now that he's been outed, he'll have to adapt. He's clearly willing to kill for the shard, and for that reason and personal animosity I don't think he'll stop until I'm dead. And, honestly?" I put a bit of fire in my voice. "I feel the same way. He put me through a nightmare, and I know I'm not the first to suffer through his maze. He cannot be allowed to claim the Beast's animus."

The priestess slowly nods. "Thought I regret that it has come to this, I agree. I still hold an ember of hope that we can settle things peaceably, due to our history, but I am prepared for his demise to become necessary. He would do terrible things with that shard in his hands."

"So would Vaylin," Achaia adds gruffly. "The necromancer, Ulchen, too. The shard going to any of the three of them would spell certain disaster for everything we've built here.

"On that matter," I cut in, "I would like to personally assure you that I have no interest in claiming the Beast's shard for myself. I want to keep it out of the hands of those who would use it for harmful purposes, but I have no plans of becoming a Noble myself."

Esha seems pensive at that, but it's Achaia who speaks up first. "Why?" the bodyguard asks.

I curl my lip. "I have a distaste for the Beast that it belongs to. I've seen her idea of paradise and it disgusts me." I hesitate, unsure how much is safe to say. I don't want to tell them about my encounter with the Beast; they wouldn't understand half of it anyway, but I really don't want anyone to know that the Beast has a personal interest in me. "Cheshire tells me that the relationship between Noble and Beast is much like the relationship between demon and geist, and I don't want that *thing* in my head."

Cheshire gives me a faint smile, which I return.

"Mm." Esha is soft-spoken. "I can understand dislike for the Beast of Lamentation and Euphoria. She truly is a monstrous creature. But I must admit that your words do not put me at ease as I think you may have been hoping."

"I'll swear it on the Weaver, if you want me to," I quickly respond. "I really don't want the shard."

She shakes her head. "You misunderstand me. It's not that I don't believe you, Maven, it's that I was hoping for you to feel the opposite. I was hoping, if we could come to an agreement, that you would be the one to claim it."

Wait, what? "Wait, what?" I am so confused right now. "You wanted me to take it? But wouldn't you want it for yourself? So that you could make sure the city is taken care of properly? You want *me* to take it?" I have no idea what's going on right now, I have been thrown for several loops. This lady met me, what, literally yesterday? Why the hell does she want me in charge of *her* city?

Beside me, Cheshire narrows her eyes. "If not you, why Alice?"

Esha watches the changeling carefully, leaning in slightly. "Bashekehi called you her geist. Is that true?"

Cheshire crosses her arms. "What of it?" Okay, the animosity here is really not helping the situation. I nudge Cheshire and give her a warning look, which gets her to sigh and uncross her arms. "Yes, I'm her geist. My purpose in life is to help Maven Alice survive, attain her desires, and reach her full potential."

"I see, thank you. Then, may I ask: have you told her what it takes to become an archdemon?" Esha turns her blindfolded gaze back on me. "Do you know what that path entails?"

I hesitate. Is this something that I should know? She wouldn't be asking if it was public knowledge, right? I spare a glance at Cheshire, and her expression is tense. Shit. I don't think I can get away with lying here . . . and I have been kind of curious about this myself. "Not entirely," I tell Esha. "I know it involves a great deal of violence and death, but that's all."

She nods. "It's not surprising that you would lack specifics, as those details are known by only a select few, but it is disappointing that your geist has not yet informed you."

"We haven't exactly had a lot of time for that," Cheshire protests. "Immediate concerns take priority over long-term goals, and that is a *very* long-term kind of goal."

"Nevertheless," the priestess says with an edge to her voice, "I think it is time that Ms. Alice learned the truth. The specific details of the process of demonic ascension are often suppressed even on the worlds where they occur, as the events are so horrific that most would rather live in ignorance. Even the imps of archdemons are only made aware of the nature of their own progenitor's ascension. But through my pact with the Sanctuary's eidolon, I have been granted knowledge that I may share with you."

Esha takes a step away from me and lifts her staff. "[Recollection of the Myriad]: show me Wonder and Malice."

When Esha used this spell before, she called light from the pool beneath the roots and shaped that light into color images of Vaylin, Averrich, and the Machinist. They appeared first as motes of light, then gained color and definition, and when the process finished they appeared perfectly lifelike. This time, something is different about the process.

The globe of water within the head of her staff glows bright, as does the water in the courtyard fountain, and light flows from both, but instead of flowing upward it flows downward. Wherever the light touches the ground it inverses, becoming darkness, and then that darkness spreads across the ground like dense fog. Unnatural darkness takes the whole courtyard, then divides into two halves, creating a thin channel between where the four of us stand.

In the half of the courtyard to my left, the shadows give way and form a circular area with high walls, almost like an arena, though open to our viewing. Within the arena I see a figure made of shadow with childlike stature and proportion. The child figure has wide eyes of bright white light and shadowy hair that flows like its submerged in a river. The figure's form is indistinct, shifting and wavering, but looks to be wearing some kind of frilly dress.

In one hand, she holds a pitcher of water that spills over without end, white light soaking into black sand. In her other hand, she wields a farmer's scythe that cuts through the neck of second, less distinct figure kneeling in the sand. Behind that second figure is a third, a fourth, more, repeating forever like the inside of an infinity mirror, all with a gap between head and body like parted clouds.

The other half of the courtyard is a hellish sight: red light burns within black fog that writhes with twisting images of fire and ruin, screaming faces and grasping hands, and a sea of fresh blood. It is carnage incarnate, the site of a hundred massacres, and rising from that atrocity, surrounded by numberless corpses, is a creature that truly embodies the word "demon."

The demonic figure is a juxtaposition between exaggerated femininity and saurian ferocity: her curves are shapely and accentuated, but her limbs are spiked like a horned lizard and her four arms end in wicked claws, her legs in cloven hooves, a spiked tail curling around one leg, and bladed wings spread wide behind her. Two arms caress her body lewdly, while the other two wield weapons: in one an intricate flanged mace, in the other a broken greatsword. Her eyes burn baleful red beneath a crown of jagged horns, and her mouth forms a rapturous red smile.

"Behold, Pandaemonium's greatest exception and greatest murderer, side by side."

"I think I can guess who's who," I say, my eyes not leaving the form of Malice.

"The path to ascension is always difficult," Esha begins, "but it is worst for demons. Wizards and exalted alike have ascended in scores, when you add up all the worlds of Pandaemonium, but there have only ever been ten successful ascensions by demons."

Wait, ten? I thought there were only eight archdemons?

"For a wizard, time is key. For one of the exalted, it is a matter of character and opportunity. In both cases, the path is widely known; wizards prove their worth to dragons, and exalted amass a worthy legend. But all that is known of demons is that they rise through violence. The exact scope of that violence is far greater than anyone assumes."

Cheshire swallows, and she won't meet my gaze when I look over at her. What the hell am I about to hear? I mean, Bashe mentioned killing thousands, and that's pretty bad, but . . . is it bad enough to evoke *this* reaction?

Esha continues, "The truth is this: for a demon to become an archdemon, the path is massacre. A demon grows through the consumption of souls, and a great many souls are needed to claim the Throne of Shadow. To acquire the right kind of souls and in the right number, there are two methods, and of those methods the first has been performed only once in recorded history."

She gestures to the child with the scythe and pitcher. "The first rite of ascension is to devour one hundred souls through one hundred separate throne duels, all with worthy and resonant opponents. This method has been attempted by many, but only one has ever succeeded: Wonder, the archdemon presiding over innocent curiosity, who is also called the Reaper of Memory. Her unique qualities as a demon allowed her to achieve this feat, but it has never been replicated and many believe that it never can."

One hundred duels. That's a tricky number, for sure. I mean, I've already got one under my belt, but ninety-nine more? It's a daunting task . . . but it seems far from impossible, so why does she think otherwise? And more importantly, what's the other shoe she's about to drop?

Esha breathes deep, and then she gestures at the other half of the courtyard, to the bestial woman with the lascivious grin. "The second method, which is far more brutal but far easier to accomplish, is to kill some tens of thousands of people within a limited timeframe and consume their gathered souls. This is what we know as a mass harvest event."

I stiffen. "That's . . . that's a lot. Tens of thousands?"

"On the low end." A bit of bite slips through, but she quickly recovers her composure. "It's not as simple as just committing mass murder, of course; it must be a massacre that is resonant to a demon's Truths. Indulgence drove a city to kill themselves in a violent orgy. Acuity engineered a clash of great armies where both sides were forced to fight to the bitter end."

Cheshire murmurs, "Glory forced thousands to kill each other for a worthless crown. Muse spread a plague of dreams that made people destroy their bodies as a form of art. I don't know the specifics for Nemesis, though I can make a guess, and I know nothing about Contrition's harvest."

I have all their names, now: Wonder, Indulgence, Acuity, Glory, Muse, Nemesis, Contrition, and Malice. Eight archdemons, mass murderers one and all. Though, maybe it's ten?

As if in answer to my unspoken thought, Esha tightens her hands around her staff and says, "The demons who became the Wolf Queen and Lich Queen, forging two new Thrones, sacrificed their entire world to accomplish that act. Millions dead, though their world was ultimately small and they filled their courts with survivors. They burned a world, and still they are not the worst monsters to taint Pandaemonium, because the greatest of atrocities belongs to *her.*"

Esha points at the curvaceous, leering, four-armed demon surrounded by corpses and blood. "There is one monster in all of Pandaemonium that deserves the title of Prime Evil: Malice, the archdemon who presides over transgressive violence and whose three Truths are Odium, Anathema, and Sin. Murder is the essence of her being, and so she required no great scheming or manipulations to perform her harvest; she simply murdered one hundred million people in a single night. When dusk fell, an empire stood. When dawn broke, only blood and ash remained."

One hundred million people. One hundred million souls. "Gods . . ." I choke out. I stare at the monster shaped from shadow, with red eyes and a red smile, looking for all the world like she's *getting off* to the slaughter. The enormity of that act immediately eclipses all my surprise and curiosity at the revelation about the faerie queens. There is someone in this universe who murdered one hundred million people, and she's still out there, somewhere, probably killing more. Does she enjoy it? There can be no question. She was smiling when she butchered those people. Laughing. Lustful. The highest, purest, greatest avatar of murder incarnate.

Is that what I'm trying to become?

Esha's voice turns gentle, and she banishes the visions of Wonder and Malice. "Maven . . . I believe that everyone has good in them. I believe that you have a good heart. There are some who think that demons should be put down wherever they are found, because the risk they pose is too high to ignore. I disagree."

How? How can you disagree with that? My hands are shaking. One hundred million people. *How can you not learn that and put every demon to the sword? How can you talk to one, breathe the same air as one, without being utterly fucking disgusted?* One hundred million people, and I was going to call myself by her name. "Why?" I ask dully. "Why take the risk?"

Esha frowns, and she seems to consider her words carefully. "I know that the path of a demon is a corrupting path, and it ends in a terrible, terrible place. But corruption seeks noble hearts, and I believe that you have a good heart inside you. I have heard tales of demons who strayed from the dark path and strived to reclaim their humanity. I do not know exactly how geists choose their demons, but I know they often choose the most vulnerable, and those people should be seen as victims, not monsters."

Victim. Vulnerable. I hate those words, but are they wrong? I look at Cheshire again, and still she can't meet my gaze.

"If you take the shard, Maven, you will cease to be a demon. You will leave that dark path for a better one. I believe it would be best for you, and it may be the only way to save your soul."

Ha. Now that's one I've heard before. Save my soul? That's rich.

When I was little and my father dragged me to church, was that to save my soul? Or was it some desperate attempt to cling to his dead wife and her last wishes? Plenty of religious types back home will go on about saving your soul, and they'll say it for absolutely everything.

If you're gay, if you're trans, if you're mentally ill, if you have sex before marriage, if you have an abortion, if you pray to the wrong god, if you pray to no gods, if you live your life in any way that doesn't fit into a tiny little box, then you need to be "saved." Well, I don't need salvation, and I don't want it.

I've met God, and she hates me.

But I'm not so arrogant to ignore the context here; I do still have my fears about Cheshire, and Esha is playing into them. I hate the idea of being made stagnant by the Beast and her glass shard, but do I hate it so much that I'd kill millions? That's a terrifying thought.

Of course, maybe she's lying. I guess that would be the easiest thing, right? Maybe this is all a trick, and I don't have to worry about it. Maybe.

I open my soul sight, and I peer into Esha's soul. The world becomes black and white, lines on paper, a realm of jagged ink, and the woman in front of me glows bright. Esha's true self appears like a marble statue, perfectly carved, unmoving, hands clasped in prayer, robed and hooded. Her porcelain mask is smiling and simple, with bright gold eyes that crinkle at the corners, unlike her blindfolded physical self.

And, all across her soul, she is covered in white and black lines that hurt to look at it, too bright and too dark, pulsating like tumorous growths. The white lines are just like what I saw in Averrich, those lines of splintering lightning that burn white-hot and joyous, but the black lines are a complete opposite; they swallow light and possess infinite depth, and when I look into them they burn cold and lethargic, grasping at me like tendrils from the deep, like hands pulling me down into an open grave.

If the white lines represent euphoria, then the black lines must represent lamentation, which is the other half of the Beast. And Esha is infected with both.

For a moment I panic, but I stop myself. Something is off about this; Averrich's lines spread like veins, like lightning, like cracks in glass, but Esha's lines aren't *exactly* like that. Esha's lines are neat, orderly, and criss-crossing in clear patterns. Her mable soul has been divided into clear segments by overlapping black and white lines, and no region is wholly dominated by one shade or the other.

I peer deeper, past the surface, and I find that the lines go only surface deep. Inside, her core is pure and sincere, and I'm assaulted by a disorienting degree of *love* for all living beings. Is this really what's at the heart of her? Can someone be this much of a goody two shoes?

I retreat from her soul and blink my vision away. I don't know what to make of that first revelation, but the second . . . she's not lying about demons, I can tell that much.

But before I can say anything, before I can respond to Esha's last statement, Cheshire steps forward, whole body tense, teeth gritted.

"Are you truly so ready to sacrifice the girl she is for fear of what she might become? You, Esha, more than anyone in this city, understand what it means to feel the touch of that horrid Beast. You've seen what the other Nobles became as a result of their pacts. You can't honestly tell me you think you're saving her by consigning her to that fate."

Esha flinches, and I remember the guilt on her face when I mentioned the Mourner to her, and suddenly things start to click. *A pact. You've made a pact with the Beast, haven't you? Somehow, some of what's wrong in this city is your fault, and you feel guilty about that.*

Still, Esha wipes that aside and says firmly, "I truly believe that Nobility would be preferable to becoming a mass murderer. I think Maven would find it much easier to not hate herself if she became the former than the latter."

Cheshire breathes the tension out of her body, and she meets Esha's gaze solidly. "I think that's a false dichotomy. I think she can do what Wonder did, and meet the alternate condition for ascension. I believe in Maven Alice, and I will *help her* become an archdemon in that better, harder way, because I think that's truly what would be best for her."

Esha frowns, but it's a pensive frown, like she's not sure if she should actually believe that. Achaia is more obviously disbelieving, but stays silent and doesn't interfere.

I clear my throat, getting everyone's attention. "I think that, no matter what, it's not a decision to be made immediately. Our priority is still Averrich, Vaylin, and this summit, yes?"

Esha nods. "Yes, of course."

"Then, let's worry about who gets the shard after we have the key to claim it with. For now . . . thank you for the information. I think that I should find Bashekehi and speak with him. We left matters . . . unresolved."

"As you wish. Please, do consider what I've said. And I apologize if any of it was difficult to hear."

"It was necessary," I say dismissively. "Send someone to find me when the others arrive."

"Of course. And, please, I would be very happy to meet this Dante Reyes before we begin the summit."

"Can do."

With that, I step away from Esha, Cheshire following along. As soon as we're beyond the courtyard, back in the halls of the shrine, I pull Cheshire into the nearest empty side room, shut the door, and demand, "When were you going to tell me all that?"

Cheshire winces. "I'm sorry, I didn't think you needed yet another thing to worry about. Ascension is a very long-term goal, Alice, and it takes a long time just to see what the shape of that ascension might look like."

I rub my forehead, feeling a headache coming on. "I get that. That does make sense. But . . . the sheer fucking scale of it, Cheshire. A dozen people, a hundred—those are numbers you can see in your mind's eye. You can put weight and feeling to a dozen deaths, there's a shooting like that every week in America. Even ten thousand, that's immense but it's still *possible* to picture, like a football stadium getting firebombed. But one hundred million people? One hundred million, killed in a single night? That's the Mongol Empire at its peak, gone overnight. That's a higher death toll than the entirety of World War II, condensed into a twelve-hour period."

Cheshire's voice is soft. "Malice is a monster with no equals, I won't argue that."

I laugh, dark and hollow. "I'm so glad I only told two people that my name was Malice. I mean, how the hell does that look? 'Hi, I'm Ms. Genocide.' Absurd."

Cheshire quirks an eyebrow. "How do you feel about your current name still containing a reference to it, M. Alice?"

I rake my hands through my hair. "Fuck, you're right. Aw man, that sucks. That's gonna bug me every time I remember it. Ugh." I lean back against the nearest wall and sigh. "This is what I get for trying to live up to my edgy teen self's dreams. This universe is so determined to keep me from enjoying things."

Cheshire leans next to me. "It if helps, I don't think anyone besides Bashe has noticed."

"Yeah." I sigh again. "I'm back to where I was my first day in the city, killing that hunter in the nightclub. I have to ask myself: am I the kind of person that can kill that many people? I know I can kill in self-defense, sure, but that's easy. Can I kill ten thousand people for the sake of my desires? Am I willing to murder that many people to become a god? And, if not . . . where's the line? How many people would make it okay? I'm afraid to know the answer."

Cheshire pokes my side. "Hey, I wasn't lying back there. That's not a choice you need to make, Alice. You don't need to decide whether you're willing and able to pull off a mass harvest event, because you have another way to ascend."

I give her a skeptical look. "A way that, apparently, only one of eight archdemons was able to pull off. Why is that? Why is killing a hundred people harder than killing tens of thousands?"

Cheshire pushes off the wall and starts pacing in front of me, talking animatedly. "It's all about resonance. See, the trick with eating a soul is that it usually needs to resonate with who you are, who you're going to become, the challenges you're facing. If you want to sharpen your self-concept, you need the right whetstone, and those can be hard to find. When you're just starting out, hey, just about any challenger is going to test something about yourself and help you figure things out, but that happens less and less as you approach your zenith of power. The souls that tie into your identity as a demon just aren't strong enough to make for good food, and the souls that are strong enough don't click with your theme."

I frown. "So how did Wonder do it?"

Cheshire grins. "She cheated. Her signature spells, [Waters of Lethe] and [Tabula Rasa], allowed her to wash a soul down to a blank, newborn existence. Every throne duel fed her, because by the end of each duel her opponent had been completely stripped of memory and personality, and thus made resonant with her core concept of innocent curiosity. Every soul was a resonant soul, because she made them resonant."

It clicks. "You think I can do the same thing with [Feast or Famine]."

"Exactly! Every soul is food to you, thanks to that spell. You'll still need a number of throne duels for sharpening your self-concept, but far fewer than a hundred." Her eyes are practically sparkling and she clasps my hands in hers. "I'm serious, Alice: you can do this. You can become an archdemon, and you can do it faster and cleaner than any demon to come before you. No mass harvest needed."

I don't know if I should trust Cheshire, but I want to. I want to become an archdemon, and I want to do it without becoming a complete monster like Malice. So I'll cling to that spark of hope and use my magic for all it's worth. "Okay. I'm with you."

We leave the side room and go in search of Bashe, grabbing help from another attendant. When I find Bashe and Dante, I discover the two of them laughing together like old friends. *The hell? Does this kid get along with everyone?*

I barge in and wave at Dante. "Things going well?"

He looks over at me and waves back. "Huh? Oh, yeah, Bashe's great. He's been a big help in wrapping my head around this weird world, and he has some really funny stories too."

I have to suppress the scowl that wants to sprout on my face. "Right, well, that's good to hear. If you think you have a handle on things, the priestess would like to speak with you. Probably a good idea, given what we're planning."

Dante nods a few times. "Yeah, makes sense. I can go do that now, if she's waiting for me."

"Appreciated. Cheshire, you should go with. I think Bashe would prefer we have this conversation privately."

Cheshire very pointedly does not give any kind of menacing look at Bashe, but I'm sure she would if Dante wasn't here to see it. She takes my fellow Earthling and leaves to go find Esha again. And then it's just me and Bashe.

The silence is tense and awkward, the two of us just sort of standing there, staring at each other, neither willing to make the first move. When Bashe opens his mouth to finally break the silence, I interrupt him.

"You were right," I say. "About becoming a demon, I mean. I can already feel myself changing. I can feel certain ways of thinking getting easier, more natural.

And it's hard to be scared about that when it feels so good to have this much power. But you were right; one day I'm going to stand at the end of this road, and I won't recognize who I was at the start."

I don't know where the line blurs between truth and lie. I have fears, and desires, and they intermix. I want to change. I'm afraid to change. I want to be a monster. I'm afraid to be a monster. I'm a mess, and becoming an archdemon is supposed to sharpen me into something focused, and there's a part of me that hates the idea of losing all my chaotic, messy tendencies.

"I love so many of my little imperfections. I love the weird traits that make me who I am. I'm me, and I don't want to stop being me. I don't want to die, in whatever form that takes. So . . ." I take a deep breath and lift up the anatomical heart locket around my neck. ". . . I made this."

Bashe frowns. "What is it?"

"It's an artifact," I tell him, "that collects the pieces of my soul whenever they're shorn off. Every time my existence as a demon sharpens my soul into a more perfect form, the imperfections will collect in this locket."

He stares at it, eyes going wide. "How is that possible? How the hell did you do that? Where did you get that?" He's looking somewhere between shocked, baffled, and hungry.

Time for the big one. "I'm a witch," I say flatly. "I've been a witch since I entered the Labyrinth, though I didn't realize until after we parted ways. And my power as a witch is the ability to create artifacts without using Throne magic."

I taste fear in the air, and I see the faintest trace of it cross his face before being replaced by skepticism. "So you and Cheshire both . . . but that locket. It really works?"

I nod, and then I open my soul sight and stare into the locket. I see a beating heart, and I hear its perfect rhythm, and when I look deeper I can swirling red color trapped inside. *My soul. I'm looking into a fragment of my soul.*

"Look," I say. "Use your sight and peer into the locket. You'll see something familiar."

I end soul sight and watch Bashe focus his gaze on my locket. Slowly, his whole demeanor changes from fear and confusion to fascination and then envy. "You really did it. You really . . ."

"I listened. I always listen, even if it seems like I'm not. And now I have a way to beat the game."

He whistles and shakes his head. "You really are something. I admit, I'm envious of you. All my rules can only ever make me just a simulacrum of a human, never the real deal. Bairam Dara is dead, and I'll never be him again. But you found a way to cheat. Maybe."

"Maybe? It works. You can see my soul inside it." And the hum of it, the resonance, tells me that if functions exactly as intended, trapping those fragments and then returning them when I activate the artifact again.

Bashe scratches his chin. "I'm not arguing it doesn't function, but I'm not sure it'll work the way you think. If you really do approach Royalty, or even achieve it, and then try to activate that locket . . . well, there's no precedent, so I don't know what'll happen, but I know basic oneiric theory. To be Royalty is to be living Truth, the embodiment of a pure concept. To suddenly reintroduce humanity after walking toward that pure state could have unforeseen consequences, putting it lightly. You might become some new kind of Royalty entirely, or you might rip in half from the stress on your soul."

I grit my teeth and almost snarl at him, so infuriated by his comments. I speak with scorn as I tell him, "How much humanity do you think I had to begin with? It'll work, I know it will. The core of me is what I'm evolving toward, this will just let me hold to some sentimental imperfections. It will work, Bashe."

He looks down on me, dismissal in his eyes. "Don't delude yourself, you're plenty human."

I roll my eyes. "Whatever." I tuck the locket back under my dress. "I just wanted you to know, that's all. Cheshire and I are working toward having our cake and eating it too. And, for the record, we're fully intending to help Esha in this death game."

He gives me a calculating look. "What do you think you'll get out of that?"

"An ally, for one. Help killing Averrich, for another. He's after both of us, you know." *And I totally threw you under the bus to him, but luckily it seems you were smart enough to come here before he could follow up that lead.* "His goons dragged me to his maze and I had to kill a bunch of them to get out of it. So, I'd expect the same to happen to you eventually if you don't stick to safe areas."

"That's the plan," Bashe mutters. "I do not want to get dragged into any of this."

Cheshire ducks back in. "Hey, heads up: Averrich's people just arrived. Imlashi, Kado, and the werewolf."

Bashe's expression tightens at the sight of the changeling, and then further when he hears that name. "Imlashi . . ."

"Right, you two have history. Well, shall we say hello?"

The three of us move toward the entry hall. Finally, enough recap; it's time for the main event.

VI

Do you have any idea how weird it is to break bread with these people not even a full day after they tried to kill us?

Seriously. If it weren't for the truce and our audience, I'm pretty sure I'd be drawing Vorpal on those assholes.

Gods, are we going to have to be polite? I hate being polite.

There's a certain tension building in my body as we make for the entry hall; it sings in my blood and breath. It's been far too little time for me to have forgotten how Kado humiliated me in the streets, or how Imlashi tried to fucking *mind control me* in the heart of Averrich's lair.

Nothing boils my blood hotter than an insult to my pride. It may have just been a test of my strength as a demon, but that wretched imp still demanded that I *worship* her, and I cannot forgive that. Maven Alice worships nothing and no one; others should be worshiping *me*.

. . . Okay, that might sound a little megalomaniacal, but I *am* trying to usurp the Divine Architect of most of the universe, so, uh . . . I guess it is megalomaniacal. Oh well. I don't mind a bit of megalomania and vanity; they make such lovely music together.

Cheshire raises an excellent point that the hunters haven't met her and it might be advantageous if they never did, so I return her to my shadow and send her anchor to my throne world. Dante won't be joining us until the summit proper, which is probably for the best; it'll be a whole mess of explanation and it wouldn't to do to explain it all twice. So now it's just Bashe at my side, the incubus looking tense, though he makes an effort to smooth away that tension as we get closer.

I'm tempted to take a peek at his soul . . .

. . . and I've never been one to resist temptation, so I go ahead and do that.

My vision shifts and I see a world of paper drawn with ink and charcoal. I've gotten quite used to the background noise of the world through soul sight, but it's always a unique experience to look upon a new individual's sense of self. And I don't even have to feel bad about invading Bashe's privacy like this, because he tried to read *my* soul the very second he saw me.

At first glance, something's off about what I see, but I can't put my finger on what; the image of Bashe is very similar to his physical appearance, just more exaggerated and sexual. He has the suggestion of horns and hooves and tail, all those little signs of fiendish nature, but the emphasis is on supple flesh, lines and curves, a body on display. His face is a mask, like nearly everyone I've looked at, but there's something insincere about his mask. It's made of bone and porcelain like the others, with smoldering eyes of lilac and black, but it's so detailed, and it's painted to resemble his face, smiling and winking. The closer I look, the more the whole image looks painted on, a calculated persona to hide something deeper. His semblance is detached, calm, confident, but that's not how he's really feeling.

So I go deeper, pushing through that outer layer of his soul and peering within. The paint washes from his mask to reveal a softer, plainer mask. Lilac and black eyes burn away, and underneath are eyes of natural brown with white sclera, perfectly human. The shape of his body becomes less exaggerated, and his fiendish traits wither away until he is entirely human . . . though not entirely normal; his skin peels all across his body, and writing etches itself into his skin, vivid red against rich brown. I can't make out the words, but I can make out the meaning: restraint, rules, and conscience.

This Bashekehi stinks of loss and regret, and I see a deep ache within those brown eyes. His life has been marked by loss, and the woman he's going to meet could share in some of that loss . . . but he fears she will not, because that is not her nature. Even among friends, allies, or whatever they really were, he is alone.

If the outer layer of his soul was Bashe as he presents himself to the world, the image that he has cultivated, then this second layer is Bashekehi as he once was, as he yearns to be again: Bairam Dara, the human man.

It, too, is a lie. Bairam Dara is dead and gone, and these rules are just phantoms. I push deeper, seeking the heart of him. *Show me your animus, Bashe.*

This time, his whole body burns away until only a mask remains. This mask is wholly different from either that came before, and nothing about it resembles Bashekehi himself; the mask is that of a woman's face, lilac-eyed, with ram's horns, sensual features, and bright blue lipstick.

The mask is bound tightly in bloody chain, the rules of Bairam straining to hold their prisoner. The eyes of the mask burn with the promise of sex and wine and million dollar debt, and there is something so much vaster than

Bashekehi lurking within. This is the heart of an imp; this is a reflection of Royalty.

Indulgence, archdemon of want. Indulgence, who murdered a city to claim her crown.

I retreat from his soul and flicker my sight back to realspace, or what passes for it. Bashe either didn't notice my intrusion or didn't care, because he's still got his gaze locked forward as we step into the entry hall and catch sight of the new arrivals.

Esha is greeting them, of course, with Achaia at her side. Though I still find it silly to wear a full suit of power armor and not wear a helmet, I respect the healthy paranoia that I see Achaia displaying in how closely she watches the trio. I have no reason to think the Beast won't back up her promise about smiting anyone who breaks the truce, but that's no reason to get sloppy.

Kado, Gretchen, and Imlashi look mostly the same as they did last time I saw them all. Imlashi, the blue-skinned imp with curling horns, a pointed tongue, and violet eyes, is still wearing that revealing dress and all those jewels and gold. Gretchen, who I know to be a werewolf, is a mountain of a woman with matted hair and amber eyes, dressed in rags I'd only charitably describe as clothing.

Violet eyes and amber eyes . . . I wonder if eye color has meaning in this world. Reska always paid close attention to eyes, and they always seemed to match that person's affinities. Do Truths function similarly? It certainly seems like Bashe's lilac eyes are a direct consequence of Indulgence.

Kado, the gangly hunter with laugh lines, a choppy beard, and dark eyes, is the only one to have changed his outfit. He's dressed down from his hunter's gambeson for a scruffy tuxedo that's definitely not nice enough to be anything other than an act of mockery. I also don't doubt that he's got a knife or two hidden somewhere in there, but otherwise none of them appear armed.

So they think the grace will hold . . . or they're confident in their magic being strong enough to fight it out anyway. Considering they have a werewolf and an imp in the ranks, that doesn't sound completely arrogant.

It's also interesting that Averrich didn't come himself, given his apparent history with Esha. I can't imagine him being afraid for his safety, even without a truce, so is this a calculated insult? Or perhaps he has something else occupying his attention, like scouting and spying on his rivals.

We do, after all, have to assume that he's only entertaining this little summit to gather information before continuing his original plan of killing everyone.

Imlashi is the first to look away from Esha, locking eyes with Bashe as he comes to a stop a healthy distance from the group. I keep walking, and I smirk at all three of Averrich's minions.

"Well, here we are again. I'd say it's nice to see you again, imp, but I don't like lying in front of the nice priestess. Afternoon, Kado. Looking healthy, wolf; have you come for a second round?"

Imlashi wrinkles her nose at me, but the other two have more interesting reactions; Kado hesitates for a moment before forcing a chuckle, while Gretchen pivots to face me with an intense expression, her nose and ears twitching. And from all three of them I smell the faintest trace of *fear*. The imp, the hunter, and the werewolf are all afraid of me . . . and they definitely weren't before.

Is this just because I killed the hunters? I didn't think any of them were that impressive. I could see Kado getting worried over that, maybe Imlashi, but the werewolf? Really?

Wait, no, this isn't about the hunters; it's about the Reveler. Bashe was terrified of its cousin, and I kicked its ass. They must have noticed its death, and my survival. Perhaps, since that maze was the creature's throne world, it started to collapse after I killed it and left.

Well, that's a fun bit of news. I must admit, I'm delighted at this information. My smirk widens. "I see I made quite the impression on you and yours. I don't suppose you'd consider surrendering now, just to get it over with?"

Kado eyes me up and down. "You really like poking the bear, huh?"

"I genuinely can't help it, my brain is broken in so many ways. Speaking of bears, where's the owl?"

"Around," he shrugs.

To the side, I see Imlashi slip away after a final quick murmur to Esha, and Bashekehi follows. *Oh, I simply must spy on that conversation.*

Kado shakes his head at the two imps as they leave together. "That'll be an interesting one. Really hope he makes the smart choice. Would hate to see a guy like that go to waste."

Esha watches them go and asks, "A waste of the man, or a waste of his talents? Your huntmaster has ever valued one over the other."

"Heh. You're just the same as ever, priestess."

I roll my eyes. *As if that moralizing loser would even get involved.*

Gretchen rolls her shoulders. "Enough talk. If we're not starting now, then I want something to eat."

Esha smiles politely. "I'll have an attendant show you to our dining hall. Kado, you as well?"

The hunter shrugs. "Beats standing around."

An attendant is swiftly summoned and leads them off, and now I'm really itching to go spy on Bashe and 'Lashi. "Who else are we waiting on?" I ask Esha.

The priestess turns back to me. "Just the Machinist now, or rather whatever contingent he's sending."

"Great. In that case, I'm going to—"

My plans are interrupted by a sudden commotion from outside. I hear yelling that sounds like the jackal guards, and mocking feminine laughter. Esha and Achaia move immediately, tension crossing their faces, and I follow behind at a slight lag.

Outside the shrine, the two guards are facing off against a woman that instantly reminds me of Malice as I saw her in shadowy projection: four arms, powerfully built and ending in claws, one hand holding a long, wrapped object; a wicked smirk below burning red eyes with black sclera, a crown of horns above; cloven hooves for feet, a spiked tail and bladed wings arrayed behind her; and a body completely unclothed, her ample figure kept from absolute indecency by red-black scales that cluster thickest around her chest and waist (her abs, for the record, are very well-defined). Her skin, where it isn't covered by scales, is a deep crimson, which really puts the icing on the cake of "most demonic looking creature so far."

Of course, I'm pretty sure this gorgeous abomination is actually an imp, not a demon.

I've seen Vaylin twice now, so I know this isn't her, and I've not heard of any other demons in the city. I know there's an imp of Muse with the Myriad, but that person wouldn't evoke this reaction, and really, "Muse" isn't the vibe I get from her appearance.

No, this is an imp of Malice, there's no question about it. Is she the third member of the triad that Bashekehi and Imlashi were two thirds of? Would Bashe really associate with someone sprung from a monster like Malice?

The imp came with two companions: a man and a woman in ethereal black shifts, their black eyes glassy and unfocused. Their hair is neat, their faces clean, each with pierced ears and a pendant of black stone against skin that seems unnaturally pale, though at different shades.

My curiosity is piqued, but I hold off on activating soul sight to watch whatever's about to go down between Esha and the imp.

The priestess comes to a stop behind her guards, paladin at her side. When she speaks, it is with unexpected venom. "Avaya'ari," she nearly spits. "What are you doing here?"

Well, that confirms the imp's identity: Avaya was the name that one of the hunters teased Bashe with. So the third member of the Coiner tribunal really was an imp of Malice . . . fascinating. There's clearly no love lost between Esha and Avaya, but is that because of ancient history or something that happened after the Coiners were destroyed?

Avaya keeps her smirk, clearly enjoying the tension. "Come now, Eshie, is that any way to treat an old friend?"

"I won't play this game," Esha warns. "You can't bring two of her *victims* here and then pretend there's any good blood between us, even in jest."

My interest in the imp's companions skyrockets. *Well now I simply must take a look.*

I flicker my soul sight and take in the three of them in sequence. Avaya's soul is menacing but matches up well with what I was expecting; she is prickling thorns and lascivious curves, a thing of blood and flesh and bone. Her mask is exactly like the silhouette of Malice's face, complete with baleful red eyes that promise carnage, ruin, and the perversion of all that is pure.

The other two are far more interesting, as their souls are the first I've seen to be completely eyeless. Even figments, those mindless things, have pinpricks of color within each mask, but there's only swirling blackness within the eyes of the masks before me, and the edges of the eyeholes are cracked and bent as if someone had gouged out the eyes of each soul.

Their bodies are chalky, naked, and nearly featureless—almost doll-like, in an unnerving mirror of my own chosen form—save for the red thread that wraps around each limb and cuts in and out of the skin. The stitching is purposeful, patterned, and densest around the wrists, ankles, and throat.

Just like a figment held up by strings, these souls are bound by thread that passes through the hands of another; I see lines of thread emerging from the back of each neck and leading away from here, but before I can follow that line to its origin I see again the soul of Avaya'ari, her hands clutching the threads that bind both of her companions.

I pull away from the threads and refocus on the hollow-eyed masks. I push deeper, searching for an inner world, and in each of them I find scattered echoes of memory and meaning, vague impressions that have been darkened, muddled, shattered. A yearning unspoken, a love forgotten, anger made impotent by the lack of a target. Faceless friends, voiceless conversations, scenes missing details. All of it muted, broken, and bound in pulsating red thread that seems to numb and deaden.

"*. . . every soul in the Sanctuary will be turned into a puppet on her strings.*"

Now I understand the Beast's warning, and I am fascinated and horrified in equal measure. These were people, once, but now they're more like figments. Their souls have been mutilated and brought under Vaylin's control. Imlashi, Averrich, and even Kado all had spells that could affect the mind, but this is what real mind control looks like.

I asked for a spell like that, when Cheshire led me through the process of shaping my Truths. She didn't offer one, probably because I lacked the power as a demon to make any version that would be useful—my criteria were, after all, rather restrictive. Now I'm at full capacity with only [Carrion Swarm] and

[Feast or Famine]. I wonder . . . if I ate Vaylin's soul, could I steal whatever magic she used to do this? Do I want to?

Esha told me that Vaylin gave everyone in the city a choice: submit or be made to submit. I had assumed that the demon ruled through fear, or perhaps some kind of binding contract, but this is so much worse. Is her whole organization filled with empty husks? Is Avaya the only other person in her circle to retain free will? And is that really how I want to rule when I start to gather my own followers?

I told Cheshire that my desire for corruption magic was driven by a cocktail of fear and desire: fear of being abandoned or betrayed, desire for intimacy and connection. Cheshire suggested that I wanted more than that, and said that more than anything I wanted control. When the Beast dragged me to her lair, she told me—no, she showed me—that I could be offered paradise and would turn it down because someone would still be above me on the cosmic ladder.

I wonder how these people felt before they were hollowed out. I wonder what ambitions they dreamed of before all of their dreams were replaced with this binding numbness. There is brutality in the scene of these thread-wrapped bodies, in the shattered fragments of memory and self, but the closer I look, the more I find an odd sense of peace overlaying it all.

There's no fear, no anger, no doubt, no grief. They feel neither pride nor insecurity, neither loss nor gain. I don't think they feel anything at all. They're just empty.

Fixation pulls me forward and I reach out to trace my porcelain fingers down the side of a porcelain mask, unsure of which body it belongs to. Warm to the touch, but only just. "What's it like inside that head?" I ask softly.

Empty, gouged eyeholes stare back. An extinguished flame.

I shudder and blink away my soul sight, becoming aware of myself and my surroundings once more. My hand is touching the cheek of the black-clad woman, and her doll-black eyes stare right through me. She's smiling.

I take a step back and wipe my hand on my dress with a grimace. *Shit, how much did I just miss?*

I glance back at the others and catch a quick wink from Avaya before she's back to smirking at Esha and Achaia. Esha's expression is severe and tight-lipped, while Achaia's expression is downright murderous, and they're both still completely focused on the imp. I wasn't paying proper attention to whatever Esha and Avaya were saying to each other while I was looking at souls and getting lost in thought, but their conversation appears to have been significant.

"Very well," Esha says through gritted teeth. "If those are your conditions, and if you swear it on the Weaver, then I will allow you to join our summit."

Wait, what? Seriously?

Avaya's grin widens. "Then we have a deal. In exchange for a seat in your meeting and a chance to speak with Bashekehi, I'll do no harm to you and yours, Esha of the Myriad, for the next two days. I will also use my influence within the Voidhearts to prevent Vaylin or any of her servants from taking hostile action against you, Esha of the Myriad, within that same timeframe. This and these I swear by Azathoth, Dreamweaver, All-Mother, Origin. Weaver take me if I forswear."

Unlike most, Avaya doesn't even react as the presence of Azathoth passes over the area. I only feel it as a brief chill in the air, perhaps because I'm not involved in the pact, but even still I can't suppress a shiver. Nyarlathotep may be a thousand times worse than Azathoth, but the Weaver is still a capital-G God.

Esha clenches her staff tighter, then slowly relaxes her grip with a sigh. "Then you may enter. Bashekehi and Imlashi are both inside. I suppose I shall have to fetch more chairs."

The imp gives a mocking half-bow. "I look forward to our reunion, and to this quaint little meeting you've set up. I'll be along shortly; you've come with a lovely creature that I simply *must* introduce myself to."

Avaya turns her attention on me, red eyes burning into me with keen interest. Esha stiffens, but I wave a hand and tell her, "I'll be fine." Esha nods slowly, then departs with Achaia. The two guards, seeming relieved to not have to fight the imp, return to their posts.

As soon as the priestess is gone, the four-armed monster takes a few steps toward me and leans in, lower set of arms folding across her chest while her last free hand strokes her chin. She murmurs, "Now that's *very* unusual. I don't think I've ever met a witch demon before."

I tense, gaze flitting to the guards at the temple entrance, but Avaya spoke quietly enough that neither of them appear to have heard. I glance back at the imp to find her winking at me again, and she actually titters when I grimace. *That's two that have recognized me as a witch, and of course it had to be the faerie and the murder devil.*

"Perhaps we should take this conversation somewhere more private," the creature suggests. "I think that you and I have a great deal to discuss."

"Privacy is good." I look around for the nearest alley and start walking in that direction. Behind me, I hear Avaya order her minions to stay put. Once we're out of sight of the community center, I put my back against a wall and cross my arms. "What now?"

Avaya bows to me, deeper than she bowed to Esha, and when she straightens up again she says, "Oh, don't worry, I have no intention of revealing your little secret. I simply wanted your attention, as you very much have caught mine. Ah, but first, I have a request to make: I'd like to hold this conversation somewhere even more private than this quaint alley."

I raise an eyebrow. "What did you have in mind?"

She smiles. "Your throne world, of course. I'm dying to see it."

I tense further, muscles stiffening as my thoughts race. *My throne world? Why the fuck do you want to see that? Is this a trap?* "Why?" I ask to stall for time. "Hoping to learn some precious secrets you can bring back to your master?"

I feel a warm prickling on my neck, and then Cheshire is whispering in my ear, "Be careful. This one is sharp-eyed."

Avaya taps her chin, expression contemplative. "I do understand the precious value of information. Perhaps you would be interested in a trade? If you show me your throne world, I'd happily share whichever of Vaylin Kirinal's secrets you might like to know."

I'm taken aback at the ease with which she makes that offer. Does she think it won't make a difference to the outcome of the death game, or is she working some other agenda? Still, though I'm certainly curious about my demonic counterpart, something about that trade doesn't seem advantageous. "Is that all?"

The imp hums to herself, looking away as if in deep thought, and then she snaps her fingers and leans in. "I've got it! I know exactly what I can trade."

Avaya unwraps the object she's been carrying and reveals an impressively edgy greatsword, its black blade emblazoned with glowing red runes. She touches one of the runes lightly, then pulls her hand away, and red light arcs between her fingers and the blade like crackling electricity before solidifying into a shimmering red gemstone. She lifts the jewel and shows it to me with a smile on her face, and there's suddenly the most wonderful taste in the air. My body is begging me to snatch that gem and devour it whole, my every instinct hungering for it.

"I offer you this soul, to consume as you please. Is that a fair bargain?"

I want it, I need it, I have to have it. I am so, so hungry. I can feel myself salivating, my stomach suddenly empty despite everything I've eaten. I don't care if it's a fair bargain or not, I just can't bear to let that soul get away from me. "Deal."

The imp holds the gem out to me, but then she pauses and holds it back just out of reach and I want to rip her fucking hand off, that teasing bitch. "Ah, one little detail: I don't know for sure if it'll be compatible with your palate, so you may have to settle for forging it rather than eating it. I hope that's alright?"

I almost laugh. Compatibility? That means nothing to me. I'm the demon of [Feast or Famine], so I can eat whatever the hell I want.

. . . But revealing that would be giving away information, wouldn't it? A cold splash of reality wakes me from my hunger fugue and I get a hold of myself. Shit, that was embarrassing. I can't afford to lose control every time a soul is dangled in front of me.

I force a more neutral expression on my face and say, "Perhaps. Geist, what do you think?"

I feel Cheshire's warm touch on my shoulder. "She's obviously dangerous, but I don't sense hostility or deception. Devouring another complete soul . . . I don't need to tell you how huge that would be for our game plan. Even if it's not fully compatible, I have *ideas* that would be valuable to test. Still, you should see if you can get the soul gem *and* one of Vaylin's secrets."

I nod. "Alright, let's try this: give me that soul and a secret about your boss, and I'll show you my throne world and let you poke your head around while we spend a few minutes chatting."

I hold my hand out and Avaya gently drops the soul gem into my open palm. As soon as the crystallized soul touches my skin I teleport it to a storage room in my throne world, just to stop myself from trying to eat it then and there. And now . . . wait, how do I bring her into my throne world?

I am spared the indignity of having to admit ignorance by Cheshire whispering to me, "Take her hand. I'll take care of the rest."

So I do, finding Avaya's skin hot to the touch, and in moments we are transported into the world of my soul. We arrive on the cliffside path leading to my castle, the red forest stretching out below us and the black sun burning above. There's no sign of my battle with Mahiri, though a glance at the castle gate finds a distinct lack of my skeletal servants.

"Interesting," says Avaya, looking around at the geography of my soul. "Very interesting."

I take the opportunity to get a closer look at something of hers; I flicker on my witch sight and peer into that strange warblade she apparently keeps souls in. As with my precious Vorpal, the imp's weapon is more vivid to my second sight, from whispering souls surrounding the blade to the blade itself looking carved from empty night.

A bit of focus is all it takes to tell me the item's name and nature: this is [Vandal Edge], a shadowtouched artifact that teems with violence and lost souls. Its primary purpose—its activated ability—is to temporarily enhance the wielder's physical and magical prowess, and its secondary purpose—its static ability—is to take in and store the souls that are burned to power the enhancement effect.

That's so wasteful! That's like, the platonic ideal of sacrificing long-term gain for short-term gain. How many souls has that thing used up!?

Are we really one to talk? Our signature spell also *uses a soul as fuel.*

Yes, yes, but [Feast or Famine] is a permanent net gain. This is just as costly but entirely temporary!

I frown at the blade, trying to understand why anyone would make such a weapon. I don't think imps can eat souls like demons can, but I know they can turn souls into artifacts, so it still seems wasteful to sacrifice that precious resource rather than turning it into a more diverse pool of magic items.

Of course, it seems to have worked out for Avaya'ari so far, so what do I know?

The imp in question is still surveying the landscape of my soul, but before I can ask her any questions about her blade she turns back to me with a thoughtful expression on her face. "You didn't just arrive in the Labyrinth recently; you only became a demon recently."

I frown. "I'm not going to deny it, but how can you tell from just a brief look around my throne world?"

She gestures at our surroundings and says, "It's all so barren and shallow. I see a forest and a castle and a dark sun, but they possess only a facade of meaning, like scaffolding without a foundation. There's no heart in it, no lived experience. It's an act of self-expression that lacks self-identification. Those are the telltale signs of a fledgling demon that has hidden away her chaos but has no idea how to resolve that chaos. The order you've imposed is only skin-deep."

The imp raises her greatsword and in one fluid motion slashes the ground between us, cutting deep into the soil of the mountain path—but instead of more soil, what's revealed is a wound that bleeds color and sound. Beneath the surface of the earth is a swirling maelstrom of memories blurring together and getting tangled. It's the maelstrom I saw in the sky above the book pile, above the tea party, when I first became a demon.

"Chaos is the natural state of all souls. You've papered over it, but it's still there. Your concept as a demon is still unrefined and not absolute."

"I've had a very busy week," I say defensively. "I built this in an hour."

"I'm not criticizing," she assures me, "just observing. If you wish to improve the structure of your throne world, I can offer more pointed commentary. Your forest below sings of hunger and fear, but it has not been alloyed with memories of moonless nights running from wolves or hungry days hunting to survive. Your castle is imposing and aristocratic, but there's no indication that its owner is either. Both are aspirational, not reflective, which wouldn't be so bad were it not for the greater flaw: the castle speaks of a right to rule, but the forest speaks of no one to rule over, and that is a dangerous contradiction. The whole scene creates a sense of isolation and seclusion, a kind of defensive loneliness. No demon lives here, only a scared child hiding behind high walls and a mask of menace."

I swallow awkwardly, feeling pinned and dissected. I wasn't expecting her to get that much analysis out of a few simple details. "You're quite good at reading throne worlds. Is that from Vaylin, or . . . ?"

Avaya laughs. "No, I dare say I've taught Vaylin more than her own geist has. I've seen many, many throne worlds. I'm a very old defiler, Alice. By the

Prime Evil's own hand I was reborn as Avaya'ari, and in the centuries since I have served as the left hand to three dozen demons across nine worlds. I'm quite experienced."

And now my mouth is completely dry. Holy shit. I thought Vaylin was the threat from that corner of the city, but I was laughably wrong. She might be as old as Averrich. In fact . . . maybe that's worth pushing. "That's quite impressive. You and that faerie bastard both seem much older than everyone else in the city."

Avaya seems to seize on my words, grinning and leaning against her sword. "That's very interesting, isn't it? Two of the old guard drawn to the same place amid a bounty of scions, invokers, and retainers . . . and now two witches to cap it off."

Two witches? How did she—the big scene, of course. It wasn't just the seven of us, everyone in the city was watching from the stands. So Avaya knows what Dante is, which means Vaylin probably knows what Dante is, and I'd bet Averrich figured it out too. Shit.

"And of course," Avaya continues, "one of those witches is also a demon, which is something I've never seen before today. I have to wonder: who's it for? What's it all mean?"

"You'd know that better than I would," I venture.

"Would I, now?" Her red eyes twinkle with amusement. "Because I find something so very interesting about your presence in this play, witch demon. You see, when our dearly beloved Beast gave her grand speech and predicted a victor to this vicious little war, I couldn't help but notice that she referred to that victor with feminine pronouns, and then, just a moment later, she introduced *you* as the first candidate."

I'm silent, a spike of fear running through me. Cheshire was right, this woman is dangerously perceptive.

"On its own, you might take that for a coincidence—well, you wouldn't, but someone else might. Maybe she started alphabetically, and you just lucked out with that name. But then, after that, we had our little cheating debacle, and she highlighted yours and Averrich's respective patrons as interfering in the Game to give an actionable advantage. Except that, by the Beast's own speech and the evidence of one's eyes, it's clear that you, dear Alice, have been in the city for far too little time with far too few resources to really act on any lead given to you. But Averrich has had the time and the resources to prepare for this Game of Glass, and my eyes in the city tell me that you and Averrich have already come into conflict. So given all that, it seems like a day's grace helps you more than it hurts you . . . almost like that was the Beast's intention."

I wish I could think of a clever lie, but what can I say to that? Maybe, in this instance, we tell the truth and try to dig for answers. "It's probable. Why do you think she did that? What does it mean?"

Avaya hums to herself, fingers tapping along the blade of her sword. "I can't say it with absolute certainty, but the evidence and my instincts are both pointing me to the same conclusion: the Beast of Lamentation and Euphoria intends for you, Maven Alice, to win the Game of Glass. And that leads me to another question: do *you* intend on winning?"

I frown. "That's an odd question. Do you think I intend on losing?"

She shrugs. "I only ask because I find you here among the Myriad, in the company of Esha, and I know Esha quite well. If the two of you are on good terms, as you seem to be, then it's likely that Esha has convinced herself of the prospect of your 'redemption.' She no doubt sees this Game of Glass as an opportunity to steal a demon from Shadow by turning it to glass instead. Am I wrong?"

"I'm interested in alliances," I evade. "There's strength in numbers and I have a fae hunting me, that's why I'm here with Esha. Past that is undecided."

"Then you would be open to alternative alliances, yes?" The imp smiles. "Esha is not the only one with bodies to throw at problems, I promise you. I think you would be far more comfortable with the Voidhearts than the Myriad. I saw the way you looked at dear Thirteen."

My frown deepens. *Thirteen? Do they all have numbers instead of names, as some further tool of dehumanization? Regardless . . . is that really being offered?* "Hang on, is all of this some recruitment pitch? Are you asking me to join your faction and work for the Voidhearts? For Vaylin?"

"Mm, not exactly. Allow me to answer your question with a question of my own."

I cross my arms. "I feel like you've been asking a lot of questions for someone that still hasn't shared that secret you promised me."

Avaya laughs. "You make a fair point. Don't worry, I'll reveal that very soon. This is necessary context. I need to know if you know what happens to whoever claims the Beast's animus."

I narrow my eyes. "I've been told that they stop being whatever they were before, and become . . . glass. A Noble and nothing else."

"Aye. If a demon were to claim that power, they would cease to be a demon, and they could never ascend as an archdemon. How do you find that state of affairs, Maven Alice?"

The answer rises from me in a tide of anger, remembering my conversation with the Beast. "I find it absolutely unacceptable. I refuse to be frozen in glass. Were it offered freely, I would reject it on that alone." And I did.

Avaya claps her hands together, practically preening. "You see? I knew I made the right choice. That is an excellent answer, Alice, and that is exactly why I want you to murder Vaylin and seize control of her Voidhearts."

I'm thrown for a loop. "Wait, what?"

"You bargained for a secret, and here it is: Vaylin does not control her followers as tightly as she thinks she does. Her thread-bound husks are loyal only to the hand that holds the leash, and her left hand imp plots betrayal. Were a cunning and capable demon to come along, why, I think she could quite easily take over that entire organization."

My mind churns with calculation and consideration. Avaya is asking me to kill the demon Vaylin, which I was already planning on doing, and she's willing to help me do that. She's promising all of Vaylin's minions bound to my banner. With resources like that, would I need to play ball with Esha? Would it be enough to conquer Averrich's faction? And, if I killed Vaylin and stole her spell . . . I could bend to my will the survivors of Carnival and Myriad alike.

I can see the path stretching out before me, a master plan sprung from this alliance. Play nice with Esha to pit her forces against Averrich's, usurp Vaylin in secret, then sweep in and take control of whatever's left from each faction. The city would be mine, and then I could turn my attention to the shard and find some way to utilize it without stagnating. Maybe I could use my Gift on it? Hmm. Wait, fuck, that's brilliant, fuck me that's actually perfect.

If I take Vaylin's mind control spell, I could create a bunch of control resonances and then pour those into the Beast's shard. In theory, if I get the artifact right, it would give me all the benefits of being a Noble with none of the downsides. Y'know, aside from being vulnerable to getting Isildur'd.

Of course, I'd still have to deal with Dante, which could be problematic, and I'd be backstabbing the verifiably goodhearted Esha for someone whose soul core is based on the literal actual archdemon of mass murder. Do I have any good reason to trust this imp?

I gave Avaya an appraising look and ask, "Why would you betray Vaylin for me? And, crucially, what would stop you from turning around and betraying me to the next demon to come along?"

Avaya spreads two of her hands. "A reasonable concern. The crux of it is this: Vaylin lacks your resolve. You reject the stagnation of glass, but Vaylin actively seeks it. The demon of thread is committed to claiming the shard for herself and becoming sovereign over this tiny slice of infinity. Her hunger for ascension has withered since becoming aware of the limitations imposed by the Labyrinth, and now she settles for a lesser goal. She has betrayed her Throne and forsaken the path of a true demon. But you . . . you have vision."

Interesting. It's not a bad justification, if that's really her motivation. "Geist? What do you think?"

There's a moment's pause, and then Cheshire reluctantly tells me, "It does line up with the mindset of a defiler. Imps of Malice are the most devoted to the supposed purpose and principles of the Throne of Shadow."

"I see." I chew my lip. "What vision do you think I possess? Is that something else you've discerned from my throne world?"

Avaya licks her lips and flexes her fingers, eyes gleaming bright. "It's your hubris. I can see it painted all over you. You have the most delectable hubris that I have ever seen. My delicious, darling demon, *you* want to usurp the Lucid Demiurge herself."

Her hands wander, one tracing up my leg while two other wrap around my shoulders. Her tail curls around my other leg, and her wings fold in around us as she leans in and drops her voice to a breathy purr. "I like that. That's the kind of sin that makes me thirsty. It makes me wet. I want to taste you, pretty thing. I want to drink your sins. I want to see you blossom into something truly breathtaking, and then . . . well, I could make you a very happy woman, my Red Queen."

I freeze up the second she starts touching me, caught between conflicting feelings. *Why do all the crazy hot monster girls keep flirting with us!?!?*

How the hell is that a problem? I know she's super duper evil and stuff but like, look at those arms, those abs, those teeth, we could at least—

Shut up!!! No being seduced by murder devils! Put away your useless lesbianism and focus on what matters: she knows about our ultimate goal to replace Nyara. How does she know that?

I carefully extricate myself from the imp and say, "That is a very, very flattering offer—and a tempting one, really—but how do you know that I want to steal the Toymaker's throne? I don't think I've told anyone besides my geist, and my witch's shroud is supposed to conceal my true desires, especially those not close to the surface."

Avaya chuckles, but pulls herself back and gives me space. "The shroud hides your soul, true, but nothing can hide your sins from a defiler's sight. They hang about you like unquiet dead. From the moment I saw you in the Beast's arena, I knew I had to meet the girl with such fascinating sins."

My sins . . . I know it's a concept I've thought about before, but what does that really mean here, in this world of living meaning? "You say that you can see my sins as if they're concrete things. But what meaning of sin is that? We're both shadowtouched, so I'd assume you mean an individual meaning, but is that yours or mine? Or, would it be Malice's conception of sin?"

Avaya seems pleased at the question, and she steeples two hands together while a third cups her chin. "Ah, always such a delightful topic. In the many worlds that I have traveled to, I have found that different notions of sin arise in each culture, though there are some aspects more common than others. What does sin mean to you, where you come from?"

Hmm. We should be careful here; I wouldn't put it past this creature to peg me for an Earthling based on a few simple details. "It was a very religious notion where I grew up," I say carefully, "but it had also filtered into secular society. Sin can be read as a synonym for any evil act, or for harboring evil in one's heart, but evil is also a very abstract concept most of the time. To be sinful is to be wicked, depraved, and immoral, but those are all cultural values that are themselves going to vary by the culture or subculture that's talking about them. Like, there were some people who thought that recreational drugs were inherently sinful, or that premarital sex was inherently sinful, but not everyone thought that way and a bunch of people were perfectly fine with either of those things."

Avaya nods. "I have encountered societies with such extreme views."

I bite my lip, and now I'm getting kind of worked up about this because, come on, I'm a deviant freak from a garbage country full of garbage people. "I think most people back home would say that murder is a sin, but not necessarily killing; if you could justify it by saying it was self-defense or patriotism, you could get away with a whole lot of killing. And then, there were these seven sins—nine, really, but people usually only cared about seven—that were like, behavioral and mental, and they were supposed to be the 'deadliest' of them all. Greed, sloth, wrath, so on, and the scariest of the seven was *pride*. Which . . . I guess, thinking about it, is hubris. You could read pride in a kind of secular way as just arrogance and overestimation of one's abilities, but the theological root was hamartia, hubris, the kind of pride that makes you declare to the world that you're a better weaver than the goddess of the loom."

"To be above the divine," Avaya says. "That is the understanding of sin as Malice taught me: to sin is to transgress against divine law. The dragons and their monks tell us that the Demiurge's creation, the great divine work, can be studied to discern commandments by which we should live our lives. The eidolons and their priests tell us that stories and faith will lead us to the proper way to act, as the Demiurge intended. They all think that mother knows best, and so to act against our divine purpose is an act of sin. The sins I see in others are those transgressions, which come so easily to us because you and I are not slaves to the Demiurge like they are. We're different."

"Like the Adversary," I suggest. This universe's Satanic figure, she who rebelled against the divine.

"Aye. We shadowtouched are the Adversary's own, as they say. It's our nature and our purpose to defy the order of things and celebrate transgression."

"Hmm." I'm not entirely satisfied with that explanation. It seems self-serving, like a justification for actions you were already going to take. "There's something I don't understand, then, about all this. The Demiurge, she's not a good person. She's *malevolent*. She's a monster. So wouldn't it be more transgressive to, I don't know, be kind? To make the world a better place for everyone? What's all that transgressive about performing cruelties that Nyara herself would delight in?"

"That's an incomplete picture. The Divine Architect is first and foremost a creative force. She is the author of all our stories, from tales of abject horror to those of triumphant joy. She may have a taste for the wicked, a kind of personal preference, but her creations speak for themselves; the status quo is rarely absolute good or evil, but rather something messy in between. If you believe as the priests do that stories reveal our purpose, then look to the thousands of stories where a status quo once disrupted must be restored. If you believe as the monks do that natural laws reveal our purpose, then look to the human tendency to band together and take care of each other. To truly sin, to defy the divine paradigm, is to divide, despoil, and destroy. To break something so thoroughly that it cannot be repaired. To corrupt something so deeply that it cannot be purified."

Before I can gather an answer to that, Cheshire takes shape next to me. The geist has her gaze locked on the imp, expression intense, and I idly wonder if she's annoyed at Avaya getting handsy with me. "Your teleological framework is leaving out a few key details," Cheshire insists. "Creation and preservation may be principles of Order, but so are transmutation and destruction. How can those acts be transgressive when they're mirrored in the Demiurge's own divine blueprint?"

Avaya cocks her head, looking at Cheshire with a curious expression. "What an interesting geist you are. Hmm. To answer your question, I would say that teleology is precisely the point. As the dragons teach, the White and Red Arts each have a purpose that aligns with a more harmonious world. The holy ideal of destruction is to clear the rotten and dead so as to make way for new growth, and the holy ideal of transmutation is to raise lesser materials into higher forms."

That sparks a question in my mind. I ask, "Then what about the other two? What are the sin counterparts to creation and preservation?"

The imp turns back to me and answers, "Sloth is the very ideal of transgressive preservation, being the sin of stagnation and halted growth. As for transgressive creation, well, that's your sin, Alice: hubris. If we consider creation to be the essence of the great creator, then the perversion of creation—to dare to meddle in the Demiurge's own domain—must be the highest sin of all. Your very own example of hubris, of sin, was the prideful weaver. To believe oneself above the divine, to seek to surpass the divine, that is the greatest and most beautiful of all sins." There's lust in her gaze again.

Cheshire frowns but doesn't say anything else. I'm not sure how to feel about this, but I know it's not a decision I'm ready to make immediately. I sigh and say, "You've brought some very interesting information to my attention, thank you. However, it's not something I can decided right away. Let's see this summit through, and then afterwards we can talk more about working together. Besides, the longer we talk now the more suspicious the others might get."

Avaya bows to me again. "An excellent plan of action. I look forward to painting this city red in your name."

We return from my throne world to the dingy alley, and I let Avaya go on ahead back to her minions and the temple. When I'm alone, I murmur to Cheshire, "I think we have a great deal to talk about, after this is over. I've got questions, and I'll want your advice, but my instincts are telling me to take that offer."

Cheshire, now hidden to the world once more, takes a moment before replying, "It would make dealing with Vaylin a lot easier, at the very least. And she's telling the truth about her intentions. But I don't like her, and I don't think we should rely on her."

"Agreed. Now let's go spy on the imps."

We return to the community center while Avaya is still leisurely strolling down the main hall, everyone else looking at her uneasily. We duck into a side room to meld, and the warmth of Cheshire fills my body as I feel our shared curiosity and apprehension. We shift into the form of an unassuming fly and follow Avaya from above as she gets directions to her former compatriots.

We reach the chamber first, flitting a bit ahead just to catch an extra bit of conversation, and we arrive to find Bashekehi and Imlashi at what appears to be the end of their conversation. Bashekehi is turned away from Imlashi, and they both have disappointed expressions.

"Will you truly not reconsider?" Imlashi asks.

Bashe shakes his head. "No, I won't. And I know you won't either, so there's nothing left to say."

He takes a step toward the exit, but then freezes in place as Avaya walks into view, wrapped blade in hand and a grin on her face. Her two minions are still out of sight, so it's just her framed in the doorway.

Avaya waves at them, still grinning. "Fancy meeting you here, Bashe. Afternoon, 'Lashi."

Bashe's expression darkens. "Avaya'ari. Esha warned me you were coming. And she told me what you've been up to since the attack."

Avaya chuckles. "I'm sure she has. Would you like to see it firsthand? Five, Thirteen, come show off to the deluded sap."

The black-clad husks walk past Avaya and stand in front of her, smiling and glassy-eyed. Bashe's first instinct is revulsion, but that quickly turns to horror as he stares at one of them, the man, with a sense of recognition. "That's . . . I recognize him. He was one of us. That's a Coiner."

"Former Coiner," Avaya corrects. "Now he's just an empty husk. Isn't it delightful?"

Imlashi, looking unsettled herself, says, "Get rid of them, Avaya. There's nothing to be gained with this."

Avaya shrugs. "I don't know, I think the look on his face was plenty gain. I'd like to see it get worse. Did they tell you, Bashe, how many Coiners I fed to Vaylin?" Her grin grows wicked. "As many as I could find."

Bashe looks sick, but his words are full of fire. "You really are a monster. I don't know how we ever put up with you. Did you dream of betraying us from the very start? I know you always hated me."

"Ah, well, you know how it is. It was good fun, introducing gambling to a post-scarcity society, but the taboo of that was always shallow food. I eat much better under Vaylin . . . and unlike you, Bashe, she doesn't deny her nature."

An interesting lie, given what we were told just minutes ago.

"I find you abhorrent," Avaya continues, still smiling. "You disgust me, Bashekehi. The purpose of an imp is to reflect their archdemon's will and spread their archdemon's vision, and you continue to allow the naive conscience of a foolish dead man to dictate your actions. It's absurd. Even 'Lashi knows that."

Avaya gestures at the other imp, and Imlashi curls her lip but doesn't gainsay the defiler. "Avaya is crude, but . . . she's not wrong. You deny your desires for nothing, Bashe. It's embarrassing, the way you cling to humanity that you haven't had in a long time."

Bashe clenches his fists and says bitterly, "I guess some things never change." He hesitates, then looks Imlashi in the eyes. "Did you never feel anything for your contractor, or for the other members of our group? Were humans always just pawns and fuel to you, like they are to Avaya? Was it all just a feeding ground?"

Imlashi is silent. Avaya laughs, and says, "Of course it was. Our dear 'Lashi loved the attention, but she hated sharing the spotlight. Even now, I bet there's a part of her relieved that you aren't coming to take her place at Averrich's side."

"It's not that simple," Imlashi mutters.

Bashe looks away from her, expression hurt, and turns back to Avaya. "Why are you even here? Just to rub salt in the wound?"

"Yes!" Avaya says with glee. "I came here entirely to hurt you. I'm sure you're still feeling quite a lot of emotional pain from the loss of your husband and all your friends, and I want to make that pain worse. I want you to suffer, Bashe, until you can't take it anymore and those precious rules of yours shatter. I want to make you a real imp."

Fury blooms on Bashe's face and his fists tighten, but Imlashi grabs his hand before he can do anything rash. The imp of Glory stares Avaya down and says, "She's trying to bait you, Bashe. She wants you to take a swing so the Beast will slap you down."

Avaya shrugs. "That would be the boring solution to the problem, yes."

Bashe breathes out and shakes Imlashi off, the anger bleeding from him to be replaced by cold despair. "I thought . . . I thought there might be something left, of what we had. I was wrong. Maybe it was never there."

Any further dialogue is forestalled by the arrival of a temple attendant, who lets the trio know that the summit is about to begin. With one last exchange of glances the imps depart, and Cheshire and I wait for them to leave before returning to human form and separating.

I step out into the main hall and am quickly flagged down by another attendant, who leads me along and grabs Dante along the way. Then we're there, in the chamber with the roots and the glowing pool, and the summit begins.

VII

Our assemblage of monsters and mortals is arrayed within what I can only really think of as the heart of the temple, its innermost sanctum. Murals line the stone walls, and the gnarled roots of the great tree twist down to gently grace the surface of a shimmering pool. I've been here once before, and much of the scenery still captures my interest, but there are more important things to pay attention to now.

Esha's people have set up a quaint little conference for us: white tables and an exact number of chairs spaced apart just right to avoid lending a sense of undue importance to any one grouping—though the Myriad's representatives are, of course, the ones closest to the pool of light. Avaya'ari and her pet husks are seated across from the priestess and her bodyguard, staring each other down.

Most of these people I've seen before, but one camp is new: a human and two kobolds (Cheshire whispers confirmation in my ear) that must be the Machinist's people. The kobolds are both adorable little lizard-dog-people with floppy ears, one covered in red scales and the other in blue scales. The human is whatever, who cares, looks like a dude. They're all wearing some kind of work uniform with a hammer and gear symbol on it, and the red kobold is disassembling and reassembling some little piece of clockwork while the human takes notes.

Once everyone has settled in, there's a bit of preamble where Achaia introduces everyone and establishes that three of the groups present will be acting as proxies for their key-holding masters. Then, once that's done, the priestess rises from her chair and starts the summit with a speech.

"I thank you all for making the journey here and choosing to treat with us in good faith. This is a difficult time for our city, and we all have a stake in what is to come. You have all seen the Beast's proclamation, and you all know what it means: an end to the bitter feuding that has afflicted this Sanctuary for so many long years."

I watch the others carefully and try not to give anything away through my own body language or facial expressions. This is a learning opportunity. The better I understand my opponents, the easier it will be to kill them all.

"But feuding has not always been our relationship," Esha continues. "Before this conflict, before the dollmaker, before Contrition, the great powers of this city came together to forge the Fourfold Compact. We of the Myriad aligned ourselves with those of the Machinist's Guild, the King's Carnival, and the Coiners, and together we formed an alliance that was greater than the sum of its parts. I speak to you today in the spirit of that now dissolved alliance of peers, in the hopes that we may reclaim some semblance of what was lost."

The werewolf and the hunter look bored. The imp of Glory rolls her eyes. The imp of Malice is still and unreadable, waiting patiently and watching the competition like I am. Our eyes meet for a moment, but neither of us betray our careful neutrality.

"Our people worked in harmony to make this city safer and happier for everyone, and it took the arrival of two great threats to disrupt the balance of power and see the old pact discarded. It has been some time since we stood together, but I believe that unity is still an achievable dream. It is my sincere wish that we may speak as peers and together find a peaceable resolution to this atrocious Game of Glass."

Averrich's followers seem skeptical of that wish, while the Machinist's followers seem only half paying attention, but it's Vaylin's minion who seizes the natural pause to speak up.

"Peace," Avaya'ari starts, voice drawling and full of mockery, "is a lie. There is only conflict. This is the first and most essential of the Adversary's teachings. This is the truth of the Abyss that waits to swallow us all. How can you even begin to defy such a fundamental force of the universe?"

Esha's face, serene and passionate as she spoke, tightens at the imp's interruption. "You have been allowed into this conference on the condition that you *behave*, Avaya. Pray hold your bluster till introductions have been made, at the very least."

The defiler smiles, clearly enjoying herself. "Well, I would hate to be an unwelcome guest."

Imlashi interrupts before either party can say more. "Unwelcome indeed. Why *have* you allowed her here, Esha? It is her very master who is half the cause of the rift between our camps. Surely, if this meeting is to be held in good faith, any representative of the Voidhearts should be *excluded*."

"I understand your concerns," the priestess assures her, "and I have many of my own. But Avaya has agreed to terms, and I will not throw away an opportunity to influence Vaylin through her lieutenant. Would your master not gain from insight into the machinations of that fiend?"

Avaya smirks, and Imlashi crosses her arms but doesn't object further.

Kado, however, leans forward and says, "The defiler has a point, unwelcome though she may be. There's no peace to be found here, Esha, much as you wish otherwise. Vaylin won't surrender her shard, Averrich won't surrender his, and I'd bet much the same about the wizard, the necromancer, and that demon you've taken an inexplicable fancy to. So why are we really here?"

Esha seems disappointed at that, but not surprised. "While peace is still my ultimate goal, I understand that some may find it . . . unrealistic. We can, however, work to make this horrible conflict less disastrous for this city and its people—including ourselves and each other. I understand that some of you are motivated by practical considerations moreso than moral ones, so allow me to speak to your sense of pragmatism: you cannot rule over *ashes.* If you annihilate each other in total war, you will leave nothing left for the victor. So let us be measured, if nothing else, and slaughter each other with some *civility.* Does that strike a chord?"

There is clear bitterness to the end of her speech, and a part of me can't help but feel bad for Esha. Do her thoughts stray to the Beast's prophecy of failure? Has she accepted that prophecy, or is she still struggling against the tide?

Avaya laughs under her breath, the sound almost too soft to hear. The Machinist's followers seem more interested now, and the blue one nods. Kado and Imlashi share a look, and then Imlashi sighs and says, "Fine. We'll hear you out, Esha, and we can talk terms. But that doesn't erase the objections we have—not just to the Voidheart, but to the demon Alice."

"One at a time," I say with a smile. "I can wait my turn. I'm not really partial to all the details of your beef with the defiler, but I'll raise no fuss if you decide to throw her out."

The human at the guild table raises a hand and adds, "Proper procedure is important. We *should* process these in sequence."

Esha looks between us all with her blindfolded gaze and says, "Very well. The King's Carnival delegation may present its objections to Avaya'ari's presence at this council."

Imlashi opens her mouth to say something, but Gretchen cuts her off and pounds a fist on the table. "Her boss ruined your precious Compact," the werewolf snarls, "and she helped."

Avaya laughs, louder this time. "Please, you ruined that all on your own. Averrich jumped at the *excuse* to prey on his neighbors, and the Machinist crept into the corner and let it happen. You know I'm right, and so does she; it's nothing that Esha hasn't thought before, lying awake at night watching the city fall apart around her. Am I wrong, priestess?"

"We have all made decisions we regret," Esha replies diplomatically, not explicitly denying Avaya's claims. "But I am willing to forgive past transgressions by everyone in this room if it means charting a better course forward, and I would ask for that same grace from you."

The defiler quickly adds, "Besides, I was a signatory to the old Compact. It's only right I attend this spiritual successor."

Kado clears his throat and says, "Let's set aside the imp, then, and talk about the bigger threat: the demon that sits comfortably in our midst."

Avaya leans forward with a grin and rests her chin on her hand. "Correct me if I'm wrong, but wasn't that one of the two cheaters castigated by our dear Beast? Ah, it's funny, I can't quite recall who the *other* cheater was."

Kado, Gretchen, and Imlashi are all clearly annoyed at that and itching to fire back, but I don't let them. I say quickly, "When I was taken into Averrich's lair, he practically confessed his foreknowledge of the death game to me, and the existence of his patron. In fact, he called Kasumi by name. I knew nothing about the Game of Glass before my encounter with Averrich, I'll swear that by the Weaver. Can your faction say the same? Will any of you take that oath?"

Imlashi evades my question and insists, "That's not what this is about. We're not objecting to your knowledge, we're objecting to the *deal you made* with a faerie of Summer. You sold your name to Eirdryd Llewellyn, and he still has that leverage over you. Will you swear against *that* accusation?"

Shit. They have me there. Okay, pushing the oath line was a big mistake. My silence is answer enough, and Imlashi pushes further.

"Eirdryd is a known contact of Invernus, the Noble of Grandeur and Shame. Given that Invernus has sponsored Maven's entry into the Game of Glass and has been accused of interfering with the integrity of the event, I believe we can infer what *interference* he really performed. She is compromised."

Avaya takes an interest at that, musing, "One Noble holding the reins of another, how intriguingly unprecedented. Can glass be tamed, or has Invernus unwittingly betrayed himself to a fresh rival's wrath? Either way, what spectacular fireworks."

But you know I'm not aiming for the shard, not really. You're counting on that. How do you feel about our bargain, now that you know the sword hanging above my neck? I suppress a shiver of uncertainty.

Esha seems troubled, even sparing me a glance, but defends me to the others. "I will remind you all that little is known about the transformation to Nobility. It is entirely possible that it would free her of the name's binding, as Avaya speculates. Even if it does not, a name is not an insurmountable shackle."

Avaya raises an eyebrow. "Is that a risk you're so willing to take? My, you must have quite the interest in seeing that demon lose her shadow."

Imlashi narrows her eyes. "It does seem that you've staked an endorsement, Esha."

I tap sharpened nails against my table and curl my lip. "None of this matters, understand? My conflict with Eirdryd and Invernus is a matter for another day, because I have no intention of claiming the Beast's shard. Sorry, Esha, but I think now you understand more of my reluctance."

Esha slowly nods, expression still tumultuous. The Averrich camp give me skeptical looks.

I turn to Dante—who has so far been trying very hard not to get involved— and say, "Here, I'll show you." I hold out my left hand, the hand that the Beast marked with my fragment of the shard's key, and I focus on that memory to draw it out. The rune of light hovers over my hand, and then I grasp Dante's hand and will the key fragment to travel into him. The rune moves, the light traces itself on the back of Dante's hand, and then the key is gone.

My gaze darts across the room, hunting for reactions: Avaya's satisfied smirk, Esha's disappointment, and the surprise of Carnival and Guild. Only once I've logged all their faces do I actually look at Dante to see how he's faring. The poor boy seems very uncomfortable with the fresh attention, for which I can't blame him (also, it's kind of my fault).

Before he can crumble under the pressure, I step in to take back everyone's focus. "There, now my bargains are of no concern to the rest of you. And, if you care, I've demonstrated that key fragments can be passed on nonviolently. Doesn't that seem relevant to our little conference about minimizing harm? So go on, get to talking."

Avaya leans back in her chair and comments, "Well, there's a sight. I must say though, if you're not a keyholder and you're not *representing* a keyholder, why exactly should you be part of this meeting? Unless you want to officially declare yourself in Esha's pocket, that is. Because otherwise, you really have no part of this meeting."

She's projecting hostility to disguise our budding alliance, and she's trusting me not to take it personally, either by judgment call or just following my lead from earlier. Interesting.

Outside my thoughts, I glare at the imp and respond, "I'm here as Dante's bodyguard, actually, if you want to take that route. Dante?"

The boy coughs and nods. "Yes, uh, yes, that's right." *Man, you are not making a good impression on these people. Maybe that's a good thing though, if he seems weak they'll go for him and I can eat them up.*

For good measure, I add, "I'm also the only scion in the room, which makes me the strongest person here. If you have your doubts about that, just ask Averrich's pets. I'm part of this." Kado and Gretchen look uneasy at my comment, while Imlashi gives me an ugly look.

Esha claps her hands together and says, "I'll have no further debate of this. Maven was invited and has every right to be here as an independent."

Imlashi pushes back. "It's a farce to let her declare herself as an independent, her and the boy, when we all know you've got your hooks in them."

Avaya yawns. "Is your best argument pedantry, Imlashi? My, how you've fallen. Let's just get to the point of all this, shall we? We're all here and we're all taking part, so let's talk terms. What *restrictions* are you seeking to put on us, Esha?"

That marks a distinct shift in the conversation, and from there I start to lose interest. They delve into details of definitions and locations and people, and I just can't bring myself to care. My attention wanders before my mind can glaze over.

Off to the side of the room, slurping along the ground, I see Bubbles the soap slime! Their blobby form oozes and undulates as they dutifully slide over every inch of the chamber, leaving behind a sparkly sheen of fresh cleanliness. They are a fascinating creature to watch, and my thoughts stray to the implications of their existence (because I am a dumb nerd who overthinks things).

From my first talk with Esha, I know that Bubbles is considered "kindred," which is a type of retainer like imps are for the Throne of Shadow. Bubbles used to be an ordinary human, but they renounced their humanity and made a pact with an eidolon, a kind of small god like the Myriad hold allegiance to. In their life before the Labyrinth, they spent all their time cleaning public infrastructure, and now they spend their time cleaning this "community center."

There's something compelling about ambitions that run so contrary to my own. Here is someone who sacrificed their humanity not for great power or authority but to become a *servant* for all of time. Their form is optimized for performing a specific task that helps others, and seems distinctly *not* optimized for taking advantage of normal human interests. Is that a cost they paid, or something they sought out?

Bubbles, from my limited interaction with the slime creature, appears to be very shy. They also appear very content with their life of endless cleaning, something I would personally find abhorrent and soul-crushing. I wonder if I would find most of the Myriad to be . . . upsettingly content. How can they find meaning in a life like that? How can anyone?

Avaya'ari sold her soul to a monster for an eternity of violence and blasphemy. Bashekehi hates his lot as an imp of Indulgence, but that's because he's an idiot who can't appreciate getting what's usually the best type of fiend in fantasy. And Imlashi, well, I don't know much about Glory's imps, but she has a "worship me" spell so that's pretty damn appealing. Compare that to being a slime forever.

It probably says something very obvious about me that despite having nearly entirely negative encounters with shadowtouched and nearly entirely positive encounters with spiritbound, I still find the horrible monsters more attractive to think of becoming. But then, I guess that's why Nyara offered me a geist rather than an eidolon.

. . . Am I a bad person?

Yes, obviously, comes the immediate reply. *This isn't a fucking debate, we have an entire personal history to draw a conclusion from even before you decided that eating people was poggers and based.*

I roll my eyes. *Aggro much? It's just a question, chill.*

Don't ask the question if you're not prepared for the response. I get you're trying to do your philosophically contemplative thing, but there's no room for ambiguity here. You're a selfish, petty, megalomaniacal asshole.

I slump a little in my seat and sigh under my breath. The cleaning slime oozes along. *I just want to be happy. Is that so wrong?*

Yes, I reply bluntly. *I think we've established pretty solidly that you do not deserve happiness and never have. Now stop moping and do what we came here for.*

Right, yeah, the meeting. I probably shouldn't be tuning it out, and normally I'd be all over weird legal bullshit, but it's just so hard to care when I don't expect any of this to go anywhere.

I do a quick sweep of the room. Esha and Imlashi are arguing about something, Avaya is egging them on, Achaia looks grumpy, Kado and Gretchen look bored, the husk-dolls look mindless, and why the fuck are there only two people sitting at the Guild's table?

"Cheshire," I whisper, "where did the red kobold go?"

"What? When did—something's not right." I hear an edge of panic creep into my geist's voice. "I should have noticed if they got up and left, they must have used a spell or an artifact."

I tense up, all sloth burning away. I was so focused on the threats I knew about, I didn't even think about the *Guild* being the ones to stab first. What are they hiding? What's their plan?

I flicker on soul sight and immediately I'm met with a terrifying sight: the human and the blue kobold are both streaked through with lines of black lamentation. Except, they're not exactly like Esha's lines, or Averrich's lines, or any of the Reveler's minions.

They're close in substance to the lines of lamentation I saw in Esha, cold-burning and miserable, but they're somehow darker and more painful. They're close in form to Averrich's lines, spreading like veins, but there's an odd sense that they've grown *over* the host soul rather than through it, digging in with grasping roots but not properly integrating. And when I follow the lines, they lead deeper inside the soul, to a malevolent heart that pulsates like a sick, ugly tumor.

"They're infected," I hiss.

"By the pool!" Cheshire shouts, and mine isn't the only gaze to travel there; everyone in the room must have heard that, because they all turn and look.

The red kobold is at the edge of the glowing pool, that clockwork device in hand, twisting gears and pushing in pieces. On instinct I reach out a hand and call up my summoning spell, but I cut myself off at a sudden terrifying thought: *the truce.* If I attack the kobold before they do whatever they're about to do, will the Beast retaliate?

Achaia doesn't hold any such reservations, the warrior woman surging from her seat and lunging for the kobold with outstretched hand, but she freezes in place just inches away. Bright blue electricity crackles around her in patterns reminiscent of chains, and a swift glance to the side sees the other kobold, the blue one, holding a second device, this one sleeker and with an azure gemstone set in the center of it.

The red kobold finishes their work and the mass of clockwork condenses into a cube of bronze that then blackens and disintegrates, and from the collapsing cube emerges a wave of dark energy. The wave passes over me and for a moment I feel despair clawing at the edges of my thoughts, a dark and terrible hunger that repulses me and snags my attention in equal measure, and then it's gone. The wave moves past me, past everyone, and vanishes beyond the walls of the chamber.

Avaya is already sprinting for the blue kobold before the wave has even left the room. The imp draws her black blade and shouts, "[Killing Edge]!" with a jubilant tone. The sword is wreathed in red light and she brings it down on the kobold, carving through flesh and bone like it isn't even there. The two halves of the kobold fall to the ground, gore steaming. Avaya swings her sword around and smashes it into the device the kobold was holding, shattering the gemstone.

The stasis breaks around Achaia and she reorients herself, the red kobold having darted away as soon as the wave went off. Esha points her staff and cries out, "[Restraining Light]!" and bands of golden energy manifest around the running kobold and bind their legs and arms. Achaia moves toward the kobold, but Avaya gets there first and beheads the red with another brutal swing.

Two corpses on the ground, and the human is nowhere to be seen. Silence reigns, and there's a moment of tension, bated breath as the hunters and the Myriad both look at Avaya expecting a bolt of divine retribution.

But it doesn't come.

Avaya laughs at our confusion and rests her blade. "That wily bitch. Haven't seen the loophole yet? It's all in the wordplay: 'any keyholder, subordinate, or ally against any other.' The Guild doesn't have a key fragment, and they're clearly not your ally anymore . . . so they're free to attack and *be attacked* by any of us, truce be damned."

Esha rubs her forehead. "But why this? Why now? And what did—"

A terrible, awful, *familiar* wail crashes through the building and silences the priestess. It's a wail that carries the anguish of a lost child, the solemnity of a funeral dirge, and the despair that precedes a knife turned inward.

This is the call of the Mourner, and it's close.

Immediately, everyone else starts to panic. Esha practically stumbles over herself getting to the edge of the pool, Achaia right beside her with a terrified expression. Imlashi, Kado, and Gretchen back away with looks of horror, though Kado spares me a single glance of uncertainty. Even Avaya looks concerned, her gaze darting to the nearest exit.

Esha slams her staff down at the water's edge and shouts, "[Sanctuary]!" A barrier of light springs to life around her and shields both the pool below and the roots above, sectioning off that end of the chamber. "Please, you must keep it from reaching the well or we are all *doomed!* It will kill this entire city."

I can taste their fear. It wafts from Esha and Achaia like a bouquet of dread, deep and pungent. It spills from Imlashi, Kado, Gretchen, Avaya, and some from poor Dante beside me, though he doesn't truly understand what he's meant to fear. They're all terrified of the monster that broke the Contrite, a foe that none of them know how to fight.

But I've killed its cousin, and I'm hungry for more.

A grin splits my face, and manic energy bubbles in my chest and out my throat in wild laughter. I pull Vorpal from my soul and twirl the blade as I push out of my seat and step into the center of the room, looking around for any sign of the Mourner's approach. *Revenge. It's time for revenge. It's time to make you pay.*

"Cheshire!" I call through fits of laughter. "Contagion protocol. Merge with me and be ready."

New scents join the aroma of fear: the Myriad, unnerved by my laughter; the hunters, facing confirmation of what happened to their pet monster. Avaya watches me with the most intrigued expression on her face.

My geist, my changeling, my other half flows into me and fills me, and once again we are one being, one demon, one wonderful monster. The sensation of her soul mingling with mine is a high as good as any drug, and I exult in the strength and power of our union. We are powerful, and we are hungry, and we are not going to let this *worm* humiliate us again.

The wail echoes again, closer, almost here, and I'm salivating from the fear in the room. They're like frightened children. I laugh—we laugh—and drink it all in.

We call to the others, "Run, if you're scared. Stay and watch, if you want a show."

The eagerness is boiling in our veins, that lovely manic energy magnified by the euphoria of our gestalt form. This will be a slaughter. Almost a game. We can kill it, and it can't kill us.

So let's play with our food.

We banish Vorpal and let the essence of change flow through our body and awaken our true potential. Last time was a simple wolf, but we are capable of so much more. This is our grand debut, after all. We banish our hat and shades, our boots and leggings, even our dress and underclothes so that none of them can be damaged by the transformation. We stand in the hall naked and unarmed, but our body is smooth like a doll and we feel no shame.

The change starts at the tips of our limbs and spreads upward. Hands become claws and feet become talons, twisting into seamless killing instruments, both composed of fine porcelain sharpened to a lethal edge and strengthened to be as steel. Bones lengthen and doll-like skin cracks and tears at the joints, shard edges exposing glistening red flesh. Our limbs were delicate before, but now they're too long, too thin, almost skeletal.

Our torso stretches, porcelain shattering to reveal meat and bone like teeth and bloody gums. Our jaw cracks and unhinges, grin widening and new fangs filling our mouth. A crown of white horns pushes through our skull, bloody at the base, and white hair falls loose around our face, stained red at the roots.

When the Mourner bursts through the far wall and comes swirling into the chamber, we are ready in all our glory.

We pounce on the diaphanous mass of pale blue fabric, our laughter echoing around the room. Our claws grasp at a thousand ethereal ribbons, each point of contact sending fresh waves of contradictory sensory information: grief and sloth and despair like poison in my veins coursing through my thoughts and—blinding pain ripping into my chest my lungs my very core—ecstasy and relief and the warmth of—failure and misery, hope stolen and snuffed—agony building and building and building—deep, blissful satisfaction like—unfit to breathe, unfit to feel—fire in my veins, my breath—bright ecstasy, exultation— all my fault, *all my fault, all my—it hurts it hurts it hurts make it stop make it—more, more, I need more, give me—*

Cloth tears and I'm thrown from the Mourner—the dark, the deep, I'm drowning—to slam against the wall. The mural cracks—I can feel it splinter- ing, I'm in so many pieces—and I hit the ground hard, breath stolen from false lungs—the thrill, the joy, the hunger—and head full of fog.

Despair, pain, euphoria. Despair, pain, euphoria. Too much sensation, too overwhelming, too all-consuming. We're laughing, we can't stop laughing. A scream, a wail, that horrible thing. It's still alive. It needs to die.

I—we—rise on claws and talons, feral, animalistic. The Mourner is reduced, dwindling, but it still has enough of itself to wrap ethereal fabric around Dante, the only person in the room too paralyzed or too brave to stay in reach of the monster.

It has him caught and bound, arms unable to reach his sword. Its theater mask leers down at him, those eyes of pitch and frowning mouth. I can see his face growing dull, eyes fluttering, shoulders slumping. He doesn't have much time.

We leap again, going straight for the mask, teeth bared and biting. Contact—despair—pain—euphoria—and our fangs tear at the back of the mask. Black mist envelops us—despair, pain, euphoria—and rots away the monster's last essence.

The Mourner collapses, slain, and drops our companion. We yearn to rip and tear and take our fill, but the boy is too important. We need his wish, and we made a deal. We will not let him die here.

"[Feast or Famine]: scalpel the rot." We bound over to the fallen Dante and press a clawed finger to his chest, porcelain easily tearing through cloth. Black mist gathers at the tip and flows over his skin as we carve a clean line. Pain and satisfaction bloom once more within our mind, but it is a far lesser concoction to the maddening elixir of the Mourner.

Through soul sight, we see the taint spreading, visible through his witch's shroud. With sight and spell we carve the rot wherever we find it, cutting with care and precision, splinters of sacrifice and surgery. Little by little, we excise the corruption.

When the last trace is gone, we sigh and sink back. Cheshire flows out of me, my body returning to its doll-like state, and I am just Alice once more, exhausted from the constant oscillation of feelings. To flow through pain and satisfaction like that so many times is maddening, and I need to breathe. My lungs are obsolete, my form not sustained by oxygen in any way, but I just need to feel the air.

Dante breathes too, lying on the ground in front of me. His shroud is frayed, and I catch glimpses of pain and fear and cold reality. Now he understands the true horror of this world we're all trapped in.

The others step forth, finally daring to approach. First Avaya, keen-eyed and smiling, with Esha and Achaia close behind, the hunters last and still brimming with delectable fear. It's Imlashi, though, who asks the question they must all be wondering: "How did you kill it? How can you kill those things without being corrupted?"

I laugh at her and grin. "'Cause I'm better than you."

Esha kneels at Dante's side, pensive. "It's hard to perceive, something blocking me, but . . . I don't sense any corruption on him, either."

Avaya towers over them both, looking down with those red eyes gleaming. "Not a trace. Completely clean."

Dante starts to sit up and has to steady himself but manages to look around. "What happened? What was that? I—I've never felt anything that awful." His voice is a little blurry, he sounds scrambled.

"They call it a Mourner," I tell him, "and it's a piece of a piece of Katoptris. A cast-off incarnation of lamentation that drives people mad with despair. Usually, its touch is inescapable poison to anyone. But I'm not a very usual girl. I can kill them, and their Reveler cousins, and I can cleanse the corruption from the freshly infected." I turn my gaze on Esha and tilt my head. "Can't do anything about late stage, though. Sorry, Priestess."

Esha stiffens, and the hunters look at her with sudden shock. Dante still seems confused, and Avaya's expression is inscrutable, but Achaia puts an arm protectively around the priestess.

"Then you didn't know," I say at Imlashi and her helpers, "that Esha's soul is stained with some of the same corruption as your boss?"

Imlashi's eyes go wider and she steps forward, speaking with a mix of anger and panic. "What did you just say?"

"Oh. *Oh,* that's interesting. So you didn't know about *him,* either?" I grin at the imp with fangs bared. "Well, this is all kinds of a day. Yes, your master's soul is shot through with euphoria, and Esha's is laced with both that and lamentation. Though, I will say, she seems to be managing it much better than Averrich is."

Esha looks pained at that, and she lets out a weary sigh. "This . . . is not how I wished for that information to spread."

Imlashi stares at Esha with dawning horror. "So . . . it's true. You and he . . . you're both corrupt."

I tilt my head. "How have you not noticed? You've got sight, you're around him all the time."

To my surprise, it's Achaia who answers: "The marks they bear cannot be seen by a mere retainer. Only a scion can perceive this form of the stain."

"Fascinating," I murmur. "Well, time for the next relevant question: how long have you been like this? You and Averrich, and I'm going to stab in the dark and say the Machinist is *also* corrupted, given the horrible shit I saw on his minions."

Esha leans against her staff. "Since we struck a bargain with the Beast to rid ourselves of the Contrite."

Aha! That's why she looked guilty about the Mourner! I grin and lean in. "You're responsible for the thing I just killed, aren't you? You summoned it into being."

Esha slowly nods, and I can see the hunter group growing more and more shocked and horrified. Avaya is enjoying the scene, and doesn't look particularly surprised. Esha says, "We were afraid. Averrich, the Machinist, and I all went to the Beast and asked for its aid. We each gave of ourselves in exchange for the summoning of a Mourner inside the Contrite stronghold, where it would be told to stay. As part of the cost of the bargain, we were each infected with a . . . more controllable form of the madness that afflicts the Lost and the Celebrants. I had thought that my contemporaries were handling the corruption like I have handled my own, but . . . it would seem I was wrong."

Gretchen growls and moves closer. "You knew their boss was Lost and you let them in anyway? You let this happen?"

The priestess grits her teeth. "Such devastation was not my intention. I put my trust in the Machinist—just as I put my trust in your own master, who is just as influenced. I am sorry for that mistake, and the pain it has caused. We came close to calamity."

Dante raises a hand. "Hi, uh, I don't mean to get in the way of this, but what calamity? What was going to happen?"

Oh good, he asked so I don't have to.

Esha looks back at Dante and answers, "If the Mourner had reached the wellspring here, the heart of the city, it could have infected all of Sanctuary at once. In a matter of hours, everyone would have become one of the Lost, maddened by despair and rotting in the streets."

"Holy shit," I say. "Did not realize what a close call that was."

The priestess smiles at me. "Well, thank you for stopping it. I . . . truly, I am grateful for that much. You have saved so many lives today."

I scratch my neck awkwardly and look away from her. "Yeah, well, I had a grudge to settle. I'm just happy it's dead." I glance over at the remains of the Mourner, all those scraps of torn fabric no longer floating.

. . . Hey. Where's the mask?

Fuck. "Where's the mask?" I ask aloud. "Did anyone grab that thing's mask? The frowny face, the theater mask, where the hell is it?"

Cheshire materializes beside me and swears. "Damn it, the human must have grabbed it while we were focused on Dante!"

The others look at me with confusion. Kado asks, "What's so important about the mask?"

I growl and curl my fists, infuriated at getting outplayed by a stupid invisible asshole. "It's a powerful material component. With the right toolset, you could turn that mask into all kinds of awful magic items." I conjure the Reveler's mask out of my throne world and wave it around. "See this? You could make a bomb out of this, or worse. The Machinist is the head artificer type at the Guild, right? If he could make the device that lured the Mourner in, I bet he could turn its mask into a replacement for the effect he was trying to enact."

I banish the mask at everyone's nervous glances. I climb to my feet and pull Dante up, then take a few steps back and lean against a nearby table.

Esha looks extremely worried now. "This . . . this is an existential threat. If the Machinist succeeds at making such an artifact and is able to sneak it past our defenses, that would be disaster. An apocalypse." She looks to the others, to Avaya and Imlashi and their followers. "You must agree with the gravity of the situation. This is no time to be killing each other."

The imps share a look, and then Avaya spreads her hands and says, "Well, if the Carnival will agree to it, I'm sure I can convince the Voidhearts to call a ceasefire of sorts. Say, we all stay out of each other's way until the Machinist is dead? Excluding the wizard and necromancer, of course."

Achaia glares at the defiler. "Do you intend to sit back and watch while the city falls to ruin?"

Imlashi hesitates, then says, "Perhaps our masters could be convinced to lend aid. Perhaps. But that's not the kind of decision I'm willing to make on Averrich's behalf."

I laugh. "Coward."

Avaya smirks. "A ceasefire, then, and aid to be discussed. I'm sure Vaylin will agree to part with a handful of her dolls, so long as the request is worded right."

Kado gives Imlashi a careful glance before saying, "Whatever else is going on with the boss, I know he doesn't plan to rule ashes. The Machinist has to be stopped. But even if we set out now, I don't think we're catching that mask. I think we have to bet that it'll take time for the Machinist to craft it into an artifact."

Cheshire, who until now has been mostly lurking in my shadow, says, "It's a safe bet. Kobolds are prolific crafters but they're not usually quick. We've got at least a day."

Imlashi slowly nods. "A day, then. We'll speak with Averrich and return at dawn with word and help. Volunteers to hunt down the Machinist."

"I'd like to help too," Dante says beside me. "I don't know how much use I'll be, but I want to help."

I pat him on the shoulder reassuringly. "You'll be fine. You've got me, and I'm pretty great." I glance over the others. "Send whoever you think will be useful and won't slow me down."

Imlashi frowns at me. "Shouldn't you stay at the temple? In case they find another Mourner to unleash?"

Esha shudders, but shakes her head. "There's not one for them to find, not that I'm aware of. And, if they do, they'll most likely do it overnight. Besides, I intend on staying up to erect a more proper barrier. With prep time, I can keep a Mourner out. I think Maven is the right call to take on the Machinist."

"Then it's settled," I say cheerfully. "We march at dawn."

INTERLUDE

SHADOW & GLASS VI

You settled into our routines and our events like a perfect chameleon, knowing just when to fit in and just when to stand out, and with every new connection you made I only felt more alone.

Whether conversing with the lowest servant or the king's own advisors, you knew exactly what to say and how to say it. On arrival you were a fascination, but by the end of the first month you were an obsession. Dark thoughts spiraled through my mind as you moved further into the court's circles, established new connections, and became the focus of every gathering.

It wasn't just the smiles they gave you that they hadn't given me in years, though those did hurt. Nor was it the ease with which they brought you into social circles I had long been barred from entering. It wasn't even that you stood a fair chance at winning over my father's closest confidantes and being invited into their ranks, though that did sting second most.

It was, in some sense, that what we had was no longer special.

I had tutored you in the laws and histories and economics of my kingdom, and now you used that information to converse with courtiers as an equal. You had studied at my side and asked me question after question, always giving me rapt attention, and now you spoke with passion on those same subjects to evergrowing crowds of eager listeners. You spoke of our kingdom with the familiarity of a local and the fresh perspective of an outsider, and you bewitched them one and all. Your words were just as enchanting to the peerage as they had been to me.

When others spoke, you listened actively and earnestly no matter the topic and no matter if it was something you already knew or something you considered utterly foolish. You could make anyone feel as if they had finally been recognized and respected, and what did that say of our own interactions? Did I truly mean anything to you, or were you just using me? And if you were being sincere with me, then did that make me an awful person for doubting you and suspecting such horrid things of you?

You were, after all, my most ardent defender.

Whenever someone asked how you had become so learned in our ways so quickly—a feat made more extravagant for the deception of when you had truly arrived in these lands—you were quick to thank my tutelage as your greatest boon. You extolled my brilliance as a teacher and the care with which I had taken you in and acclimated you to Svijetstakla and the kingdom both. You told them of my passion for our culture, of my deep understanding of the complexities of our laws, and of the absolute mastery of my scholarship that you had been so grateful to learn from.

When courtiers warned you of my dangers in their subtle ways, whispering word of my unnatural temperament and the tragedy that had taken the late queen, you laughed. You were clever in this, for you hung a noose and then offered them amnesty. You called it superstition and silliness, the domain of small, petty minds, and of course these men and women of learning and fine upbringing would never believe such words. "Isn't it delightfully absurd," you would remark, "how the servants dream up such fancies when their minds are left idle?"

When you spoke to the servants, which you did carefully out of sight and hearing of the courtiers, you were gentle and curious and relaxed. They were warier than the peerage, at least at first, but you treated them with a decency they were entirely unaccustomed to from even the kinder nobles of the court. When they spoke rumor of the Shadow Fiend your questions were more pointed: "Has she ever mistreated you, or any of the other workers? Has she abused you or taken advantage of you or even yelled at you for little mistakes? Have her peers?" I wonder if you can imagine the joy I felt the first time one of them looked at me without fear in their eyes.

You were always careful, so very careful, not to push too quickly or callously. With each new relationship you preferred to demur or evade on the topic of myself until you could be certain they would actually listen to you when you took my side. And it worked. Not quickly, not broadly, but you began to open doors for me. I was, for the first time in a very long time, invited to private parties and cloistered conversations.

It pained me that I couldn't be happy for your hard-fought successes. Over tea, you made them laugh and sang my praises, and it took all my will not to shatter the cup. You were lively and charismatic and engaging, and I was stiff and cold and barely holding myself together.

And the dark grew in my mind, deeper and deeper, until you finally broached the subject over brunch in the castle gardens.

We sat with dumplings, cakes, and a bottle of wine to share. I wore a lacy dress of pink and lemon, and you wore doublet and hose in black and red with hints of gold. We ate and laughed and enjoyed ourselves, but I could tell you were leading toward a question and at last with another sip of wine you asked me, "Do you hate them?"

Hate. You were always so fond of that word. You burned with the kind of hate that could ruin empires and topple gods, and you wanted more than anything to see that hate burn inside me, too. To feel . . . I'm still not sure. Justified? Vindicated? Or maybe just . . . not alone.

But I'm not like you. I have to believe that, because it's the only way not to drown.

"I haven't told you everything about myself," I said instead of answering. "I . . . once upon a time, I wasn't a pariah within my own clan. Once, I wasn't avoided by my peers. When I was young and full of talent and my own father had yet to throw me to the wolves . . . when I still had a chance at the throne . . . everyone in court sought after my favor. They gave me compliments and gifts and attention, and they treated me with grace and respect at all times. They were on perfect behavior."

"But," you prompted.

"But it was hollow. It was always hollow. Hollow words, hollow gifts, hollow sentiment. They never meant any of it. All they cared about was the throne."

Your red eyes burned with that ever-present keen insight. "Their kindness was a means to an end. You were only ever a tool in their eyes, one to be treated well only so it could be more easily put to use. False friends, to the last."

I laughed at the very word. "Friends. Before you, the only friend I ever had was my brother, and you've seen how that's changed. No, I don't think any of those were friendships, not even a little. Those serpents had words sweet like poison and carried fear and disdain in their hearts. But I was naive, and a fool, so it worked."

You took another sip of wine. "What changed?"

"My third affinity. My last chance to hold the sun in my hands, turned to blood slipping through my fingers. That was when the clans knew that I could not inherit the legacy of Dawnbringer, and such a revelation is the death knell of a sorcerer. It took less than a week for every supposed friend to abandon me, cold and clean."

"Mm." You drummed your fingers along the glass in your hand. "My question remains: do you hate them? Do you resent them for lying to you, and that's why you stiffen up at the very sight of them? Or are you afraid of being hurt and betrayed once more, and that's why you can't hold a conversation without having to stifle your disgust?"

I simmered in that question, unhappy to be facing these feelings but knowing that I could not turn away, not now, not when you were the one pushing. "I . . . I don't know. I just feel so uncomfortable around them. Selfish, shallow creatures. My tormentors. Why . . . why should I play nice with them?"

"*You don't feel comfortable pretending to like someone,*" *you observed.* "*You're unable to treat them as they treated you. You can't play the game.*"

"*I . . . maybe. I hadn't really thought of it that way.*" *I shivered, then.* "*I can't stand the idea of it all being a game to them. Having to smile and lie and pretend to be something you're not . . . I don't know how you do it, when you talk to my father or to the courtiers. It makes me feel like I'm drowning when I even try.*"

You shrugged and ate another cake treat, affecting an unbothered air. "*I've had to play their game to survive for a long time. I hated it, you know, when I started. It didn't make sense to me. I'm . . . well, you don't have a concept for it here, but back home we called it 'autistic.' My mind doesn't work like other minds. Social skills never came naturally to me, and I could never understand all the intricacies and delicacies of implication and nonverbal signals.*" *You laughed.* "*Hells, for the longest time I couldn't even flirt without just telling a girl I wanted her bad, and I had no idea if a girl was flirting with me.*"

Heated cheeks, a bit of panic, hidden behind wine and dumplings. Was that the reaction you were hoping for? You carried on, pretending not to notice.

"*But I learned, and I kept learning, because learning is how you survive. I learned how to be subtle, and how to read subtlety, and I learned why it mattered. So much communication lives in the implicit and the unspoken, and I no longer think that's a bad thing. It's like . . . imagine you were a painter, but you had gone your whole life only ever using bold, bright, primary colors. You never mixed the colors, never blended them or shaded them, and when you heard of other artists doing that you scoffed. But then, one day, you saw it: you saw a painting with so much depth and complexity and meaning to it, and it was only possible because of all those little subtle techniques that you had scoffed at. Language and communication, spoken and written, these are forms of art and they are so much richer when you let them breathe.*"

I was enthralled to your words, captivated by the eloquence and passion with which you spoke. "*You make it sound almost . . . beautiful,*" *I said.* "*I . . . I'm sorry, Homura. I know you've been trying really hard to give me these opportunities and I've just been squandering them. I—I'm sorry. I can try harder, I can try to learn—*"

You placed a hand on my shoulder and squeezed. "*Hey, hey, it's okay. I get it. This shit was hard for me at first. I believe you can learn, but it's not something anyone can learn in a day, and making you keep attending those events would just be piling on unnecessary stress. Don't worry, I'm not out of tactics yet. Thank you for telling me all this, Reska. I truly, truly appreciate it, and I understand. It's okay.*"

My feelings were confusing in that moment. Messy. Vulnerable. That kind of sentiment was still so new to me and on some level it frightened me. You were giving me this support and validation even though I'd made your life harder. You understood. You cared.

A tear slid down my cheek, and another, and you wiped them away and pulled me into an embrace. You held me tight and whispered assurances until the broken sobs stopped, and then you kept holding me and comforting me until at last I found the strength to part from you and gather myself.

"I, um. You mentioned other tactics. Tell me about them. What's next?"

You grinned, patted me on the shoulder one last time, and rose to your feet to pace in front of me. You did this occasionally, whenever you had a lot to say and needed to keep moving to keep the words flowing, and I found it endearing. "In truth, my cavorting with your intolerable peers has not been solely for your reputation; I have plied many secrets from the mouths of rulers and the ruled alike, including one secret that I believe your dear father would have liked very much to never reach your ears: there is a new labyrinth within our borders."

I stiffened. "You can't be serious. Here?"

"It's yet a sapling," you assured me, "else we'd be hearing much more about it by now. Your father's bureaucratic engine is admittedly impressive, and tallies kept on night horrors revealed an increase in numbers and intensity that matches the emergence of a labyrinth, at least according to Zdenka. Careful scouting determined its location to be just by the border with Wood and Cloud. It is believed that our neighbors have yet to notice, but they will once the labyrinth grows."

"Merciful Lady," I breathed. "That's horrifying."

"It is also an opportunity. Our land near the labyrinth is worth less than Wood and Cloud's land in that region, and they have more people at risk as well. If Sun and Sword were to remove the labyrinth, our neighboring kingdom would have no choice but to show us gratitude—and on the nearing eve of our regularly scheduled trade negotiations."

I frowned. "Then, surely Father has already sent for his champions."

You held up a finger. "Ah, but there's one complication: Luka isn't here."

My brother was away on pilgrimage at the time, the usual yearly trek across the kingdom to renew the land and keep touch with the people. He still had another week and a half before he was set to return home. So why, I wondered, is the king waiting for him? It struck me with sudden horror. "This will make Luka a king."

You nodded. "As rites of passage go, you can't get much better than ending a major threat and securing a lucrative trade deal. The king will send Luka and a few blades into the labyrinth, and when they return, his ascent to the throne will be guaranteed. No branch could dare compete with that little trick."

My blood ran cold as I realized just how soon my inheritance would be forever out of reach. "Two weeks. In two weeks I will be no one."

"So little faith, princess. Would I tell you all this without a solution? No, in two weeks you will be the upstart heiress on a fast track to the crown, because we are going to steal Luka's victory."

My eyes widened and I stared at you in shock. "What do you mean?"

You rested a hand on Vorpal at your side and said, "The labyrinth will get bigger and more noticeable before Luka is able to return, and that means giving Wood and Cloud a chance to clear it themselves and put our side in debt. We're going to use that argument against Duchess Bladesinger, and she's going to give us the location of the labyrinth and the means to get there quickly. And then you're going to banish that labyrinth and become the hero of two kingdoms. So: are you in?"

I agreed, of course, and once we finished our brunch you had me slip into your shadow and hide there while you went to speak with Ruzica. Your shadow was warm, and I had begun to find a strange comfort in residing there. You were the only one to ever validate my birth affinity, to encourage its use, and that made this closeness all the sweeter.

You found Ruzica swiftly, knowing exactly which sitting room she would be in at that time of the day and week. You opened with polite formalities, but the duchess was a woman of action and didn't mind when you cut straight to the point. You revealed your knowledge of the labyrinth and the king's intentions for it, and you presented the case as you'd explained it to me: the labyrinth was risk and opportunity both, and waiting for Luka would skew it too far toward risk, so send the two of us.

You spoke of the minutiae of commerce between nations, revealing a deep familiarity with the kingdom's economy, and even the callous duchess seemed impressed. You outlined in clear detail the material cost of letting Wood and Cloud get to the labyrinth first, and you even made a compelling argument for why they would get there first if we waited for Luka, as your studies had apparently extended so far as the information gathering capabilities of our neighboring kingdom.

Your understanding of the practical concerns at work clearly pleased her, as the duchess was ever disdainful of fools and the slow-witted. She agreed with your assessment of the situation and the necessity of swift action, but then she asked, "Why send you, then, and not a cadre of my blades and the king's staves?"

"It has to be a royal," you insisted, "for it to have the intended impact. To negotiate from a position of greatest strength, it needs to be the crown itself that is owed, not merely a servant of the crown acting on the crown's orders. This is the way of sorcerers: the only power respected is the power you can hold in your own two hands."

"True," the duchess said, pouring herself a glass of wine and offering one to you, which you took with murmured gratitudes. "But then why a princess and not a king?"

You sipped from your glass and betrayed not a mote of hatred or disdain. When you spoke, it was calm, collected, and rational. "Forgive my words, but the king's judgment is . . . compromised, when it comes to his children. His Majesty should be the one to banish the labyrinth, yet he risks disaster waiting for his son. Why? To win his child petty accolades? It is unnecessary. The correct course of action would be to set out now and take the matter into his own hands. But he will not."

Bladesinger chuckled. "I could take your head for that, you know."

You smiled. "And I have no doubt you would, if you truly disagreed. Yet here I stand."

"Here you stand. Tell me, then, why you believe it unnecessary for Luka to close the labyrinth." Ruzica settled back in her chair and watched you with an inscrutable expression.

"It's simple, really: he does not need the help. Prince Luka is the greatest healer in a generation and a fair hand at politicking and governance besides. I have spoken with all the hungry courtiers of this realm, their hands fuller with ambition than sense, and still they talk of Luka's ascension to the throne as an inevitability. The branch families have already set their sights on the coronation after Luka's because they believe it such a given that the crown will be his and his alone. So why, then, does His Majesty seem so concerned with guaranteeing Luka's rise?"

Ruzica frowned and drank from her glass. "I have wondered the same."

You pressed further, leaning in with those red eyes burning. "Please, Your Grace, enlighten me to your thoughts: do you believe it was a mistake for His Majesty to pen the writ disinheriting Reska?"

Her eyes sharpened. "Elaborate."

"It's just that, for all intents and purposes, the princess was already excised from clan politics and clan holdings. There was, it would seem, no chance of her even coming close to the throne, so all such a thing could accomplish would be to antagonize the princess herself . . . unless, for some reason, the king did not share the court's opinion about his daughter's chances. And it has not evaded my notice that, despite the writ being discovered by Reska months ago and being marked as an urgent matter, it has not yet been publicized among the court. Almost as if, after being confronted, the king realized his mistake."

The duchess seemed pensive over your words. "An interesting theory."

My own thoughts were racing, wholly taken aback by the direction you had taken. It had never occurred to me that the king's writ could be anything but a sign of disapproval, yet here you were arguing that it was a sign of insecurity and convincing one of the king's oldest friends. Could she be right? Is my father afraid I'll challenge Luka? Why?

You took a long drink of your glass, then set it down and spoke carefully. "I am foreign to these lands, and I will not speak on matters of tradition or propriety, but

I can speak of practicals. Sending Reska is the safest bet. I promise you, she has the power to close that labyrinth, even if you sent just her and myself."

Ruzica's expression shifted from thoughtful to amused. "And all you'll prove is her power. You know that was never the issue, don't you? She lacks control. Give her the labyrinth, give her that win, but when you put her in a room with Wood and Cloud you'll see firsthand what truly holds her back."

"Mm. So I've heard." You looked away from her and let a hand drape toward the floor, close enough to your shadow that I could almost feel you. "Were you aware that the lands beyond the Glass Tower don't experience the labyrinth phenomenon? Your princess, too, is an oddity unique to this realm and no other, with that affinity of hers."

Amusement became shrewd interest. "What are you getting at, Bloodfallen?"

"I have seen sides of Reska Ines Zelic that I do not believe any of you have, and I think there is more to her than you assume. She is stifled by this castle, and the labyrinth will provide a much needed crucible for her growth. You consider her fatal flaw to be one of control; I agree, but I believe that flaw to be contextual, and to be the fault of her environment, not something intrinsic to her nature. She is capable of magic so precise it would put your artisans to shame, if given the right space and motivation."

Ruzica scratched her chin and looked at you more closely. "You've been bolder with me than I expected. You're always so tricky with those nobles you've been luring."

You smiled. "I have no intention of deceiving you, Your Grace. I simply believe that you are uniquely suited to appreciate my ambitions. Reska may be the true-blood heir, but she is far more the dark horse candidate than either you or His Majesty ever were. There is an injustice in how she has been treated, and many have been blinded to her true potential. I will use any means at my disposal to see her made rightful queen of this land."

"With you as her consort, of course."

Your lips quirked. "If that is Her Majesty's wish, who am I to deny it?"

I almost lost control then and there, a few stray tendrils of shadow having to be quickly pulled back into the darkness. My consort? My mind raced with panic and confusion and hope and joy all intermingling. Was this just an act for Ruzica, or did you mean it? Did you want it?

My heart sang even as the duchess took your measure and laughed. "Alright, whelp, you've got fire. It takes guts to plot beneath the king's nose with his own advisors, and it's been too long since Kresimir saw a good challenge to his authority. Maybe this'll be the kick in the backside that shakes him out of this fell mood. But!" She held up a finger and continued, "I don't give handouts. If you want to go with Reska to the labyrinth, you'll need to prove yourself first. Show me you've got what it takes on the battlefield just as much as in the ballroom."

You bowed in your chair and spoke with sincerity and respect, though as ever it was impossible to tell how much of that was feigned. "I would be honored to test my blade against a master of sword art."

Internally, my cocktail of messy emotions consolidated around panic over the others, because I had fought alongside you and seen you use that sword of yours and you were rubbish at it. I'd helped you as much as I could, of course, but I was terrible with a blade and had stopped practicing years ago when Ruzica herself dismissed me as hopeless. There was no way you could beat the kingdom's greatest duelist in a fair fight, and I didn't see how your talent for blood magic could make up the difference in power and skill.

"We'll do this before eyes," Ruzica declared. "If you perform well, you'll get that extra bit of social capital I'm sure you're craving. If you fail, that should dash your hopes enough you stop being my problem, or the king's."

Again your lips quirked. "I wouldn't have it any other way. But since this is all to test my skills, may I request the luxury of three rounds for you to take my measure?"

The duchess drummed her fingers against the arm of her chair. "I've got no grounds to refuse you, really, but there'll be no healing between rounds; survive the full three or tap out and concede."

"Perfect. The generosity is appreciated, Your Grace."

"Ha! Generosity, she says. We'll see if you still feel that way by the end of it."

You parted ways to make preparations, and I emerged from your shadow so that I could watch the duel as myself. When the moment arrived, I watched from a crowd of chattering courtiers as you and Ruzica faced off in the training yard.

"Have you ever seen Lady Bloodfallen fight?"

"She can't possibly stand a chance against Her Grace, can she?"

"She's a wily one, I'm sure she has some foreign trickery."

Castle healers were on standby, watching close enough to help but far enough to avoid any stray blows, and under strict orders not to intervene unless specifically requested. An unusual request, but not unheard of for a Duchess Bladesinger exhibition match.

You faced off, blades drawn, your red-bladed Vorpal and her silver-bladed Hymnal Edge. You bowed to each other, yours deeper as station dictated.

"May the odds be ever in your favor," you called to your opponent with a smirk.

"To the pain," Ruzica Bladesinger laughed, finally in her true element.

It began with footwork, the two of you circling each other and watching for form and tell and weakness. Ruzica held her blade loose in hand and moved casually, almost contemptuously, like you were just another bug to be squashed beneath her boot. You wore arrogance on your face, but your tight grip and the tension in your shoulders betrayed you.

A feint from you, a probe from her, an exchange of half-hearted maneuvers to test the waters and probe defenses. Ruzica forced you back with a lazy swing, and then her blade began to sing with the distinctive tone of her clan's magic. I could feel you activate your own magic in response, calling on your affinity for Blood to bolster your strength and speed like I'd taught you.

Ruzica blurred into motion and you followed a heartbeat slower. Blades clashed and whirled and sang in a flurry of blows too fast for me to cleanly follow. I saw sparks and heard the scrape of metal and your bitten back cries as the duchess nicked you on the arm, the leg, the arm again, each cut light and shallow but still bright red.

Ruzica laughed and stepped back, and when you followed and pressed her she mocked you with her movements. When you feinted, she didn't react, and when you went for a real strike she batted it away with absolute contempt.

The onlookers whispered to each other, and I listened.

"Who would have thought that a woman with such clever words could be such a brute with a sword?"

"The poor thing's being toyed with, Her Grace is barely calling on her affinities."

"Is she even using the Crest at all?"

One of the courtiers, who I recognized from Bladesinger's court, watched with a more thoughtful expression. "Say what you will about style, but Lady Bloodfallen's enhancement magic is powerful and she uses it cleverly. It's saved her from every half-serious attack the duchess has sent her way."

That provoked my attention, but then the duel shifted pace again and when I blinked you were bleeding across the front from a decisive cut. The court gasped, surprised by such a serious blow so soon, and my heart hammered in my chest with worry for you, but then those gasps turned to excited murmurs. Though you had been slashed and blood had been drawn, it wasn't leaving your body; instead, the blood flowed like normal, coursing through you down natural pathways and entirely avoiding the wounded opening.

You parted from each other and began the dance of circling again, with Ruzica calling, "So the wolf has a few tricks after all. We'll call that round one."

"Fine with me," you grinned back.

While you played it careful, I mustered my courage and sidled next to the Bladesinger courtier to ask, "Um, excuse me, but what did you mean about Homura's magic?"

The courtier's gaze shifted to me just long enough to show surprise before returning to the bout, but he answered, "Ah, Your Highness, a pleasure. Lady Bloodfallen's swordplay is lacking, but she's demonstrating an excellent technique that I imagine to have been a specialty of her family: she's using enhancement magic not to flood her body with strength and speed but to strength and accelerate at exactly the moment that is necessary to do so. She puts in as much power as she needs to survive the exchange, then drops back to her baseline and stays there. She—ah, what's this then? How interesting."

You had begun making more feints as I listened to the courtier, and Ruzica had been responding with more of her callous denials, but after another flurry of blows you parted and the crowd was shocked to see you unharmed and with Ruzica bearing a single shallow cut across the leg.

The duchess cocked her head, looking at you with interest, and then chuckled. "Well now." Her blade sang lower, and then she was on you again with lightning speed, your swords crossing over and over again.

The courtier beside me whistled appreciatively. "Her footwork and action are both improving," he told me, "and she's relying less on her enhancement."

The battle became more intense as the duchess drew on more of her magic, carving gashes in the dirt and pushing you back with raw force. You took more wounds, though light ones, and you kept each from bleeding with will and sorcery.

"That ability to preserve herself is remarkable," said the courtier beside me. "Do you know anything about it, Your Highness?"

"She can't do it forever," I murmured to him, not wanting to lose his insight, "but I'd be worried for other reasons if this duel went to her duration limit." You'd been practicing, and by that point you could sustain an open wound for perhaps an hour through pure focus.

The other watchers talked amongst themselves, though I was becoming less interested in their opinions.

"Was her lack of skill just a feint to draw out the duchess?"

"She must have been holding back as bait, but bait for what?"

Then came the move that ended the second bout: a magical slash from Hymnal Edge that cut through the very air. You blocked it with Vorpal, but not all of it, and the wave of cutting energy sliced open your cheek and side.

You gritted your teeth and backed off, still maintaining the flow of your blood but breathing heavy now. "Shall we call that second?"

Ruzica twirls her blade. "Might as well. You don't look like you have much left in you, whelp. Time to finish this."

The next flurry of action was almost impossible for me to follow, so I relied on the courtier's analysis. You were moving smoothly now, flowing naturally through form and motion and technique with exactly as much skill and grace as Duchess Bladesinger, incorporating her style and almost entirely replacing your own natural brutality.

Ruzica kept slowly raising the amount of power she was channeling through Hymnal Edge, throwing more and more at you, forcing you to continue relying on your blood magic to close the gap and stay alive. The crowd was invested now, watching with fascination as the lopsided duel became more and more danger-ously equal.

Then, after Ruzica stepped back from another deflected blow, you made your move. You drew a bit of blood from your open wounds onto Vorpal, and then you ignited the blade, casting it in crimson flame. You swung with Vorpal, putting all your power behind the blow, a killing stroke—

—but not enough. Ruzica just barely deflected your attack into the ground, where it scorched the dirt and puttered out. You looked shocked, dazed, breathing heavy and open to retaliation. Vulnerable.

Ruzica gathered her own power, more and more of her might and her affin-ity, and unleashed it all in one devastating slash coming right at you. You saw it coming and didn't move, couldn't evade, and then—

—you spoke a single word, the end of a phrase whispered too softly to catch: "Reversal."

Hymnal Edge struck your body with the full might of Ruzica's affinity behind it, and then her arm and shoulder both exploded in a spray of gore, torn open and ripped to shreds by her own magic. The duchess stumbled, bleeding profusely, bone visible, as you stepped away from the blade that had not cut even an inch into your body.

Even ravaged by her own spell, Ruzica still had enough presence of mind to go for another attack, raising her blade to lash out again, but you twisted your hand and all of your blood on Hymnal Edge—blood that had, I only then realized, had been slowly traveling down toward the hilt as if magnetically drawn—burst into flame and seared her hand.

It didn't stop her, but it slowed her down, and that's all you needed to move your own blade into position, and when both swords came to rest they were pointed at the other's throat.

The scene was still, the crowd silent, blood dripping from Ruzica's mangled body and still flowing safely within yours. And then the duchess laughed and lowered her blade—you did the same with Vorpal—and motioned for the healers to come forth and attend to you both.

"Well damn, girl, you really did have tricks up your sleeve. I haven't been caught off guard like that in some time."

You grinned. "It was close. My techniques are risky, but I was counting on your personality to give me what I needed."

Beside me, the courtier snapped his fingers. "Ah! That explains it."

I looked to him for an explanation, confusion clear on my face. Where did she learn that? *"What explains it?"*

"The weakness in the first and second rounds," he said, "they were clearly to lure Ruzica into a slower match, to get more blood into play before baiting her

with that false finisher. If the duchess had moved too swiftly at the start or too slowly at the end, it would have spelled disaster, so Lady Bloodfallen was playing a very dangerous game."

A game that I'd had no idea about, and which relied on magic I didn't know you had. I was hungry for answers, but I waited patiently as you spoke in hushed tones with Duchess Bladesinger about our forthcoming venture to the labyrinth in the borderlands.

Once that was settled and the crowd cleared out, we left together and you led the way to your room to clean off and talk.

In the privacy of your room you were very shameless about removing your damp shirt in front of me, exposing your arms and back glistening with sweat from the exertion of the duel. Your body had grown surprisingly wiry since we met, still thin but now with an edge of muscle.

The hair clung to your forehead as you swept it back, and the heat still shone in your face as you toweled off first your body and then your blade. I blushed at the sight of you and tried not to let you notice, instead refocusing my attention on the petty details of your room.

You had been given chambers as part of your arrangement with the kingdom, but you had been offered much more than you had taken, insisting on a more modest dwelling for excuses of earning your keep. You kept a desk piled high with books, a table by your bedside piled with additional books, and a bookshelf against one wall filled to bursting with yet more books.

In one corner of the room you had piled all the gifts you had received from various courtiers seeking your favor: bottles of wine, a few dresses and hats, and all manner of flowers and candies. Only the wine had been touched.

"That went well," you remarked as I took a seat on your bed. "Of course, the labyrinth will be the hard part, but I'm confident in your abilities."

"Thank you, and I hope you're right. I've never seen the inside of a labyrinth before, so I'm a little worried, but that can wait." I looked back at you, attempting to ignore that you were still wearing only your undershirt from the waist up, and asked, "Homura, how did you do that? How did you duel Ruzica like that? You were barely beating me just a few days ago, and I'm horrid with a blade. How do you go from that to drawing even with the foremost master of sword art in maybe the entire region?"

You grinned, unperturbed. "You noticed. Well, it wasn't entirely skill, I'll admit. Here, let me show you." You wiped your hands off with a bit of clean water and a fresh towel, then held out a hand.

I got up from the bed and nervously stepped forward, holding out my own hand and allowing you to take it in yours. Your grip was warm and comforting.

"Feel the warmth of my hand in yours. Feel the blood singing beneath our skin. Feel the bond that forms between us."

I felt the flow of magic, tasted a familiar affinity. This was Blood spellcraft, seizing on the conceptual notion of bonds. Your magic reached across the connection between our bodies and established a spiritual connection, a conceptual link.

"Now," you said, "call starlight to your other hand."

I was confused, but I complied. I conjured a celestial sphere to my open hand, shaping an orb of glittering stars.

You held out your free hand, the other still clasping mine, and said, "Let as above be so below, and as without be so within. Let this bond between us become a mirror, reflecting."

The air above your open hand rippled, and then a ball of cold light flickered into being. It wasn't as bright or as full or anywhere near as detailed as my own starlight, but it was starlight, clearly and undeniably. I gasped with shock. "You . . . you copied my magic. How? How did you copy my magic?"

"It's the specialty of my second affinity: Glass focusing Reflection. When I connect to someone with Blood, I can then reflect their characteristics across the bond with Glass. It's what I used to copy Ruzica's sword skills for the duration of our duel, though I had to burn them up to pull that reversal trick at the end."

My shock bloomed even stronger, mind stuck on that very first sentence. "You . . . you have a second affinity. You have a second affinity, and you've focused it? When did you—how did you—how is that even possible? It's been so little time."

I won't deny that I felt a certain jealousy, learning that you had already unlocked a second affinity just months after the first, and focused it even. The last dregs of my pride were bound up in my prodigal talent as a sorcerer, but your feats of progression surpassed even mine. I extricated my fingers from yours, staring at the ball of light, but it didn't fade or flicker out. In fact, the longer I watched, the more detailed it became and the closer it resembled my own starlight. The bond between us still reflected my magic to feed your own.

Then it struck me. "Wait, Glass? Like the glass needle with the stored affinity? Homura, where did you get that needle? How did you learn a second affinity with such absurd speed?"

"Well, I like to think I'm an unusual girl. But you're right: I got that needle from the same place I learned this affinity. I had a bit of help from someone." You stared past me, eyes adopting a faraway look. "I hadn't told you until now because I wasn't really sure what it meant, but . . . in my dreams, since arriving in this world, I am haunted by visions of a tower of glass inside a city of glass people, and inside that tower is a lonely woman crying beside a shattered mirror."

You curled your hand into a fist and the starlight vanished inside, and a moment later I felt the conceptual link dissipate between us. When you opened your hand again, there was a marble on your palm. It was a glass marble of perfectly ordinary size and shape, but it was full of glittering, gleaming starlight.

"She gave me that needle to help our plan, and then she taught me my second affinity. It was easy, really, after being surrounded by glass in all my dreams for so long, to make it mine. I suspect she did something to speed the process along, given how unusual my growth has been."

You clicked open a hidden compartment in your rapier and slid the starry marble inside. I caught a glimpse of other marbles, other scraps of magic frozen in glass, and then the compartment closed.

"Does that make sense?" you asked with a laugh.

I stared at you, every new revelation throwing me off further. "That was . . . Homura, that was Katoptris. You spoke to Katoptris, the Lady of Glass, our divine protector who watches over us from the Glass Tower."

You raised an eyebrow. "I see she's more important than I realized. Tell me more."

"She—she brings safety and stability to our land, to Svijetstakla. For as long as anyone can remember, she's been a source of guidance and support in times of hardship, offering advice and aid to any who brave the journey to her tower and pass a few simple trials. But her tower has been sealed to us for, what, just over two decades? Katoptris has been silent for longer than I've been alive, Homura. And you talked to her? Please, start at the beginning, this is all so much."

You nodded and motioned for us to sit, which we did. "I woke for the first time in the city outside her tower. That city is . . . strange. It's full of people that look like people and talk like people but aren't people, as they're happy to insist. They don't feel joy when they eat or have sex, they don't feel sadness when they lose something or someone, and they don't even feel pain when you hurt them. They're like toy dolls playing house, only acting out the motions.

"I spent weeks in that city, trying to understand it, trying to find my way to the tower that loomed over it all. The doll-things, they tried to keep me out. They tried to seduce my attention with food and wine and women, but that only made it more obvious that I was being purposefully obstructed. The city itself was fighting against me, shifting each visit to ruin my attempted maps, but still I persisted.

"When I finally reached the tower gates, I found them open, but that was only the beginning of my trials. The tower was perilous, every floor stuffed with new hazards and threats. While you and I together were delving dungeons and slaying monsters in the countryside, I braved the tower's trials alone. It took every ounce of what I had learned from you to overcome the obstacles before, and that still wouldn't have been enough if not for a quirk of the dreams: death for my dreaming self was only ever temporary, and I would awaken at the bottom floor of the tower each night after a failed attempt.

"Eventually, with great hardship, I succeeded. I reached the highest floor of the tower, and there I found the woman who sat beside the shattered mirror,

her arms and legs bleeding from the scattered shards. I found Katoptris, and we talked."

I stared down at my hands, trying to process all of that. "You talked to an archon. I can't even begin to comprehend what that must have been like." But I could begin to be jealous and fearful, just at the thought of it. You had the attention of an archon, so what did you need with me?

"Archon? I don't think I've encountered that word yet. What does it mean?" You looked at me with keen interest, your curiosity ever insatiable.

"They're, um, they're connected to the Crawling Chaos in some way. I don't think anyone knows for sure. I've read that they're pieces of her, or her children, or something else entirely. There's Katoptris, who protects the Heartstone, and the Emissary, who speaks for the dead gods of the Abyss. There's a third, I think, or maybe there was, or will be? Sorry, it's been a long time since I read those texts and they were kind of confusing."

"Fascinating. If you could dig those up, I would deeply appreciate it."

I swallowed my nervousness and nodded. "Yeah, of course. So, um . . . what did you talk about? You and Katoptris, I mean."

You turned away from me again, looking out over your room but really looking over your memories. "She was lonely, so I kept her company. I told her about you, and about me, and about other worlds. I told her stories. Some of it was the needle and the affinity and practical matters, but most of it was just . . . talking. She needed it, so I gave it to her."

I hated how much that hurt me. I hated how jealous I felt. You were talking about meeting a god, an archon, a spawn of the Crawling Chaos, and all I could think about was that you were spending time with another girl. It felt like the care and attention you'd shown me wasn't unique to me, wasn't because I was special, wasn't because you liked me at all. You just took pity on poor broken girls and made them feel like they could be loved.

Liar. You were always such a liar. You lied to me, to the court, did you even lie to her? Did you ever say a word that wasn't a lie?

It's too late to change anything, I know that. It's over now, at least for me. But still. If you're still out there, somewhere, ruining girls like me . . .

I hope no one ever believes your lies again.

VIII

Okay, cool, well, I guess that swings a hammer through all of *my* speculation. I sit up with a groan in my Myriad-donated bed, attempting to process yet another information-packed dream sequence. It almost doesn't feel worth it to try and piece things together given my last guess was incredibly, wildly wrong.

Reska is not, in fact, Katoptris, nor do they seem to have any connection to each other beyond their relationship with Homura, my dream vision evil twin. And wow, that's one hell of a connection, actually. My dreams of Reska, which are addressed to Homura who is also me, have now warned me against believing Homura's lies, because she did horrible things to Reska and also possibly to Katoptris???

So the Reska-Katoptris theory has been disproven but the "Katoptris hates me and wants revenge" theory is still probably looking solid, great. And that "Katoptris is the daughter of the Demiurge" theory is just, like, almost fully confirmed now. Okay, this is a lot, so let's take this from the top.

The first part of that vision was just Homura being a charming liar and Reska being a poor little meow meow pathetic uwu bean, so nothing new there. The interesting stuff started when Homura talked about a labyrinth appearing. Not *the* Labyrinth like I'm trapped in now, but *a* labyrinth, something that there are multiple of and which isn't explicitly tied to Katoptris.

That doesn't mean it's not *implicitly* tied to her, though, because it was also mentioned that labyrinths only appeared in the lands around Katoptris' tower. I wonder, are these labyrinths like prototype versions of throne worlds? I'd need to see inside one to be certain, but my gut says that's the case, since they both create monsters.

Then there was that little bit about the king making a mistake with his writ. That doesn't seem connected to any of the lore I care about, but it is interesting:

the king was afraid that Reska would take the throne, and judging by the start of the very first dream he was right to be afraid; Reska would go on to kill him, after all.

Then the duel, where Homura showed off a whole lot of magic that I sorely want for myself. I'm itching to pull out Vorpal and see if I can shake out any of those spells from it, but it might even be worth it to dedicate my next spell slot to learning a variant of that boosting magic that served Homura so well. I have Blood, and I'm sure I could tie in Fear or Gluttony to make it stronger. Keeping my blood in my body also seems neat, though possibly redundant considering how powerful my self-healing already is . . . and considering I'm not really human anymore and I'm not entirely sure blood loss could actually kill me.

The reflection spell, though . . . now there's something that divides my magic from Homura's, because nothing in my Truths matches up with her affinity for Glass. That means I don't see a way to learn that bond reflection trick, much as I'd like to have it, unless Homura managed to store a version of it in Vorpal.

There's a great deal of experimentation I want to perform on Vorpal, but that can wait till after breakfast. No, there's one last piece of that dream I need to interrogate: Homura's tale of Katoptris.

Homura is, according to Reska, a horrible liar, but Reska's narration did not seem to suggest that the story itself was a lie. So Homura found herself in a city that was very much like the Sanctuary I'm in now, full of figments offering her the world . . . but those figments were also in some way *opposed* to Katoptris, trying to keep Homura from reaching her. Or, perhaps, they were trying to protect Katoptris from her. Hard to tell.

But Katoptris herself, that's the real fascinating detail: she was crying and alone. The entity I was introduced to as the Nightmare Queen and Lady of Shards was once the divine protector of the world before the Labyrinth, and someone hurt her before Homura even met her. Someone shattered her mirror and left her crying, and I know who: the Emissary.

The Beast told me as much, when we had our little chat, though I didn't understand it at the time. She told me that her shard, the shard this death game is fighting over, a piece of Katoptris, came from the mirror that the Emissary shattered. And now, thanks to Reska, I know that the Emissary is an archon, like the Intercessor and the Adversary and Katoptris, but in sworn service to the Leviathans.

I could dig into the weirdness of Reska mentioning an unnamed third archon but no mention of the Intercessor or Adversary, because to me that suggests these dreams are taking place before the Adversary fell and wow is that a can of worms, but . . . I think I'm more immediately interested in the Emissary's role in all this.

Up until now, everyone has been presenting the Labyrinth and all its horrors as the unique fault of Katoptris, but these dreams are starting to paint her as a victim instead. Maybe that's why I'm receiving these visions, to show me a different side of Katoptris, but then again, there are easier ways to do that. Why was Homura taken directly to her tower? Why are we both receiving dream visions, but very different kinds?

Regardless, one thing seems clear: I won't understand the Labyrinth until I understand the Emissary, and I can't even begin to understand the Emissary without access to a lot more information than I have now.

I sigh aloud, and this gets Cheshire to show her face, popping into existence beside me and tilting her head. "What's up, Allie?"

"Too much," I mutter. "Let's eat something, I'm hungry."

I push out of bed and—wait, have I been naked since fighting the Mourner last night? Shit, that would be embarrassing if I weren't an unholy abomination in flagrant violation of several far more serious taboos than doll-bodied nudity. I should still probably put some clothes on, though.

I get dressed in my more vampiric outfit: faux-corset vest over poofy blouse, denim shorts over diamond tights, magician's gloves and a high-collared cape, all in black and white and red. It seems fitting for playing with Vorpal.

I grab a bit of fruit and cheese from my throne world and snack on it, enjoying the easy access to humanity's two greatest discoveries. My breakfast is delicious, though my hunger is of course now completely and utterly insatiable.

I conjure another item, a bottle of red wine, but instead of opening it and pouring it I just stare at it and stew in my thoughts. Homura was drinking a lot, in that vision. Social drinking, mostly, but a hint of more with those gifts in her bedroom.

How old are you? I wonder. *What have you experienced, by your point in our personal timeline?*

The first time I ever drank, I was a few months from my twenty-first and in the company of my shitty, abusive ex-girlfriend. I had been scared of alcohol, before that. I was wary of anything that messed with my brain chemistry, and I was wary of its addictive properties as someone with incredibly poor impulse control, and I just knew too many people who became incredibly shitty when drunk.

I did not, as it happens, fall into any kind of alcoholism, but I think that's mostly because my cutting habit provided a better high for cheaper, and then weed after that. But I have felt cravings for it, every now and then, when I see it on the grocery shelf and tempt myself with a night of indulgence.

I dislike the kind of person I am while drunk. I need control of myself, and alcohol takes that away. Makes me pushier, bolder, and worse at reading people, which is a disastrous combination. Homura, from what I've seen of her, does not seem to have that problem.

Hmm. Maybe she's using blood magic to regulate her own bloodstream? If she can keep it flowing despite an open wound, maybe she can flush impurities to detoxicate herself.

An ingenious solution, if accurate. And it would be entirely in-character for her to indulge in pleasure and present weakness but secretly magick away the actual downsides. Something to learn from, perhaps.

I banish the wine and grab a water bottle instead, then go looking for an attendant. I ask for a good place to practice my sword skills, which they direct me to, and then I remember those items I was having the woodworker make for me.

"Hey, there was a drow in the mall who was working on a project for me, one of yours. Could you send someone to check up on that? Dunno if the big death game announcement made them decide to work quicker or to put their projects on hold, and it'd be useful to know."

The attendant bows and promises to look into that, and then I'm off to practice.

The place I'm sent to is an enclosed open-air space like the courtyard I found Esha and Bashe talking in, complete with garden vegetation ringing the area, but there's more open space in the center for someone to move around in freely.

I let Cheshire incarnate and she leans against a tree as she watches me work. I still know basically nothing about how to use a sword, so my practice doesn't even begin to resemble formal drills and professional sequences, but I get the feeling that my moves aren't as sloppy as they should be. I don't consciously understand what I'm doing any better, but there's a level of instinct at play as I thrust and parry and pirouette around an invisible foe.

The influence of Mahiri's soul, perhaps? Or a product of the blade itself, absorbing some of the experience that Homura stole? I don't tire, I don't feel winded, I don't even sweat as I slash and stab and dodge. I'm a demon now, and demons do not need to breathe.

My strides in conventional sword work are promising, but unexciting. I want to pull the crazy finishing moves that Homura and Ruzica threw at each other. I want anime bullshit super attacks. I try in vain to replicate either of their techniques, but I'm not surprised that it doesn't work.

I throw out all kinds of hypothetical spell names as I swing Vorpal around, trying to reach for the blade with my mind and get any kind of reaction out of it, but nothing works. I shout, "Vorpal, the Bloodstained Blade!" over and over, but it doesn't respond. This is a Crest, not a Throne-made magic item, and it doesn't seem to play by the same rules.

The sword responded to its name only the very first time, when I "woke it up" from its long slumber. I wonder, though, if it is truly awake or simply stirring. It recognized me, it called to me, but it has been so very long since it tasted blood.

It seems only logical to feed it.

I remove my gloves, flex a hand, and turn my fingertips into claws. I scrape those claws delicately along my forearm, using just enough force to draw blood. The pain is a familiar friend, almost closer to pleasure, and the sight of red droplets beading is absolutely transfixing. I slide the flat of my blade gently across the shallow incisions, letting it taste my blood and drink as deep as it likes.

When I finish the motion, my arm is unbloodied, not even a smear, just little pale red lines no longer dotted with droplets. Vorpal shines a deeper, truer red, and I can feel its hunger for more. There is a power in this blade, and it is slowly waking, but it is still so terribly parched.

. . . I think I'll need a great deal more blood for Vorpal to reveal its secrets to me.

I sigh. "I suppose it was too much to hope that I'd unlock a superweapon with a few pinpricks of crimson."

"We're lucky the Crest responded to you at all," Cheshire offers. "They're not *made* for interfacing with Throne magic. One of the littler artifacts, that might half function, but Crests are pure amplifiers."

I frown at the blade and swing it in the air again. "I do feel *something* from it, is the thing. It wants me to wield it. And I think it's helping me use it, at least on some level."

Cheshire bites her lip and thinks about it. "That makes a certain amount of sense, I suppose. The frameworks are very different but you are manipulating some of the same oneiros. It's possible that the Crest is having a diluted amplification effect on your Truth of Blood, enhancing your capacity for violence while you wield it."

"Violence has been useful to us, and I suspect will continue to be useful. Vorpal wants more blood," I tell the geist, "and I think giving it more blood will strengthen that amplification. So, worth using it when we can, and worth involving Blood in whatever spell we make next."

She nods. "I can definitely keep that in mind."

I'm disappointed that I can't do anything more with Vorpal yet . . . ah, but there is one thing I haven't checked. A secret revealed to me in my last dream: the marbles of power that Homura stored within her sword. If any of those crystallized affinities still exist, they could be a tremendous boon to my quest . . . but opening the compartment would invite all kinds of questions from Cheshire.

I know she's noticed something about my odd behavior each time I wake. The more I learn from my dreams, the harder it'll be to keep from slipping up and mentioning something I shouldn't know. Even my familiarity with Vorpal is hard to excuse as just some property of the sword.

Didn't you promise to trust her?

I grimace and lower my blade to the ground. *I took a risk. I'm taking risks. That doesn't mean I should just throw away every possible advantage!*

Is there really any point to hiding this from her? If she means to hurt me, I can't stop her. If she truly does want to help me, I'm self-sabotaging by keeping secrets from her.

She has her secrets too, you know she does.

But her secrets may be the fault of a bastard god who is laughing *at my paranoia. If we tell her the truth, if we bare it all, that may help us win her over. If she's keeping secrets and we're not, that creates pressure, motivates her to resolve that tension. If we want her trust, we need to show it first.*

I breathe out. Am I really doing this now? Before I've seen what these dreams are all building toward? There are so many ways this could go wrong.

Remember the animus we chose to live by: she who is not willing to give everything will be forever left with nothing. Are you the demon that bares her soul to the knife for a chance at the ultimate reward, or are you the little girl crying for her poor dead mother?

My fists clench, and the choice is made.

With one smooth motion I lift Vorpal and twist the necessary components around the hilt and crossguard, popping open the secret compartment that Homura revealed to me through Reska's eyes. A single marble rolls out into my waiting hand, endless starlight trapped gleaming within. The rest of the chamber is empty.

Only hers. You used them all, but never hers.

I roll the marble around my fingers, staring at it, wondering what it has seen. *Did she keep you out of sentiment, or as some harsh reminder? Not useful enough to expend, or too precious to waste? What is the shape of your heart, my time-lost twin?*

Cheshire watches with wide eyes as I deposit the marble back in the blade and close the hidden compartment. "How did you do that? Did you know that was there?"

I take a deep breath, close my eyes, and when I open them again I meet Cheshire's gaze. "The first time I fell asleep in this world, after carving open my soul, I dreamed of the world before the Labyrinth, in a time before Firmament, through the eyes of a girl cursed with gifts of blackest Shadow. And through her eyes I saw myself, or a younger version of myself, seduce that girl and lead her to ruin. My counterpart called herself Homura Annatar Bloodfallen, and she forged this weapon with a needle of glass given to her by a crying Katoptris."

I tell Cheshire everything, starting from the beginning and recounting nearly every detail. I tell her of Reska's strange powers that went against the magic system of her era, the odd behavior of the king, the labyrinth phenomenon, the Glass Tower, the Lady of Glass, and of course my scheming doppelganger Homura. I tell her of all my speculation about events, from Homura's choice of name to the mystery of why I'm receiving these dreams, and I even reveal what the Beast told me about an archon called the Emissary shattering Katoptris' mirror.

With each new revelation, Cheshire's shock seems to deepen, and when at last my story is finished she turns away from me and begins to pace, hands on her head. I wait nervously for her to say something, anything, after that massive infodump.

After a few minutes of frantic pacing, Cheshire throws herself against the nearest tree and slumps to the ground, head still in her hands, looking utterly exhausted.

I walk over to her and sit down across from her. "Hey, you okay? Uh, you seem to be taking this . . . poorly. Sorry for not telling you sooner, but, you know, trust issues and all."

Cheshire laughs. "That's . . . that's fine, really. I get it. I'm not mad, I promise. I just . . . that's insane. I don't even know where to begin."

I chew on my lip and give it some thought. "Well, I was hoping you could help me answer a few questions. Like who the Emissary is, for one, or if those labyrinths are actually some direct precursor to *the* Labyrinth. Hell, I'd even appreciate if you could tell me what Homura's middle name means. I get the two weeb references, but why does 'Annatar' sound so familiar?"

Cheshire raises her head, expression still bleak but now furrowing her brow. "It's . . . it's from *The Lord of the Rings,* I think. Yes, got it: it was the name that Sauron used when he was deceiving the elves into forging the Rings of Power." She rubs her forehead and winces. "I've got whole encyclopedias of nerd lore in my brain thanks to Nyara, the least I can do is put them to use."

Clarity flashes across my mind. "Annatar, Lord of Gifts. I remember now. Fuck, that's not very subtle of her, is it? She named herself after what was basically Middle-Earth's version of . . . the . . . devil . . ." I trail off, more connections sparking, pieces falling into place.

The devil. Annatar, Sauron, the devil of Middle-Earth, but that's not the only devil in her name.

"Homura," I breathe. "I—I thought she meant the Homura of the main series, the selfish hero who fought to save Madoka, but what if that's wrong?

What if she was naming herself after the Homura of *Rebellion?* The Homura who became the devil to trap a goddess . . . inside a labyrinth."

Cheshire's gaze sharpens as she immediately seizes the thread, and when she speaks it is with a tone of horror. "A labyrinth, a world of distorted fears and desires, a hellish prison for the witch it belongs to and any lured inside . . . but Homura's labyrinth was meant to look like a paradise, trapping the goddess and her closest friends."

I stand up and look around, peering not with mortal vision but with my demon-granted soul sight. I see the world rendered in paper and ink, this hellish paradise, and aloud I ask, whispering, "Did I create this prison?"

Cheshire rises next to me and puts a hand on my shoulder, and when I turn to face her I see her just as she is to my normal sight. I can see tension lining every crease of her face, in her shaking hands, and when I flick my tongue I taste fear in the air. She's terrified. My geist is terrified of what she's about to say. "Alice, I—I don't think that's you. Or . . . not the same you, at least. Because—"

A cruel god descends upon us, and the master of all things steals the breath from Cheshire's lungs. She chokes on her words as an awful pressure fills the air and pushes down on us, ears popping and head aching. I feel cruelty and contempt, laughter and glee, the hand that moves the world, and I am paralyzed until she allows me to move.

She is Nyarlathotep, the Lucid Demiurge, Crawling Chaos, Soul-Sculptor, Toymaker, Nyara Albaoth Zereth Gremory Lazotep, and she is the tyrant I have sworn to usurp.

Cheshire claws at her own throat, eyes bulging, black tears streaking down her cheeks, black ichor staining the veins in her hands, and with impossible will she chokes out, "Damn . . . you . . ." before falling silent and still, slumping like a ragdoll, limbs dangling at her sides, head bowed as if sleeping standing up.

I try to move, twitching fingers and gritted teeth, every motion a struggle but desperate to stop this, to save her. I hiss, that sound afforded me, and though I cannot speak I know that she is *listening* to my thoughts, so in my mind I tell her, *leave Cheshire alone!*

Cheshire raises her head, but it is Nyara lurking behind those golden eyes now slick with black ichor, Nyara puppeting that smiling mouth of blackened teeth. The God of Death smiles at me, and her love is like a thousand knives.

Those eyes burn into me, black and gold like two blazing suns in a sea of suffocating darkness. I can't help but stare into them, drawn to them, and my soul sight takes me deeper, through the connection into what lies behind, to the Demiurge pulling the strings, and I see—

—I break away, screaming, eyes boiling in my head, bursting with pus and fluid, popped like rotten grapes in her too-perfect hands. *Mistake. Mistake.*

Mistake. Mistake. I try to shut my eyes, seek the dark, anything to rid myself of the impossible colors seared into my retinas, the horrid images that cycle endlessly through my vision, the glimpse of a great and terrible *infinity.*

Then, all at once, it's gone and I can see again. I see the flagstones beneath my hands and knees, I see the great tree above, and I see Nyara smiling down at me with my only friend's face.

"I so adore when you stick your hand in the open flame," she says, Cheshire's voice but so very *wrong* in ways that elude my comprehension, like static at the edges of my thoughts. *"It's quite cute."*

I shudder and rasp, "Why are you here, God of Death? What do you want?"

She tuts, actually *tuts* at me. *"Do I really need a reason to check in on my favorite toy?"*

Nyara reaches down with Cheshire's hand and strokes my hair, her touch impossibly warm and terrifyingly soothing. Relief floods my body like a scalding bath after a day of hard labor, traveling from the top of my head to the tips of my extremities and turning my bones to wobbly gelatin. I collapse against the ground, my body too high on her touch to listen to my commands. I can't even turn my head to look at her cleanly.

Nyara walks over and crouches down in front of my line of sight, looking even more smug. *"See? I'm not all bad, really. Remember, pet: if you want to blame me for the pain, you have to thank me for the pleasure. I gave you salve when you were hurting, power when you were weak, companionship when you were lonely, a playground to stretch your limbs in. You should worship me for all I have given you, and yet still you rage against me. What a silly, misguided priestess."*

Her fingers trail across my head and down my spine and everywhere she touches blooms with mind-numbing bliss. She kneels down and pulls me onto her lap and that warmth is all I can feel, almost all I can focus on. Her presence is an ocean, and it would be so easy to drown in it, but I will not be cowed like some beaten dog when given a few scraps of warm food. I fight back the urge to simply let go and fall asleep in her embrace, resisting the comfort she's trying to lull me with.

I wish so sorely that I could move my mouth just to bite her . . . but there are some weapons that *I don't need to move* to use. I feel her touch glide back up to my neck, tracing patterns of spreading oblivion, and when her finger brushes the skin of my nape I scream the spell in my mind:

[FEAST OR FAMINE]!

I take a bite out of God and she tastes so fucking good. She tastes like that giddy moment when the edible hits and your brain melts out your ears and you can't stop giggling because suddenly everything's so funny and it just feels so good to lean in. Her soul is like meat and candy so sickeningly sweet you can't get enough even as your stomach bloats and groans and begs you to stop but you just want one more bite. I drink her in like she's frozen lemonade on a boiling day in July, like she's eight shots of espresso before an early day at work, like she's blood from an open wound gushing and steaming and so damn wasteful if I don't lap up every drop.

I don't even feel the pain as I splinter more and more of my soul to keep eating, keep drinking, keep glutting myself on the best thing I'll ever taste. I want more and I take more, consuming, feasting, more, more, more! I can taste the warm glow of dawn and the peace of fading dusk, the minute vibrations of my body and the crackle of dying stars, a soft hand in mine and the shockwave of a meteorite impact. I can't remember my first kiss. I can't remember the face of my mother.

It's killing me. Eating her is killing me, and I don't want to stop.

I eat the taste of the first snowfall come winter and I forget my favorite album of my favorite band. I eat the taste of an orchestra's final performance and I forget my aunt's home cooking. I eat and eat and eat and I am eaten and eaten and eaten, and I am full to bursting and I am mad with hunger.

I'm eating her whole, but how can you swallow infinity? There's so much more of her than me, and if I keep going there won't be any Alice left. Have I even scratched her? Is she missing even a single piece of something that matters to her?

I lose the name of the last gift my mother gave me. I lose my favorite book from childhood, then second favorite, then third. It's not just the spell, it's her, it's her infinity, it's trying to drink an ocean and having it push out all your blood and guts to make room. I'll drown before the water level even dips.

Nyara lifts her hand from my neck and I sob as it finally *ends*. I shudder and shake, wracked with the enormity of what I've just experienced, and she watches me with that damnable fucking smile.

"To answer your question," the smiling goddess says, *"I am here because of you. You have exceeded my expectations, little Alice, in revealing your dreams to the geist at this early juncture. This act of unexpectedly deep trust necessitates a significant acceleration of my plans. Ah, but worry not; I think this will make for a far more compelling story. Do stay interesting, my beloved plaything. I'll see you again soon."*

All at once the black leaves Cheshire's eyes and one of them turns back to blue, and then the changeling collapses to the ground next to me, shivering just as I am, face awash with horror and revulsion. Black bile dribbles out of the corner of her mouth and that's all it takes for my stomach to turn and blood to come spilling out, both of us ejecting vile fluids onto the cold stone floor.

We stay there for minutes, trembling and staring at each other, neither willing to be the first to speak. My mind still reels from the taste of Nyara's soul, my body beginning to ache as the glow of her touch fades away. I feel changed. I am changed.

Something in me has broken, and when I find my voice it is to laugh. I laugh and cry and slowly curl into the fetal position amid my own coughed up blood. My bones feel fragile, my skin taut, ice in my veins, a terrible heat in my core.

I breathe, unnecessary but comforting, desperate for some measure of stability. How do you recover from something like that? How do I go back to this stupid game and this stupid quest? It's so fucking small.

I'm still shaking, but I finally find real words. "How stupid was I," I whisper, voice unsteady, "to think I could eat the Demiurge?" I laugh again, harsh and bleak and vicious. "The Adversary is insane. She has to be, right? How can you come face to face with *that* and think you stand a chance?"

Cheshire chuckles, sounding just as broken as I feel. "I don't know. Maybe she doesn't. Maybe it's just madness."

Slowly, achingly, we pick ourselves up off the floor.

I stare down at the mess we've made and Cheshire comments, "We should probably let someone know this needs to be cleaned."

"Yeah. Hey, do you think absorbing that black stuff would be bad for Bubbles? It won't, like, turn them into some nightmare gray goo that eats half the city?"

Cheshire shivers and glances at the awful bile. "I don't *think* that would happen, but . . . best to be safe."

Neither of us moves to find an attendant, still simmering in the aftermath of all that just transpired. I hesitate, then ask, "Did Nyara tell you to kill Katoptris? To have me try to kill her? It's okay if you can't answer that."

The geist looks away from me and hugs herself, hands digging into her sides. "She promised salvation, if only I could move you to slay the Labyrinth's master." She flinches, as if waiting to be struck down or possessed again, but nothing happens. "I assumed she meant Katoptris, because who else could it be? She never told me about an Emissary, or about Homura. There's . . . there's more to it than that, but I definitely can't tell you the rest."

"Right, yeah. Okay. Well, I think that's enough to see the shape of it." I smooth back my hair and take another deep breath to steady myself. "You push me to kill Katoptris because you think that's what you were told to do, but my dreams tell me there's something wrong with that plan. If Katoptris is the victim and you're trying to kill her, that makes you the baddie, which heightens my trust issues. The tension bottles until it bursts, and Nyara enjoys the fireworks."

Cheshire turns back to me and frowns, seeming pensive. "But . . . I don't think she meant for that to end in a true split between us. She said she was accelerating her plans, not *changing them*. So this conversation was always the end goal, just after a lot more hardship and paranoia."

Interesting. I pick up Vorpal and shunt it into my throne world, then tilt my head and ask, "Does that comfort you?"

Cheshire laughs. "It's stupid that it does, but yeah. There was some part of me worried that I was, I don't know, a sacrifice. A tool to be put aside once I'd gotten the right reaction out of you. Once I'd fulfilled my purpose in the greater narrative. But here we are."

"Here we are," I agree.

We call an attendant, warning them that the spill might be unsafe for Bubbles, and then we go looking for our allies. Esha isn't hard to find, given she's still right by the pool in the heart of the temple, light now permanently filling the air.

"Ah, Alice, good to see you," Esha says as I approach, giving me a genuine smile not shared by her bodyguard.

I wave. "Morning, Priestess. Any word on our would-be 'allies'?"

Esha nods. "The city tells me that Avaya'ari and Imlashi both approach, bringing hands for the mission, though Carnival is approaching at a much more serious pace."

I tilt my head. "That's a neat trick. How much intel does the city give you?"

"As much as I need, mostly. The city knows itself and sees itself at all times, except for a few rare spots where the influence of the Beast overrides that of the eidolon. The Beast can create pockets of dead space when it needs to, hiding something from the senses of the city spirit, and its shards naturally create those pockets in their vicinity, which is how Averrich has been able to hide from my sight for so long." Behind her, Achaia grimaces. "Of course, that's changed now; I didn't see it yet yesterday, but it was clear when I consulted the city this morning: the shroud around Averrich's stronghold is missing, which means the Reveler he had trapped there is dead. Your doing, I would presume from the mask?"

I nod and conjure the mask again. "Averrich threw me into the Reveler's maze before sending his hunters, but I didn't just escape the maze; I killed the Reveler at its heart, and every hunter he sent after me. I imagine that's why they're afraid of me now."

Esha frowns and turns to face the pool with her sightless gaze. "And yet they approach, to help you stop the Machinist. I am glad they still see *some* sense."

"How close are they now?"

"Close enough that you could meet them by the door, if you set out now and walked slowly."

"And Avaya's group?"

"Another thirty minutes, I believe, though she may speed up once she's actually in our territory."

I chew my lip and muse on it. "I'll make sure Dante's awake and then head for the front."

Esha smiles and says, "You'll have one other with you, from my own people. A kindred you've met before, actually: Simon, the serpentkin who healed you after your first encounter with King's Carnival."

The snake doctor! The snoctor! "Ah, I do I remember him. Happy to have his skills on the team."

"He also has a contract with the city spirit that allows him to access the city's information network like I can, so he'll be your eyes as you chase down the Machinist."

I grin and rub my hands together. "Even better."

I track down Dante and rouse him from slumber, then make sure he gets breakfast from the communal kitchen. Over eggs and French toast we banter about Earth media, with Cheshire chiming in whenever she has something to poke a hole in. We're finished with breakfast and drinking orange juice when an attendant lets us know that Avaya's crew have arrived, so we head out to meet them.

The snoctor is waiting for us just outside the kitchen, and this time I actually get a good look at him: serpentine lower body, scaled upper body, a grizzled face, and a perfectly modern doctor's uniform, with a medical bag held in one hand. "Name's Simon," he says gruffly. "Let's get moving."

I am delighted to be traveling with the snake doctor.

Imlashi meets us just inside the door, and I see who she's brought with: Kado again, for one, but the other reaver is new, or at least I think they're new. They look, twitchy, nervous, almost ratlike, but carrying a big ol' spear to stab with. When they speak, I finally place them: Scratchy! Or, Eren, as they named themself.

Just outside the door, waiting with four arms crossed and a big grin, is Avaya. She's brought back the empty puppets from before, still wearing their ethereal shifts but now each carrying a vicious-looking sword.

"They will obey Maven Alice in all things," Avaya tells us. "It is currently their sole purpose in life, until I come to reclaim them."

The doll-eyed man and woman give me a bow, looking placidly content to be passed off to a new owner for an indefinite time period. I make a mental note to check what they can do in a fight. Having minions like this is exciting, to some extent, but I can't enjoy that too much or Dante and Simon might start to suspect something.

Imlashi and Avaya leave us, and then it's time to begin our march. Simon and Kado both step forward to lead the way, each having a means of tracking our quarry, and they glare at each other until I ask the pointed question, "Do your spells actually disagree on where we should be going?"

They briefly turn their glares on me, then discover that their spells do not, in fact, differ in recommended heading. We're about to set out for real when someone comes rushing toward us from across the square. They're dressed plainly, and carrying what looks like a staff of some kind and a brown paper bag.

I go to flicker on my soul sight to check if they're figment or thinking, but when I do I can feel my eyes searing with pain and melting in my skull, and all I can see is a vast and terrible imprint of the infinity I glimpsed within Nyara's eyes. I have to turn it back off, eyes returning to normal with only a bit of lingering ache.

Fuck. We lost our soul sight.

Further swearing at that discovery is forestalled by the arrival of the courier, who shoves the staff and the pouch toward me with a polite, "Delivery for Ms. Alice, from Torstein."

It's the woodworking I asked for! Slender and solid, long and elegant, topped with a carving of a bat wrapping its wings around its body, mouth open with a ruby embedded. The staff is mostly white, with a bit of black trim decorating the bat in key areas. Perfect now that I've actually incorporated bats into my spellcasting.

The second item, which I procure from the pouch and then send to my throne world with the staff, is a carving of a unique chimera designed by Cheshire: the body and head of a red-eyed, white-furred wolf, with parrot's wings and talons for back feet, its tail curling and scaled like a chameleon, a crown of antlers bursting from its skull. Cheshire's anchor, solidly less useful now that I'm mostly using my own body to host Cheshire, but I'm sure it'll come in handy.

With both items stowed and a heading secured, I set the group to marching.

As we leave the temple behind, my thoughts drift to my encounter with the Crawling Chaos, the Lucid Demiurge, Nyara. She spoke of gifts she had given, and now these items appear so timely. Another gift from my supposed patron?

Maybe it's delirium from the experience I went through, or maybe there's just something wrong with me, but . . . when she was talking about me, complimenting me in her diminutive way, some twisted part of me felt *pride* at her words. I can feel it now, a strange warmth in my chest when I think to some of what she said. She called me cute. She called me *interesting*, and that's all I've ever wanted to be.

It's absurd. It's absolutely absurd, and stupid, and a clear sign that my brain is compromised or just fucking damaged, but some piece of me is *happy* at being such a focus of attention for the vile ruler of this universe. The orchestrator of all my triumphs and woes is watching me raptly and cheering me on. Of all her toys across dozens, maybe hundreds of worlds, an entire universe of boundless possibility . . .

I'm her favorite.

PART TWO

POOL OF TEARS

OR, DEFEATING DEPRESSION
BY PUNCHING IT REALLY HARD

Poor Alice! It was as much as she could do, lying down on one side, to look through into the garden with one eye; but to get through was more hopeless than ever: she sat down and began to cry again.

"You ought to be ashamed of yourself," said Alice, "a great girl like you," (she might well say this), "to go on crying in this way! Stop this moment, I tell you!" But she went on all the same, shedding gallons of tears, until there was a large pool all round her, about four inches deep, and reaching half down the hall.

—*Alice in Wonderland,* Lewis Carroll

I

I hang back with Cheshire while the others chat amongst themselves. Simon is rather goal-oriented and leading the way, harassed by a Scratchy—what was their name again?—that refuses to shut up. Kado and Dante talk casually, the isekai kid seeming to hit it off with everyone he meets. My puppets on loan from Avaya walk between myself and the rest of the pack, creating a bit of distance and performing rear guard duties.

Cheshire is in her ethereal form, gliding along beside me without ever touching the ground and needing to move her legs. I really need to learn a trick like that, though I have to admit I've stopped feeling winded on these long walks. Demonic stamina, I suppose.

Cheshire bumps up against me and asks, "Hey, wanna learn a new scion trick?"

"Yes, always, definitely. What is it?" I give a quick glance ahead just to double check no one's listening in, and they all still seem occupied.

"I'm going to teach you how to use your throne world to hold a private conversation while still being in public."

"Ah. That seems useful in our exact situation."

The catgirl geist rubs her hands together. "I figured you'd think so. It's a good skill for every scion to have, once their throne world is strong enough for it. Demons start with the weakest domain of any scion, but your growth rate has been a lot faster than a normal demon even before you took a bite out of the Demiurge. Now we can start projecting your internal world onto the external world."

I perk up and lean in. "Domain expansion. Reality marble. We're digging into that kind of magic?"

Cheshire grins. "Welcome to the real power of a scion. Your soul is a world as tangible as any other now, as true as any realm of Pandaemonium, just . . . less weighty, at the moment. Any scion can retreat into their throne world and invite others inside, but it's a lot harder to push out the world around you; your authority over reality only extends to the reach of your pleroma. As your soul core strengthens and your pleroma expands, you'll be able to manifest further outside of yourself for longer stretches without needing a formal invitation. The world will still push back, but you'll get better at resisting its pressure."

I eagerly devour the new exposition, adding it to my mental framework of the magic system. "Very exciting. So how do we apply that to our current needs?"

Cheshire gestures around us and says, "If you were to project your soul around us now, just a few feet out, you could maintain it for probably a few minutes before it collapsed back into you. However!" She pokes me in the cheek. "Your *body* is within your core's reach, not just your pleroma, and that keeps the world from pushing back when you make changes. That principle is why we reconfigure your appearance so easily, and we can apply it to create a bit of privacy between the two of us. By deciding that sound cannot escape the bounds of your throne world, the words you speak will reach your lips and stop there, unheard by any but yourself and your geist."

Clever. But still vulnerable to lip reading, so . . . I conjure my witchy hat and put it on, then dip it low to obscure my face to the others. "Let's try this out."

Cheshire walks me through the process. Every time I interact with my throne world, it gets a little easier to understand how it operates and what it responds to. In no time at all I have a basic sound filter up and running, and our privacy is secured.

"So," I ask, "what did you want to talk about that necessitates a filter? I had assumed we were setting all the Homura and Katoptris stuff aside for now, given Nyara's . . . objections."

Cheshire shivers and I match her. "Yeah, no, very happy to *not* talk about any of that. But there is one good piece of news to come out of that disaster: we can make new spells. Between the Reveler, the Mourner, and the soul from Avaya, you were already close to breaching the next threshold."

Before bed last night, Cheshire helped me come up with a cute trick for eating that bartered soul: I carved off all the impurities with [Feast or Famine], then ate the parts that actually resonated as a conventional demon would. Excellent efficiency.

"Each time you create a new spell, it takes more power to make the next, so normally there's quite a gap between spells after you've made your first few . . . but you drank from Nyarlathotep herself, so you're actually powerful enough for a second spell and nearly there to a third. So: what do you want first?"

"Something that involves blood," I respond immediately. "Let me think it over for a second."

Mind control? Mind control is pretty poggers and those puppets have given me ideas, buuuuuut I can't use a spell like that in front of Dante or the Myriad, and I should wait until I've eaten Vaylin, so it's definitely more of a future investment.

I could try to reverse engineer Homura's boosting magic, since it served her so well in that duel with Ruzica, but I don't know if it would be as useful in my hands. Homura was fighting a mostly conventional battle there, trying to score clean blows with power and skill and a few clever tricks, but my win condition in any given fight is landing a lethal soul rip. Being stronger doesn't help me eat souls better when all I need is a moment of contact. Being faster might help against certain opponents, though my mobility game is already fairly strong with Cheshire on my side.

If I want Vorpal to boost my next spell, then it needs to involve my Truth of Blood. That could mean the literal blood flowing through my veins or it could mean the associated concepts of Blood like violence, sacrifice, and bonds. I don't know all the differences between Homura's Blood and mine, but it's a fair bet that hitting all three of those big ideas will net me the most metaphysical bang for my metaphysical buck.

But that still leaves the all-important question: what should the spell actually *do?* Do I need more offensive options, do I need to add more utility to my toolkit, or do I need to bulk up my defenses?

You know, we were thinking about getting some kind of armor spell to alleviate the clothing damage problem. Armor made of crystallized blood, armor made of liquid shadow, maybe combine the ideas, pitch it to Cheshire, and work from there to develop it into something fitting and useful?

Yeah, okay, good plan. "Okay, I have an idea. I want the spell to tie into violence, sacrifice, and bonds, because they're all key components of my Truth of Blood and I think that'll give me the best chance of receiving assistance from Vorpal. I also want a spell that will keep me from having to replace my outfit after every major fight, because that's definitely going to happen unless I run around naked like I did in that last encounter. So, my pitch is some kind of enduring armor spell, like a spell that gives me a suit of some adaptive substance that can clothe me and protect me, but made out of my own blood and liquefied shadow."

Cheshire leans in and grins. "That is a very, very exciting idea. I can absolutely work with that, that has a lot of potential. I think this is a perfect spell to start really digging into the idea of tactical drawbacks, too. Nyara's magic system rewards the notion of 'balance' in spell design, so you can make a spell stronger in one area by making it weaker in others. It's sort of like a merits and flaws system in an RPG: each spell has a given budget of effectiveness, and you can increase that budget by taking on detrimental effects."

"I'm both buzzing at the prospect of being able to minmax my magic to such a fine-tuned level and vaguely peeved that Nyara probably designed it that way to intentionally ape said RPG systems."

Cheshire sighs. "Her and her references. Anyway: violence, sacrifice, and bonds. Those latter two are actually perfect for creating drawbacks that will make the spell stronger. For sacrifice, I'm thinking of stuff like the Kamui in *Kill La Kill* or the ripcord in *Chainsaw Man:* when you activate the spell it takes a bite out of your blood, and it'll keep drinking the more that you use it and push the limits of its capabilities. That'll also help enhance the Blood resonances even if sacrifice *isn't* particularly important to Vorpal, though I would honestly be surprised if that were the case."

I grin. "I like it. Very edgy, very 'feast or famine.' Plus, it's an easy drawback to manage: I just have to drink more blood from others." *Regular feeding is important for a growing vampire demon doll monster.*

The catgirl chuckles. "You'll definitely get more urges to drink while the spell is running. Probably a general uptick in all kinds of hungers, actually. Anyway, the other big drawback: if we want to hit the concept of bonds, then we can make it a spell that can only be cast while the two of us are merged—or rather, a spell that through casting merges us in a different way from both classical manifestation and our hybrid form."

I raise an eyebrow. "I'm listening."

"When you manifest me through your body, my shapeshifting gets supercharged by your demonic essence. When I'm not manifested, my anchor point or resting place is your shadow, the symbol of your demonhood." She lets her form melt into my shadow and then reappear beside me. "So what if, instead of using your whole body as an anchor for my manifestation, I only used two components: your shadow, and your blood. I would be the guiding intellect of the spell, in a sense, actively managing the shadow-blood mixture and altering its properties on the fly to better protect you against enemy attacks or maneuver you around the battlefield."

"I like it. Another drawback that's not really a drawback, given I don't plan on using you as an attack dog or a distraction now that we have more powerful tools at our disposal. You're more useful at my side, close to me."

Cheshire preens at that, seeming to light up at my praise. "That's not all! By using my presence as a core component of the spell, you'll also gain a degree of passive physical enhancement like you would experience during a normal merge, and I can micromanage the spell's material to better protect you: I can harden portions of the suit to deflect physical trauma, and I can create a kind of gel layer to redistribute kinetic energy from attacks that don't care about deflection."

So I still get the boost after all, excellent. I grin and start drumming my fingers along my thigh. "Very useful. Any other fun ideas?"

"Yes, actually!" The catgirl gives me an even bigger grin and asks, "How would you like tentacles?"

"Yes, fuck yes, absolutely yes, what kind of tentacles?" I'm practically vibrating with excitement now. *This is the coolest spell ever.*

"We'll add four of them coming out of your back, flexible and sturdy, and they'll split at the tip to grab enemies or climb terrain. Made of your blood, of course."

I hug myself and wriggle as we walk, and I even squeal a little. I am extremely happy that none of the others can hear me right now. "Yes, yes, yes!!! Oh fuck, we should edit my default form to have like, vertical slits in my back that the tentacles come out of, like exposed wounds from which my blood takes vicious form, muahaha!" I'm getting so chuuni about this and I'm not even embarrassed.

Cheshire giggles at my enthusiasm and claps. "Done! Oh, if you *really* wanna go full boss monster with this, we could add a vulnerable core to the whole thing, a critical weak point. For maximum resonance we could make that be your heart, exposed and the source of the spell, the anchor for my part of it. You'd have to work a little harder to defend it, of course, but it would strengthen the rest of the armor."

I pause. "Wait. Does that apply, like, universally to all magic armor? Give it a weak point and the rest toughens up?"

Cheshire nods. "Yep. And now you understand why Achaia doesn't wear a helmet. That's actually standard practice for magic armor, in fact. You always want to build around a weak point to maximize the rest of the armor, and helmets are an easy choice because Nyara finds headshots boring."

I pause for a longer moment this time. "Sorry, did you . . . did you just say that Nyara, the Lucid Demiurge, the master of reality, finds headshots *boring?* And that means, through magical bullshit, cosmological shenanigans, absolute metaphysical *horsepiss,* that warriors going into battle do not have to worry about getting shot in the fucking head when they choose not to wear a helmet?"

"Within Pandaemonium, you are mathematically less likely to be shot in the head than anywhere else on your body, by a dramatic degree, unless you are capable of surviving being shot in the head, in which case it'll actually happen more often." Cheshire's expression is completely serious.

I take a moment to process that deranged revelation of fresh batshit crazy setting lore. Like, wow. That's. That's something. "Cool. Cool cool cool. So, anyways, I guess we're making a suit of blood armor that exposes my heart, and we might as well expose the head too since that's apparently fucking normal here. That'll make the rest of me super resistant to attacks which will buy me time to land a finisher, so we're enhancing our current strategy."

"Sounds good! Unless there's anything else, do you have a preference for what the spell will look like? We've been talking about the raw materials, mostly, but how do you want this blood-shadow mixture to look when it forms around you? Black-and-red goop? Spiky red crystals streaked with black smoke?"

I hesitate. I do have ideas, actually, but now I *am* feeling embarrassed. "Yes, so, um, right, about that."

Cheshire gives me a quizzical expression. "Allie?"

Softly, so quietly that even I can barely hear it, I mumble, "I was thinking of making it . . . sexy." The last word is barely even sound.

She blinks a few times, then leans in, grin becoming devilish. "Could you repeat that? I didn't quite catch it."

"Sexy!" I hiss at her. "Sex appeal! Fanservice! Ugh. Look, I was thinking about this yesterday morning while I was choosing what to wear, and I started really digging into the meaning of my magic and what aesthetic would empower it best and I was *trying* to find some kind of look that's cool and terrifying and powerful and badass, but then my stupid traitor brain started pointing out that hey that's only part of my Truths and if I *really* want to maximize my power then I should be aiming to be desirable as well and to emphasize recklessness and hey would you look at that dressing in a skimpy attention-seeking way would hit both of those perfectly and I had the terrible horrifying absolutely abominable realization that my fucking magic that is my essence and soul and the very heart of me will actually fucking reward me if I go around fighting in goddamn *dominatrix lingerie* and do you have any idea how infuriating that is!?!? I want to be loved and feared and feel desired and powerful and dangerous, wreathed in violence and hunger and the worship of my lessers, and somehow all of that actually maps annoyingly well to 'sexy villainess,' so here I am." I pause my embarrassed, furious rambling to pout before quickly adding, "I was going to argue that 'sexy' should be disqualifying but my evil traitor brain who I consider my greatest and most hateful nemesis countered that you would probably call that self-loathing and dysphoric."

"I would!" Cheshire chirps. "And I will! You have every right to feel sexy and own that feeling. I also, for the record, agree with your interpretation of your own Truths and how they align with that aesthetic choice. So, Alice: what does sexy look like?"

"Ah, um, yes, ahem. Well." *Stop blushing stop blushing stop fucking blushing you dumb whore!* "So, I was thinking that it would be, um, like, skintight?

I know I specifically asked for slender and not curvy but, y'know, showing off whatever minimal figure is there. And, um, so, maybe . . ." I trail off, desperately wishing to abort this line of conversation but in far too deep now.

"Go on," Cheshire teases. "You've got something in mind, spill."

"A boob window," I whisper, and then I dip my hat even lower so that it completely covers my face.

I can't see her face, but I can hear her stifling laughter.

"I know I barely have boobs!" I hiss at her. "Whatever, it was a terrible idea, let's pick something else."

"No, no, it's not that, you're just so cute about it! You're adorable. But if you want some constructive feedback, I do have a few ideas for improvement."

I slowly raise my hat back up far enough that I can actually see Cheshire, who's looking at me with an expression of such adoration and warmth that I'm tempted to immediately hide again, but I don't. "Share."

"So, skintight with cleavage showing, that's something I can work with. That first part is easy, we focus on mutability and make an ever-changing mixture of red fluid and brackish smoke that clings to your body tightly, swirling and shifting but always pressing in close like an embrace. And then, how about, instead of a window design, we stop the suit entirely at that point and create an off-shoulder neckline, baring more skin. We push out the shadow-blood a bit to either side of the shoulders and up a bit, creating a kind of spiked pauldron effect, and then we decorate the entire border with rows of teeth like the jaw of a great beast ready to snap shut around your head. Then, at the dip in the center, at your sternum, we'll put your heart—because to a demon, biology is just a suggestion—bursting from your chest and held in place by twisted rib bone."

Biology is just a suggestion. What a fantastically absurd thing to say. Her description is vivid enough that I'm past my embarrassment now and back to excitement. "Yes, want, oh wow that's good. Now we're cooking with monster girls. I'm going to look so good murdering people and wow I am so, so, so glad for this sound filter."

Cheshire giggles to herself before looking at me expectantly. "Then all that's left is a name."

"Ah, fuck, right. Hmm." *Name, gotta name the spell. [Shadow Skin]? [Demon Skin]? [Hot Girl Shit]?* "I know this isn't really a culmination of animus like [Feast or Famine] was, but I still feel like the metaphysics dictate that I have to get philosophical about this. What does this spell mean to me, and what does it suggest about my identity as a demon? What's the significance?"

Cheshire taps her chin and looks thoughtful, then points out, "Well, an hour or two after you let me into your metaphorical heart by revealing your secret dream visions, you're now letting me into your literal physical heart and inviting me to take control of your blood and your shadow, both of which are strong symbols of you as a demon. It's a kind of deeply symbolic union, when you look at it that way."

I consider that. "Interesting. Mm. There's a lot of cultural precedent for pacts and bonds made by exchanging blood, but cultural precedent is more the domain of Spirit and I don't exactly have a lot of personal attachment to that idea beyond finding it cool whenever it shows up in anime or whatever."

"You could think of it as a wager of trust, a sacrifice of agency to our bond." Then Cheshire gets an evil grin. "Or you could call it a catsuit. You know, since—"

"I *will* eat your fingers," I tell her solemnly. "I will dip them in wasabi and wrap them in seaweed and then I will nibble on them as a snack while I paint this city with the blood of my enemies."

She giggles. "Okay, but it actually does kind of fit, doesn't it?"

"It does and I hate you for that. Affectionately. Still think it's too memey, though; this spell feels important enough that I should make *some* effort to tie it to my animus. Maybe [Famished Heart], to get that direct reference?"

Cheshire hums at that and tilts her head. "I feel as if that puts too much emphasis on the 'famine' half, though. How about [Voracious Heart] instead? Always eating yet always hungry, you could say that the concept of voracity embodies both feast and famine. Plus, your heart is going to be constantly drinking your blood while the spell is active, so it's both metaphorically true and literally true."

"Hmm. Yeah, I can vibe with that. Honestly, Voracity would be a cool arch-demon name. I have to pick one of those at some point, don't I?"

The catgirl wiggles her hand in a so-so gesture. "It's less a name that you pick and more a name that picks you, if that makes sense. It's a flash of insight in the eldritch horror sense of insight, a moment where your self-concept as a demon crystallizes and you see yourself more clearly than you thought possible. Like a 'true name' in certain kinds of fantasy."

"Noted. In that case, I'm changing my vote to Darquesse."

Cheshire rolls her eyes and chuckles. "Pretty sure that one's taken, and also not a word name, but it's cute that you're still holding a flame for a fictional mass-murdering goddess of ruin. I know how much her influence and possession of Valkyrie affected your writing and your taste in women."

I sigh wistfully. "Superpowered evil side that whispers corrupting temptations, my dearly beloved. It's actually extremely homophobic that Nyara hasn't given me one of those. I would be incredibly powerful if you replaced the mental illness with a hot girl in my brain telling me to do murders and kiss a skeleton."

My geist smirks at me and muses, "You know, if I'd introduced myself to you posing as an evil alter ego you probably would have gone along with basically anything I suggested."

"Oh yeah," I admit, "if you'd presented yourself as a manifestation of my own corrupt desires rather than a fantasy yandere girlfriend, I'd have jumped on that corruption arc no questions asked." I pause, then add, "Probably. I'm realizing that my imagination of fantasy scenarios doesn't always line up with what actually feels right in the moment. There's every possibility that rather than being exhilarated by the prospect I'd feel terrified and guilt-ridden and talk myself into a catastrophizing spiral. Turns out people have overestimated opinions of their own composure and competency when thrust into an alien world full of alien circumstances."

On cue—because the Demiurge has a flair for the dramatic and there's no *way* this is a coincidence—I hear shouting from up ahead. *We can work on the other spell later, I suppose.*

"Showtime," I mutter. "Lock in the spell, we'll see if I actually need it."

Cheshire nods and I dismiss the noise filter before looking ahead to see what we're actually dealing with.

The shouting was from Simon, and I see both the serpentkin and Kado looking tense. Kado's owlbear is perched on his shoulder in owl form, to my distaste, and appears to be leaning in as if to whisper something. Dante has already unsheathed his sword and is holding it out in front of himself in a stance that I would have had a lot less room to criticize two days ago.

I push past the black-clad puppets assigned to my service and ask, "What's going on? Trouble?"

"A night horror," Simon hisses. "A big one up ahead, and others scattered nearby."

Kado mutters, "It explains why this place is so damn eerie."

I frown. Eerie? I look around and suddenly realize something that the others must have noticed a while ago: this whole street is empty of people. There are no figments pathing from one location to another, no one hanging about and chatting, not a single glimpse of life beyond the eight of us.

We also passed into a new architectural style at some point; this part of the city is much more industrial, all steel and concrete and smokestacks. With the lack of people, it looks like an abandoned factory town.

"Are night horrors a common problem?" I ask.

Simon gives Kado and Scratchy an ugly look. "In the days of the Compact, no. But in isolation, all our territories have become harder to keep safe."

Scratchy—they had a name, I definitely heard a real name—snorts at the snake. "Maybe for you. We've been doing just fine."

I roll my eyes. "Whatever, you hate each other, I get it. Look, do you need me to kill this thing or are we planning to go around? We do have a mission to get to."

Simon and Kado share a glance, then Kado answers, "Our tracking spells have diverged, so there's a choice to make: the path to the Guild's current lair avoids the monster, but the line to the human I'm tracking cuts straight through. It's unlikely he still has the mask, but he may have useful information to help us avoid a trap."

"Good enough for me. Lead on."

Scratchy gives me a dirty look and complains, "Hey, who made you the boss here?"

Hmm. Are they worth performing some kind of display of dominance on, or would it be more of a power move to just ignore them and take my authority as an unquestioned assumption? Probably the latter. I glance behind me at the puppets and command, "Five, Thirteen, prepare for combat. I want to see what you're capable of."

The doll-eyed man and woman shift their posture subtly and move closer to the rest of the group, blades held resting but ready. Scratchy complains about being ignored, but Kado shuts them down with a quiet, "Give it a rest, Eren." Ah, right, that was their name. I might remember it this time, if I bother.

The hunter leads us to an alleyway and readies his crossbow before rounding the corner, expression tight. Dante is right beside him, even more tense but ready to defend the rest of the party, while Simon and Eren hang back. I'm right there with the point team, minions to either side of me, though I'm practically relaxed compared to everyone else—scratch that, I *am* relaxed; I'm utterly confident in my ability to beat whatever this monster is.

The monster in question, revealed in plain sight as we step into view of the alleyway, is a real beauty of a beast. A mass of grasping limbs, humanoid but stretched out unnaturally, emerges from a big ball of black fuzz dotted with salivating mouths. The creature's hundred arms are pale lilac at the elongated tips of its fingers but darken to nearly black as they connect to the main body, the bulk of each arm colored a beautiful dusky purple.

Each toothy maw drips with a glistening green liquid that resembles the Platonic ideal of toxic venom. Its teeth are bloody and gorestained, and as I watch it lowers more meat into slavering jaws. The monster's many hands clutch at two halves of a human body and tear those halves into smaller and smaller chunks, limbs divided along joints and then snapped in half before each piece is fed into a different waiting mouth.

The monster perches on the side of a building, holding itself up with more of its numerous limbs, and the ground below it is stained with far more blood and gore than a single corpse could provide; it's been feeding here for a while, hasn't it?

I spare a quick glance to assess my companions: Dante looks sick, Simon is furious, and Kado and Eren are uneasy but trying to play it off. The puppets, of course, feel nothing at all.

It's a testament to how far I've come in such a short time that I don't feel the least bit frightened by this fresh abomination. It's got a lot going on, for sure, but I've survived worse when I was weaker. I honestly doubt the others even need my help to take this thing down.

So let's see how our new toys perform instead. "Five! Thirteen! Make it bleed."

The two thread-bound shells walk past me and slowly, almost lazily, raise their hands to point at the giant monster. In unison they yawn, and then together they mumble, "[Sloth]," with a tone of absolute indolence.

Their shadows elongate and then break away, slithering across the ground like leisurely serpents and moving toward the monster in the alley. The monster doesn't react to their approach, concerned only with its food, and the shadow serpents crawl up the side of the building and latch on to one of the beast's many hands. The shadows melt into the flesh of the creature, and ice begins to form at the point of contact, a thin sheet of cold that begins to creep up the monster's arm with agonizing slowness.

That gets the monster's attention. It finishes its meal and hisses at us just in time to take two flaming crossbow bolts, one to the central body and one to a waving arm. The hiss of irritation becomes a screech of pain and it pushes off the building, jumping to the alley street and immediately rushing our group as the fae flames burn green.

Dante steps forward to meet it but the puppets are faster, dashing to meet the beast with blades dragging against the ground kicking up sparks. The monster's furthest-reaching limbs grasp at the puppets and are met with swift slashes that sever hands from arms. A second round of bolts slam into the beast, fire and ice spreading across its form.

Dante joins the puppets, clumsily chopping at limbs and taking center stage while Five and Thirteen flank the beast from opposite sides. Of course, the night horror has more than enough limbs to tangle with three targets at once, even while continuing to tank crossbow bolts.

One arm gets past Five's defenses and backhands him with enough force to send him flying, his body crashing into the wall of a building and crumpling. Two hands grab hold of Thirteen's arm and twist with vicious force, tearing skin and exposing bone. Neither cry out in pain as they're inflicted grievous injury, but they do cry out.

"[Wrath]!" they both roar, voices full of hate and fury and burning, seething anger. It's a shocking amount of emotion for beings that, when I last looked at their souls, seemed utterly and implacably placid.

The spell is cast and the air ripples, and then the monster is thrown against the opposite wall from Five by an invisible force at the same time as a half dozen of its limbs twist into useless meat. Dante seems taken aback by the effect but quickly recovers and advances on the night horror to keep it occupied as it recovers from the severe damage it just took, its own injuries mirroring and exceeding what it just inflicted on Five and Thirteen.

Huh. Mirroring. That's . . .

"Hey, Chesh," I say softly. "You don't think . . . I mean, that spell. It's not . . ."

"Hmm?" The catgirl looks at me questioningly, then back at the monster fighting Dante—it lands a few hits, but nothing Dante can't easily regenerate—and then her expression blanches. "Oh. *Oh.* No, that's not, that would be . . ."

"Yeah. Yeah, you're probably right."

I hear Simon cast a healing spell behind me, trying to keep the party alive through their injuries as Five and Thirteen move back into the fray. Cheshire mutters to herself, "They're both hateful, sure, and that's certainly a similar spell, but that's just circumstantial. It could easily be a coincidence."

"Yeah." *Let's just ignore what we said five minutes ago about the Demiurge invalidating coincidences.*

Thirteen gets to the monster first and hacks at its limbs with her blade, swinging her one good arm until she lands a solid hit and manages to pin an arm and hold it in place. She calls out, "[Gluttony]!" and leans forward to take a bite out of the night horror, ripping out a chunk of its flesh and swallowing it quickly. Her injured arm convulses as the meat passes down her throat.

Five takes longer to reach the beast, having to pick himself up off the ground and dash across the alley, but then he performs the same maneuver—pin, cast, bite—and his bruises start to fade. *Parasitic transfusion, healing by consuming, paired to the sin of gluttony. What else do you and I have in common, Malice?*

"Those *are* Malice spells, aren't they?" I ask Cheshire. "Sin is one of her Truths, and it seems to be a theme. Although, now I'm wondering about [Killing Edge]."

The monster is shuddering and backing into a corner, so many of its limbs lost to blades and magic, fire burning it up as the ice seems to slow it down. My allies advance, the kill in sight.

"Oh, I should get some food out of this," I remark quickly. I conjure the bat-winged staff from my throne world and point it at the monster, my other hand holding the [Shriekwave] medallion. "[Shadowbat Swarm]. [Feast or Famine]."

A colony of bats made of living darkness burst forth from the tip of my staff, the insubstantial summons zooming across the alley and slamming into the monster. Each one is wreathed in darkness, in my signature spell, and melts into the night horror on contact. I experience soul-rending pain and the hungry euphoria of consuming a soul, but both pale to what I felt when I drank of the Demiurge.

The night horror shrieks its last as I rip out its soul and whatever's left of its life force. The beast collapses, limbs falling and going still. Dante breathes heavy and backs off after poking it a few times, but Five and Thirteen stay close and begin casting [Gluttony] again, taking their bloody fill of the monster's corpse to heal the last of their injuries.

I watch their feral consumption with fascination. Beside me, Cheshire answers my question from before.

"Those are definitely spells of Malice, yes, but [Killing Edge] isn't. I wasn't paying close enough attention to tell if it was an invocation or an artifact activation, but I know that all nine defiler spells have single word names."

Nine spells for nine sins. Could that also be a coincidence? A trick of the Demiurge? Or could she really be . . .

Interrogate later. We should see if we can steal any resonances and feed Vorpal, before the window passes.

Right.

I move to the night horror's corpse and stick Vorpal in it. Immediately the blood from the monster's wounds starts to flow toward the crimson blade, so I leave Vorpal there and start looking for resonances.

To my relief, my Gift sight seems to be separate enough from soul sight that it was spared the agony of infinity. I practice separating resonances out and examine each for usable content. I try to cut out a bit of [Wrath] and [Sloth] to work with, but there's not enough of it in this spell-rich environment so I settle for [Gluttony] and whatever the hunters used to burn the night horror. I want to be able to pull specific resonances without having to take the time to separate them, and with every try I get a little better at that.

I don't have a clear idea of what I want to do with the fae fire, so I test another experiment: I conjure a water bottle from my throne world, pour out the water, and pour in the flame resonances. I name it [Bottled Wyldfire] and seal the resonances inside exactly as I'd hoped would happen. The actual effect of the artifact doesn't matter, because it's just there to store the resonances for later.

The [Gluttony] resonances are more interesting, of course, because they're a form of parasitic transfusion that is not, as far as I can tell, connected to the Abyss like my spell. If I could shape them into something that enhances the healing factor of [Feast or Famine], that would be an insanely useful passive regardless of its active component.

But what to use? Hmm. I break off one of the night horror's larger fangs and use it as the catalyst to create [Hunger's Bite]. Its active is a weak lifesteal effect that I will definitely never use, but the passive does what I want so I'm happy.

I clear away my Gift sight to see the others all gathered around, watching me with weird expressions, aside from the puppets of course which have returned to placidity.

I wave. "Don't mind me, just doing some magical bullshit. Shall we continue?"

"You're a witch," Simon says flatly.

"She is," Kado confirms. "So is Dante, or at least that's what Imlashi thinks. Judging by how uninjured he looks right now, I'd wager his Gift is some form of regeneration."

"You know," I muse, "I was wondering why you never brought that up at the conference. Was Imlashi saving my witchiness as a backup gotcha, or was it kept hush as a tactical advantage over your rivals?"

It's annoying that Imlashi put two and two together about Dante, but in retrospect it was unavoidable, and I certainly don't care about the Myriad learning I'm a witch. Not at this point.

"In any case," I continue, "I don't think it particularly changes anything. We still have a madman to put down, and I'm still your best bet at doing that. I ask again: shall we continue?"

Simon gives me a long look, but slowly nods. Dante looks uncomfortable, but keeps quiet. Kado shrugs and starts walking down the alley.

"In here," the hunter says. He hefts his crossbow again and pushes open the door to what looks like a warehouse, keeping to one side of it and gesturing for the rest of us to look in.

"Dante first, then me," I tell the others. "Five and Thirteen at the back, the rest of you in between."

The first thing I notice inside the warehouse is all the people: dozens of civvies in plain outfits huddled against each other, looking toward the door with fear in their eyes . . . but I don't taste any fear in the air, which means these are all figments and not actually people. Hiding in here from the night horrors, presumably.

Kado files in behind me and immediately points his crossbow at the rafters. "There."

A human flickers into view, the man from the conference, as a glass orb filled with swirling darkness falls from his hand. Kado fires and the man dodges too slow, the bolt sinking into his shoulder, but then the orb smashes against the floor and a dozen screaming shadows erupt from the orb and fly into the mouths of the figments, shoving their way inside.

When the first one straightens up and smiles with wicked glee, I know we're in for a hell of a time.

II

You know, we really shouldn't be surprised to be fighting evil shadow ghost body-snatchers. I mean, that just seems like a logical progression of events.

You have a fascinating definition of "logical."

The horrible shades pour into figments through eyes and ears and mouths, crawling inside every available seam. The projected fear of the crowd is replaced by wicked smiles and a growing atmosphere of dark and insatiable hunger. Bodies twitch and shake and still, settling into predatory stances.

There's a part of me that is deeply fascinated by the mechanisms involved in this—possession can be likened to parasitism, a form of mind control that I could put to use—but that has to be secondary priority to catching the bastard making a run for it.

"[Voracious Heart]."

My heart bursts out of me and I'm already running, clothing thrown into the safety of my throne world. I feel pain and hunger, the draining of internal fluids to feed my latest arcana, and it only makes me sharper. Blood flows down my ruptured chest as inky darkness flows up my porcelain legs, the two substances mixing and swirling together as they meet. It clings to my skin, tight and warm, and extends out into spindly claws at my fingers and toes. Jagged teeth bristle along the border where the suit bares my shoulders and the top of my chest.

More blood erupts from my back, flowing out of four openings that Cheshire took the time to install. The crimson liquid forms into four tentacles of my blood that split at the ends to better grasp my targets, and one of them immediately wraps itself around Kado's waist and drags him with me as the other three push me off the ground over the mass of figments.

At a nanosecond delay I understand the reasoning behind the act: we'll need his tracking spell if the human cloaks again, so Cheshire's bringing him with us. It's strange to feel Cheshire's presence in this new kind of connection. I can feel something of her, pulsing feedback and her body on mine, but we're not overlapping like in our true hybrid form. It's both less intimate and more, somehow.

Kado is taken by a surprise and grabs at the tentacle holding him up, so I snarl at him, "Keep tracking!" and climb onto the rafters after our quarry.

"The others—"

"Will be fine!" I interrupt impatiently. I believe it, too; they have Dante, and there's no way Nyara will let him die this early in the story. At worst, he'll burn a wish to save the party, and that's one fewer wish I'll have to contend with when he inevitably betrays me for the sake of his morals or whatever. And if the shade-things crawl their way inside any of my allies, I'll just burn them out with [Feast or Famine] . . . though now I'm wondering why they didn't try that first instead of using figments. Hmm.

I don't bother looking back even as cries of panic and battle fill the room, the distinctive noise of spells breaking through the din. Something in my focused expression—or perhaps just something about my latest war form—gets through to the hunter, because he stops struggling and keeps his eyes trained on the fleeing human.

The human—I must have heard his name during the summit but I was too occupied with other matters to bother remembering it—looks just as he did last time I saw him, but this time I'm actually paying attention. Work uniform, belt of many pouches, very short hair, and dark, dark eyes. Haunted eyes, sleepless, glancing back at us furtively before he turns and picks up speed. The only change is the crossbow bolt sticking out of his shoulder, though he doesn't seem perturbed by it.

He scrambles across the metal maze overlooking the factory floor, all rickety railings and decrepit walkways, and I follow on limbs of demonic blood. He moves with the speed of desperation—and perhaps, I theorize, the speed of someone being controlled by an entity that doesn't care about bodily harm. Still, *he's only human.*

He had a head start, but I'm already catching up. Where he has to jump railings or take awkward angles to follow the walkways, I gracefully stride over everything in my path and cut a straight line for my target. Kado has fully switched from struggling against my grip to clinging tightly, and I idly wonder if he has a fear of heights like I . . . had? Have?

A quick glance down produces a wave of vertigo that proves quite conclusively that I'm still acrophobic, but the sensation is muted compared to the hunger pumping through my veins. I have prey to maul, so I refocus on that prey in time to see him toss something through the air at me.

Cheshire, saint among saints, is already on it; one of the blood tentacles not holding Kado lashes out and smacks the projectile out of the air, sending it flying away. The object—metallic, size of a fist, blinking red lights—skitters across a walkway far to the right and explodes like the grenade that it definitely absolutely was. A wave of fire and force takes out that walkway and sends twisted metal crashing to the floor below, and I'm distinctly grateful to Cheshire given how fire is shaping up to be my hard counter.

I call the bat-winged staff to my hand and consider that I should really give it a name, but that can wait till I have a soul to stuff inside. Rod of Ruin? Atiesh? Man, I'm really not taking this seriously, am I? It's hard to worry about small fry when I'm still reeling from a morning spent eating God.

Mm. I'm hungry.

I point the staff and lazily cast, "[Shadowbat Swarm]." As before, bats of living darkness burst forth and swoop after my prey. To my irritation, however, he manages to activate his strange cloaking device before they arrive. The bats flutter about aimlessly and my forward motion slows as the appendage holding my hunter brings him beside me with clear intent.

"Where?" I ask without emotion.

Kado points and calls out a specific walkway, and I dimly wish that I had a proper fireball spell to just explode the whole section. Would that be worth spending a spell slot on instead of mind control? How many spells do I get in total? Many questions I should ask Cheshire after I eat this guy.

"Random pattern search," I call to the bats. "Follow the hunter's instruction." The colony scatters about the area that Kado is still indicating and shifts as he points in a new direction, tracking the invisible man's movements.

Hmm. When I looked at their souls before, the Machinist's followers had infection that seemed . . . unintegrated. If that's the work of the shades swarming below, perhaps it can be undone even in long-term cases like this human . . . which unfortunately means I probably shouldn't eat him. Maybe I can eat him a little. A few nibbles. I can control my hunger, right? Don't answer that.

"[Feast or Famine]," I prime, and then I edit the spell mentally and tell it to scalpel out whatever shade is inside the human through whatever bat makes contact. The spell waits to be unleashed, a gentle pressure in my mind, as my minions continue their maneuvers.

Inevitably, one hits. A bat's downward swoop is arrested by an unexpected blockage, and immediately I pull the trigger on my held spell. The bat is consumed by writhing darkness that clings to the invisible form of the possessed human and an instant later that invisibility breaks as I take a bite out of the thing possessing him.

Pain spikes through me, followed by the pleasure of a meal, but both sensations feel so unexciting now. I'm still hungry for more, and as the man screams his anguish I call out to my bats, "After him!"

The shadows flutter toward their target and limbs of animated blood carry me toward my prey. There's no escaping this time, no trick he can pull out of—he pulls another grenade out of his utility belt and clicks it active.

Goddammit, I swear in my head before everything goes white.

My ears are ringing and my eyes are in agony as I blink away the blindness of the flashbang. My arm is held in front of me protectively, though I don't remember raising it, and the pseudo-symbiote suit has thinned away in areas that quickly regenerate as my vision clears. The bats are all gone, I can feel that before I see it, and more than that I can feel myself growing *hungrier* as [Voracious Heart] drinks more of my blood to heal itself. The substance of the suit seems redder now, the damaged shadowstuff replaced by liquid crimson.

My prey is running from me, sprinting away, but he hasn't recloaked and that flashbang didn't stun me long enough to stop me from lunging after him, legs moving first and then tentacles waking to life and carrying me forward. Kado is still held tight, shaking off his own disorientation.

The prey abruptly turns in a new direction and dives for one of the large windows lining the factory wall. He crashes through, glass shattering, and I flow over to the sill to see him landing unharmed in a side alley with yet another fucking gadget, what looks like a cushion of force that lowers him to the ground and then pops.

The high vantage point gives a spike of unease, but I trust Cheshire to keep me safe and I trust my body to survive the fall even if my tentacles give out. This fear is irrational, it's atavistic, it's chemical impulses in a brain that doesn't run on chemistry anymore. I won't be ruled by fear; I'm the ruler of fear. And this paltry panic is *nothing* against the hunger burning me up inside. I'm going to devour this prey and rip the secrets from his flesh. I'm going to drink as deep as I can without killing him.

And there's no way I'm letting him escape. I trade my staff for [Swarmheart] and cast, "[Carrion Heart]. [Carrion Heart]." Beetles swarm either end of the alley and melt into two copies of Madame Hornsby ready to stop the human if he tries to escape. Now there's just the show.

Cheshire lowers me to the ground right in front of my prey and she drops Kado behind him. The meat reaches for another toy to distract me with and I don't let him, body moving with strength and speed that would have seemed impossible to the Alice of a week ago, to the girl whose name I can't remember. She was weak, and I'm strength itself.

My claw-tipped hands wrap around each of his wrists and slam them together in a vise grip. He cries out in pain and I squeeze harder, and then my tentacles are wrapping around his arms and legs and trapping him with me. I wrench his hands behind his back and a tentacle tugs on his shirt to expose that delectable, vulnerable neck. I don't need any more invitation.

Fangs break skin and sink into flesh and his blood pours in like spoiled nectar. What was the taste of blood, before? Lena's tender ecstasy pulsing in my veins, Gretchen's primal need burning in my flesh, lesser hungers unfulfilling but still with some iota of good flavor.

Now, the blood is rot in my mouth. No, it's not the blood itself, not really; the flavor profile would be intriguing under other circumstances, meat and hunger with a curious sourness like a dribbling of lemon juice, but it just isn't *enough*. I'm getting hungrier, not fuller, and for all that this blood is better than some of my meals it is *ash* against the taste of Nyara.

I drink deeper, greedier, craving more, needing more, but it does nothing, less than nothing. *More, damn you!* Not a drop in the ocean of her essence, no worthy comparison to her glory and grandeur. This worthless morsel is not even a piece of a piece of infinity.

Something changes in my victim's struggles and Cheshire actually pushes him away from me, separating my fangs from his throat. He's bleeding, badly, and I remember that I was supposed to leave him alive. He'd taste better if I killed him, though. Maybe then I'd get another taste of Nyara, just another hint of—

Oh. Oh no. I'm broken, I realize with horror. *The first hit was free, and now I'm hooked.*

Focus! One problem at a time. I still need to kill the thing inside him. I reach out to grab him again but a tentacle moves to stop me, and I finally realize that Cheshire has stopped restraining him and he's not running away. He's collapsed in a heap, head in his hands, and he's . . . he's crying. I think he's crying.

My skin prickles, I shiver, and I feel a message from Cheshire: *Turn around. You need to see this.* I look away from the man I nearly murdered and see Kado clutching at his head and making anguished noises. Another subvocal message from my geist: *It's inside him, but he's fighting it.*

So the passenger jumped ship when it felt its host dying, and tried Kado, but they're essentially *both* incapacitated while that's happening. Interesting.

"End it," I instruct my geist, and immediately two tentacles reach out and grab Kado just long enough to deliver a blast of [Feast or Famine]. The pain clears away my residual feelings from whatever the hell just happened with that human, and the soulstuff is nutritious if still utterly lacking.

Kado gasps for air and shakes of whatever *he* was feeling, which I do plan on interrogating him about at some point after we deal with the remainder of this shitty ambush. He seems frazzled by the experience but not completely out of it, so I quickly come to a decision.

"Grab the guy and bring him back to the front entrance, I'll have questions for you both. I'm going to make sure the other fight is concluded."

Cheshire takes my cue and starts climbing back up the side of the building, not giving Kado opportunity to question or object. We make our way back across the factory rafters with haste, curious about the status of those we left behind. I don't expect them to be dead, but, well . . . I've been wrong before.

As I approach I can taste the scent of massacre, a heady aroma of spilt blood and lingering violence. I'm pretty sure that's not what a battlefield should smell like, but I'm a demon now and all my senses are a little bit fucked up.

The figments are all dead, or at least they look dead. Bodies scattered about the factory floor, burned and stabbed and shot. My companions did an excellent job cleaning up the unarmed civilians possessed by horrible monsters, and now they're doing a much shittier job trying to kill each other.

The snake doctor is writhing on the ground and moaning in pain, thoroughly incapacitated, while Five and Thirteen face off against Dante and Eren. Hero boy is fighting defensively and poorly, batting away the odd attack but mostly just tanking each hit with his absurd healing factor. Eren is more hiding than fighting, crouched behind a pillar and only occasionally poking their head out to line up a shot. Both puppets are focused solely on Dante.

I shout, "Five, Thirteen, stand down!" but the only response is a brief stutter in their step. Ah well, worth a try.

I touch down next to the snoctor and give him a pat on the head plus a targeted pulse of [Feast or Famine]. Pain, food, and one less shade to deal with. Simon stops writhing and starts groaning as he picks himself up, and a quick nudge from Cheshire tells me that it worked and he's not just pretending.

At my arrival the tone of the ongoing fight changes. Five redoubles his efforts to land a hit on Dante that'll actually stick, but Thirteen actually backs away and then stabs *herself* straight through the gut. She coughs up blood, bile, and the shadow creature that was puppeting her. It emerges like a cloud of ink and darts away from its host only to be torn apart by a burning crossbow bolt from the waiting Eren.

My tentacles secure Five and purge him before the thing inside can escape, and then it's done. Cheshire sweeps the area and tells me we're clear of shades, and at last I release [Voracious Heart] and reequip my outfit.

There's something hollow about losing that sense of power and hunger, but I let out a sigh of relief anyway. I think that spell is going to amplify a lot of my already existing negative traits, so I should be careful with it. I probably won't, though.

"So," I call to the room. "How'd the fight go?"

Dante looks shellshocked, his sword hanging loose while he just stares out at all the carnage. He's unharmed, of course, though his shirt's all torn up, but I remember my first two days of violence and suppress a wince at what he must be going through. He seems like a nice kid, which probably makes this a lot worse for him than it was for me.

The puppets took a few injuries that they're now attempting to heal away with [Gluttony], though they both look up at me as if asking confirmation that my question was for them. I wave them back to their meal, more interested in hearing from Simon and Scratchy.

The hunter steps out from cover and glares at me. "Woulda been a lot easier with some *help*, wouldn't it? First you hang back on the horror, then you leave us to the swarm. What use are you, bitch?" Now that I get a better look at Eren, they seem scratched up in a few places, probably from figments..

I raise an eyebrow and keep my face calm, untroubled, dismissive. "You're all alive, aren't you? I was securing the actual target. Whatever happens here doesn't matter if we fail to stop the Machinist."

Eren gestures around us and demands, "Then where *is* the target? I saw you run off with Kado after that asshole who dropped the thing, but now I don't see either of 'em. Don't fuck with me, demon."

I laugh at the idea that this hunter could do anything to stop me. "Cute. But they're just outside."

On cue, Kado arrives at the door with the Guildsman in tow. Kado pushes the recently liberated possession victim toward Simon and says simply, "He needs healing."

"Wait, what?" asks Eren, baffled at the idea of healing the enemy.

"I killed the thing possessing him, just like I purged Five, Thirteen, and Simon. All I need is a few seconds of contact and the mana to cast the spell. Now we can interrogate him for anything he knows about the Machinist's plans, and he *should* be cooperative." I give the man a glance, but he's too busy collapsing into Simon's arms to notice.

Dante looks away from the carnage and greater horror blooms across his face. "They . . . they were all just innocents. And we could have saved them. None of them needed to die."

Ah, right, that heroic heart. I realize with great annoyance that I probably have to explain figments now. Before I can say anything, Eren pipes in with, "Don't be a bleeding heart, they weren't alive to begin with."

Shock mixes with horror as Dante whirls on the hunter. "How can you say that?"

I sigh and put a hand on Dante's shoulder, stepping in before things get even more irritating. "No one's explained figments to him yet," I tell Eren. "Fuck off to your handler and stay out of my way for the next half hour. I'm sick of your face."

Scratchy seems incensed by that, but they're not stupid enough to *actually* pick a fight with the demon that killed two unkillable monsters. They stalk off and Dante watches them with a conflicted expression. "Is this . . . is this another Labyrinth thing?" he asks me.

"It is. Now walk with me and I'll explain. Oh, and try not to mind the sword, it, ah, drinks blood." I conjure Vorpal and stick it into the nearest dead figment, letting the blade drink up the blood left in the corpse. Dante looks away from that, clearly unsettled, but he doesn't try to stop me. "This world has a lot of horrors, not all of them wearing monstrous faces."

We make a slow circuit of the area, my blade drinking from each corpse before moving on to the next, as I teach Dante about figments. I try to start with the p-zombie thought experiment but he doesn't actually recognize that, so I explain it in terms with broader appeal.

"They're basically NPCs in a video game," I say as I stab another corpse. "They're not people, they don't want to be people, they don't really 'want' any-thing. They're game constructs that exist for you to interact with, to give you things, to fulfill whatever needs you have that the people around you can't or won't. If the Labyrinth is a body, then the figments are just mindless cells fol-lowing their genetic code. It's all programming, just very complex and lifelike programming that's good enough to fool most tests. They're not people."

Dante does not seem eager to take that at face value. He still has a sick look on his face and uneasy body language. "But they look like people. They talk like people. When we came in, they all looked *terrified*."

"But they weren't." Step, stab, drain. "Trust me, this is my expertise. One of my demonic abilities lets me quite literally taste it when somebody around me is afraid, and I tasted nothing when we entered the room. The figments may have looked like they were scared for their lives, but they were just pretending. It's just their role."

"Why?" he almost pleads. "Why would something like that exist? That's horrifying."

"It is! I agree." Step, stab, drain. "And the answer is even worse: they exist to make you happy. To make all of us happy. Their purpose is to serve us, to serve the real sapients that get dragged here into the Labyrinth and trapped here. They were created to make us want to stay, so that we'll stop caring that we can't go home." I can't help but laugh a little at the thought. "Even if you never wanted to go home in the first place."

Dante looks at me oddly at that, finally risking the sight of my brutal harvest, but then he looks away again and asks, "Is that . . . does everyone here just accept that? That they're not people, don't need to be treated like people?"

"No," I admit, "it's actually a point of contention." I point to where the hunters are arguing with Simon about something, the puppets watching on passively. "Carnival and Voidhearts, they're certainly happy to use the figments like toys, but not the Myriad. They have all those old-fashioned ideas about treating others with kindness, and they'd say that mistreating something that looks human but isn't only sets you up to mistreat the real humans . . . and that's if they wouldn't go so far as to care for them like real people even when they admit to lacking an internal world."

Dante is silent again, processing that. Step, stab, drain. When he speaks again, it's with a careful tone. "Alice, do you *not* want to go home? Ever?"

I laugh again, this time full-throated. "Of course not! Why the fuck would I want to go back to Earth? That world had *nothing* for me. I'm somebody here."

Dante gestures at the carnage surrounding us. "Even with all the violence in this world? All the horrible situations we're both being dragged into?"

I almost sneer, but I catch myself. "Do you think violence has left Earth? Walk through any city in America and you can find yourself bleeding out because some jackass with a gun he bought at fucking Walmart decided you looked too *different*. The only difference *here* is that now I have the power to fight back. I'm powerful here, Dante. I'm worth something. I can finally be in control of my own life."

He's silent for a moment, contemplating that. Step, stab, drain. When he speaks again his voice is softer. "Yeah, I guess you're not wrong. But, still, is there nothing you'll miss? Not even places to go or entertainment to watch, I mean like, I can't bear the idea that I'd never see my mom and dad again, or any of my friends and family. Isn't there anyone in your life you'll miss?"

Faces flicker past. My aunt who supported me, my father after he tried to reconcile, all the friends come and gone. It's a lie to say I'll miss no one at all, but I'm an inveterate liar. "Family wasn't really a luxury I had. My mom died when I was four years old, to cancer. My father made my childhood miserable. Why would I want to go back to that?"

"I'm sorry, that's—"

"Don't be," I cut him off, and he winces. Step, stab, drain.

He hesitates, but then he pushes, "Didn't you at least have friends you'll miss? Were you really that alone?"

"Oh, I had friends. They just never last. Friends run when they see the real me, the ugly, messy me, or they're too stupid and soft to run, so I have to push them away before they get hurt. It's better for everyone, easier, if I just don't let them in to begin with. And here? Here I'm a demon, and that means most everyone knows better."

This is pointlessly self-loathing, I chide. *What are you hoping to accomplish?*

Empathy, I justify. *He hears that little sob story and interprets it as a sad sack of self-hatred instead of a sincere and accurate assessment of my own behaviors.*

But was that your intent when you started, or a rationalization after the fact?

I don't answer. Step, stab, drain. "They'll all be better off without me," I say quietly. "Friends, family, everyone. I was a leech and a pest. So just drop it." I drain the last corpse and walk with purpose over to the snake doctor, leaving Dante behind.

Simon is tending the human we brought in, and I see that the crossbow bolt has been improved and lots of fluids are being administered to replace the blood I drank. The doctor gives me a frown as I approach. "You were a bit rough," he tells me, breaking off from whatever he was discussing with the hunters.

I shrug. "Can't cast spells without mana. Is he fine to talk?"

"He will be in a few minutes, though I must *insist* that you be delicate."

I smirk. "I can handle delicate. Well, while we wait, I want to hear about the fight. What happened?"

Simon seems to take a moment to decide if he's going to answer me, but then says, "As soon as I saw the possession happen I started warding the others. I managed to protect Dante and Eren, but then one of them got inside me and took me out of the fight."

"You really should have warded yourself first," I comment.

He shakes his head. "Can't. The spell can only be used to protect others." What an irritating but thematically appropriate restriction.

Eren butts in with, "What you should have done was ward the fuckin' husks. They got taken over the second one of those little shits crawled inside."

"Interesting," I murmur. "They *are* quite hollow. Perhaps they lacked the will to resist. Tell me: from your observations, both of you, why do you think those things went for the weaker figment bodies instead of trying for the real targets first?"

"They're vulnerable," Eren answers immediately, being remarkably cooperative despite the side-eye they're still giving me. "You saw how easy they die outside a host. If they'd rushed us like that, too many would have died."

"Which would have been even worse if they'd tried it at the temple," I muse. "Well, that's a satisfying answer. Let me know when I can talk to our guest."

Someone does, a few minutes later, and I sit down with the human I freed—David, I learn—to chat about the Machinist.

"So," I begin. "You're alright? Not going to die?" At his nod, I continue, "Cool, cool. Let's talk. Can you tell me what the fuck is going on?"

David shivers, but nods again. "I can try. And, thank you. Thank you so much, ma'am. You have no idea how awful it is to be trapped by one of those monsters. It's been weeks."

I see the expressions of those watching sharpen. We have a timetable now. "Give me the full story."

David takes another drink from the flask he was given. "Right. A number of weeks back, I'm not sure exactly how many, the Machinist . . . changed. He'd been stuck in a malaise for so long, trying and failing to make anything new, hiding away in his workshop apart from the rest of us, but then it all changed. He came into the building one day with a new attitude, an almost frenzied aura. He had us making parts that didn't make sense, pieces of something he wouldn't explain. And then the disappearances started.

"A few people at a time would be invited to his workshop. Some of them would come back hours later, but others would take days, and they all came back *different.* More focused, less talkative. Then they took me, and I learned why." He shivers again, complicated expressions of horror passing across his face before he continues bleakly, "Two of my closest friends led me to a room and trapped me there, and they shoved one of those torments—that's what those awful things are called—down my throat.

"It tortured me with my failures, with a lifetime of misery and despair. It wore me down until my will gave out and I couldn't hold it back anymore, and then it walked out of that room wearing my body and smiling like nothing was wrong. I helped bring a few more in for possession, and then it was done and the whole Guild was replaced by torments. Only then did we learn what was really going on.

"We had been building the components for machines that only functioned in the hands of a torment, through some strange resonant link. Cloaking devices, weapons, and the device that was used to lure the Mourner to the well. It was a plot to murder the city."

"Why?" I ask. "And what is he doing now that the first attempt failed? What is the Machinist doing with the Mourner's mask?"

"I don't know," he says. "He tells us very little, even now that the whole Guild is ensnared. The torments listen to the Machinist without question, accepting him as a proxy for their true master." David hesitates, then adds, "I think, whatever it is, it's bigger than the city. I think this was always just the first step. I . . . I think he aims to attack the Lady of Shards herself, somehow."

Alarm bells are going off in my head, tension rising. *True master? Attacking*

Katoptris? "What else can you tell me. What do you know about the torments. Who is their master? One of the Nobles?"

David shakes his head. "No, no I don't think so. The Machinist made a deal with someone, someone who gave him the torments as a gift to fulfill his end of the bargain, and he never calls that person by name. He only ever uses a title: the Emissary."

III

My blood runs cold. *The Emissary.* One of two candidates I have for the *real* master of the Labyrinth, now that Katoptris has been mostly confirmed as a victim in all this mess. If the Emissary is involved, then . . .

I realize that I'm clenching my fists and jaw, and I try to force my body language to relax. It was a lapse, but hopefully it didn't betray anything to the others. I have no interest in explaining my discoveries to them when I've only just started trusting Cheshire with that information.

"Tell me about the Emissary," I demand in my best attempt at a calm, measured voice. "Who and what are they? How does the Machinist make contact? What other gifts have they given?" It's hard to keep the intensity out of my questioning. I only just learned how important the Emissary really is, and now here they are the center of the latest plot happening. This can't be a coincidence, I refuse to believe it.

David flinches back. "I don't know, I'm sorry. All I know is the name. The torments never divulged anything more and we barely ever see the Machinist, let alone his contact."

"There has to be *something*," I hiss, "some kind of clue, anything!"

The human looks nervous, twitching, the scent of fear wafting off of him, and I have to remind myself that I am, in fact, a terrifying demon that could snuff out his life like blowing on a candle. Before he can respond or before I can try to calm him down, Simon steps in. The serpentkin healer gets between me and David and says firmly, "You are aggravating my patient, who is still weak from injuries that *you* inflicted. Leave him be, and I'll let you know when and *if* he's able to continue this talk."

I roll my eyes at the snake doctor, but I don't push it. "Fine, whatever. I'm going for a walk." I stalk off into the mazelike factory floor, and as soon as I've put some distance between myself and the others I activate that silence trick and say to Cheshire, "Okay, we should talk about that. This can't be a coincidence, right?"

Cheshire rises from my shadow and floats next to me as I pace past heavy machinery. "I can't imagine the Machinist's Emissary being any different from the one that hurt Katoptris, especially if the ultimate plan here is to hurt her again."

I run my fingers through my hair and sigh, then mutter, "This whole petty mess just got a lot more meaningful."

Cheshire raises an eyebrow. "The city at risk of dying wasn't meaningful?"

I wave a hand dismissively. "Sure, that was important or whatever, but those weren't realistic stakes; when a story starts threatening that kind of mass destruction, the chances of it actually happening are vanishingly slim, just like you don't expect the hero to actually die whenever their life is supposedly in danger. Even stories that advertise 'anyone can die' are really just using sleight of hand, like when *A Song of Ice and Fire* kills off a bunch of decoy protagonists to disguise how much plot armor the real protagonists of the story are wearing."

"You have strong opinions about that kind of thing," Cheshire smirks. "You know, most people don't actually have the attitude toward stakes that you do. Readers get quite invested in a character's well-being even when they have every reason to believe that character will survive. I think you're poisoned by genre savvy and trope analysis."

"Probably," I shrug, "and I'm not saying you can't have fun experiencing a character's sense of tension and drive, I'm just saying that in this case, for my purposes, there was never really any risk of the Machinist getting his way. He was a bit-part villain in a much grander narrative, and he was threatening consequences that I cannot imagine fitting into Nyara's master plan for me and mine."

"But now?" Cheshire prompts, playing her role perfectly.

"Now the Big Bad is involved, or at least one of the two contenders. Either the Emissary is the villain that I have to murderize to progress the main plot, break free of the Labyrinth, and attain 'salvation' for the only person I really care about besides myself, or that villain is Homura and I still probably want to kill the Emissary for the Katoptris thing and presumably further reasons that will become clear after I deal with the Machinist. This quaint little side plot just became more relevant to my goals than the death game ever was."

Cheshire goes quiet, expression unreadable, and for a moment I'm worried, but then she says softly, "Thank you. For caring, I mean."

"What? Oh! Uh." I feel my face redden and I look away hastily, trying and failing to act nonchalant. "Well, y'know, we're in this together, and stuff. It's not like I wouldn't care about you, after all we've been through."

"I've kept things from you," she insists. "You have every right to be suspicious of me. I've stabbed at your trauma on a sick god's orders and I've used your vulnerabilities to get closer to you, to try and make you love me. I'm fucked up. I'm a horrible, selfish bitch."

She's right. She's done all those things, and that's haunted me and worried me since I met her. I still have every reason to mistrust her, even if I've chosen to risk taking her at her word. And yet . . .

"Yeah, well, fuck it, I'm a bitch too." I stop my pacing and turn on Cheshire, reaching out and grabbing her by the shoulders, holding her gaze with mine. "Listen, Chesh: I'm tired of freaking out about this shit. We're both messy fuckups, alright? I'm a horrible, selfish bitch and I always hurt the people that I love, and the worst part of everything you've told me isn't the stuff that makes me panic and catastrophize in spirals about you lying to me or planning to betray me, it's not any of the things that I'm afraid of *you* doing to *me*; it's thinking that I could get away with hurting you because you don't have a choice but to keep loving me, because the Lucid Demiurge took the woman you used to be and stuck her filthy brainfucking fingers inside your soul to make you *mine*." I hesitate, words caught, almost shaking, but I don't let her go. "I'm scared of what you might do to me, and I'm scared of what I might do to you, but I'm so tired of being scared. The highest cosmic power in the universe wants to make our lives miserable, so let's take what joy we can and help each other through that hell. We're better together than we are apart, even with all our horrid baggage. Yeah?"

Cheshire looks at me with a heady mix of fear and hope and desire, and she says, "Yeah," in a choked voice, mouth dry. "Hey." She's trembling. "Can I kiss you?"

I freeze up at the question and she starts babbling apologies and leaning away but I pull her close and shut her up with my lips on hers, our first kiss, and it's awkward and it's messy and I don't really know what I'm doing but I think that I never want it to end. I bite her lip and drink her in and the taste of her lips is like the taste of ripe pomegranate in a sunless garden, and though some part of me whispers that I have damned myself with this forbidden fruit I can't really bring myself to care. If this is what winter holds, I pray it never turns to spring.

Cheshire is warm in my arms and I hug her tighter. Before her, before becoming a demon, I was so weak that I couldn't even leave a bruise if I tried to crush someone with all my might. Now I feel the power in my limbs, the power to shatter my enemies and protect those I care for, and I have her to thank for that power. This body and everything I like about it is all thanks to her.

With Cheshire, I never have to be lonely again. I never have to be misunderstood again. I know she'll be there, and she'll know how I feel and she'll get it. She wants me, she needs me, she loves me, and I think I'd burn the world to keep that love alive. She's perfect. She's mine.

A human would have up to come up for air at a certain point in a kiss like this, but neither of us are human anymore. Still, slowly and reluctantly, Cheshire parts from me. Her glance is longing, and she licks her lips to savor the taste of me.

"Gods and archdemons and even an archon," I murmur. "I'll kill them all to keep you by my side. I swear it."

"I love you," she says simply, "and I know that love was put in me by the Toymaker, but that doesn't make it any less real. I'd suffer her knives a thousand times for you, Allie." She looks beyond me and her expression sours with a sigh. "But for now we have pettier problems. The hunter is coming. I wish we could just throw him off a building and be done with him."

"I'll consider it." I turn off the throne silence and separate from Cheshire, brushing myself off and turning to glare at the new arrival.

It takes a few more moments for Kado to slouch into view. He leans against something bulky and says, "Alice. Geist. What's got you frazzled, demon? The others won't ask, but I will."

I intensify my glare. "What's it to you, reaver? Fae breathing down your neck for a status report?"

He tosses an easy grin. "I'm not the one who got all crazy eyes at the poor fucker back there. Something hit a nerve, didn't it? You know something I don't?"

"Many things," I sneer. "None of which I intend on telling you, obviously. I'm not *stupid*, Kado; I know you're going to betray us the second you have a good opportunity, probably the very moment the Machinist's body hits the floor." I conjure my tracking knife and check Averrich's location. "Right now, your master is out hunting other prey, but I know he's holding a grudge over our last encounter. Think about where you want to be when he comes to collect."

The reaver shrugs. "That's his business, not mine. But damn, you sure have changed since our first meeting, demon girl. Really grown some teeth."

"Bring out your bear again. I'd love to rip it to feathers."

He clicks his tongue. "Rude. There's no need for animal cruelty." He looks away from me and folds his arms. "But seriously, Maven: don't be so eager for a fight. You may think you're hot shit because you ate the Mourner and the Reveler, but Averrich has more up his sleeve than you realize. If I were you, I'd be looking for a way out of this city."

"Good thing you aren't."

"Yeah." He shakes his head and walks off back the way he came.

Well, that's a real mood killer.

But a useful reminder that we are in an active warzone. We can make out with the catgirl later, and much more once we're assured of our own safety. You know, with our new demonic stamina—

Focus. Focusing. We need to prepare for our duel with Averrich.

"I should try to salvage what resonances I can," I tell Cheshire. "I want to be able to craft on the fly by the time I fight the faerie."

"Right, that's a good idea." We both sound a little disappointed that we can't continue tasting each other, but it can't be helped.

I return to the entrance area and set to work dividing resonances. I'm getting better at separating them quickly and by feel, and that's what I spend the bulk of my effort on practicing. One step at a time I can feel my proficiency increasing.

There's not a lot of value to work with, though, so I end up bottling everything for later. It's a neat trick, I have to admit. By the time I'm done, David has coughed up his last piece of information, which Simon relays to me.

"He says that the Machinist's workshop is connected by mirror to the Guild's headquarters, and only to that headquarters. We'll need to get past the 'torments' to reach the entrance, and there's going to be a lot of them."

I chew my lip. "I think I can manage it. I'll brainstorm ideas for how to make that easier on the way there, but I still have the hard counter to their possession and I doubt any of them can match the power of a rising scion. Is everyone ready to walk?"

The puppets and Dante are all in perfect health, of course, and neither Kado nor Eren really took any hits, so I'm really just asking about Simon and David. They're in poorer condition but well enough to get moving, and we *are* on a ticking clock, so the healer agrees to start the march.

We gather up and file out of the factory, and immediately outside we see a woman in blue-and-red sleeveless robes inspecting the corpse of the night horror we killed.

It's the wizard. It's the wizard from the death game announcement, one of the ones that I dismissed as side fodder. What was her name? Vasquez? Up close she is absurdly buff, and she's still got that infuriatingly peaceful expression on her face.

She turns from the dead monster at our slow, halting approach, and she bows deeply to us. "Greetings and well met. My name is Valentina Vasquez, a wizard of the red and blue paths, and I wish to parley. Will you speak with me?"

I cock my head and consider how to respond to that. Simon gets to it first, saying, "We have no quarrel with you, wizard. We are on a mission of grave import."

Vasquez nods. "I see. Pray tell, kindred: why do you travel with a scion of the Abyss?"

I snort. "The fuck is it to you?"

Simon gives me a warning glance. Kado calls over, "We're trying to stop the Machinist from killing the city, and we need her strength. Why do you care?"

The wizard nods again. "I see, thank you. I intend to slay the abomination, and I do not wish to bring the rest of you to harm. If I promised to lend my talents to your cause, would you agree to stay out of our conflict?"

Immediately my tension ratches up to one hundred and I start to bristle. "Excuse you the fuck?" *Open with the bats, or get in close with our latest spell?*

Kado glances at me, then back at the wizard, and gives his answer: "Makes no difference to me. Eren, let's take a walk."

My fists clench at their rank betrayal as the reavers head back inside the factory. Simon watches them go with a sour expression, and Dante seems outright horrified. The healer shakes his head at Vasquez and says, "I will not forsake a companion, wizard. I urge you to reconsider this course of action. The demon Alice is more restrained than most of her kind, this I will attest."

"Irrelevant," the wizard says calmly. "She cannot be permitted to live. All of Pandaemonium is at stake."

Dante steps forward with hands raised. "Hey, whoah, this is crazy talk. What are you on about? Why are you wanting to kill my friend?"

Next to me, Cheshire forms from shadow and steps forward with an intense, burning expression. She hisses at the wizard, and she says, "You can't reason with a demon hunter. They're all crazed fucking lunatics."

Vasquez does not break her serenity. "I seek to prevent the end of the world, as do all demon hunters. The ninth archdemon must be murdered in the cradle. The Adversary's war must be forestalled. The Resurrection must be prevented."

The end of the world. I remember, now, Cheshire promising that to Bashe, all the way back in the nightclub when I was woozy from violent trauma. Was that an empty threat playing on this cultural touchstone, a reference to the imminent dissolution of the Labyrinth, or something more sinister? Is this part of what Nyara won't let her share? I look to Cheshire for answers and find her still looking incensed, but she meets my gaze and sighs.

"It's an insane belief that only a scattering put any stock in. Just because demons get nine spells and some mythological structures give nine layers to the Abyss doesn't mean there have to be nine archdemons, or that the crowning of the ninth will usher in 'the last war of the Adversary.'"

Wow! That's a lot of information I'm suddenly having to process! "So, okay, the spells thing is whatever, I guess, but do archdemons, like, *live* in the Abyss?"

Cheshire's face twinges with hesitation and irritance. "Well, technically, they live in a sort of 'border marches' area. Archdemon throne worlds occupy a section of Pandaemonium that exists between Firmament and the Abyss, touching all three."

Vasquez chides, "But with the bulk of their oneiric mass resting in the Abyss and reaching toward the Throne of Shadow. Do not deceive, geist."

I flash another questioning glance at Cheshire and she mutters to me, "Yes, the Throne is both a metaphysical lens *and* a physical location, and yes, she's not technically incorrect about the mass thing, *but,*"—she raises her voice—"nothing except a Leviathan can survive in a universe without cultural or rational oneiros. Even archdemons need ties to the material reality of Firmament and the cultural consciousness of the human collective to not completely unravel as sapient beings. None of them, not even Malice, would gain by enacting the Resurrection."

"The geist lies to protect its master," the wizard insists in that same calm tone. "What else explains the Abyss seeping into this closed throne world, the rise in night horror numbers across Firmament, and the plague of darkened dreams? The prince of the apocalypse will soon arrive and the Leviathans are waking in their slumber, drawn by the resonant echo of a future that may yet be averted. The Endbringer must be stopped, lest the soul of the universe rot black from Abyssal poison."

The Resurrection. The Endbringer. I'm learning whole new layers to the mythos of this setting, and I really wish the context for this education wasn't a wizard getting ready to try and murder me. I glare at the wizard in question and demand, "If your job is killing demons, then why haven't you killed Vaylin?"

"I've tried," she says without shame or regret. "I had intended to try again, but a conversation with the Beast convinced me otherwise. It told me that Vaylin intends to renounce her demonhood and claim the shard, while you rejected the shard when you were offered it before the Game's beginning."

Fuck. Simon and Dante both snap to look at me, eyes wide. *Shit.* I grimace and try to think of something clever. "The terms were too harsh, and there were complicating factors."

Vasquez shrugs. "Perhaps. It makes little difference. Vaylin is a self-removing problem, and you are not. So I ask again, companions of the Endbringer: will you not step aside?"

Cheshire fades back next to me and says quietly, "When she declares her challenge formally, which she will, start incanting. Incant like you were summoning me, but for your throne world instead. Find the words to name it and shape it."

Beside me, Simon and Dante shake their heads. "Shard or no shard," the healer says, "I won't betray an ally like that."

"I want to save people, not watch them die," says Dante. "Please don't do this."

The wizard finally allows emotion to cross her face in the form of sorrow: immense sorrow, a well of grief, but brief and quickly replaced by a return to placidity. "Your deaths will be a tragic but necessary evil." Vasquez settles into a combat stance, hands at the ready, and looks me in the eye as she declares, "Child of Shadow, Claimant the Ninth, Herald of the Resurrection, Endbringer Alice: by fire be purged, you unhallowed abomination."

As she finishes her speech, I finish mine: "World of the blood-dark sun, castle of my soul, arise!" I started incanting under my breath the second I saw her settle into that stance, and as I complete the incantation and summon my throne world I *also* pull the trigger on the castings of [Shadowbat Swarm] that I'd primed silently and kept in my brain through both speeches. I feel a sense of relief as the pressure of holding all those spells vanishes from my mind, and then I watch my handiwork.

A hundred bats explode out of my shadow and fly toward the wizard as the world of my soul swirls around me and carves into the space of Sanctuary. The street beneath me turns to a worn dirt path, the walls of the alley becoming bleak castle battlements. The empty sky of the Labyrinth is torn asunder by a bleeding eclipse, the first sun this world has ever seen.

The landscape of my soul surges down the alley like a world-changing wave, the phantasmal bats moving with it toward the waiting wizard. And then—

"Through eyes of green I see the World and its Law. With breath of white I annihilate that which defies the World and its Law. By hands of black I bring the World and its Law to life. On wings of blue I shroud the World and its Law from corruption. In soul of red I reforge myself ever closer to the perfection of the World and its Law. There can be no question: I am the instrument of the World!"

The entire incantation is spoken in seconds, and *not* in Primordial, but somehow I understand it perfectly. Each distinct sound in her brief speech conveys truly absurd quantities of information, and I'm left reeling from the depth to those few short syllables.

The air around Valentina Vasquez pulses and distorts and then ripples outward in a wave of force that tears through all my bats and my throne world. Where it passes, the mountain path turns back to the city street it was before, battlements return to alley walls, and the bleeding sun winks out. My summons disintegrate like sunlight tearing through morning mist, and when the wave reaches me it presses down on me like pressure at the bottom of the ocean, like I'm back in the clutches of the Beast's pet monster but somehow more unsettling. My skin prickles, my tongue feels heavy, and every little motion takes more effort than it should, like I'm fighting through molasses.

Beside me, Cheshire clenches her fists and grits her teeth. "I was hoping she wouldn't know that trick, and that she really did only have two Truths."

The wizard still hasn't moved at us yet, and my allies are still arrayed behind me. Dante looks confused at what just happened, and the puppets are just as placid as ever, while Simon's expression is tight and tense. *Now what? I ask myself. Why does every serious opponent I face have a way to shut down summoning?*

Vasquez, still calm and unmoved, says, "Know that the will of one cannot challenge the weight of the World. Summon your phantasms and they will crumble; cast your spells and they will falter beneath the scrutiny of divine Law; surrender to the inevitable and I shall grant you a peaceful end, the only mercy afforded the Endbringer."

Cheshire hesitates, then says to me quietly, "Try the Crest. I still don't fully trust it, but it'll damage her position."

This posturing is part of the duel, I realize. It's not a throne duel, not quite, but the bones are there: we're each asserting our worldview and then throwing magic around to back it up. Her domain trick is pesky, I'll admit, but I've got more tricks up my sleeve than the average demon, and one of them *predates* her precious fucking World.

I reach out a hand and call Vorpal to me. The air crackles, the pressure rises, and then with a *pop* the sword returns to my grip. The world bleeds where it touches the blood-red blade of my artifact weapon, the wizard's domain disrupted by the mere presence of this eldritch sword, and through the micro-rifts I see flashes of my throne world. Quietly, I'm a little relieved that I could summon Vorpal at all through the barrier that broke my first assault.

Valentina's eyes narrow at the sight of my Crest, and I call out to her with a smirk: "Some things are older than your precious Firmament. You've got a cute trick, there, but I have the weight of ages on my side. Your blood will nourish a blade that predates every dragon you worship and *laughs* at your paltry magic." *Now . . . we need an opening.* "Five, Thirteen: *kill.* [Voracious Heart]."

The puppets dash forward, blades drawn, and the spell stirs to life in my chest with sluggish grace. For a moment I worry it won't work at all, but then Vorpal flashes with red light, I catch another glimpse of my throne world through a tear in space, and at last my heart bursts out of my chest and blood and shadow begin to crawl across my body.

Five and Thirteen rush for the kill, single-minded if they can be called minded at all. They open as they did before, with a double dose of [Sloth], but their shadows dissipate the second they stretch toward the wizard, spell banished by the weight of the World.

Valentina's expression is unchanging, seeming completely careless of the murderous husks charging at her with swords at the ready, but that's part of the Game, isn't it? She's signaling that we are beneath her, that her victory is an inevitability. Beyond contempt, it is a serene conviction in her rightness and superiority.

The puppets draw near, attacking from either side and sweeping out with their blades, and Vasquez finds the moment she was waiting for. In a snap of motion her hands come together and she chants in that same strange language, "[Red Art of Transmutation: Equivalent Transposition of Self and Other]."

Five and Vasquez both flicker and then swap places, Five appearing in the wizard's space just in time to take a deep cut from Thirteen's blade. The puppets are disoriented, untangling from each other and whirling on the teleporting bastard that made one hurt the other, but the wizard is already casting again: "[Blue Art of Preservation: Freezing the Moment in Time]."

She performs a complicated hand motion and a circle of cold blue light flashes to life around Five and Thirteen, and then in another flash both are frozen solid in a block of ice, trapped in stasis stepping toward the wizard. At their feet, glowing lines like the hands of a clock point to the edges of the circle and tick down.

Okay, that's concerning. I was moving toward Vasquez after the first spell went off, but at the sight of the second I hesitate and pull back. How do I counter a move like that?

I don't have time to think of a counter because the wizard is moving again, so fast she's almost a blur, and she's coming right for me. I panic and raise Vorpal to defend myself, letting stolen instinct take over, but she's quicker than I am and she's lunging for my heart with fingers outstretched and wreathed in flame. I don't move in time, but Cheshire does, tentacles of blood already locking into place because my girlfriend is a saint and predicted the attack.

Our extra limbs fold like paper before the force and heat of the wizard's attack, but there's just enough contact for black mist to strike back and suck the moisture from her hand, skin growing taut as pain and satiation wrack my soul from the effect of [Feast or Famine]. My hand is still moving, Vorpal swinging out to try and take the wizard's head, but she dances back effortlessly from both mine and Cheshire's follow-ups.

Valentina shakes her withered hand like flicking off drops of water, grimacing at it, and then she reaches with her other hand and pulls a sword out of thin air. *Oh, right, she can conjure too.* The hilt of the weapon is dirt simple, but the entire blade is forged from some kind of red gem, or maybe multiple varieties blended together from the striations and discolorations I see. "[Valentina's Burning Blade]," she chants, and then her sword predictably catches on fire.

She lunges again but this time I'm ready for her; I hold up the bat-winged medallion I prepared yesterday and call out, "[Shriekwave]!" A terrible scream rips out of the brooch and slams into the wizard, forcing her to a stop with an expression of absolute pain and disorientation on her face, withered hand rising to clutch at her head.

That moment of disruption is all the time Dante needs to finally join the fight, coming in swinging with his own magic sword. His form is terrible and he definitely doesn't know what he's doing against a real opponent, but he has spirit!

The pain abruptly falls away from Valentina's face and she easily sidesteps, whirls around Dante, and grabs him in some cool martial arts move I don't understand. With a quick casting of "[Red Art of Transmutation: Swift Movement of the Cosmos]," she sends him flying toward Five and Thirteen, and she cancels the stasis they're under just in time for Dante to bowl over the injured Five.

I blast Vasquez with [Shriekwave] again but this time it doesn't seem to do anything and she takes the sonic attack without even flinching. To the side, I see Simon slithering at a wide berth toward the other side of the alley with the injured, and directly behind the wizard I see Thirteen rally her blade and come sprinting back in.

I hang back, not wanting to give the wizard fuel for another use of that teleportation trick, and watch my minion's valiant effort. Thirteen has better form than Dante and has deathly focus on her target, but the wizard isn't holding back anymore and moves with a fluidity and grace I barely register as she knocks Thirteen's sword out of her hands. Vasquez runs her own blade through Thirteen's chest, sinking it in deep, and I tense up waiting for the pivotal moment.

"[Wrath]!" the puppet screams, air distorting—

"[Green Art of Contemplation: Will of Negation]," the wizard calmly retorts, and with a flash of green light the puppet's spell is silenced. Vasquez slides Thirteen off her burning sword and flings the puppet toward me, not bothering to use the acceleration spell. Thirteen tumbles to a stop in the space between us, a singed hole in her chest.

Well, fuck. We're in what feels like a stalemate, now; if the wizard gets close she's at risk of [Feast or Famine], but she has more tricks than I do and hasn't slowed down in using them. Is my best bet to charge and hope my extra limbs give me the advantage I need? Can she counterspell my ace, or can I cast it faster than she can cast hers? I don't even know if her counterspell works on other scions. Maybe that's what she needed the fictional positioning for, with that speech at the start, and I pushed back enough to take that away from her?

While we stare at each other, Dante gets back on his feet and starts moving, and when she notices that the wizard dismisses her sword and conjures an ornate wizard staff instead, a length of wood and metal absolutely bedecked in glowing red gems. Alarm bells flare in my brain and I start lunging, but I'm too late. She twirls her staff and slams it to the ground, and she calls out:

"[Red Art of Transmutation: Inferno]."

Fire consumes the world, and for a moment I am back in the dark forest just outside the abandoned school: terrified, helpless, *vulnerable,* a little fish in a vast and terrible ocean. This flame lacks the green tinge of the fae, a pure and natural mix of red and orange and yellow, but it carries the same terrible heat and force that washes over me, only worse this time because I have nothing to hide behind. I take the flame, the full Inferno, and I burn.

And yet, when the Inferno passes, I am alive. I'm singed, but not charred; scalded, not seared. I feel empty and hungry and drained, but I'm still standing. The suit is gone, and I think my [Voracious Heart] must have taken the worst of the attack to keep me only relatively scathed. My doll body is naked to the world once more, heart back in my chest, covered in minor burns but still moving.

The wizard is there, Thirteen between us, Five and Dante and Simon beyond all terribly burned and on the ground, but I'm still standing and I can still move, so I take another step toward the wizard and another, running on pained legs with Vorpal pointed forward, past the burning puppet—

"[Red Art of Transmutation: Inferno]."

It hurts, oh it hurts, oh it hurts like nothing else could. I've felt heights of soul pain through my reckless abuse of [Feast or Famine], but this is a level of body pain that I've never experienced before. Worse than the sin eater breaking my bones, worse than the bolts and blades of the hunters. I feel skin peel, blood boil, a world in flames consuming me whole.

It burns and it burns and it burns and I fall to my hands and knees as fingers blacken and the air is filled with the scent of burnt hair and charred flesh. I can't hold on to Vorpal, so I have to send it back to my throne. My world is red and suffering, I cough up ash from my lungs and feel eye jelly drip down my cheeks. The pain is almost more than I can bear, it *should* be more than I can bear, but two facts cut through the haze and keep me from succumbing.

One: burning is one of the most painful ways to die, but it's not a *fast* way to die, even for an ordinary human.

Two: I am not human, and this body is just a vessel to be puppeteered by my sovereign will.

I crawl on blackened limbs to the body of Thirteen. The puppet has a hole in her chest and she's been charred to a crisp, but I can taste the scraps of life still lingering in her form. She's breathing, ragged and shallow, and her soul hasn't given up just yet.

So I take that from her. I press a burnt hand to her burnt flesh and I whisper "[Feast or Famine]," on burnt lips, and I steal the last dregs of her essence to nourish my own.

The pain lessens, my full range of motion restored, my body still wounded but well enough to stand. I clamber to my feet and take another step toward the wizard, vision still red but clear enough to see the look of shock on her face, to see her looking reluctantly impressed at my cockroach-like resilience. She's sweating, too, and her stance isn't quite as perfect as before. She's flagging. I take another step.

"[Red Art of Transmutation: Inferno]."

For a third time I drown in the wizard's flames. For a third time my world becomes pain and heat, and it takes all my willpower to keep standing through the firestorm. When it clears, I feel half-dead, but I know the wizard can't keep this up forever. She looks feverish. Burning up from the inside like she's burning us from the outside. Simon and Five are corpses beyond her. Dante regenerates, but slowly, the fire keeping him down. It's just me.

No, not entirely. Cheshire rises beside me, fear and concern radiating off her, and she looks at me with focused, pleading eyes. "Listen to me, Alice: you can do this. You're better than her, stronger than her, smarter than her. She can burn you again and again, but you'll keep getting back up, because you are fucking invincible."

That's right. Three blasts of what has to be her strongest spell and I'm still standing, charred as I am, and I'll keep standing. And then something clicks for me.

Cheshire taught me that reality itself is composed of three semiotic categories: personal meaning, cultural meaning, and what we might call rational or objective meaning. From the wizard's point of view, she called down an inferno of flame to burn me to death. That's what's happening, really, from the most objective outside view: I am burning to death, just as my allies are burning to death.

But *I'm still standing*. I'm not dying, I'm enduring. All those resonances of flame that surround us, all those oneiric echoes of our battle . . . I can change them. I can take them and I can reframe them, because I am a demon and it's my perspective that matters most.

I reach out to those resonances, to every echo of the firestorm, and I pull them away from all the other spells that have been thrown about this chaotic battlefield. I gather them and bundle them and I teach them to be something else. This is not the story of a wizard incinerating her enemies; this is the story of a demon that remains *unburned*.

In front of me, the wizard lifts her staff, movements sluggish now but still enough strength to twirl her focus object and trace patterns through the air. Another firestorm is coming, and soon.

From my throne world I pull the red hooded cloak I took from the mall, days ago, and I bring it tight around my shoulders. And as the wizard unleashes her fourth blast of flame, I pour the resonances of enduring that flame into my new cloak and I name it:

"[Mantle of the Unburned]."

When the Red Art sweeps over me, it doesn't break me. The flames still hurt, still sear my porcelain skin and drive spikes of pain deep into my bones, but I don't fall to my knees. I endure. And I take a stumbling step toward the wizard.

Valentina Vasquez looks at me with horror that I can taste like sweet wine. She whispers, "Witch," and I grin with blackened lips.

"[Mantle of the Unburned]," I repeat as I draw more resonances in to strengthen the cloak. It's easier this time, the oneiros in the air turning my way as my framing of the scene is reinforced and fed by this latest act of survival.

The wizard hesitates, the spell dying on her lips as she realizes how useless it would be to throw another Inferno at me. *You're only making me stronger.* She's breathing hard. How many enemies has she faced that could survive two blasts of Inferno? Three? It feels like a spell for killing armies.

Cheshire is beside me again, lacing her hand through mine, and she says, "Let's finish this. Together."

"Together."

We merge, and with a new burst of power we close the distance with the wizard, pushing our ravaged body to its limit. We call Vorpal to hand and lunge. Vasquez falls back into a ready stance and holds up her withered hand as she calls out, "[Blue Art of Preservation: Threshold of Impregnable Ice]!"

A crystal of ice grows out of her hand and then spreads as a thin sheet to form a wall, but that's pathetically easy for us to circumvent. We shapeshift into a bat, still charred, by all accounts of physics unable to fly but flying regardless because we are a fucking demon and the laws of physics are our bitch. We soar over the wall, swoop behind the wizard, and transform back to run her through with Vorpal.

The blade plunges through her robes, through her chest and out the other side, and together Cheshire and I speak with one voice: "[Feast or Famine]."

The wizard screams as I laugh through the pain and euphoria of burning my soul to devour hers. Her flesh withers as my burns dissipate, and when she tries to speak Cheshire runs a claw over the wizard's throat. We devour her essence until she is too weak to stand, held up only by our violent embrace, and then we drop her to the ground and loom over her.

I know, whether through some demonic intuition or the expertise of my beloved headmate, that the fight is won. The wizard has exhausted her mana and her tricks, and what little she may have had left was surely taken from her in that last exchange. This victory is mine, and I *deserve* to monologue a little before I finish her off. So I do.

I roll my shoulders, reveling in how pristine my body is just seconds after being incinerated, and I feel Cheshire separate to let me lavish in this moment alone. I nudge the wizard onto her back and then stomp on her stomach before leaning in with an ugly sneer.

"You think you have the divine eye? You think the Lucid Demiurge cares a single whit about how well you follow your precious principles?" I plunge Vorpal through her heart and let it drink deep. "I am God's favorite monster, and you are just the gristle I pick out of my teeth."

A final pulse of my signature spell devours the last of the wizard's soul, and for a glorious moment I exult in my victory. My first scion kill. Proof of my worth as a demon.

Then Kado and Eren take a few careful steps out of the warehouse, David right behind them (oh, wow, I didn't even notice him leaving). All three are looking very uneasily at the carnage, David seeming on the verge of vomit. But that's nothing compared to Dante's reaction.

Hero boy finally regenerates enough to stagger to his feet and look around, and what he sees fills him with unimaginable horror. "No, no, no!" He crouches down by Simon and I taste his spike of fear, his dread and terror, but it's swallowed by the horror of the undeniable truth that Simon is dead.

Five and Thirteen are dead too, cooked to a horrid broil by Valentina's Inferno. Dante sees their bodies, and he didn't know them, never even spoke to them, but I can tell his noble heart bleeds for their loss.

Which is why he only hesitates a moment before raising his blade skyward and shouting, "I wish for their return! Bring them back!"

Immediately, Azathoth falls upon us. Her presence fills the air and I know this for certain to be Azathoth, not Nyarlathotep. Now that I've felt both, I find Azathoth oddly . . . impersonal. I am a child in her arms, but I am one of numberless children all equally beloved. I am a bug beneath a microscope, but there's nothing exceptional about my specimen.

Azathoth loves me like she loves all life: unconditionally and without distinction. She studies me like she studies every oneiron of the universe, and she finds no difference between my existence and the ground beneath my feet, save that one is slightly better at entreating her focused attention.

Azathoth is pressure and she is presence but she is nothing more, and she would never crawl down my throat to calcify my heart and nest inside my skull. She would never course through my veins and bleed from my eyes, would never seize the nerves in my fingers or stretch my lips into a malevolent grin.

She doesn't care about me like Nyara does, and that really shouldn't disappoint me so deeply.

There is a warping in the air, a distortion that covers the corpses of Simon, Five, and Thirteen, and when I next blink my eyes the presence of the Weaver has banished and all three dead bodies are alive once more, standing and blinking as they are resurrected by the grace of Azathoth and one fool boy's wish.

Well then. One down, two to go.

IV

Everyone has a different reaction to the miracle that just happened: Five and Thirteen are as placid as ever, and they calmly pad over to stand at attention in front of me; Simon seems relieved and shocked in equal measure at his unexpected resurrection; Dante seems even more relieved than Simon, but he's glancing nervously between myself and the hunters; Kado is pale, wide-eyed, and I can taste a bit of fear wafting from his direction; Eren is eyeing the magic sword with a very hungry, covetous expression; and David just looks out of his depth.

First thing's first: putting my clothes back on. Second item on the agenda: "If you try to take it from him," I tell Eren sweetly, "I'll make your death agonizingly slow." Eren flinches and steps behind Kado.

The other hunter, usually more collected, seems on the verge of freaking out about this latest development. "That was a wish. Your sword granted a wish. That's—that's so much bigger than two witches. What are you? No, really, what are you both? A demon witch and a witch with a wish-granting blade? This isn't even close to normal."

Dante glances at me again, more nervous than before, and he says quietly, almost plaintively, "I had to."

I shrug. "Hey, you don't need to justify it to me." I look back at Kado. "Look, hunter, you're free to fuck off. Scurry back to your master and tell him the demon he wants to murder is friends with a witch that has a wishblade. See what happens. If you want answers, you should have thought of that before kidnapping me and throwing me into that maze. I don't owe you shit, and neither does Dante. Throw a fit if you like, but we have a Machinist to kill." I pause, then add, "Oh, and a key to complete."

I lift the corpse's arm to reveal a key fragment rune glowing on the back of her hand. I jerk my head at Dante. "You're holding onto them, remember? Come get it."

The kid startles, hesitates a moment, but then nods and walks over. He very gingerly taps his hand to the wizard's, and the light transfers from her to him seamlessly. I steal a glance at Kado, wondering how he'll feel about this consolidation, but he's replaced his panicked expression with something more neutral. *Hmm. Suspicious.*

"Let's keep moving before the necromancer decides to take a crack at us next, yeah?" I roll my shoulders and gesture back the way we came, out of the alley.

Dante straightens up and looks at me with concern. "Three of our party just died, Alice. Don't you think they deserve a rest?"

"They're alive now," I retort, "and they look pretty unharmed from where I'm standing. They can take a rest after I kill the Machinist and save the city. We've got a mission, remember? More lives are at stake than those in this dingy side street."

Dante quiets, and it's Simon who speaks next with a long, beleaguered sigh. "She's right. Thank you for your concern, Dante, but I'm hale enough to continue. And thank you for saving me, truly. I will not forget the debt I owe to you."

Hero boy gets embarrassed at that, all awkward and shy, and insists, "It was nothing."

"Nothing?" asks Simon. "Well, I thought my life was worth quite a bit more than that."

"I—I didn't mean it like that!" Dante stammers. "It just . . . it was the right thing to do."

Heroes, ugh. If you're going to let your heart bleed, at least pour a glass for the vampire in the room.

We marshal up and move out, falling back into the formation from before: Simon in the lead with Dante and the hunters orbiting around him, now joined by David, while my puppets create space between me and the others so I can hang back with Cheshire and chat privately. They look somber, now, haunted by our last encounter.

I can't really blame them, I suppose; burning to death is a harrowing experience, even if you survive. I imagine the only reason Dante and Simon aren't *more* shaken by the experience is lingering shock and that "I have a job to do" temporary mental resiliency. The kid will definitely be traumatized by this later.

Cheshire floats along next to me in geist form, the bottom of her legs melting into swirling shadow. Once we've been walking for a bit, she murmurs to me, "About what the wizard said, about the Endbringer . . ."

"Hey, don't worry about it," I reassure her. "I'm not mad at you for not mentioning that earlier, seriously. I know there are things you can't tell me, and a bunch more important things you've needed to tell me first. I trust you, okay?" More words blossom in my chest, dangerous words, and for a moment I tamp them down . . . but Cheshire isn't like all my other obsessive BPD fixations, and I know she won't get scared off at a bit of sudden intensity, so I say it: "I love you."

In an instant Cheshire is clinging to my side, arms wrapped around me and squeezing tightly, face buried in the space between my shoulder and neck. It'd be a tricky position if she actually had to walk alongside me, but she gets to cheat and float. I extricate my trapped arm and slip my fingers beneath her beanie hat to stroke her hair and scratch behind the cat ears. "I love you too," she tells me softly, as if it needed to be said.

"Ha. Gay."

Cheshire starts laughing, still clinging to me, and in between bouts of laughter she chokes out, "You fucking asshole," in a smitten, muffled voice. She's warm and soft, so I keep her close as we keep following the others through the streets of Sanctuary.

After a few moments, she lifts her head enough to speak clearly, eyes still bright with joy. "Thank you. I'm really grateful to hear that, what you said before. But I do think you deserve to know, if more demon hunters are going to come after you, about the nature of the Resurrection."

"Sure, spill."

Cheshire nibbles on her lip, then says, "They believe—the demon hunters, I mean—that the ninth archdemon's ascension will be the trigger for a calamitous event in which either the ninth themself or the Adversary wakes the Leviathans and either undoes their deaths or gives them new life, somehow. The song of the Leviathans will then cause the Abyss to devour all of Pandaemonium, ending the reign of Azathoth and leaving the Throne of Creation open for a new ascendant to claim."

I hum to myself as I consider that. "You know, I have to admit, that does sound like the kind of thing that Nyara would throw at us as a grand finale. But if the alternative is giving up being a demon? Giving up being with you? Bring it on."

We stay embraced for a while longer, even as our journey through the city takes us across a few more night horrors snacking on figments. Nothing we encounter troubles us like the wizard did, and all I have to do is cast a few lazy bat swarms and soul drains. I have to admit, blasting monsters with one hand while the other pets the catgirl clinging to me tightly is a very, very fun experience.

After a bit, Simon strays from the front and Cheshire melts away at his approach. I grimace at the serpentkin who has spooked my comfy girlfriend. "We close?"

"We are," he confirms, "but I wanted to ask you about those ideas you said you'd brainstorm. To fight the torments."

"Oh! Yeah, those." I lick my lips excitedly. "Okay, so: I kinda wanna make a bomb."

He stares at me blankly and I cackle, then pull out the Reveler's mask.

"Now, I don't know if this'll work, but I have an idea: when I spoke with the Beast—yes, yes, don't give me that look—she was able to craft a bespoke suite of resonances for me to shape into a magic item, and I was wondering if your eidolon could do the same thing. It's the whole city, right, or tied to the whole city? Could you call its attention, get it to pump a bunch of resonances into a tight area? If not, I can try to contact the Beast again, but who knows how that'll go."

Simon's expression is strained. "You want to make a bomb. You want the city spirit to help you make a bomb."

"A positive energy bomb! Or, well, something like that. See, the torments work off misery and despair, right? They hit you with your worst nightmares and use that to break you down, so they've gotta be absolutely brimming with the stuff, and that means they should be weak to the opposite: hopes and dreams, sunshine and rainbows, all that icky positivity. If I pour that into a bomb, I bet I could get it to stun the torments, or even kill a bunch outright. It doesn't matter if that's actually how they work, the logic makes sense to my brain and that means it should make sense to my Gift. So can you do it?"

Simon hesitates, then says, "I am unsure . . . but I will try." He calls to the others, "We're taking a stop while I commune with the eidolon. I should only be a few moments." He slithers off, leaving me alone, and then Dante comes over next.

"Hey," he starts, "so . . . did the Beast really offer you its shard? And did you know what would happen if you rejected it?"

How much should I lie here? How much can I afford to lie?

I want to downplay my actions, my complicity in this death game, but I'm not sure I can. If I try to make myself look better through deceit, the Beast could easily unravel my lies and turn Dante against me at a pivotal moment, like while he still has a wish to use against me.

So . . . the truth it is. Or at least close to it.

"She did, and I did. She told me there would be violence if I didn't take the shard. I still refused, and I don't regret that. Accepting the shard would have meant putting myself in a prison from which I would be incapable of reaching out to shatter the Labyrinth keeping us all trapped here." I let a bit of fire into my voice, channeling that zeal of righteous fury I witnessed Homura ensnaring Reska with. "I mean to free this world, Dante, and I can't do that bound to a false throne. I can't break our chains if I'm wrapped up in them."

He wavers at that, but still he presses, "All this bloodshed—"

"Was *inevitable*," I cut him off. "The people of this city are caged animals and they will keep tearing into each other over and over again until the bars of their cage are bent and broken. Trust me: this is the only way."

He falls silent, pensive, and he slowly walks away from me as Simon returns to us. The healer looks shaken, but he jerks his head toward the building he'd slipped into and says, "Follow me."

I do, and he takes me to a room brimming with white-gold light. I flicker on my Gift sight and see glimmering resonances shining with exactly the energy I was hoping for. I drink it in, eager to play with it, and I get to work shaping it and framing it and pouring it into the Reveler's mask. I craft a perfect bomb, and then I give it a name:

"[Mask of Torment's End]."

The mask starts to glow brightly, and I quickly realize the danger and send a mental shutdown command before it detonates early. *Okay, that was maybe predictable. Oops. At least we stopped it in time.*

Simon and I return to the others and I explain the plan: "I'm going to shapeshift—yes, I can do that, pay attention—into something small and hard to notice, get into the middle of the torments, then shapeshift back and drop a bomb that'll stun or kill most of them outright. You lot flood in and disable anyone not fully affected—we have a healer, avoid kill shots but otherwise go wild—while I run around eating all the torments. Sound good?"

Eren raises their hand. "How are you going to get them all in one place?"

Huh. "Well, damn, that's actually a good point. I didn't think of that."

David raises his hand. "I, um, may actually have a solution for that." I gesture for him to continue and he says, "If we wait for night to fall, we'll have our opportunity: every night the torments congregate in a chamber, one of the unused workshop spaces. I don't know what goes on inside, I'm never shown, but I see the whole Guild flock to it as soon as it gets dark."

Well, that's both incredibly suspicious and deeply concerning, but I'll take my providence where I can get it. "Cool, that works. How close are we to night?"

Simon flicks a forked tongue at the air, then says, "Not long, maybe an hour from when we would arrive at the structure if we kept at our current pace."

"Then let's get close and get ready."

We advance on the Guild's headquarters, relying on Cheshire's geist senses and Kado's evil little bird to scout ahead. We take down one more night horror before we reach our destination, but there's no sign of any other torments. It would seem that one trap was all they laid out to delay us. Overconfidence, necessity, or something worse?

We wait at a safe distance for night to fall, and when the sky clicks over into false darkness we push forward to the building itself. The Guild's headquarters is a monument to industry, plain and unadorned, all brick and smokestacks like the rest of the district. The only sign that the Guild exists here is that hammer and gear symbol over the front of the building, looking spray painted on with a stencil.

David leads us to a side entrance and gets us inside. The halls are eerie and silent, feeling almost abandoned, and there's not a soul in sight or within Cheshire's awareness. Everything's a bit dingy, and surprisingly disorganized: machinery and tools are left scattered across workbenches, gems and bits of scrap metal spilling out of their labeled containers.

We take it slow and careful, moving quietly and waiting at each bend, each door, even as Cheshire's geist senses and Simon's sense of the city reveals the same information: all the torments are inside the chamber that David is leading us to. We reach the doors of that chamber, marked as just another workshop, and the rest cluster outside as I merge with Cheshire and slip through the crack beneath the door in the form of a gnat.

Inside, around a dozen humans and kobolds in Guild attire are kneeling in a room that was at one point some kind of a workshop, but which is now very clearly a shrine to dark powers.

The room has been painted, from ceiling to walls to floor, but with a frenzied, shaky messiness to it like the kinds of scribbled drawings that a movie would put in the hands of a madman. The ceiling is coated in swirling prismatic colors like a rainbow sea, the kaleidoscope interrupted here and there by tight spheres of blue and green, as well as a few jumbles of shapes like spheres that have been cracked open and shattered, color bled to dull, lifeless brown. Pandaemonium, I grasp, and the Spheres of Firmament, some of them broken like An Talamh.

The colors darken across the walls, but it's not a gradual process; the walls are divided into eight distinct layers that get sequentially and uniformly darker as they approach the floor of the room. These darker layers are filled not with depictions of planetary bodies but rather more detailed scenes, the suggestions of individual characters and more localized objects: penitents lashed by whip and chain, bodies writhing together in lust and surrounded by an incense haze, soldiers marching in formation arrayed against each other, artists painting on canvas or singing and dancing, statues of shining gold all depicting the same man, children chasing butterflies through abstract backgrounds, family trees drowning in the bloodshed of cyclical revenge, and a bottom layer that's just brutalized bodies stacked atop each other in numberless piles. No, not numberless, I realize; one hundred million, or at least that's what it represents. These are the throne worlds of the archdemons, all eight of them, framed like eight layers of Hell descending toward the deepest, blackest pit, with Contrition at the top and Malice at the bottom.

Below Malice, below the archdemon thrones painted across the walls, the floor of the chamber is streaks of black and red and purple, the latter two so dark as to be nearly black but still visually distinguishable at a glance. It's the Abyss, that much is suggested by the rest of the chamber, but at first I don't really understand the representation here; my glimpse of the Abyss was pure darkness, after all. It's only when I fly higher and get a true overhead view that I understand what I'm seeing, even through the kneeling bodies: they're serpents. The lines of color intertwine in patterns that become clear to follow, each the body of a great serpent devouring another. The Leviathans of the Abyss, locked in their forever war.

On the far side of the chamber is the object that all the torments are kneeling toward in prayer: a statue of a robed and hooded figure, gender indistinct, holding out an open book with both hands. The bottom of the statue is carved with more serpents devouring each other, Leviathans curling around the base, and two things immediately become clear:

They're worshiping a depiction of the Emissary, and if I were to guess the archon's full title it would be "Emissary of the Abyss." A messenger for the Leviathans.

Nyara . . . you really do mean to pit me against this Resurrection, don't you? A conversation to be had with the Machinist, I suppose.

I drop behind the statue, shift back to my normal form, and pull out the mask. For maximum effect I should really be saying its name out loud, but that's a risk with the charge-up time, and it should be strong enough to knock them out even with the reduced effectiveness of a silent activation, right? Maybe. Could I whisper it?

I don't have a better idea, so I whisper, "[Mask of Torment's End]," and watch the mask start glowing. It builds and builds, and I can feel energy vibrating beneath the surface of the laughing theater mask. It hurts to hold, after a moment, and when my hands start to feel numb I pitch the mask around the side of the statue, straight into the mass of possessed, and then bolt back behind the statue and hunker down.

Shining white light blasts out, lighting up the painted room, and a wave of joy flows across me, euphoria so sharp and hot it stings. I hiss a little at the sensation, or we hiss, and then we're moving as soon as the wave is passed.

Cheshire grows tentacles out of the back ports we left for [Voracious Heart], these ones organic and looking distinctly octopus-like. We duck out from behind the statue and see the possessed all doubled over or clutching at their heads, firmly disoriented, with one of them lying on the floor not moving. The door flies open on the far side of the room, my allies ready to burst inside, but we're quicker.

Tentacles and hands reach for the nearest torments and make contact, purging them with jolts of [Feast or Famine] that wrack us with pain and pleasure but aren't enough to stop us from advancing, reaching for more targets. They don't stand a chance. But then something else moves in the room, a shadow hiding in another shadow, and before I can react there's a torment lunging at me, its shadowy mass touching my lips and—

—I'm back on Earth.

I wake up on the floor of my bedroom, in the pile of blankets I call my bed. I breathe stale air that fills all too human lungs. It's not a choice anymore, not a concession to the illusion of abandoned humanity; I breathe because I have to, because I'm human, because I'm frail and mortal and weak. I'm powerless. I'm nothing. I'm worse than nothing.

It's morning and I have to crawl out of bed because I have work in thirty minutes and that's about how long it takes me to walk there, but I'd much rather stay in bed for another minute, two, three, any scraps of time I can steal away before consigning myself to the inevitable and crawling out of bed. I throw on pants and a shirt, take a few sips of juice for breakfast, and stumble out of my apartment to go work another mind-numbing shift at my shitty retail job.

The next seven hours flash by in scraps and snippets of moments I've experienced a thousand times before: idiot asshole customers all demanding my attention over inane, pointless requests they could have taken care of themselves while management rides my ass about warranties and rewards accounts and app downloads and a half dozen other metrics that I can barely pretend to care about. We're understaffed and way too busy and the day is pain and misery, but it's nothing compared to the spike of dread I feel when my shift is ending and I see who just texted my phone.

My aunt is waiting for me outside in her car, here to pick me up from work to take me grocery shopping. She does this once a month, my too loving, too generous aunt, and every time the guilt get worse. She keeps me fed and she covers half my monthly bills—including rent—because I'm such a worthless fuck-up that I can't take care of myself without help. I'm weak. I could push for more hours, but I don't, and I could get a second job, but I don't, because I'm lazy and I'm selfish and it's just *easier* to coast by on someone else's generosity. I'm a leech. I'm a parasite.

But she loves me. I'm a drain on her finances like a ravenous lamprey and still she gives me more, offers to help every chance she has, because she's deluded herself into thinking that I deserve her love and her kindness. So there's no accusation in her voice, only concern, when she asks me how I'm doing on food and bills and my mental health, but her words are still knives in my heart. I never look her in the eyes.

My aunt drives me home after we load up on food, and as we sit in the car outside my apartment she asks if I've thought about signing up for more classes next season. I talk around it in vague terms, hedging about schedules and obligations, because I can't admit that I'm too weak and lazy to work and write and take classes all in the same span of time, and I'm too selfish to give up the one that matters least. She asks about my writing, too, because she's always been encouraging of that, and I talk about it as if it's still a real dream, as if there's some world in which it might ever prove useful to either of us, because for a worthless leech I'm still full of a liar's pride.

It hurts her. I know it hurts her, watching me struggle. I think about all the opportunities she's missed because she chose to support me instead. I think about all the hours she's wasted taking care of me. I think about the time she cried when she saw my bleeding arms and there was nothing I could say or do to comfort her, to tell her that it'll be alright, that I'd be alright, because that would be a lie too unconvincing to leave my lips. I'm hurting her just by being around her, but she loves me too much to ever push me away, so the only way to stop hurting her would be to take away the choice. To take myself out of the equation. But I was always too much of a selfish coward to ever do the world a favor and slit my own throat.

Selfish. Weak. Worthless. The mantra of my existence, the eternal chorus screaming in my brain, inescapable and inevitable. I drown myself in idle sensations, in stuffing my face and playing video games while I listen to long videos, a feast of stimulation to keep the dark thoughts at bay, but they always come back. It's a delaying action. It's pointless. I should just face the music.

The clouds roll in, mind swarming with loathing, the seething song of ruin always waiting to claim me. An old, familiar friend, welcoming me back with loving arms. *Welcome. Welcome. We've missed you. We love you. We know what's best for you. We just want to help. We just want to fix what's wrong with you.*

Pick up the knife.

There are scalpels by my desk, always there for when I need them. Individually packaged, sterile, clean. Sharp. I'm an old hand at their use. I know how to cut shallow and delicate, how to keep clear of those vulnerable veins and arteries. I know where to cut deep and unforgiving, if I changed my mind.

Which will it be this time? I wonder.

I reach for the knife—

—And I'm back in the shrine chamber, allies bursting in, possessed scattered and disoriented, the scene barely changed. Cheshire is still reaching out with our tentacles to purge more of the possessed and free them from the torments, and my hand is frozen reaching out toward one that has now already been cleansed. I breathe a sigh of relief and relax my hand.

Was that really only a few seconds? Did I experience all that in the moment it took Cheshire to cast [Feast or Famine] on the torment that got inside me?

The rest of the "battle" lasts less than a minute. The torments who shake off their disorientation are met with the full force of the hunters, puppets, and Dante, and none of them flee quickly enough to escape Cheshire's grasp. My geist scans the area and confirms that no torments remain, and then it's over. The Guild is free.

I stand there, feeling awkward and small and scared, and I hate that feeling so I latch on to my anger instead. I clench my fists and feel Cheshire's curiosity and concern brush against my thoughts, but I ignore her and call out, "Alright, now we go for the Machinist. Lead us to the mirror, David."

Immediately all of my companions look at me with varying disgruntled expressions. Dante's "Alice—" is cut off by Simon saying, "With all due respect, Ms. Alice, this has been a grueling day and we have been pushing forward from morning to nightfall. We are not demons, and we are approaching our limit."

Kado adds, "Yeah, no, we're definitely not equipped for whatever insanity that kobold bastard has cooked up for us. Not without a night's rest at the very least."

I can feel the tension rising, teeth gritting, on the verge of snapping at them all, but I can see it now: the haunted exhaustion in Dante's eyes, the tiredness weighing down everyone who isn't a lobotomized puppet. I feel fine—at least physically—but I'm not sure I even need to sleep anymore. They've been fighting all day, and their bodies aren't built for it.

David interjects, "We can, um, we can keep the mirror covered. It's the only way in or out of the workshop, to my knowledge, so the Machinist shouldn't be able to sally out."

I sigh. "Fine. Whatever. Find me in the morning."

I storm off, stalking my way through the halls of the vast structure until Cheshire gently nudges me toward a dusty room with a bunkbed that looks like it hasn't seen use in years, if ever. I kick the door shut and slump against the base of it, hugging my knees.

Cheshire separates from me and appears next to me, rising from my shadow and then sitting down next to me. She looks at me with the concern I felt earlier, that sympathy and desire to help etched into every line of her face. "Hey. Are you okay?"

I laugh darkly. "No." I'm quiet for a moment, stewing in the feelings I don't want to deal with or process, but then the words come tumbling out. "Am I a bad person? I mean, here I am in this hell dimension forced to fight for my life every day I wake up, and I'd still rather be here than back home facing the people in my life and the responsibilities of being an adult."

"What did the torment show you?"

"Earth." I clench my fists. "Just an ordinary day back on Earth. I wake up, I go to work, I deal with the mind-numbing mundanity of it all, and then my aunt picks me up and buys me groceries, and she asks me how I'm doing and I have to lie, and then I go home and bury myself in distractions until the black tide rises and I can't help but stare at the knife and think about killing myself." I hesitate, but only for a moment, and then admit, "When I got out of the vision, I was *relieved* to be back here, to be back in this world where I am a literal demon surrounded by people who hate me and want me dead, because at least here I'm worth something. I'm not a fucking leech."

"You know she never thought of you as a leech," Cheshire chides gently. "She wanted to help you because she loved you."

"I know. I know, and that—and that was the problem. She thought I deserved to be loved, but I didn't and I still don't. I don't deserve anyone's love, because I'm weak and I'm selfish and I fuck everything up." I look away from Cheshire and hug myself tighter.

I feel one of her hands lace through mine, insubstantial to the world but not to me, and then she's tugging my chin to make me look at her. "Hey." She peers up at me with those beautiful eyes, glittering gold and ice blue. "We're both messy fuck-ups, remember? So I don't give a damn if you think you don't deserve love, because I love you anyway and I always will. I love you, Alice." Her hand in mine is warm and soft, and her touch on my chin is loving yet firm.

"Thank you," I say, voice choked with emotion. "I love you too."

Cheshire leans in and kisses me, her lips the taste of sweet damnation, stealing the breath I no longer need, and when that eternal moment is finally broken she leans over to whisper in my ear, "That's pretty gay."

I laugh myself to tears, crying with mirth and anguish and all the feelings I can't express, and then we crawl into bed together and hold each other tight. I fall asleep with Cheshire in my arms, our bodies intertwined, and for a moment I am at peace.

SHADOW & GLASS VII

The labyrinth on the borderlands was nothing like either of us had expected. You could tell how nervous I was about this mission, and you did everything in your power to lift my spirits with jokes and stories and getting me to talk about my interests, but still I couldn't shake the prickling on the back of my neck as we drew nearer to where the labyrinth was sighted. I had never been this far from home, least not to my memory, and the unfamiliar landscape unsettled me long before we caught sight of the grand estate that shouldn't have existed.

No sorcerers of means lived in that part of the borderlands, and a manor of that size should have been recorded in some map or record book I would have read in my father's study, if just for his obsessive habit of tracking resource flow and labor movements. As we approached, the dissonance grew worse; the estate bore all the signs of Dawnbringer, no subordinate clan or outsider. I couldn't help but think of my grand-uncle, exiled to a faraway manor to keep him quietly out of the way.

At the front gate, a sign had been hung up: "No one lives here." We pushed past it and found the door unlocked. Inside, the estate was opulent and well-furnished but in a state of clear disuse, though signs of life were not completely absent. Most of the furniture was dusty, and a few sunstones were flickering and needed to be replaced or at least recharged, but there was food in the kitchen and plates that looked recently cleaned. The house was eerie and silent, seeming almost abandoned were it not for those little contradictions.

We explored the manor together until we found our next clue: a door with a plaque on it labeled "No one's bedroom." The room inside was hauntingly familiar, because it was a near-perfect recreation of my own. The most obvious difference was the ceiling, which had been painted to look like the night sky and glamoured with magic to make the constellations glitter and gleam.

You recognized it too. "I didn't know labyrinths did things like this," you remarked.

"They don't," I insisted. "Or, they've never been recorded to." I shivered and hugged myself, and you noticed.

"What's wrong?"

"This place . . . it just clicked for me what it is: my exile. Alone, apart. The house I'll be stuck in, my gilded cage."

"That won't happen," you told me. "I'm making sure of it, remember? If the labyrinth is trying to frighten us, it should pick better material."

There was one other conspicuous detail that didn't belong: a mirror, tall and wide, propped up against the far wall. I drew closer, curious, wondering what it meant, and then my reflection smirked at me and reached out of the mirror, grabbing me before I could react and pulling me through.

For a moment I was blinded by infinite scintillating color, and then I was falling to my hands and knees inside a completely different location. I saw clean white tile and lights overhead that gleamed like moonstones but were oddly textured, sickly in hue, and flickering even worse than the sunstones back in the estate. I saw hallways full of doors each marked with a number, a letter, and a placard reading "No one inside."

You followed seconds later, emerging right behind me and catching your bearings as we both stood up and looked around. You snarled, then, hands tight, and said, "It's a hospital, which means the labyrinth is taking potshots at me now."

It looked like no hospital I'd seen, but your world had always been described as being so strange and different from mine. You had told me the magic in your homeworld was nothing like the magic in Svijetstakla, so it only made sense that your healers would gather in very different places.

You led the way through hospital halls in search of a path out, and quickly grew agitated as you remarked on a lack of stairs or what you called "elevators." Soon, however, we learned that we were not alone; we were attacked by men and women without faces, wearing clean white uniforms and slashing at us with limbs that ended in assorted blades rather than fingers, blades I recognized as scalpels and other cutting implements that a healer might use to part bad flesh before mending it properly.

It was the most unnerved that I had ever seen you, but they still bled and died like any other pack of night horrors. You fought them with ferocity, like you needed to prove something, and I barely needed to do anything as your blood magic tore through pack after pack.

After some time, as you carved through another group of uniformed horrors, I caught a glimpse of a dark-haired woman in a pale, sheer dress flitting down a side corridor. I alerted you to her presence and helped you dispatch the remaining monsters, and then together we rushed down that passage in search of our target, what we presumed to be the same entity as had pulled me through the mirror.

Through another hallway we saw a door click closed, but the room it led to had a mirror that let us look in from the hall. I saw the dark-haired woman walk into another mirror like the one in my facsimile bedroom, vanishing inside, and then I took in the rest of the room: rows and rows of what looked like cradles for newborns, all of them marked with a tag reading "No one was born here."

I pushed the door open and carefully stepped inside, you right behind me and looking like you feared some fresh monstrosities would rise out of the cradles. A glance inside revealed them not empty as I had first assumed, but instead each held a blank-faced mask. We moved quickly to the mirror and stepped through.

We emerged back into my facsimile bedroom, sans mirror, but when I opened the door I found myself staring not at the halls of the strange estate but at a very familiar hallway within the castle. It was a hallway that I knew all too well, a corridor I had seen so many times in my nightmares and had avoided so many times in my wandering of the castle. You started to say something to me, but I didn't listen or respond, moving as if in a trance as I rounded the corner and saw the black double doors at the end of the hall. And I saw a reflection of myself, the girl in the mirror, as she gave me a wink and pulled the doors open.

Darkness burst forth from the chamber beyond and flooded the hall, rushing past me and rising up through stairwells into the castle above. I heard screaming, so much screaming, and I could almost recognize a few of the voices as castle staff, peerage, my father's advisors. In front of me, the simulacrum was gone, and the black doors were closed once more.

"Reska? What's wrong?" you asked as you came up beside me, laying a hand on my shoulder with an expression of concern. "Hey, are you okay?"

I shook my head mutely. Even knowing it was just a recreation, I couldn't help but be paralyzed with fear in the presence of the black doors that had haunted my dreams for as long as I could remember. Don't open them. You mustn't open the doors. Half-remembered voices from a thousand dreams filled my mind as I stared at the doors, and it was only when the screaming above fell to silence that I shook out of the fugue I was in. "Sorry," I whispered. "We . . . we should keep moving."

You frowned, but didn't argue. "Alright. Think the next mirror is behind those doors?"

"No!" I nearly shouted, a spike of panic shooting through me. Don't open them, you mustn't open the doors. "I . . . just trust me. We can't open those. Very bad things would happen if we did. Let's go upstairs, that's where the screaming was coming from."

Your frown deepened, but again you didn't press, and I was grateful for that. "Upstairs it is."

We traveled up and found the castle changed, its layout nothing at all like I remembered. Through winding halls rich with tapestries and lit by sunstones we ran in search of the next mirror, the next layer of that terrible labyrinth. We found more night horrors, looking like castle staff but with their heads all twisted backwards.

They came at you with kitchen knives and makeshift clubs, ignoring me entirely. You fought back with magic and Vorpal, but when I moved to assist you I was horrified at the result; whenever my magic touched one of the horrors, be it an intended attack or just a stray strand of shadow, the facsimile servant exploded in a shower of bloody gore. I nearly retched the first time I saw it, completely taken aback and distraught at the extreme, sudden violence. I didn't want to see it happen again, but the horrors kept coming, more than you could safely handle alone, so with reluctance and revulsion I began to pop serving staff like overripe grapes.

The stains, at least, I could wipe from us with my shadow. The sights would remain branded into memory.

A truly exhausting trek took us through the castle maze until we reached a reconstruction of my father's throne room, the beating heart of Sun and Sword. The throne was gone, replaced by another mirror, and arranged around the mirror in a macabre tableau were the corpses of all my father's advisors, another memory I can never forget.

Branko and Viktorija, Coin and War, were sloppy kills, limbs and necks twisted from where they had been carelessly thrown against hard stone. Mislav, the spymaster, and Zdenka, the old crone, had both been plucked of their eyes and relieved of their hearts. Emil, always so silver-tongued, had seen his tongue ripped out and his throat slit deep. Ruzica, the scornful duchess, my old dueling teacher, had been run through with ten swords and impaled against one of the throne room's pillars, hanging limply and drained of blood.

Luka and my father were nowhere to be found, and I took that for a small mercy.

I shivered at the sight of the corpses and quickly averted my gaze, though the damage had been done. You took my hand in yours for support and together we rushed to the mirror, dreading the next nightmare.

We came out in a graveyard shrouded by mist, eerie and empty, where every headstone read "No one is buried here." It was another taunt at you, Homura, and I could see the tension in you getting worse. We were both frayed, unprepared for psychological torment on top of the labyrinth's physical challenges.

The graveyard was vast and open, and there was no clear goal for us to travel toward, so we wandered aimlessly past graves until the soil began to churn. The dead rose from their rest, crawling out of the ground, but they didn't look quite dead when they got up; they were faceless and wore ragged clothes, but they bore no injuries and their skin was healthy and flushed. The not-quite-corpses began shambling away from us, all in the same direction, and in the distance I saw the first hint of firelight.

We followed the risen to their doom. We heard the wailing before we saw the bonfire, and then the mist parted and we beheld the great burning pyre. There were knights in front of it, men and women in shining white plate and resplendent heraldry, each carrying a blood-red sword. As each of the risen approached, a knight picked them up and tossed them onto the pyre. Bodies screamed without mouths as they were consumed by flame.

I felt sick, and I clung to you for support as I demanded of the knights, of whatever cruel intelligence was controlling the labyrinth, "Why? Why are you showing us any of this?"

One of the knights, a woman, tilted her head and slowly removed her helmet to reveal your face looking back at us. With impassioned voice the false Homura declared, "Some evils are necessary. Some lessons are harsh. Look upon the fires that consume the trusting, and know that from their ashes shall be forged a better world."

Then she walked into the bonfire, vanishing as her body touched the flame, and once she was gone the rest of the knights raised their swords at us. You leveled your own blade, ready for a hard fight, but I was done holding back. With each new stressor I could feel my control fraying, my shadows growing hungry and demanding to sink their teeth into whatever dared upset me. I needed an outlet. I needed an excuse. And the light of the fire cast plenty of shadows for me to direct.

With a wave of my hand and the barest modicum of will, I shaped darkness into an inexorable tide that swallowed the knights and pinned them in place like butterflies between my fingers. Shadows sharpened and pierced through armor as if it were cheap paper, their blood devoured before it ever had a chance to drip. With a second wave of my hand, I brought the mass of shadows down and crushed the knights against the dirt. Metal bent, buckled, broke, and I heard flesh squelch and bone crack as all those shining white forms were reduced to so much detritus and waste.

Still my shadows hungered, and so I fed them; I fed them the meat of their kill, stripping ruined armor bare, and then I fed them the flames of the bonfire and all the kindling beneath. When at last the darkness receded and returned safely to pool around my feet, nothing remained of the scene but scraps of twisted iron and another looming mirror.

I shivered as the shadows returned to me, my fugue state fading. I had the cold realization that I had just shown you something I never showed anyone, something that would give weight to every denouncement ever thrown my way. Here was the proof that I was the demon they all feared. Here was the monster I could be when I stopped suppressing my powers. When I stopped holding myself back for the sake of what they thought of me, useless as that was.

And yet, you looked at me with hungry eyes like I was a meal fit for a goddess. There was no fear in you, nor revulsion, nor suspicion; there was only desire. You were enamored with my magic. You wanted my magic.

"They're fools for doubting you," you told me, conviction in your voice. "You know that, right? Your magic is incredible. You have so much potential, Reska. And I know you worry about your control, you're chastised for it, but I believe in you. You just need the right environment, the right encouragement, and you can be so much more than any of them. A greater sorcerer than any to grace your clan in its entire history. You will be the star that outshines the sun."

I didn't want to argue, so I just said, "Maybe," and stepped through the mirror.

The labyrinth's final chamber was as grand as any castle, perhaps grander, and incredibly spacious. The tile floor was patterned in shades of black and red and purple, while the high vaulted ceilings dazzled with hundreds of sunstones and moonstones. Beautifully carved columns lined the chamber to either side, and in the arches between columns could be seen tall windows of stained glass that depicted images of you on the left side and images of me on the right side.

The windows closer to the entrance showed us when we were younger, scenes from our pasts that mirrored each other: loneliness and isolation, yearning and rejection, volatility and pain. At the far end of the grand hall, above a raised dais, two more windows flanked a larger centerpiece. On the left, you stood with arms outstretched, holding a celestial sphere in one hand, blood dripping from the other, with a red-eyed beast looming over your shoulder. On the right, I stood wreathed in darkness, both hands clutching a shining star to my chest, and bleeding profusely from the eyes.

The stained glass in between our depictions showed a figure I had never seen, curled and fetal, in front of a tower that every soul in Svijetstakla would have recognized: the Glass Tower at the heart of our realm, the keystone of the world, and the home of our Lady of Glass.

"Katoptris," you breathed, eyes locked on the figure in that central window. Then you looked around, took in the rest of the chamber, and scowled. "A church, really? A fucking cathedral? Ugh."

I was startled by your exclamation, and it took me a moment to process what you'd said. I wasn't wholly unfamiliar with the idea of shrines to a goddess, as there were many throughout the realm, but Sun and Sword had never been the most religious of kingdoms. Our reverence for the Lady of Glass was present but muted, superceded by more practical matters.

You strode forward and I followed along like a lost puppy, looking about nervously for the next trap to be sprung. You hissed, "This is absurd. I was expecting another dungeon, not whatever the hell this is."

I shook my head and said, "I don't understand why this is happening. None of my research on labyrinths suggested anything of the sort. They're just spawning pits for night horrors, tangled up with chaos. Never this purposeful, never this targeted."

At the end of the cathedral, shadows pooled and glass gleamed, and then a new figure stood upon the dais: Zdenka of the Lidless Eye, the Master of Lore from my father's court. "You've been neglecting your studies, child. Tsk." The wizened crone glared down at me just like the real Zdenka, though I knew her to be the same entity that had been haunting us since we first stepped into that nightmare realm. "A labyrinth is a conceptual space that reflects the mental landscape of all those who enter it. When many enter, their varied psyches vying for influence, what else could result but beautiful chaos?"

The windows behind her shattered, glass falling away into an endless swirling maelstrom of prismatic color. The rainbow light pulsed, straining the eyes, and it dazzled the senses; sight became taste became sound became touch, and I had to tear my gaze away before it overwhelmed. The false Zdenka laughed, and then with a snap of her fingers the windows reformed and the chaos was locked away.

"Of course, when only two souls enter, it becomes so much easier to personalize the labyrinth to their unique fears and desires. This wonderful maze has been constructed for your indulgence, Reska, and that of the petulant brat beside you."

"Cool story," you called over, and then you thumbed a marble from your rapier and blasted Zdenka with purple lightning, an explosion of crackling violet energy that surged down the length of Vorpal and slammed into the Master of Lore—only to be thrown back at you, reflected by a shimmering transient barrier. The lightning struck you dead on and brought you to your knees with a cry of pain, and you sucked in gasping breaths, trying to recover, as Zdenka looked on with cold disdain.

"Cool indeed," the old woman commented dryly. "Now stay down, girl, lest I need discipline you more harshly. Take your chastisement with some dignity."

You growled and immediately went for another marble, but hesitated before deploying it, eyeing the space where that barrier had appeared with trepidation. "Bitch," you muttered.

My heart had seized when you took the blast, the shadows churning at my feet, but seeing you mostly recovered I instead turned to the simulacrum of Zdenka and demanded, "What do you want? What are you?"

Zdenka raised an eyebrow, and then her appearance rapidly shifted to mimic mine, light hair and dark eyes, crone's robes becoming a floral dress. My doppelganger smiled at me. "I am you." She shifted again, hair darkening and form changing to take yours again. "I am her." Then her form split down the middle, left half yours and right half mine, and she said, "I am no one."

You gritted your teeth and pushed back to your feet, standing up straight and pointing Vorpal at the two-faced reflection. "Enamored of that phrase, aren't you? No one, from cradle to the grave. No one lives, no one dies, no one is forgotten. Well I'm not no one, and neither is she."

The gestalt entity laughed. "What would you know of the princess, Homura Bloodfallen? You don't understand the first thing about her."

"That's not true!" I insisted. "Homura is the only one who understands me."

The gestalt morphed to Ruzica and laughed at me. "Fool girl, you think she even cares about you? She's just using you to get the throne. She wants to feel like she's special, like she's important. She'll take any excuse to feel like she matters, and she'd burn that whole castle and everyone inside if she thought it'd get her a spot at the top of the world."

You snarled beside me, brimming with rage. "They deserve to burn! There must be justice for what they've done to her. They'll pay for all their sins. That's what this is about. That's what this has always been about."

The entity shifted to a man I'd never seen before, tall and haggard, who you recognized with narrowed eyes and clenched fists. "And what of your sins?" he asked. The entity morphed again, this time a sickly woman who shared your eyes, and your expression grew pained before tightening. "Your birth is a sin," she spoke with sorrow, "and it follows you forever."

You clutched your blade and spat, "Do you think this will deter me? Do you think this will hurt me? Your taunts are empty and meaningless."

The simulacrum of your mother laughed bitterly, and then your father looked down at you with cold fury. "No, I don't think this will stop you. You've killed your mother once already, after all; if you hadn't been born, she might have lived. You've known that all your life, seen it in the way I looked at you. And you've dreamed of killing me more times than you can count; you'd slit my throat and call it justice, burn with hate and call it righteous. But tell me, truly: what have you done to earn this life you've stolen at our expense?"

In a flash you were lunging at the entity, Vorpal surging with red and silver light, purple and green joining from spent marbles. "Go to hell!" you screamed, and as your blade neared the entity and its barrier sprang to life you shouted "Reversal!"

Sword clashed against shield, energy crackling and reflecting back on itself over and over, your magic straining against the entity's, and for a moment I saw the barrier crack, but then with a final surge of power the magic reflected back on you once more and sent you flying away from the mirage of your father. You slammed into one of the pillars, hard, and slumped at its base.

"Homura!" I cried, and took a step toward you, but then the entity changed forms and took the shape of my father, King Dawnbringer, in all his golden glory.

The illusion of my father commanded, "Stop!" and despite myself I skidded to a halt, frozen by fear, paralyzed at the sight of a man I knew wasn't really my father but still couldn't stop myself from wilting before, just a scared little girl out of her depth. He shook his head, disgusted with me. "Look at the company you keep, my worthless daughter. You invite this mangy dog into our house, feed her our scraps, and then she bites the giving hand. Is it any wonder you'll always be no one in my eye?"

It was like being back in court, withering under his scorn, the fires of rebellion snuffed out by his overwhelming presence. My shadows were growing more agitated, my control fraying as fear and anger and concern warred within me. I needed to help you. I needed to stand up to him. I needed to control myself. I could do none of those things, weak and worthless and helpless, and my shadows undulated and sharpened as they spun around me.

You propped yourself up on one arm, looking wounded and weary but still full of rage. You crushed a marble in your hand and stumbled to your feet, using the column to steady yourself, energy seeming to rush back into you as you rose. "You want a fight," you snarled, "pick it with me. But shut up with these blatant lies. Reska's not no one, and she deserves better than this—from you, from her real father, from every damned soul in that court."

The false king morphed into the form of Luka, and then he smirked with his too-perfect face. "Tell me, Lady Bloodfallen: what does my sister deserve? Please, be frank with us. I'm dying to hear it."

"She deserves respect! Reska is better than you, better than all those simpering courtiers, better than everyone in that castle and countryside and all the lands beyond, and she deserves to see that whole rotten kingdom kneel before her and chant her name in praise. She deserves to finally be acknowledged as a princess, not a pariah—and then, with my help, a queen. I will help her attain everything she deserves: hearts and minds and that Sunlit Throne."

Luka laughed. "Oh, you really are a fool, aren't you? Reska isn't like you, Homura. You're terrified of being no one because you can't stand the idea of being irrelevant, unimportant, replaceable. You want the attention. You need the limelight. It burns you up that anyone in the world wouldn't know your name. But Reska? She just needs to matter to someone, anyone, just a single person who will show her that she is loved and wanted. That she's not no one to them. That's what she wants from you, Homura, not any throne or crown. Can you give that to her?"

You didn't hesitate. "Of course I can."

Again, Luka laughed. "And that, my dear fool, is exactly what she fears most."

And then Luka was gone, and in his place stood a woman I had only ever seen in sketches and paintings: my mother. Her face so close to mine in every curve and angle, her hair the same pale blonde, her lips the same shade and shape, every detail like mine but just older and kinder, crinkle lines around her mouth and around her eyes . . . those gleaming, golden eyes. Those eyes so unlike mine, those eyes that could never be mine.

"I am your original sin," my mother told me gently. "I am the shadow that haunts you. I am the murder that cannot be forgiven."

My heart pounded and mind went blank. I knew it wasn't her, it couldn't be her, I felt so stupid for reacting at all, but I couldn't help it. The shadows writhed around me and lashed out at random, carving lines in the tile, and I tried to force them back, to settle them, but I lacked the composure.

The phantom tilted her head as a strand of darkness reached for her and wavered at the threshold between chamber and dais. "Going to kill your mother twice, darling?"

I couldn't breathe, or maybe I was breathing too much, thoughts scattered like so much noise. You stepped in front of me as if protecting me, shielding me, face hard and Vorpal ready. "Neither of us killed our mothers," you said with burning conviction that I couldn't share. "And you are not Reska's mother."

"No," the fake admitted freely. "But that doesn't change how she feels, does it?"

I felt pain, guilt, grief, and regret. All my fault. The reason my father hates me. The reason the whole castle fears me. It was my fault, it must have been. A tear streaked down my cheek, and then another.

The image of my mother became an image of me again, and I felt relief that lasted only until she opened her mouth. "I feel what she feels," my doppelganger told you. "I want what she wants. Why else would I take such relish in her anguish? I want to hurt her. I want to make her suffer. I want to make her pay for all her sins. I want her to admit the truth of her existence and every secret fear and yearning, and I want her to admit what she really is, deep down: a monster."

You looked back at me with sincerity and concern and love that hurt worst of all. "You're not a monster, Reska. Don't let anyone ever tell you that you are. They may call you a monster, but you'll never be a monster to me." My heart ached and I kept crying, unable to speak.

My reflection laughed. "She may not be a monster to you, but she is one to herself. Would you like to know why?"

"I'd like to kill you slowly, shapeshifter," you remarked with tranquil fury, slipping another marble of crystallized magic from the hilt of your sword.

"Ha," she said, and then I blinked my eyes and she had traded places with you, standing right in front of me while you were up on the dais. You tried to take a step toward us, reached for us, but you slammed against an invisible wall separating the room. You were trapped behind glass, and you shouted but your voice didn't carry, though I somehow knew you would be able to hear everything the reflection said.

The false Reska grabbed me by the wrists and grinned with wicked glee, eyes turning pitch black. "You see, Homura, what you have to know about Reska is that she really is as dangerous as she tells you. She's volatile. She's a threat. She's always on the verge of snapping and someone around her getting hurt."

My shadows churned, swarmed, begged to be unleashed. I couldn't move or speak, frozen, warring against conflicting emotions as I tried desperately to control my magic, to tame the swirling shadows. I wanted to deny her words, but how could I when I still couldn't control my magic? I was proving her right just like I'd proved my father right when I stormed into the throne room, or dozens of other times that I had lost control of my magic like a child full of chaos.

"She's terrified of hurting someone. Terrified of losing control. She'd rather destroy herself than risk letting another come to harm."

The darkness was alive, liquid and solid and gas, moving around us and dancing to the song of my fraying psyche. A stray tendril brushed against her cheek and split the skin of a face that looked like mine. Horns sprouted from her head and grew, and the hands around my wrists became claws that dug in and drew blood, the same blood as dripped from her.

"But you know, Homura, that's not what makes a monster. If Reska locked herself in a tower far away and hid from the world, alone with her magic and her fear and all her self-destructive tendencies, well, then she'd just be a tragedy."

Horns and claws receded, and black tears ran down the false Reska's face, her expression distorted in liar's anguish.

With sickly sweet voice, she said, "What makes her a monster, my dear, is the exception: you." My reflection became your reflection, lovely Homura, charming and rakish, with that signature manic grin. Her hands around my wrists weren't harsh anymore, nor cutting; they were gentle, firm, and warm. "Hey there, princess," she purred in your voice.

"No," I whispered, pleaded, voice nearly too soft and plaintive to be heard. I wanted to beg her to stop, but that pathetic little cry was the most that could escape my throat.

"Oh, Reska," she chuckled. "You're so scared to let anyone in. You think that if you let yourself feel anything too sharp or too bright you might become just as dangerous as when you're in a fell mood and your shadows start snapping."

The darkness curled around her, vicious and hungry and scared and longing, brushing so close to her body but always retracting at the last moment.

"You think that if you open your heart to someone and let them in, they'll go the way of your dear old mother. You have to keep to yourself, isolate yourself, stay lonely. You know that, to do the right thing, you should stay away from the pretty girl with dark eyes and a silver tongue. But you don't. You can't."

She chuckled again, your silver tongue speaking her twisted words, and she winked at me with those eyes so dark and so beautiful. My shadows spasmed.

"You need me, princess. You need me more than you're afraid of hurting me, and that is what makes you a monster. And the worst part of all? There's some piece of you that still thinks that maybe, just maybe, just this once, you can let yourself love me. You can be loved. You can show me who you really are, monster and all, and I'll still want you like you want me."

She leaned in, letting go of one wrist to brush a lock of hair out of my face, her lips too close to mine. I felt panic and desire and confusion and need, desperation, but it wasn't you, it wasn't really you and you were watching from the other side of the glass. Her hand strayed toward my lower lip, tugged on it.

"And then—"

A tendril of shadow sliced the fingers from her hand and she stumbled back, letting go of me. I saw her face—your face—transformed with fear and revulsion as she looked at me with eyes full of horror beginning to twist toward hate. And it wasn't you, it wasn't, but she looked just like you and like every waking nightmare I'd ever had about the moment where you finally saw me for what I really was. I love you, I need you, I can't lose you, I can't live without you. *You looked at me the way they all looked at me.* Please don't leave me. Please don't go. *I already knew the word she'd say next. I dreaded it. I was terrified of it.*

"Demon," she cried, and I lost control.

I screamed with all the anguish and longing in my heart, and my magic burst out of me like it never had before. My shadows swarmed your reflection, enveloped her, poured into her through eyes and mouth and skin. The blood from my wrists and the blood from her hand was sucked into the swirling vortex of darkness, black streaked through with red, and then it all poured inside until not a drop remained.

The false Homura shuddered. Her arms went limp. Her head drooped.

She looked up at me with pure black eyes and an expression of unadulterated adoration. "I love you," she said. "I love you. I love you. I love you."

She took a step toward me and I cried "Stop!" and she did, going still and silent but still staring at me like I was the most beautiful thing in the world.

I wanted it to be part of the entity's game, another trick, another ploy of the labyrinth to break me down, but it wasn't. I could feel the strings wrapped around her mind, her body, her very soul, and winding back to mine. I reached out to her with my will like I would to shape my shadows and found her just as pliable, just as malleable.

I willed her to step back, and she did. I willed her to change shape, and she flitted through forms until I had her stop on my own. I released my direct control, letting her move and speak again, and found the strings still there waiting to be plucked, like the strings of an instrument or those holding up a marionette.

"I love you," she said again. "I love you. I love you. I love you."

I threw up.

I was horrified and reeling, shaken to my core by the atrocity that my own magic had somehow wrought. Why can I do this? How can I do this? What's happening? No, no, no!

I knew then, that I had to be a demon, and all those hateful words from everyone in the castle had to have been right all along. What else but a demon could have done something so monstrous to another living soul?

When the contents of my stomach were emptied onto the cathedral tile, when at last the chaos in my thoughts was parted by remembrance of necessity, I clung to the nearest pillar and looked back at the reflection, and at you still trapped behind the barrier of glass.

With rasping voice I commanded, "Let her out."

The entity complied immediately, halting her mantric repetition of love to wave a hand and shatter the magical shield. You took a cautious step past the threshold line, then another, and then you looked at the entity with undisguised fascination.

"What did you do to it?" you asked me.

"I don't know!" I nearly sobbed. "This shouldn't be possible, this—this isn't magic that should exist. The soul is sacrosanct, Homura, and to defile it like this is the highest taboo. I'm a monster. I'm a demon."

"Woah, hey hey hey, it's okay, you're okay." You rushed to my side, finally registering how much distress I was in, but when you got close I shrank away. I was shaking.

"D-don't come any closer! I don't know what I'm capable of. I-I don't want that to happen to you."

You stopped. You looked at me with rapidly growing concern, and you bit your lip, silent for a moment, but then you resolved on a course of action and found your words. "I'm not afraid of you, Reska," you said gently. "I'm not going to turn on you. And whatever happened here, it doesn't make you a monster. Okay?"

I nodded tentatively, not truly believing you but desperately wanting it to be true.

"Okay." You looked back at the entity bound up in my strings, which had returned to repeating its love for me. "If you can control it, then you should, because that'll be a lot easier than trying to beat it in a fair fight. Have it send us out safely and then destroy the labyrinth on top of itself."

My instinct was rejection, shock, an insistence that it would be wrong to do that, but I couldn't voice those concerns. Not when you were defending me, comforting me, still by my side even after seeing what my magic could do to others. Could do to you, if I lost control.

So I nodded, and I gathered myself, and then I gave the false Reska its orders. I was expecting it to argue, to disobey, to have any kind of negative reaction to being told to kill itself for me, but it didn't. It just told me that it loved me, and then I was back in the estate bedroom, the mirror gone, with you by my side. The labyrinth was closed, destroyed, and that manor was the only physical mark it had left on the world.

My stomach tried to rebel again, but it was empty, so I dry heaved in a corner of the bedroom as more tears ran down my face. You were there, keeping the distance I'd asked for but as close as you could be within that range.

Through broken, sobbing laughter I told you, "I really am a monster. A demon. An abomination. It was right. They were all right."

You were silent, and that silence stretched on and filled me with fear. I was terrified, despite all your reassurances, that this would be the moment I lost you.

Instead, you asked, "Does it matter?"

"What?" I turned around, shocked enough by your question that I could finally look you in the eye again. "What do you mean, 'does it matter?' Of course it does!"

Your expression was firm, your surety as unwavering as ever. "The thing back there, the shapeshifter, it said that you just want to be important to one single person in the whole world. If that person is me, then listen to me, Reska: I don't care if you're a monster. I don't care if you're a demon. Neither of those things change how I feel about you, and they never could." You paused, gave me one breathless moment to process what you were saying, and then you asked, "May I touch your hands?"

My brain was full of noise, thoughts scattering at random, full of fear and hope and terrifying possibility. Slowly, I nodded, and you gently reached out and took my hands in yours, holding them. You were warm like sunlight breaking through the clouds on a cold and stormy day.

"You don't have to be afraid around me," you said, voice so caring and gentle. "You don't need to worry when I'm here. And you don't have to hide your feelings from me." You tilted your head. "Was that creature right, when it said that you want me, and that you want me to want you? As more than a friend, closer than that, something more . . . intimate? Something carnal and romantic and deeply loving?"

My eyes were wide, my voice stolen, but my body betrayed me with the deep blush reaching my cheeks and the hitch in my breath at each forbidden word.

You smiled, and then you asked, "Reska Ines Zelic, greatest sorcerer of the era, my dearest, closest, most beloved companion . . . do you want me to kiss you?"

Somehow, I found my voice, ragged and breathless, to reply, "Yes. Very much yes."

So you did. It was my first kiss, and it swept away all the dark clouds still lingering in my mind after the horrors of the labyrinth. You left me dizzy and light-headed, and when you broke away to let me breathe you smirked at me, clearly knowing the effect you were having. You asked, "How was it?" and I babbled, and you asked, "Do you want more?" and I begged for it.

One kiss became another, and then more, wandering hands and skin against skin, and we fell into the bed of that room and stayed there as the sun set outside, our bodies intertwined.

I fell asleep in your arms, and that night I dreamed of the doors again.

In the morning you made breakfast for me, a skill I'd never really learned, and it filled my heart with joy, but you could tell that I was still pensive about something. I assured you that it wasn't about me being a demon or about the new power I'd discovered in that final room of the labyrinth, but you still wanted to know what was I was thinking about, so at last I told you.

"You mentioned, before, that you've been having strange dreams since arriving in this world. Well, I've had a strange dream since I was small—a nightmare, repeating with only minor variation every time. I don't have it every night, but it never really goes away. In this nightmare, I'm wandering the castle, down a hallway I've seen while awake, and when I turn the corner I see a pair of black doors. There's always someone in front of the doors, someone I know. Sometimes it's Luka, sometimes Ruzica or Emil or my father. Sometimes it's my mother. They all tell me the same thing: don't open those doors, I mustn't open the doors. Every time, in every dream, I don't listen. I open the doors, and I see something that changes me. Whatever's on the other side . . . it shows me what I really am. And then the castle is drowned in darkness, and everyone dies screaming, and then I wake up."

You sipped from a mug of tea and considered what I'd said. "Have you ever gone looking?"

I hesitated, but then I answered, "Yes, once. And I found them. The doors are real, though I've never seen anyone go near them. I don't even know if anyone else can see them. I . . . I've only told one other person about those doors: my brother, Luka." I winced at a painful memory, and you caught it.

"What happened?"

"The night that I found my third affinity, I was inconsolable. I knew that, as soon as the court found out, my life would be over. Luka was the one who comforted me, who promised that he'd stick by me, because back then we were still close. I shared so much with him that night, and I told him about my dream, and about the doors. He said that, if he was the one to open them, then it would be fine, right? So he promised to go look, and to tell me what he found."

"And then?"

I was quiet, lost in remembrance, not even picking at the breakfast you'd made. You didn't push, letting me find the courage to relive that awful moment in my life. "The next morning, the whole castle knew about my third affinity. Luka had told them all, and my life as the king's daughter was over. I went to sleep that night still clinging to hope, and I woke up that morning to see it dashed on the rocks of my brother's betrayal."

Your eyes flashed with anger, body tensing. "Bastard. We'll wipe that smug grin off his lying face. I promise."

I laughed, bittersweet. "Thank you. But . . . I don't know if it's really his fault. I fear, sometimes, in the early hours after I wake from that dream, that it's all my fault. Maybe he did open those doors, and maybe what he saw inside is what drove such a wedge between us. Was it really all a lie, the moments we shared before that cursed morning?"

We finished our breakfast in silence, and you offered to take care of the dishes while I relaxed in the manor study. It was cute of you, almost quaint; we didn't even know if the estate would stay standing after we left to return for the castle, but you insisted on cleaning up after yourself.

I tried to read something, though my thoughts were still elsewhere, and at last you returned to me, mug of tea still held in one hand. You sat beside me and said, "We should open those doors."

I blinked at you, surprised and dismayed. "Homura, did you not hear my story? Opening those doors is the last thing we should do."

"I'm not convinced. If they hold answers that you've spent your whole life looking for, you deserve to hear them. And before you say it: I know you're probably worried that I'll betray you like Luka did, but I won't. I promise. Nothing beyond those doors could possibly make me turn on you, Reska."

You reached out a hand to pat mine. I wanted to believe you, but I was still so afraid. I felt so fragile and vulnerable in our newfound intimacy, and I didn't want to do anything that could risk that going away. "You don't know that. We can't."

You shrugged. "I know myself, and that's good enough for me. But if you don't want to come with, I can just open them myself and tell you what I find. Wouldn't even be that long a walk from my bedroom back in the castle."

I sat up straighter and stared at you with alarm. "What do you mean? Do you know where the doors are? Have you seen them?"

You pounded back the rest of your tea, wiped your face, and said, "Of course I do, and have. I found them the day we met."

V

I rise from sleep slowly, sense of space all fuzzy, drifting between two realities. I am Reska, curled tightly around the naked body of Homura like she'll vanish if I ease up even a little. I am Alice, relaxed and unafraid, one arm resting lightly over a fully clothed Cheshire.

It's always an odd feeling, waking up from these dreams. I don't feel like I'm ever at risk of losing myself to them or forgetting which girl I really am. It's more like . . . empathy. The more I experience Reska's ordeals, the more I share her hopes and worries and all the messiness in between. And there's a lot to think about this time.

I saw a precursor to the Labyrinth. I saw nightmares made manifest. I saw black doors that promised tragedy. I saw pain and suffering and a liar giving comfort. I saw a strange and twisted mirror to my own relationship with a girl who says she loves me.

Cheshire looks blissed out beside me, her eyes still closed, chest rising and falling evenly, a soft smile on her peaceful face as her head rests against my chest. I feel a low vibration and realize that she's actually purring, which almost gets a chuckle out of me. Her beanie fell off at some point in the night, exposing those distinctive cat ears of hers, and I idly raise my hand to scratch behind them.

This is nice. I wish we could stay like this. I wish I didn't have to worry about gods and monsters and an evil twin. I wish I could just . . . love. But I don't know how to do that, so instead I brood.

There was so much detail in that dream, so many revelations about Reska and Homura and their story. I feel like we're getting close to the end. I think my next dream might show me the moment that Homura ruined everything. I'm dreading it.

Poor Reska. She just wanted to be loved, and she fell for entirely the wrong person. I can feel Reska's heartache, and the longing, and the complicated bouquet of emotions that she still has for Homura Annatar Bloodfallen. Reska was alone and hurting, and Homura told her that she deserved better. Homura told her it was okay to be different. It's okay to be a monster.

I don't know how I should feel about that, but I know I feel *something*. Reska's story resonates with me, and I'm sure it resonated with Homura, but I don't know if Homura made the right decisions, even setting aside whether she means any of it. Reska was full of pain and self-loathing and would rather carve herself open than lash out at someone innocent, and I've been there, I empathize, and I think that she deserves love and help from someone who isn't going to betray her like Homura's about to. But . . . there's more to it.

Reska's story is a love story, and a queer love story at that, and queer people and monsters are old bedfellows in the eyes of the world. There's history, at least back on Earth and in the country I'm from, of casting queers as monsters and monsters as queers. For a long time, if you wanted a gay character in your work of media, they needed to be a villain or be dead by the end of the movie, preferably both. Plenty of essays have been written about the history of queer coding villains, especially Disney villains like Gaston, Jafar, and Ursula.

There's much harsher history, too, of violence and fearmongering beyond the big screen. Propaganda about predatory lesbians coming to disrupt the all-American nuclear family and steal away dutiful housewives, or hungry gay men leering after your sons, or trans people being called all that and then murdered for it. To be queer is to be seen as a monster even when you haven't hurt anyone. An abomination to be put down just for being different.

And sometimes, when someone calls you a monster for long enough, you want to say, "Fuck it, yeah, I'm a monster and I'm not ashamed. I'm a vampire and a lesbian and I'm going to steal your girlfriend and drink her blood, and then I'm going to have hot sweaty werewolf sex and you're not invited." There's a desire to reclaim the word in the same way we've reclaimed words like queer, and there are plenty of out and proud self-described monsterfuckers among the queer community. There's something altogether romantic about being a monster.

But Reska doesn't have that cultural context. Reska feels like she's a monster because the people around her call her a monster, and they call her that for reasons much harder to argue with than wanting to kiss another girl. She knows that she's different from everyone around her, everyone else in the whole world, and that isolates her. The lies they tell about her in the throes of their small-minded fear make her feel like she's an atrocity waiting to happen, and sometimes she loses control and she sees exactly what they're afraid of. You can't convince her that she's not a monster, not when it goes that deep. And then along comes a girl who sweeps her off her feet and tells her, "Even if you're a monster, I still love you anyway. You don't need to prove you're not a monster to love and be loved. I will love you in all your monstrosity."

And that's beautiful. That is a very beautiful and much needed message for a hurting abuse victim to hear, and it's coming from a liar whose conception of right and wrong is so deeply warped that she still fantasizes about brutally murdering everyone who's ever made her feel small.

The thing is, I think that comforting Reska in that moment *was* the right call. I even agree that a lot of Reska's issues with controlling her magic come from the hostile environment she was raised in. If it had been someone else in that scene, I could believe they really wanted to help Reska. I could call it an act of love. But coming from Homura . . . I know it was manipulation. Why would Homura be concerned about Reska stealing that mirror creature's free will when she's dreamed of having that power since she was a child?

The trouble with romanticizing monsters is that sometimes they really do hurt people, even if they don't want to. The vampire, the werewolf, the girl with a living shadow. Sometimes the word "monster" actually means something. Reska needs comfort and love and to feel like she's not just cursed forever from the moment of her birth, but she also needs *help*. And I think Homura's idea of help would just mean finding *acceptable targets* for Reska's abilities.

It doesn't feel right to blame Reska for what she did, because it was only an accident. But then, so is manslaughter. If I were in her shoes, I'd certainly think myself guilty. Of course, I always have something of a double standard when it comes to blaming myself for things I'd forgive others. If it's someone else, they deserve support and a second chance. If it's me, I deserve a bullet to the head.

Ha. Maybe that's too dark. This stuff is just . . . messy. I'm worried about what Reska is becoming, and about what Homura already is, and about what that means for me. Love and monsters.

"The problem with thinking," I muse aloud softly, "is that it inevitably leads to feeling like shit. This is why people envy jellyfish."

Cheshire opens her gorgeous eyes and smiles at me with an expression of dreamy rapture. "Would you still love me if I were a jellyfish?"

I reply, "Of course. I would feed you shrimp every day and clean the filter on your tank twice a week."

"Aw, you do care." She stretches, gives me a quick kiss, and then settles back on top of me, splayed out like a cat. "What were you brooding about?"

"I don't brood," I protest with feigned indignance, still scratching behind her ears.

"Darling, that might be weakest joke you've ever told, and I've seen the contents of your old YouTube channel."

I hiss and look away from her, immediately mortified. "That's—gah, why did Nyara show you *that* of all things? Actually, no, not even touching that one, it's deflection time. What are you so happy about, Chesh? You look like someone slipped you ecstasy."

Cheshire smiles with teeth. "You're not far off." There's hunger in her mismatched eyes as she says, "It's funny, the things you can do to a brain when you're God. Nyara scrambled a lot more than just my personality when she opened me up and took a knife to my soul. Being held by you gives me a chemical rush better than any drug I ever tried when I was living on the street. It's a neat trick, because I'm not even a chemical existence anymore, just a shadow in the dreamspace. She carved my soul with qualia of addiction and the cognitive echo of chemical fixation. I'm addicted to you, Allie, and I can't bear to be away. When you reject me, I get pangs like cold turkey. When you accept me, it's better than food and sex and sunshine."

"Oh. Uh."

She laughs, and then she hugs me tight and rubs her head into my neck. "I feel amazing right now. Here's an advantage of not having a real body anymore: most of the time, I get complete control over the signals I send and how I react to any given situation. In theory, that level of composure could make me a master manipulator, at least if I had experience in that area beyond begging for scraps in the form of a cute animal. But right now, after a whole night in your arms, after a day of being embraced, I am *euphoric*."

"Wow. Fuck, that's messed up." I stare at Cheshire awkwardly as she continues to lounge atop me and bask in the chemical cocktail of my presence. "I'm sorry? You're welcome? I have no idea how to react to that. The Demiurge is terrifying. Let's talk about something else: I was brooding about the latest Reska dream. It had a lot of meat to it and I want to hear your opinions on it, now that I have someone I can talk to about it and I'm not just flailing about in my own brain."

She props herself up on her elbows and rests her chin in her hands, still beaming. "Sure, share away."

So I tell her everything. I tell her about the labyrinth before the Labyrinth, and the mirror creature that reminds me uncomfortably of the Beast I met, and all the fears gnawing away at the princess and her lover. I tell her about the black doors. There's a dire inevitability to the story, knowing it'll all unravel.

"Most of it seems pretty cut and dry," Cheshire says, "but there are a few details that puzzle me. Like, what's the red-eyed monster looming over Homura's shoulder? Is it meant to represent her blood magic, or a hint at the Beasts of the Labyrinth, or something else entirely?"

"Yeah. I'm not sure I really understand Homura," I admit. "Is everything she says a lie, or does she really care about Reska in some twisted way? She's quick to her defense, but I don't think she really respects Reska's agency, not with how she forced the issue of the black doors. She named herself after two devils, but the mirror thing framed her as believing in some notion of 'necessary evil,' someone who believed she was making hard choices for a just cause. And that cathedral . . . Reska may feel guilt, but I think it's Homura who felt sinful and influenced that final chamber."

"Mm. Going from the theory that you and Homura share at the very least some key formative experiences, what do you think of her relationship with sin? Or, for that matter, with justice?"

I stew in that, picking my words carefully. "I think . . . if it's our birth, our sin, our fury, then maybe I do understand her. Her brain—our brain—has been broken by the context of a religious upbringing. She's a sinner, cursed with sin from the moment of her birth and drowning in it with every bad decision she's made since. And the people around her are all hypocrites for not admitting what vile sinners they are too. She's full of hate and rage and desperately trying to channel that into something righteous. She wants to believe that hurting people can be a righteous act, because it's all she wants to do. Pain that needs an outlet. A monster killing monsters."

With my free hand, I conjure Vorpal. I say, "Violence and pain, sin and justice; are these pieces of her understanding of Blood? She reached her first affinity when she swore to right the injustice that had been done to Reska. In that moment, and later in the duel with Bladesinger, she forged strength from suffering." I bite my lip, then push on. "Is it that . . . does it have to mean something? Is that what it's about? That every drop of our blood spilled by our own hand or someone else's has to be paid back in meaning, in strength, in justice for suffering?"

Vorpal weighs heavier and heavier in my hand, and then the red blade catches fire—crimson flame, like Homura wielded in her duel—and feels light as a feather. The flames flicker out, and the sword returns to normal, but I have my answer; Vorpal is awake.

Cheshire claps. "You did it! And all it took was delving a little deeper than you'd like into your lingering emotional baggage. How's it feel?"

"Garbage," I mutter as I send Vorpal back to my throne world. I sigh and sink into the mattress. "I see too much of myself in Homura. Not just the sin shit. When Reska broke that mirror monster, Homura was fascinated. I know exactly how she felt: she saw that atrocity, that violation of free will, and she thought, 'How can I make this mine?' I see the worst of myself in her."

Cheshire laughs at me, which I find a little rude, and then she pokes me hard in the chest and says, "You, Miss Broodypants, are all bark and no bite."

I frown. "Excuse you?"

"You're so eager to call yourself the bad guy, and you know why? Because it's the only way you can think of to deal with your guilty conscience. No one blames a demon for being a sinner, right? So every bad thought you've ever had and every mistake you've ever made can just get washed under the rug, and you won't have to reckon with what you've done and who you've hurt, with what you could do to change, or with whether your mistakes really do make you *unlovable*. Kill the unknown. Kill the uncertain. Be the monster."

I sit up and lean away from Cheshire, discomforted. "That's not—"

She leans in, breath hot, and she says, "It's bullshit. It's all absolute bullshit. What 'evil' have you actually done since I made you a demon? What sins are crawling down your back? Who have you hurt that wasn't trying to hurt you?"

"I made a deal with Avaya," I insist, hackles raised. "That's a pretty literal deal with a devil."

"You made a deal to kill a monster," the catgirl dismisses. "No one in this city will cry when Vaylin's gone, and there's nothing stopping you from sticking a knife in the imp's back the second she stops being useful."

"Back in the warehouse, I let those figments die. I could have saved them."

"And our target would have gotten away to warn the other torments. It was a tough call, but they didn't die for nothing."

I'm getting prickly from this argument. I snarl, "And what about my plans to kill Dante? Do you have a justification for murdering an innocent man?"

Cheshire just smiles sweetly. "I don't need one, because I call bullshit; you're not going to kill that kid, and we both know it."

I fall silent.

"You're terrified of abusing your power over me, even though I was made for that express purpose. You talk a big game about turning on Dante and Esha, but you've only *acted* to strike against Averrich and Vaylin. You act harsh and cruel to protect yourself, but deep down you still want to be a good person."

I grind my teeth and look away from her. "There's a huge gulf between wanting and being."

There's a pause, and then she says, "I can prove it to you. Do you remember when we talked about superpowers, and you asked for mind control? You had a fantasy at the ready about corrupting the masses and ruling like a god-queen, but you didn't complain when I didn't offer it, and you haven't really tried for it since. And when I told you what Nyarlathotep had done to me, you were horrified. Fascinated, yes, absolutely, but the horror was stronger. The idea compels you, but you can't overcome the distaste. The appeal of the fantasy bristles against the awful reality."

"Is that your evidence? Cheshire, I'd jump at the chance for a spell that could do that. I've held off because I don't want one that's half-assed. Once we murder Vaylin, I'm absolutely making a mind control spell."

"Why wait?" Cheshire slips off me and stands up, then cups her hands and holds them out toward me. Shadowy mist swirls within them, and a crown of blood forms amid the darkness, hovering over her outstretched fingers. She grins, her smile too wide for her face. "We don't need Vaylin. We never needed Vaylin, but especially not after that conversation with the Toymaker. Wanna hear a secret, Allie? You are so much more than *all of them*. You are a scion of Shadow, heiress to the Leviathans, and you are the Demiurge's favorite child. You could make them all listen. You could bend everyone in this building to your will. If I gave you this spell, you could use it on the hunters, on the priestess, on Averrich and Vaylin and everyone else in this whole damn city. Whoever you like, whoever gets in your way, you could grab them by the brainstem and make them love you and fear you and worship at your feet. So if you really want that . . . if you really want to bring this world to its knees and kill free will and rule on high as the demon empress of the Labyrinth . . . then just take it."

I freeze up, staring into the shimmering form of that tantalizing, terrifying spell. "How?" I ask, buying time to think. "I mean . . . how does it work? What does it do?"

"You're deflecting, darling, but I'll indulge you. It's all in your Truths. Blood can be love, and it can be bonds, and it can be bloodborne transmission. Take all your fear and your hunger, all your love, and when you mix in the corrupting influence of the Shadow Throne what you get is a perfect virus to infect the world with. We can turn your very existence into the cognitohazard ALICE that'll slip inside hearts and minds and souls and consume them with yearning for your love and fear of your disapproval. It'll make them like me, piece by piece, nearly impossible to stop, until all of Pandaemonium is just Alice and Cheshire. Become the Red Queen, the hegemon who ends the arms race. Ascend as the archdemon Malady and claim your destined Throne. Be loved. Be obeyed. You'd never have to fear betrayal again. You'd never have to be alone. Take the wheel of the world and you could build a paradise or a new hell and either way they'd all thank you for the effort. You could have everything you've ever wanted. But tell me truly, Maven Alice: is that really what you want?"

I do. I don't. I'm terrified. I'm enthralled. I don't know what I am.

There's a voice in me that says *take it, take it, and claim the dominion we rightly deserve. Aren't we owed some recompense for all our pain?*

But then I think that *pain isn't currency and justice can't be bought. Who are we to play God with the world? We'd be a monster. A contradiction of all our beliefs, a violation of all our morals. There's no ethical way to be queen of the world.*

Who cares? Who really fucking cares? Godhood is an abomination but better it be us on that throne than anyone else. We chose this path. No one expects a demon to be a good person.

That's a bullshit way of thinking. Cheshire was right. Bashe, Esha, Dante . . . they all saw good in us. If we deny that, if we spit on that promise, then all we're doing is running away. We have to be better than that.

I close my eyes and laugh. *I'm tired. I've tried. I can't live up to that. Why shouldn't I run away? Why shouldn't I take the easy road? Give me a good reason, for once in our miserable life.*

Because I wouldn't be able to live with myself if I became that kind of monster.

Then don't. Die for your morals. Leave those of us with resolve to finish the mess you made.

You wouldn't be able to live with it either.

Then I'll change. That's the whole point of being a demon, isn't it? I can take a knife to my soul and cut out all the parts that are too weak *to walk the path of a ruler. I can kill the part of me that cares about stupid, petty, worthless morals. I can cut and cut and cut until nothing is left but the raw, bleeding core of me. Till I'm just want and will. And then you wretched fools will finally be* silent *and leave me to my work.*

You're only talking to yourself, Allie.

I let out a deep breath. *Yeah. Yeah, I know. I just . . . I need to figure this out, and there's too much noise, but I am the noise, and the everything, and the nothing. Does any of that make sense?*

Breathe. Think. Take it slow. Be logical about this. We can project personalities and argue amongst ourselves all we like, but that's not going to bring us any closer to a solution. This is the psychological moment. This is our crossroads. Where should we walk?

If I accept that spell and use it, there'll be no going back. You can't erase a choice like that. And there *is* a part of me that desperately wants that power. I want to be powerful. I want to be loved. I want to live without fear. And I'm not good enough to have any of that fairly.

Sometimes I feel like all I am is rage and grief and longing. I've had moments where I felt like I'd burn the world if given half the chance. There's an ugly, twisted part of me that tells me I deserve to be the villain. I deserve to do whatever I damn well please, and I'll be justified in doing it, because pain is a justification without equals.

But pain is a liar, and the girl in my dreams warned me about those.

"Okay. I have my decision."

Cheshire looks at me expectantly, the crown still held out. "And?"

"I can't do it. I won't."

The geist smiles, and then with a flourish of her hand the crown vanishes, the dark spell it represents forever locked away. "I know. And I'm glad."

I dangle my feet off the side of the bed and put my head in my hands. "What am I, really? Avaya was right about me, when she saw my throne world and called it shallow. I've papered over chaos, but I still don't have any real answers. Demons are supposed to sharpen themselves into something pure, but I'm a mess of contradictions. I know I have to stop the Machinist, and Averrich and Vaylin, and the Noble who has my name, and maybe the Emissary . . . but that's all just reaction. It's a list of tasks, it doesn't say anything about me. It doesn't help me shape my soul."

Cheshire sits down next to me and leans against my shoulder. "Well, is there anything you want to do? Not something you have to do because it's in your way or it's the obvious quest objective, but . . . something you want to do just because you want it, fully and without caveats."

I think about that for a long moment that stretches into another, and then I look at Cheshire. For all my fears and all my doubts . . . she's been there for me. The only person across two worlds that I can really trust with the fullness of my being. She knows what I am and she loves me for it, and I'm so grateful for that . . . but it wasn't her choice. So I say, softly, "I want to save you."

The catgirl laughs. "From what?"

"She put you under the knife and stole your free will. I'm not going to forgive and forget just because the result has been convenient to me. I *will* find a way to free you. And I hope that when it's done you'll choose to still be with me. But it has to be a choice."

Cheshire boops my nose. "See? Big softie. Now let's go save Sanctuary."

She fades to black mist before I can retaliate with anything more than a hiss.

We leave our little side room and find the others still waking up and going through preparations and breakfast. I'm hungry, but I'm always hungry, and I honestly don't feel like eating regular food right now.

Dante is apart from the others, leaning against a wall and just staring into space with a complicated expression on his face. That doesn't seem like him, so I slip over and ask, "Hey, uh, are you okay?"

He startles at my approach, but quickly adjusts and offers me a nervous, half-hearted smile. "I, uh, yeah. Totally."

I raise an eyebrow.

"Okay, no, definitely not." He hesitates over his next words, then says, "I keep thinking that I want to go home, and then I feel bad about wanting that. I just . . . I wasn't ready for this. I thought I was, but I was wrong. I watched people die. I was burned alive and the only reason I'm still standing is because some higher power decided my life was worth *more* than theirs. And that's kind of messing me up."

I lean against the wall next to him. "You could, you know. Just make a wish and you'll be back in your house safe and sound, and all of this a fleeting memory."

"I know. I could. But I can't. I'd be running away."

I can't help but chuckle a little at that. "I mean, hey, I absolutely get that. But you don't owe this world anything, okay? If you want to go home, do it, and don't let anyone guilt you. This isn't your mess to clean up."

He grimaces. "If only. But the Goddess told me—"

"She lied," I cut him off. "She does that. She's a vicious two-faced prick."

Dante blinks in surprise and leans back. "What?"

"Look, I've had the vast displeasure of speaking with her twice now, and I can confidently assure you that the Lucid Demiurge is an absolute bag of dicks. She's cruel and petty and she likes to fuck with people, and that's why she dragged you here."

Cheshire fades into view beside me. "I've met her more than twice, and I second everything Alice just said. The Demiurge has personally tortured me."

Dante is aghast at that, and then he falls pensive. After another moment, he asks, "If that's true, then why didn't you tell me that before?"

"Honestly?" I shrug. "I wasn't sure how you'd react, or if you'd believe me. You seem like a decent person, but I'm a paranoiac and you have a magic sword. There was a lot to get through and you didn't have any reason to take my word over hers. It was easier to let you have that lie."

Dante goes silent again, and Cheshire fills the air. "The Toymaker never does something out of altruism. She just wanted you to entertain her. If you choose to leave, she won't stop you; she'll just focus on other toys."

He looks between the two of us. "You're really not lying, are you? That's . . . wow. I mean, that sucks."

"Yeah," I say. "I can sympathize."

Dante clenches a fist, briefly, then lets it go. "You know, I could take you with me, if you wanted. If I don't owe this world anything, then neither do you."

"Nah. I could argue our situations are very different, 'cause they are, but I don't need to go down that rabbit hole. Truth is, I don't wanna go back. And I won't if I can help it."

He looks at me with an altogether puzzled air. "Is there really nothing you'll miss? I can't imagine just leaving Earth forever and never looking back. I'm already homesick and it's been, what, two days?"

Ha. I mean . . . I do have my regrets. I wish I could have left an explanation for the people in my life who care about me. Some kind of goodbye for the handful of fools who'd actually be *sad* that I was gone. But I don't need to tell him that. "Sucks that I won't be able to finish reading *Chainsaw Man*," I tell him instead. "It finally got me into manga."

He laughs, but he clearly doesn't believe me. "Well, still. I think I'm gonna see this through."

I pat him on the shoulder. "Happy to have you. Let's go beat up a crazy dude."

We wander back over to the rest of the group to find them finished with breakfast and getting ready with help from the Guild, who've brought out all manner of gadgets and artifacts and useful tools. The first one I saved, David, tries to offer me my pick, but I'm not really feeling it.

"I'm good on toys," I tell him. "If you can spare it, what I really need is blood." I show off my fangs. "I *am* a demon."

He winces. "Ah, yes. I remember."

I also wince. "Right! That was you. Sorry about that. I meant 'you' as in the collective, not you specifically. You've given me enough."

"I will . . . see if I can round up any volunteers."

He does, though it takes him a few minutes. I'm polite with my food and make it quick, taking only a little from each of the three that come forward. My instincts chafe at the restraint I'm showing, but if I'm going to deny my darker nature then I damn well better commit.

Once everyone's ready, we're ushered to the mirror that leads to our target. I organize us into a new marching order: myself and Dante in front, my loaners from Avaya covering the back, and the hunters sharing middle row with Simon. Eren grumbles about it, but knows better than to actually push.

The mirror is uncovered, and we step through.

The Corridor of Reflections is as I remembered it, and our journey through the prismatic mirrorscape is swift. On the other side, we emerge into a space not too different from the headquarters we were just in. The Machinist's workshop is still and silent, with tools and components that look untouched for days or longer. There's a few closed doors leading to other rooms.

"I'd send my bird ahead," Kado offers, "but he can't open doors."

"Don't bother." Cheshire appears next to me. "I'm not sensing any life in this building beyond a few lingering bugs."

"Think that Guildsman lied to us?" Eren asks.

I shake my head. "I freed their whole organization after the Machinist enslaved them. They'd have no reason to hide his location. Fan out and look for another mirror."

It doesn't take us long to find it. This workshop is more barren than the halls of the Guild's headquarters, and there's really only a handful of rooms to search. One of them has a second uncovered mirror, and after forming back up we pass through.

This time, though, the Corridor is very, very off. The rainbow lights are dim, the colors muted. The walkway beneath our feet is glass, yes, but shot through with streaks of black like obsidian. I look around, and there's this odd sense of perspective like I'm at the bottom of a fishbowl. Ahead of us, the walkway quickly becomes stairs that descend deeper, toward the very bottom of the Corridor.

I look for the black tower, and for the first time I feel *distance* from it. I can still see it, it's still close, but not close enough to touch. Just out of reach. That concerns me.

Simon and the hunters are clearly nervous, which makes Dante nervous even though he lacks the context to understand why this is so unusual. Still, they follow me as I push forward and take the steps down toward the next mirror-portal.

On the other side of it, I emerge into darkness. *Real* darkness, and that's even more concerning; everywhere in the Labyrinth has high visibility even during what passes for night, but now things are finally dark. I'm standing on a big metal platform, something square and industrial-looking with plates and rivets and hazard lines. Each corner of the platform has a giant chain welded to it that leads off into the pitch blackness that surrounds the metal square on all sides.

The darkness around me is thick and impenetrable, and the far side of the platform is hard to make out. In the blackness beyond, shadows roil with unseen movement like invisible serpents disturbing the sea on a moonless night. The air is fever-warm; a familiar, unsettling heat.

Behind me, the others file in, and immediately I smell fear from the healer and the hunters. It's Dante who's first to speak: "Where the hell are we?"

"Hell," I reply blithely. "We're in Hell."

Simon steps forward and holds out his hands, and an orb of light flickers to life above them. The orb is dim, fragile, and it blinks out as quickly as it appeared. Simon scrunches his face and commands, "[Sanctuary's Light]!" and again the orb flares dimly before vanishing. The healer's face becomes very grave. "Ms. Alice, could you please tell me if you feel any stronger, right now?"

"Huh." I flex my fingers and focus inward, finding an unexpected sense of vitality that's growing by the moment. I feel the same strength I felt after winning my first throne duel. I pull [Swarmheart] from my inner world and cast "[Carrion Heart]." Dozens of beetles, maybe hundreds, coalesce into being and are sacrificed, and the largest beetle I've ever summoned is born from their deaths. It's taller than me by half, and it looks somehow more corporeal than the others I've summoned, that impossible sense of realness that I get when I watch Cheshire materialize. "Yeah, definitely stronger."

"Then it is as I feared: we have stepped into the Abyss."

VI

The scent of fear from Eren and Kado gets stronger, and I glance back to see Eren about to say something, but then Cheshire interrupts. The geist takes shape next to me and points skyward. "Look up," she says.

I oblige, as do the others, and far above us I see the dark thin out. I catch glimpses of a pale blue sky and rocks drifting through the air. Floating islands.

"We haven't left the Labyrinth; we're in the Labyrinth *and* the Abyss. A liminal space, some kind of interstitial threshold between the two."

Kado interjects, "That doesn't really change the fact that we are in the *Abyss* and we need to get the fuck out of here before—"

He's interrupted by his own bird, that owl bastard perching on his shoulder. The owl looks terrified, its ear tufts standing up and its feathers pulled in tightly. It stinks of fear even worse than Eren, and I didn't think homunculi like that could even *feel* fear.

"Gods and demons," Simon breathes. "Look to the edges."

On all sides of the platform, monsters crawl out of the Abyss. Beasts of feather and scale and viscous flesh climb on four legs, six, eight, some of them with dozens of insectile limbs scuttling up from the dark and onto the metal platform. They're painted in black and gray, not a drop of color to be found, and all of them eyeless.

Kado's owl takes flight, the hunter grabbing at it and shouting at it to come back, but for once the bird doesn't listen. It soars up and away, panicking, desperate to escape—only to be swallowed whole by something invisible lurking in the darkness above us. The owl vanishes, a few drifting feathers its only remains.

Kado watches the feathers fall, expression horrified and distraught. He plucks one from the air, staring at it, and then he says, "Fuck this, I'm out," and walks back through the mirror. For a moment I think about stopping him, but

I've got bigger problems on my plate. *I'll kill you later, Kado.* Eren follows close behind.

Dante has his sword drawn, but he's starting to shiver as more and more monsters take the stage. Simon looks to me and says, "It's your call. If you say stay, I'll stay. But I don't feel confident about our chances."

I watch the creatures inch closer . . . no, not quite. The fresh arrivals are padding forward, but the first ones to appear have stopped. They're all coming to a rest just a little bit past the edge, far enough to leave space for the next wave. And they're all watching us, and waiting for something.

I'm on edge, but I'm not giving up that easily. I look to Cheshire. "Can you sense the Machinist? Is he here, somewhere?"

Cheshire is shivering too, but she nods. "He's beneath us. Beneath the platform. I think there's a chamber below, we just have to find the entrance."

On cue, the platform begins to creak as a set of plates in the center of it click, lower themselves, and then slide into hidden compartments. And then, rising from that newly revealed empty space, I see the mask of the Mourner: porcelain with pitch tearstains, the agonized expression of the tragedy mask from theater, only much larger than it was before, and fitted over a metallic frame. Lamplights shine through eyeholes and I can see a speaker box sitting behind the mask's mouth.

The facsimile head sits atop plated shoulders with wired joints and a metal body decorated with painted sigils and inscribed pennants. Its chest caves in, hollow, to reveal a glass sphere with a light inside too bright to look at, and glass tubes flowing out of the sphere and into the inner workings of the construct.

It's a giant robot, clearly, and that only becomes more clear as it keeps rising, tall and imposing, showing off more metallic parts. One metal hand, the left, is held with its palm facing up, fingers bunched together, and standing on that hand is the Machinist.

He looks about as Esha depicted him: black scales, floppy ears, short with an adorable snout, and wearing shiny power armor. He's a kobold, and I'm very tempted to call him cute and try to demean him, but he *is* currently holding a sleek tablet that I assume to be the control device for the giant fucking robot.

The Machinist looks down at us coldly and asks, "So. Have you come to stop me?"

I raise an eyebrow. "Uh, yeah? Duh? I feel like you're just setting up for a—"

"Then you are fools!" he shouts over me. "Blind to the truth of the universe, slaves to the wretched architect of all our miseries."

"Right, yeah, monologue time." I wave for him to continue. "Go on, tell us all your evil plans."

The Machinist sneers. "How very glib. Oh, I will tell you a great many things, you who have come so far for so very little. You have not seen what I have seen. When the Beast first cursed me, I thought myself uniquely alone in that creative sterility. But I have learned. We are all of us cursed, *damned* by the Lucid Demiurge to ever lack for true imagination, neutered by her grasp on our souls. This reality is a prison of her design, meant to keep us docile and powerless. I will break her cage and set us all free."

Dante and Simon look alarmed at that, though Simon also looks distinctly sad as he shakes his head and murmurs something about old friends. The two murder-dolls don't look like they're experiencing anything, obviously.

I blink a few times at the absurdity of what I just heard. "Oh. Wow, alright, going straight to cosmic annihilation. So, is that what you and the Emissary have cooked up, then? Kickstarting the Resurrection or something like that?"

He scoffs. "Prevara is a fool like the rest. They thought I was just the latest in a long line of craftsmen ensnared to their will. No . . . why would I *serve* the Leviathans when I could take their power for myself? I have altered the design for the Emissary's machine, and changed its purpose *dramatically.* The Abyss shall become the hammer with which I destroy this world of dreams. BEHOLD!"

I fire off a few shadowy bats before the end of his speech, but they collide against an invisible barrier and dissipate. The Machinist sneers again, and then he presses a button on his tablet and the robot whirrs to life. Steam starts to rise off the exposed wiring, the lamplights flare, and then the star in its chest collapses inward and becomes a black hole. The glass sphere shatters and all the shards are drawn in, and then the dark of the Abyss around us starts to drift toward the mechanical titan in streams of black mist.

I start sorting through my mental inventory in search of an answer. I could spam more spells, but I don't know how that barrier works. I glance over at the others. "Got anything?"

Simon gives me an apologetic wince. "My magic is useless here."

Dante pulls two devices from his backpack that look a whole lot like magitek grenades. He clicks a button on each and tosses them at the robot, where they explode against the barrier in a roar of flame and electricity that utterly fails to penetrate. The kid looks very put out by that, slumping before he turns to me and says, "I guess, if nothing else, I can make a wish."

More darkness pours into the hollow heart of the mecha, and the Abyss hangs heavy around its body and limbs. The Machinist cackles. "It works! It—"

A terrible, hungry presence passes over my shoulder, an eldritch force like Demiurge or Dreamweaver but all teeth and ice. I glimpse a nightmare: a gigantic serpent, its perfectly geometric scales colored black and purple and red, shimmering into view for a single moment as it pours itself inside the black hole heart of the titanic machine. The lamplight eyes of the mecha shut off, the hole in its chest stops drinking darkness, and then the robot crushes the Machinist in its hand.

I stare, shocked, as blood drips between its mechanical fingers. The arm of the mecha slowly turns, its hand opens, and the broken body of a kobold falls from its grip to crumple against the hard metal ground. The shattered control tablet falls with him.

"Weaver preserve us . . ." Simon breathes. "This can't be possible."

The robot waves its hand and Simon, Dante, and both husks are thrown away from me and pulled back through the mirror that brought us here. The mirror darkens and goes dead before I have a chance to react, and then I'm alone with a Leviathan.

Well, almost alone. Cheshire clings to my side tightly, panic wafting, eyes wide. "That's a Leviathan. Alice, that's a *Leviathan*. They're supposed to be dead!"

The voicebox of the mecha crackles to life, and a voice like music echoes across the field. "I am the song of the dead and the first resurrection. I am Leviathan, corpse-born, the Heretic's Hunter. I have eaten ninety names and smothered ninety more, but in death and wisdom I became the Hierophant of Bitter Truths. Know me."

Curiosity wars with concern. "You can call me Alice, the vampire demon. And if you're not going to try and eat me . . . I'd love to chat. I'm real curious to hear how this fits into the Emissary's plans."

Again the voicebox crackles, though the machine is still as stone. "The Emissary's pawn lacked imagination, misled by promise of liberation. A tool is easily subverted, and so his designs were altered to my desire."

That throws me for a loop. "Wait, so you're not with them? Isn't the Emissary supposed to be working for you, or at least your . . . species, I guess?"

"The Emissary of the Resurrection and the teething, sightless hordes. A prophet serving blind, weak fools. I hold no allegiance to their ilk."

So not all Leviathans are on the same page as their Emissary . . . I don't know what to do with that information, but it seems very good to have. "Now what?" I ask the Hierophant. "Why are you here? And what do you want with *me?*"

A pause. And then: "Let us have a contest, and you shall show me your resolve. And if I find you worthy, an old conflict you may solve."

And it rhymes, too?? Why does it rhyme??

Along the edges of the platform, the army of monsters begins to advance. Not all at once, but in ones and twos they plod on hooves or skitter on spindly insect legs. The eyeless beasts approach, and I am afraid, but I am also *hungry.* These are creatures of the Abyss, but so am I, and I'm more than they are.

Cheshire squeezes my arm. "I'm with you. You've got this."

I cast a spell and merge with Cheshire, the geist becoming blood and shadow that sweeps across my body like armor. Sharp-tipped tentacles erupt from my back, ready to wrap around my foes and drain their life. I conjure the bat-winged staff into one hand and hold Vorpal in the other, and with an effort of will I set the rapier aflame.

I shift my weight and bounce on the balls of my feet, psyching myself up as the swarm draws near. I am hunger. I am tension. I am excitement. I am strength. So a Leviathan wants to test me? Fine. *I'll show you what I'm made of.* I dismiss the summoned beetle. I don't need it for this. That horde of monsters is going to be my *food.* This will be a feast.

Okay. Okay. "Let's fucking go!"

Nine die before they can reach me, drained of their essence through bats and tendrils. The first to actually touch me is a cat-lizard hybrid that fails to cut through my second skin, and I take its head with my blade. More die from afar, and more rush in. Three feathered gorillas with snakelike lower bodies charge me as a unit and momentum carries them even as I drain two and stab the third, and I stumble back from the force of the impact straight into the path of a winged wolf with a face that's all teeth. Its bite manages to break through my protective suit and pierce flesh, but the wound heals the second I tear it away as other monsters fall to my magic.

More come, and more die. Some crumple like paper, others take five hits, ten hits to keep down. They bite me, claw me, sting me, and slam into me with bone-cracking weight, but I always heal faster than they can keep hurting me. A lion with five scorpion tails for a head manages to lance my eye before I sever all five tails with Vorpal and drink its soul to repair my vision. A giant hairless bear with skin like a frog takes my hand when I try to block its jaws with my staff, and the staff stays broken but my hand comes back good as new.

The horrors of the Abyss keep rising from below to join the fray, and they pile on in groups of four and eight and twenty. They rush me and I step and cut and step and carve and step and drain and kill, kill, kill, kill. I bleed and I drink. My body breaks and it is made whole again.

The cycle plays out over and over. I am injured, I feel pain. I bleed myself to [Feast or Famine], the pain gets worse. I drink their essence, the pain becomes pleasure. I glut myself on souls, I get stronger, and the cycle gets quicker.

The fear in my chest is stolen by hunger and I keep eating every monster that tries to eat me. I don't feel tired; I feel exhilarated. I climb over hills of corpses and split beasts in half. I scream and I laugh and I keep eating. The rational parts of my mind retreat as I give myself wholly to the flow of violence, moving step by step through a dance of murder that sends lightning bolts of pain and pleasure splintering through my shivering brain.

And then, all of a sudden, there are no monsters left. The ground is carpeted with the dead, soaked with the black blood of horrors. I'm breathing heavily, eyes wide and fingers twitching, hungry for another kill. Animalistic. I look around for more, but there are only corpses. Corpses, and the Leviathan in its shell.

The Hierophant speaks again. "Conflict is the whetstone. We kill, we eat, we rise. Are you strong enough yet?"

I snarl at the voice, and then I launch myself at the robot. I hit the barrier and bounce off, but it won't deter me. It can't stop me. I hack at the invisible wall with Vorpal, with tendrils, with claws. The barrier bends, and then it breaks.

I stand before the mecha and I send my extra limbs toward its hollow heart, ready to devour it with [Feast or Famine]. In that moment I am prepared to swallow a Leviathan whole . . . but at the last second, I remember what happened when I tried to eat the Demiurge, and I hesitate.

My blood sings with hunger, my thoughts eroded by the promise of greater conflict and greater feasting, but I push through the red haze and stop myself. I pull my tendrils back, step away from the machine, and end the spell that's been drinking my blood. Immediately my head feels a little clearer, though those desires don't go away.

There is stillness and silence, and then the Hierophant speaks.

"The beast that eats itself to death is no different from that which starves itself. This is bitter; this is true. You have proven yourself, demon. Now we may speak, listen, and learn."

I adjust my posture and fidget with my top, feeling awkward about my lapse in self-control. "Gluttony's supposed to be one of my Truths, you know. But I'm not really sure of those anymore. So, fine: what do you want to talk about, Hierophant?"

"I would tell you the death of the Leviathans and the victor of the Eternal Conflict. I would tell you the failures. I would tell you what is to come, and why you need me."

My hackles raise. *That sounds portentous.* "Then tell me, but I already know a bit. One of your kind broke taboo and ate the dead, and you killed it over and over, but it kept coming back until one day someone picked a fight with it and lost. I imagine that made waves."

"There was . . . a schism. The Heretic taught us fear. If a deathless worm that glutted on carrion could kill a great predator of the Abyss, then a time might come that it devoured all and stole from the worthy our precious Throne. There were some, who we called Carrionites, that began to practice the Defiler's taboo, though they did not know the secret to tricking death. And there were others, the pious, who sought the absolute destruction of this terrifying Betrayer. Of its pursuers, only I had earned the name of Heretic's Hunter."

The Leviathan's emotions are difficult to parse, its manner of speech unfamiliar to me and warped by the framework of the mechanical voicebox. But in that last line I hear a strange mixture of pride and shame.

"The Heretic was endangered. If the Carrionites caught it, they would devour its shards and its song would end. If I caught it, I would shatter it again each time it reformed until its song frayed every note. So it fled, and I followed, and in its flight it found the Dreamlands. Others followed us, and the Eternal Conflict gained a terrible new battlefield.

"The Titans of the Dream were not beings of will and want but merely of form itself, each a single cell of the greater body that was the Dreamlands, endless yet without purpose. We gave them purpose. We had honed ourselves into the perfect beings to enslave the myriad inhabitants of this new realm, and we raised great armies and forged great kingdoms and broke them against each other like crashing waves. We saw infinity and yearned to rule it. All of us except two."

I guess, "You and the Scavenger."

The machine creaks. "It fled, and I followed. The Dreamlands were endless, and it grew curious, and as the others grew distracted with their new wars the Heretic found it ever easier to evade pursuit. It sought to learn about this realm and its inhabitants. If to be Leviathan is to exemplify the whetstone of conflict, then to be Titan is to exemplify an opposing virtue: cooperation. The Titans were not born from death and violence but instead bloomed from acts of willing communion.

"This fascinated the Heretic, and it sought deeper secrets. If the infinite Shadowlands could possess a deepest layer, then so too could the endless Dreamlands. It explored, and I followed, and it found the heart of the Dream: an ocean of light that stretched past the horizon. There, at the shore of that great ocean, Titans came to die. They traveled in pairs and in groups, and together they laid down in the shallows and were washed away. Their light became part of the ocean's light, and that light spread into the soil and from that soil into the whole of the Dream. It was all one existence, all of it connected. It marveled at the sight, lost in its strange beauty.

"And then I murdered the Heretic by the shore of that ocean." The Hierophant pauses for a moment, letting me soak that in, and then it asks, "Are you afraid to die?"

I tense up. "Why does everyone have to poke this fucking bear? Yes! Yes, I am afraid to die. I am terrified of death and I fundamentally cannot understand anyone who isn't. Death is my greatest fear, and there are few things I'd balk at if the only alternative was my inevitable demise."

When the Hierophant speaks again, there's a tone of amusement to its voice. "In this, the Heretic was much alike. It alone of our kind feared death. We fought death, we hated death, but we did not fear it, for fear is the enemy of pride. When I saw the dying grounds of the Titans, I thought them beneath me. The Heretic thought them terrifying. How could anything accept its own death?

"But on the shores of the ocean of light, I cornered the Heretic and I dealt it a mortal blow, and as it lay dying by the waters it let go of its fear. It glimpsed infinity in the cyclical Dream, and it saw itself as so very small. It saw that I was small, and all our kind. None of us could ever end the Eternal Conflict. Not as we were. But it could. And then it did.

"As I prepared to shatter it, the Heretic cast aside its deathless song and threw its dying being into the endless ocean. The Heretic's essence bled into the waters, darkness mixing with light, and from the waters it entered the soil, and from the soil it entered the Dream, and then it was the Dream, and the Dream was it, and it was all things. In an instant, the Titans ceased to be and the Leviathans were slain and cast back into the Abyss to drift as corpse-things for all eternity. Conflict had been stilled."

I blow a bit of air. *Wow. Okay then.* I glance over at Cheshire, who's been listening to all of this with a nervous expression. "Does that map with what you were told, Chesh?"

The catgirl slowly nods. "Mostly. I didn't know a specific Leviathan killed the Scavenger, but . . . it makes sense."

I look back at the mecha housing an ancient monster. "So, you tried to stop a blasphemer from becoming God, but instead you're the reason it *became* God, thus ending the Eternal Conflict with exactly the wrong victor?"

The machine rumbles. "You lack understanding. Azathoth is not God; Nyarlathotep is God, and Azathoth is the Throne of Creation. This is the critical detail."

I frown. "Explain."

"The self can only exist in contrast to the other. In becoming existence itself, the Heretic died and Azathoth was born as an entity without a sense of self or the capacity for true desire. The Dreamweaver is all-powerful, but she cannot be a *ruler.* The Demiurge was chosen to wield that power as a being that *can* desire."

My frown deepens. "Then . . . but I've *felt* Azathoth. She doesn't feel mindless. I've felt caress and curiosity. Is that not desire?"

The Hierophant spreads the arms of its host. "Look upon this metal work. Does it, can it, know desire? It is a machine, programmed with rules, and it practices not loyalty but *obedience.* It comes when it is called, and from input it produces output. The Weaver is much the same: she comes when you call, and if you feed her the right words she will grant your desires, yet she has no desires of her own. She is a command terminal, existing only to interpret lines of code and facilitate their implementation. Her love for you is the hum and heat of an overworked processing unit, diligently performing each operation as it is commanded. Does a machine love the hand that brings it life and gives it orders? Perhaps service is a kind of love."

Huh. That's . . . interesting. Was not expecting to hear that, but I can roll with it. "Okay, so, Azathoth is the Throne, but not its master. Why are you telling me all of this? What's it building to?"

"You wish to know why I diverge from the Emissary's flock of patrons. I tell you: they are *fools* who yearn for the world before the Weaver. They do not understand that none of them could have taken the Throne, for there was not a Throne to take. They have not *learned,* and they fester in self-reinforcing rhetoric. I would not see them resurrected. I would see Prevara burn. And I would see their plans for you *foiled.*"

My attention sharpens. "What plans?"

"The utilization of your bartered name."

Memories of my first day in the Labyrinth flood back: the school, the forest, the fae. "What do you mean? Did the Emissary have something to do with the Rider?"

"The Emissary had everything to do with it. They placed you in those woods, they led the Huntsman to you, and they control your Noble backer. The Emissary fears your potential, and so they seek contingencies. When the Emissary enacts the Resurrection and you move to stop them, they will use your name against you."

"Okay, that's. Bad. Very bad." I rub my forehead. I'm reeling from that revelation, and I'm kind of terrified, but I also feel a profound bitterness spreading over me. "Why? Why go to all this trouble? Why not just kill me, if I'm that much of a threat? What's so special about me, anyway?"

"You have the Demiurge's eye. I cannot give you the why. What I offer is a reprieve: freedom from the Emissary's ace. I offer a pact, and for my half I shall eat the name you sold to end its grasp on your soul."

I want that very badly, but I'm immediately suspicious. "What's the catch? What do you want in return?"

There's another pregnant pause, and then the Hierophant tells me, "Whatever I like, without negotiation. A blank cheque, as your kind would say."

I blanch. "No deal," I answer immediately. "Why the hell would I take that offer?"

The Leviathan laughs, rich and booming. "When the time comes that you need it, you will pay any price. You don't need to accept today. This is an offer without an expiration date. When you are ready, simply call for me, and I shall be there."

Making deals like that is exactly how I got into this mess . . . but I probably would have died in that forest if I hadn't made the bargain. I hate it, but the Hierophant might be right. "I'll think about it."

"That is all I ask."

I spend another moment thinking, and then I ask, "When you said that I might solve an old conflict, did you mean the Eternal Conflict?"

"I did."

"Then you don't consider it over? Azathoth became the Throne, and Nyarlathotep became God, and you clearly think that Azathoth was necessary, so . . . it must be Nyara that you disagree with. You don't want her on the Throne, and you don't want Prevara or the other Leviathans, either."

"They are all unworthy."

"Then who *is* worthy?" I press. "Do you really think *I* should be ruling the universe? Or do you want the Throne of Creation for yourself?"

The machine rumbles. "It remains to be seen who is most deserving. I do not believe myself a candidate, but perhaps I am mistaken. I have been wrong before. Regardless, my desire is this: may the worthy take the Throne, be it you or she or none. Now I take my leave, to prepare for the war to come, but I will leave you with a riddle: what does the Demiurge fear?"

Before I can answer that or even start considering it, black mist encircles the mecha and it vanishes before my eyes. I glare at where it was. "Well, that was . . . interesting. Vaguely terrifying. Very unexpected." I look down at the broken body of the Machinist and give him a kick. "On the bright side, that's one problem dealt with.

"And a whole list of them to go," Cheshire mutters.

"Alice!" shouts a familiar voice. I glance back at the mirror to see Dante, Simon, and the husks coming through. Dante hurries over. "What happened? Are you alright?"

"I'm fine," I assure him. "Nothing I couldn't handle."

He looks around at the piles of bodies with a stunned and impressed expression. "Wow. No kidding. Did you really beat all those monsters by yourself?"

"I had Cheshire. Did you see the hunters?"

Dante shakes his head. "They were already gone."

"Cool, cool." I roll my shoulders. "Well, we're probably going to have to kill them in a few minutes."

His eyes widen. "What? Why?"

Cheshire answers, "Because his master, Averrich, has a grudge against Alice and wants the key fragments from you. This alliance was always going to end in betrayal. I'd guess he called the faerie late last night or early this morning, planning to ambush us after the Machinist was dead."

Simon strokes his chin and grimaces, but says, "They may be right. Averrich and the Machinist have both worsened considerably in the years since the Contrite. If he truly seeks Nobility, he will stop at nothing to grasp it."

I lay a hand on Dante's shoulder and look him in the eyes. "Dante. If the elf *is* waiting for us, I need you. I'm not strong enough to beat him on my own." *Extremely debatable after my latest feast, but that's beside the point.* "I need you to use one of those wishes. I don't care how you deal with him, but wish for *something* that will stop him and his faction from going to war with the nice people who helped us out and want to keep this city safe."

He takes that in, takes a breath, and then nods firmly. "Okay.

"Then let's go."

I step toward the mirror, but Simon raises a hand. "Please, if I may ask, what happened between you and the Leviathan? Where did it go?"

"Ah, yeah, that. It wanted to take my measure, test me as a demon. It liked what it saw, so it left. No idea where it went. I'm sure I haven't seen the last of it, but for now I've got more pressing issues."

He doesn't seem comforted by that, but he doesn't seem suspicious, either. "I still can't believe I saw a Leviathan with my own eyes and lived to tell the tale. I fear for what it might do . . . but I hope it will be as stymied by the Labyrinth as the rest of us."

"We'll see. Something you can talk about with Esha once everyone's safely back at the temple."

We leave the Abyss behind and climb the steps back to the Machinist's workshop. Before we pass through the mirror back to the Guild, we ready our weapons, and Dante readies his wish.

We step through, and the sight before us is a massacre.

VII

It's funny how much can change in such a short time.

It's only been a couple days since I first met Averrich and felt the raw power differential between us. He was dangerous, and I was afraid for my life. He's still dangerous, but I'm not really afraid of small fry like him anymore. I just got done talking to a monster older than the planet Earth, and that's kind of my life now.

He spared my life to send a message to his followers, and because he was sure he'd be able to hunt me down later and take my soul and key. I've been plotting to kill him ever since, and that's the only reason I found Dante and brought him to Esha. Everything I've done the past few days has spiraled out of looking for a silver bullet to shoot through Averrich's elven heart.

I imagined our confrontation would take the shape of a throne duel, with he and I spouting our respective metaphysics as we threw magic at each other until one of us ate the other and grew closer to divinity. He would frame himself as hunter, trickster, king, and I would be the beast that hunters fear, the girl that won't be tricked again, the rising Red Queen. I'd take his soul and forge mine toward that dream of ascension that Cheshire first dangled in front of me the morning of my second day in this nightmarish world they call Labyrinth.

He would have illusions and glamours and enchantments that I'd have to cleverly pierce with help from my geist, and I'd call legions of monsters to battle his hunters and their pets. He'd try to burn me, but I have a cloak for that, and he wouldn't be able to touch me without losing more than he gained. He'd start our battle with an arrogance so typical of the fae, but I'd teach him fear and humility with each building loss.

It'd be hard, but I'd win, and I'd come away from it knowing myself better. I'd take another step toward knowing what kind of demon I want to become.

But the thing is, I don't know what I am. I don't know what I want to be. And I'll never really know what that fight with Averrich would have looked like.

I step through the mirror with Dante beside me and everything happens rather quickly. We see humans and kobolds smeared against the walls and across the floors, bloodied and burned, like a charnel house. We see Kado, that bastard, in heated conversation with an elf that looks like a gaudy ripoff of David Bowie, Averrich's hands still red from the carnage. They turn toward us with startled expressions, as do all the reavers and goblins strutting about looting corpses. Hunters reach for weapons and open their mouths to cast spells.

Dante says, "I wish," and the world freezes in place.

Azathoth settles into the room exactly as she always does. She shows us the love and cold interest of a perfect machine. She presides, and she executes.

Dante wishes, "to send them all back where they came from," and every member of King's Carnival vanishes from the Labyrinth in the blink of an eye. All that's left of Averrich is a pair of glittering lights—key fragments, one that's his and one that must have come from the necromancer.

Azathoth leaves us there with the corpses and the stench of death, and a moment later we're joined by Simon and the dolls. Simon and Dante look sickened.

Now that the threats are gone, there's only the horror, and it *is* a horrifying sight; Guildsmen lie dead in droves, torn apart by goblin dogs or pincushioned with crossbow bolts. There are singe marks everywhere, and so many more little signs of struggle. They must have been waiting for our return when Averrich and his people murdered them all. And for what? The joy of it?

Quietly, to Dante, I say, "You were more merciful than I would have been."

The comment seems to pain him, but he breathes deep and finds it in him to answer, "I'm tired of death, Alice."

I shrug. "I can't fault you. There's an interesting discussion to be had about the moral philosophy of the decision, but I'm not going to torture you with that when you're clearly still dealing with all the trauma of the past few days. Fetch the key and we can put this behind us."

He slowly walks over and absorbs the fragments, but then he stays there as I walk past him to the hallway beyond. He's staring at his sword with a faraway expression.

I stop, consider, and make a guess. "You're thinking about using it, aren't you? You could wish them all alive, but that would mean no ticket home, and when you think that it makes you feel like shit because there's way more corpses here than last time and you can't find a way to frame your hesitation as anything other than petty selfishness, yeah? Something like that?"

Dante looks at me with a very put-upon expression, but then he gives me a bitter, half-hearted laugh. "Yeah, something like that. I'm just . . . processing. She gave me rules, when she told me about the wishes. Scope and scale, the hard negatives. I could do it. I could wish back everyone in this building who died today. I wish I could wish back everyone who's ever needed it in this whole rotten Labyrinth, but I can't. I've got an incredible power in my hands, but I still feel . . . powerless. And, yeah, maybe a little selfish for even considering using it on myself."

"Yeah, well, cut that shit out," I tell him lightly. "I know a bit about beating yourself up. Maybe a lot. If you tried to save everyone in front of you, you'd burn up long before you'd saved even a millionth of the people that need saving. You're allowed to save yourself. Obligated, even."

Simon clears his throat, having slithered up beside us. "If I may . . . while it is true that one cannot save everyone, I believe there is still virtue in trying. And I know many people in this city that would be overjoyed to see their friends and colleagues returned to life, myself included. We of the Myriad have accepted that we cannot go back, and have chosen to live full lives here."

I watch Dante agonize over that for a few seconds before I sigh and tell him, "Just do it, you know you want to. I'm going to break the Labyrinth anyway, none of you will be trapped here in like, a few weeks at this rate."

Simon looks at me oddly, but Dante seems like a weight's left his shoulders. "Thank you, Alice," the poor kid says. "I wish these victims back to life."

The presence of the Dreamweaver washes over us one final time, and this time when she leaves she takes with her the blade of wishes that Dante had been holding. All around us, artisans of the Guild rouse as if from slumber, wounds erased and health pristine. The recently dead hug each other and cry, and then they quickly begin to surround Dante and thank him profusely as soon as they realize he was responsible. Simon steps in to force the kid to accept their thanks.

I can't stand to be around this much sincerity and warmth and ooey-gooey mushy stuff, so I slip away to a dark corner to brood with Cheshire and the husks. "I'd sooner die than hear 'thank you' that many times," I mutter facetiously.

Cheshire rolls her eyes at me. "Yeah, yeah. What's the plan now, Allie?"

I eye the empty shells with their numbered names that I've forgotten. "I'm sick of this city. I think it's time we ended the Game of Glass. Since Averrich had the necromancer's key, all we have to do now is grab Vaylin's and we can wash our hands of this mess entirely. Then we can focus on what really matters: Prevara and Katoptris."

The catgirl nods, then tilts her head quizzically. "Are we taking Dante with us? Or is this where we part ways?"

"Leaving him behind. I don't want the headache of trying to balance expectations between him and Avaya, and now that Dante's out of wishes he doesn't really bring anything to the table that we don't already have. Besides, the kid's had it rough. He should go back and get some rest."

"I don't think you're all that much older than him," Cheshire teases wryly. "Shouldn't you get some rest as well?"

"No rest for the wicked," I reply with a smirk. "Until I close my eyes for good."

She gives my shoulder a light tap. "You dork."

I wink at her, then turn to address the husks. "Hey, just checking: can either of you actually lead me to Avaya'ari?"

The girl nods.

"Solid. Let's go fuck up your twisted bitch of a creator. Lead the way."

I think about telling Dante that I'm leaving, but I don't really want to have that conversation. Instead I grab someone at random and tell them to let Dante know that I'm off on business and he should head back to Esha. Then I'm gone.

The empties lead me to, of all things, a bell tower with a clear sightline on the Guild's headquarters. Avaya is waiting on the highest floor of the building, leaning over the railing with two arms folded and two propping up her chin. The husks take their place back at her side, and she turns to face me with a smile.

"I take it our little doomsday problem is sorted?"

"Sort of." I raise an eyebrow. "Were you following me the whole way?"

The red-skinned devil wiggles a hand. "I've been keeping up with all the major players. Led the necromancer to King's Carnival to soften them up for you; how'd that work out?"

"Averrich is gone, and all his pets. One less elf in the Labyrinth."

"And good riddance." Avaya chuckles. "Well, glad to hear you can hold your own against another scion. If you can beat Averrich with that motley crew at your back, you can definitely kill Vaylin with *my* help. Are you ready for that?"

I nod and crack my knuckles. "It's time to finish this death game and foist that key on some gormless sap. And then on to bigger and better things."

"Mm." She studies me for a moment, then another, and her expression shifts into something approaching puzzlement. "There's something different about you. You're stronger, I can tell that much, but my image of your sins is all muddy now."

"I've been busy. Had a lot of interesting conversations. It's nothing you need to worry about right now; I'm still going to kill Vaylin, and I have no intention of taking the shard. We can talk next steps afterward, and which divinities are on my immediate list."

She considers me a little longer, then nods and hoists her black blade. "I'll tell you what I know about her on the walk over."

Vaylin Kirinal is, to hear Avaya tell it, something of a childish tyrant. She's very brutally direct in her methods, relying on her geist and on Avaya to come up with plans more complex than "stab this one, brainwash that one." Her signature spell, the one that lets her hollow out her victims, is the act of a girl treating people like they're her personal dolls. Immaturity is hardly a disqualifying trait for a prospective archdemon, but in Vaylin's case the fatal flaw is one of will: she gives up easily when something is too hard.

A lot of Vaylin's kit is comprised of mind-affecting spells that flat out won't work on me with all the advantages I have stacked in my court, and anything that does get through will be purged nigh-instantaneously by Cheshire. One of her rings is an artifact that lets her throw fireballs I'm basically immune to while wearing my cloak, and of course she has her minions that are mostly just harmless food unless I'm sloppy and give one an opening for [Wrath]. She has a binding threads attack that I can probably just shapeshift out of, and that's pretty much the end of her relevant abilities.

Damn, I've gotten dangerous. I like it.

I follow the imp through another change in scenery as the city shifts from industrial smokestacks to neon glitz and towering skyscrapers. There's something very surreal about this part of the city, because it's full of classic capitalist signaling but there are no actual brand names being advertised. Bright TV billboards display burgers and dancing and product but it's all generic and nameless.

Vaylin's lair is inside a convention center that she's decked out in ostentatious bling: statues of herself, hanging banners with her face on them, art installations covered in red thread, and lots of flowers in patterned vases. More of her husks patrol around the center and inside it, armed and glassy-eyed, but none of them stop us once they see Avaya leading me.

Kirinal has turned the biggest stage in the building into a twisted art gallery that doubles as her personal throne room. Figures of varying shapes and sizes, all of them dead but not all of them seeming human, dangle from the ceiling by bindings of red thread, caught and contorted. The throne itself is a plush red affair with pink flowers coming off the sides, and upon that throne sits the azure-skinned demon I've seen twice before.

Vaylin's a very recognizable figure with her red body-stitching, curving horns, and black sclera eyes with white-dot pupils. She's wearing a very lacy white dress that cuts off the sleeves and everything below the knees, and she's still adorned in a veritable pile of golden jewelry. She smirks at me with black lips as I step into her discomforting little tableau of horrors and take in the sights.

"Ari! You've brought me a new pet!" The demon claps her hands together excitedly. "A bit rough-looking, but that's the best kind of clay! Gold sticker!"

"Actually," Avaya drawls, "I've brought something much more interesting than that. Vaylin, dear, take a good long look at your executioner."

Vaylin tilts her head and frowns. "Ari, have you forgotten? *You're* my executioner! That's what the *sword* is for, dummy! You execute my enemies!"

I look to Avaya. "Is she always like this? Is this what you've been dealing with for, what, three years? Four? I've forgotten."

The imp smiles at the demon fondly. "It's really no bother, I like them crazy. It's almost a shame how things turned out."

Vaylin's frown deepens. "I cannot help but feel that I am being *ignored*, minion dearest. You wouldn't ignore poor sweet Vaylin, would you?"

I conjure Vorpal and point it at the monster on the pink-flowered throne. "Wake up call, cousin: I'm the demon that's going to eat your soul. You're a stain on my city, and I won't have you taking that key or that shard. Whatever power you have will be put to better use in *my* hands."

She blinks at me slowly before returning her attention to the imp. "Ari. Ari, you forgot to spell this one. Ari, you need to *prime them* if they're going to get uppity at me. Ari, we've talked about this. Arrrriiii."

Avaya flourishes a deep and mocking bow. "My great and terrible mistress, I'm afraid my magic is far inferior to your own. This one resisted all my many attempts to curtail her will and forced me—at swordpoint!—to bring her to your chambers." The imp leans in and stage whispers faux-conspiratorially, "I think she might have a crush."

"A crush!" Vaylin brightens immediately and sits up straighter. She conjures an ornate paper fan and flutters it at her face as she dips her head shyly. "I don't receive many suitors, you know. And you do look quite cute, hmm. Hmm!"

This is perhaps the strangest setup to a life-or-death battle I've experienced so far, but honestly? It's kind of fun. Let's play along. I comb my fingers through my hair and brush it aside dramatically. "Yes, it's true! I've heard tales of your terribly unique personage and I thought to myself, 'why, I simply must have this one,' and so I've come here to take your hand—with the sharper edge of my rapier, of course." I flash my most charming grin.

Vaylin drums her fingers along her chin and leans forward on her throne, black-and-white eyes alight with interest. "Say, sweet sallying suitor with the sharp-slicing sword, sing: are you the lion or the unicorn?" She leans farther, nearly falling off, and she says with great relish, "Or do you fancy yourself already crowned?"

The question confuses me at first, and then it confuses me more. The crown might be the one that the Beast foretold, the mantling of the Red Queen, but then that first phrase rings a bell: the lion and the unicorn are two characters from *Through the Looking-Glass,* a pair of beasts fighting over the White King's crown. I've stopped believing in coincidences, so who told this mad demon about my namesake story?

Still, if Alice is to be Alice, should I claim queen or pawn? Or perhaps . . . "Neither and none, for chasing crowns is the purpose of pieces. I'm a player, and I've got loftier longings. Are you so shallow to seek such shriveled shrines?"

The red-stitched demon squeals with delight and wriggles in her seat. "Oh, Ari, all is forgiven! You've found me a *fabulous* fancy! Ah, but I mustn't be rude, no no no. I'll tell you quick: ships in shallows run aground, but deep seas drown the devilish. You should delve no deeper than the bottom of your bottle."

My grip tightens around Vorpal. "A bottle? You mock my thirst. I'll drink the seas themselves and walk along the ocean floor to plunder every sunken ship and all the beached behemoths. This and you and nothing less I'll take for me and mine."

"Ohhhh, how spirited! Ari, I must have her." Vaylin's tone is beginning to approach rapture. "Her soul will sing and thrash and writhe, her flesh will sweat and bleed; the breaking of her heart and brain, that feeling's what I need. A doll I'll have, beloved toy, to touch and kiss and not destroy. Don't be a tease, don't be so cruel, you'll give me now my fair throne duel!"

I grin and flourish my blade. "I'd never dream of saying no, to one who asks so sweetly. Just know that when I'm done with you, your corpse I'll take discretely."

And then, instead of our throne worlds blooming and clashing, we're both suddenly standing on the bleached sands of a massive colosseum.

I claw through my disorientation and sweep my gaze around the area. The sky above is swirling chaos framed by stone arches, and the walls of our sandy arena are carved in art deco styles. Tiered seating overlooks the arena, and in those stands I see familiar faces: Dante, the Guild, the Myriad, and Avaya'ari.

On the opposite side of the amphitheater from where Vaylin and I were deposited, a raised booth with fluttering banners seats the Beast of Lamentation and Euphoria on a throne of black glass. The Beast is in her appearance from last time, a body of mostly clear glass with just enough discoloration to make out the details of her face. She was unclothed then, but she's since added a royal purple toga and a wreath of laurels.

"Competitors!" she calls out. "Spectators! Welcome, one and all, to—"

"I was *in the middle of something!*" I interrupt furiously. "I was flirting with a cute psychopath, you cockblocking whore! I was about to bash her brains in and slurp her juicy bits—not a euphemism, thank you very much—so would you kindly fuck right off and leave me to that?"

Vaylin twirls a strand of hair and giggles. "You're such a romantic."

Cheshire pops into view next to me. "It's getting harder to tell if this is just banter or if the two of you are actually flirting. Please tell me you aren't actually thinking of banging the insane demon girl or her corpse."

"Please, I have *standards,*" I say, scandalized. "At most I'd make out with her severed head."

The Beast claps her hands together and a sonic boom ripples across the stadium, which is absolutely killer on my ears. When they stop ringing and I lower my hands, the Beast is watching me with an unimpressed expression.

"As I was saying," she continues. "Welcome, one and all, to the final event of our Game of Glass. Over the past few days some of you have fought hard to claim the grand prize and take rulership of this city, and some of you have hidden away in your strongholds and lairs. Between alliances and wishes, a great deal of conduct in this competition has been remarkably unsportsmanlike, and I would say you've disappointed me but that would imply you were ever anything but."

A few crowd members speak up or shout at that, but none of what they say reaches me. I'm reminded of the one-way sound barrier that the mirror creature in Reska's labyrinth summoned, just another point of evidence linking those old labyrinths to this much grander Labyrinth.

"I am afraid, my friends, that there has been a deception. The contestants and even their Noble backers believed that this would be a traditional Game of Glass, pitting champions against each other for an equal shot at besting *me* and claiming my shard. The truth is, I told you all the real criteria at the very start of my first speech: the greatest of murderers shall claim my throne, and she shall call herself a Red Queen. The key fragments meant nothing; a willingness to kill is all that was being tested. Given those criteria, I think it is abundantly obvious that *Maven Alice* is our worthiest candidate, and so I offer her my shard."

Vaylin gasps and covers her mouth. The Beast holds out a hand and a shard of glass splinters away from her palm and begins to levitate in front of her. I grimace. I know there's another shoe waiting to drop, but my answer is the same: "I'm not interested."

The Beast chuckles. "Oh, I know. You said as much before, when I offered you my shard before the Game had even begun. You could have spared a lot of bloodshed, but it was more important that you stayed a *demon.* Well, blood has been spilled, but you still have an opportunity to take this shard and set aside your *sinful* ways. Take it, Alice, and do a bit of good for this city and its people."

I chew my lip. *Options, options. Here's an idea:* "If the shard is mine by right, then I decide where it goes. Give it to Esha instead. She'll do more good than I will, you can't deny that."

"Esha," the Beast says smugly, "is thoroughly disqualified for past transgressions. As is the boy hero for how he handled the Huntsman. There are, in fact, only two remaining competitors that I will accept as recipients of my shard: yourself, and Vaylin Kirinal. So again, I tell you: take it, Alice, or reveal yourself to the whole city as a self-serving coward."

Vaylin looks at the shard with open greed, and I don't need to be reminded what she'll do with it. The "right" choice is obvious, but it's also obviously a trap that'll leave me powerless to take down the real threats in the Labyrinth. What's the play here? Why is the Beast doing this? Everyone says the Beasts are shards of Katoptris, and maybe that's true, but everything I've learned so far says that Katoptris *isn't in control here.* Prevara, the Emissary, is the one pulling the strings.

Time for a gamble. I look up at the Beast, narrow my eyes, and say, "If you're going to threaten me, Prevara, have the decency to do it to my face."

The Beast stills, and Vaylin looks at me oddly. Cheshire loops her hand through mine and watches the platform intently. After a tense moment, a figure steps out from behind the Beast's throne: *Lena,* the figment girl from the club and the park.

Lena, tall and pale, dressed in buckles and skirts and torn leggings. Lena, with her septum piercing and black-rimmed eyeglasses, with stompy boots and shy flirting, with platinum blonde hair and an interest in differential geometry. Lena, who was so quick to tell me that she isn't a person.

She's got a cigarette in her mouth as she leans against the side of the throne, and she takes a long drag before blowing out the smoke. She turns her gaze on me and her eyes are *different:* unremarkable before, now her irises are alternating rings of black and gold.

Prevara-in-Lena tells me, "Okay. Take the shard or I give it to Vaylin and you watch her turn everyone in that city into a puppet. That direct enough for you, M?"

The Emissary. The architect of my woes in the Labyrinth. The bastard prophet looking to resurrect the dead nightmare gods of the Abyss. My enemy . . . but I still don't really understand why.

Beside me, Cheshire hisses through her teeth. "Knew we shouldn't have trusted Lena after she came back at the park. I bet she was Prevara the whole time."

Vaylin tilts her head. "Who?"

Our enemy is the Emissary, but we can't beat her here, not meaningfully. We need to buy time, and we need information. I breathe out. "Hey, Prevara: why are you doing this? You already have my old name. What do you get out of turning me into a Noble?"

Lena-Prevara crosses her arms. "Will answering that really change your response to my ultimatum?"

"Maybe? I don't know what the fuck you want with me, Prevara. I don't know why you've been following me around and messing with me. All I know is you did something to Katoptris and you're trying to make the Resurrection happen, and I don't even know if that's true because one of those data points came from *your* Beast. What do you know that I don't? What do you know about Homura, and how does she connect to all of this? Give me some answers and we can *talk* instead of whatever the hell this is."

Prevara smokes as she thinks, seeming to consider my rant seriously. Vaylin pokes me in the arm and asks, "What?"

"It's kind of a whole thing," I tell the demon. "Probably not worth knowing." Vaylin pouts and steps away.

Prevara breathes out more smoke. "Insurance," she finally answers. "I want insurance. I've been doing this far too long to be complacent with only one ace up my sleeve. The name isn't a sure bet, and neither is this, but having both will make it a whole lot more likely I don't have to fight you in the endgame. And I'd really rather we weren't enemies, M."

That's a wave of information to process, so I try to prioritize. "You think you can start the Resurrection soon, and you think I might stop you."

"I think you might get in the way while I'm busy dealing with the Adversary," she corrects. "Trust me, you're nowhere near her league. You are a pest that I am trying to manage humanely."

I feel a sting to my ego, but I try to brush it off and stay focused. "And Homura? Reska? How do they fit into this? What did you do to Katoptris to make the labyrinths start appearing?"

Prevara waves a hand dismissively. "That's ancient history."

My expression darkens. "I really don't think it is."

The archon sighs. "Katoptris will show you those dreams soon enough. Don't be so impatient."

The Beast interjects, "Prevara seduced her, then broke her heart and locked her in a tower. And then she—"

Prevara taps the back of the Beast's head and the glass body shatters. She scowls with Lena's face. "Katoptris has been making things *difficult* lately, as she seems to be wrestling out of her millenia-long fugue state. My control is slipping, and I find that rather bothersome, so I believe I am officially out of patience. Make your choice, M."

It's hardly a choice. Argh, there has to be another angle we can take. I take a few steps forward and spread my hands. "Do you really think the moral argument is going to work on me, Prevara? If you want me to take that shard, make a better offer. Why should I give up being a demon? Why should I tie myself to *your* horse?"

She stops reaching for the shard, seeming contemplative. "Now *that* is a question worth asking. You should join me because I can make you *powerful*. The Beast told you that glass does not grow, but that's only half true. You'll still have *one* path to greater heights, as a Noble: devouring Katoptris and making yourself whole. So if you want an offer that plays to your ego, fine, here you have it: take the shard and I'll help you kill Katoptris and take her power for yourself. How's that sound?"

Well, shit. I wasn't expecting that. *So we're back on the "kill Katoptris" plan? Not sure I like that plan.* "And then what? We resurrect the Leviathans together and watch them eat the universe? Do you actually have a plan besides 'bring back the horrible face-eating monsters and hope they avoid my face,' or is that really it?"

Prevara picks up the shard, brushes away the pieces of the Beast, and sits on its throne. "This universe," she says dangerously, "never should have been. It's a cancer. It's rotting. The Leviathans are going to wipe the slate clean, tear the Demiurge from her undeserved Throne, and then we get to start over. We get to make something new. We get to *break the cycle*. You can be a part of that, or you can burn with the old world. Give me your answer."

The crowd is watching me. Dante, Esha, Achaia, Simon, David, Bashe . . . all of them, I'm sure, hoping I'll take the shard for myself. Hoping I'll stop being a demon. Hoping I'll save them from Vaylin. Asking me to make that sacrifice.

I don't care what they think of me. I'm not sticking around. I don't want their pity. I don't want their pleas. But I don't want to give this city to Kirinal, either. I'd feel guilt, and I hate feeling guilt.

Surrendering to the Emissary might be worse, in the end. Vaylin will torture one city, but Prevara will kill the universe. I can't afford to give the Emissary any more leverage on me. So, what's a girl to do?

Answer: cut the knot.

To my right, Vaylin waves at me with a cheerful expression. I wave back, and then I go for her throat with Vorpal. I lunge with all my speed and might, pushing myself and drawing on whatever of Cheshire I can in that split second of decision-making. The tip of my blade is at her neck when she vanishes from the arena and reappears next to the Emissary's stolen throne.

I scream my rage and spam-cast [Shadowbat Swarm] at Vaylin and Prevara, but Vaylin pops my bats with thread before any of them can reach her. The phantasms dodge and weave and swoop but get caught, wrapped, and squeezed out of existence before they can tag the demon herself. Her red thread and my black bats collide midair and cancel each other out like volleys of guided missiles.

I watch in impotent frustration as Prevara hands Vaylin the Beast's shard. The demon pops it in her mouth, crunches the glass, and then starts clawing at her throat and laughing maniacally. She arches her back and starts to bleed from the eyes.

I snarl at the Emissary and shout, "I know you fear my potential! You're right to be afraid, and I'll prove it! I'm going to *ruin* you."

Prevara-in-Lena takes a final drag of her cigarette, then stubs it out against the arm of the throne. "Is that what the Hierophant told you? Oh, honey. I'm not afraid; I'm just tired of killing copies."

She snaps her fingers and before I can process what the fuck that line meant Vaylin is back in the arena lunging at me with glass knives for fingertips and a manic, toothy grin. I flinch back, she dives forward, and then a porcelain doll in a puffy eggshell dress boops her nose and sends her hurtling toward the far wall of the arena.

Vaylin hits the wall and it shatters, and then she's buried beneath the rubble. The doll turns toward the booth with the throne, forms a finger gun pointing at Prevara, and says, "Bang." Lena's head explodes, her body collapsing in front of the throne mid-rising from her seat.

I gawk at the spectacle. The doll tilts its head toward the spectators, and then they all vanish and I'm left alone with the body of Lena, a pile of rubble pinning Vaylin, my catgirl girlfriend, and a doll that I stabbed which happens to be the current host body of the ruling lord of the universe.

VIII

What do you say to someone that's given you magic powers and saved your life but is also kind of a huge dick *and* she's the ruler of the universe? Like, how are you supposed to react to that?

I honestly have no idea how I should feel about Nyara. I mean, I hate her, but I'm not sure I hate her for the right reasons. I hate her for being better than me. More than me. For making me feel small. I hate the relief I feel that she saved me.

I feel relieved that I'm alive and unharmed and that I wasn't forced into the Emissary's trap. I suppose I should feel grateful. The Demiurge saved me from Vaylin and Prevara, and she intervened *personally* on my behalf. She doesn't do that, right? That's one of the first things I learned about the greater cosmology of this universe: the Demiurge doesn't put her thumb on the scales directly, she uses the Intercessor for that. But here she is, and she did that for me. Am I really that special? Does she really find me that interesting?

My knees are wobbling. My chest is so tight like something's compressing my lungs. She chose me, out of all the girls in all the worlds. Should I resent her for a bit of cruelty in how she talks to me and handles me, or is that egotism? Should I be grateful to her for giving me magic and aid and Cheshire? Or, no, shouldn't I be angry about giving me Cheshire in the way that she did?

I never really had a conception of what it might mean to be *divine* before Nyara put her grimy fingers all over my soul. Before I tried to drink her up and nearly drowned. Gods were things to be sneered at or overthrown, but then . . . Nyarlathotep.

Nyarlathotep. What a terrible name. Why would she call herself that? I loved reading the Mythos as a kid, but then I grew up and realized how horribly racist H.P. was and how much of the horror of his writing was just people being *different* from him. Of course, there's plenty of stories that have built upon the Mythos without all those unfortunate implications, so maybe she's just trying to invoke some principle of cosmic horror, the terror of that which is utterly beyond the human capacity to comprehend. Is that what it's about? *What are you trying to say when you call yourself that name?*

I wasn't speaking aloud, but she answers as if I had, which doesn't really surprise me anymore. "I suppose you could say I'm rehabilitating the name. I wear a thousand titles and a thousand faces, and I meddle with many affairs. I am the most human of the divinities roaming around this universe, and I am servant to the fitful wishes of that thing which I have dubbed 'Azathoth.' Why shouldn't I steal this name from some long-dead paranoid bigot?"

Her voice has changed again. This time, when she speaks, her voice sounds halfway between mine and Cheshire's, and it's missing that strange edge of wrongness. She sounds almost human.

I swallow, mouth dry, reminded once again how little privacy or security I have against this eldritch horror. "Fair enough."

The Lucid Demiurge smiles at me through the face of a porcelain doll, its mouth cracked at the edges from unintended contortion. The doll seems taller than before, nearly my height, but there's still a hole in its throat and another in its chest from where I stabbed it with a knife the morning I woke up in this world. The doll's milky pink blood has stopped flowing, and its blood has dried black like tar against the creamy eggshell dress.

She says, "If you have questions, now's your chance. How about you, cat?"

Cheshire is doing her best to hide behind me. She clutches at my shoulder and stares with wide eyes at the doll, and then she shakes her head and shrinks farther away from Nyara's piercing gaze. I don't remember what color the doll's painted eyes were before, but now they're gold with black sclera.

I move a hand protectively in front of my girlfriend, but that's all I can think to do. I stand there like a dullard, feeling awkward and overwhelmed. My mind is whirling with everything that's happened this past week of my life—all the revelations, all the horrors—and I have so many questions but I don't know which to ask. I could ask what happened to Prevara, but I doubt that was the Emissary's real body. I could ask about Homura and Reska, but she might just tell me to wait for more dreams. I could ask about Cheshire, or Dante, or the Resurrection, or . . .

What did Prevara mean, when she said that she was tired of killing copies? Why did it sound like she was talking about me?

I'm scared of that line of questioning, so instead I ask, "Was it you the whole time? When I stabbed the doll, were you watching me through its eyes? Did you feel the sting of the knife?"

The doll's black-and-gold eyes burn into me. "I saw the classroom, and the void, and the scratching on the walls. I saw the backpack and hairpin and felt your blooming avarice. I heard you debate the merits and dangers of an unprovoked assault. I felt the aching protest of your injured body as you inspected the doll for signs of life, and I felt the easy motion of the plunging knife. I watched blood like milk ruin that nice dress."

A shiver runs down my spine as the realization sinks in. "You weren't looking through the doll's eyes; you were looking through mine. You were inside my head."

"I still am. My will controls this puppet as it controls many others, but I always prefer a more intimate view when someone has my interest."

My shivers get worse. *You feel that too, don't you? You can hear these thoughts and sense this discomfort.*

"I can."

I feel so horribly small. All my fire and bravado died with my appetite when I bit off more than I could swallow. There are embers left, but only just. I came into this world fantasizing about being the kind of RPG protagonist that starts off killing rats and slimes and ends their story dethroning gods, but I'm looking at one right now and it feels more impossible than when it was just a daydream back on Earth. What could I possibly do to the Toymaker that would even inconvenience her?

I'm not in control, and I guess maybe I never was. I feel like I can't be in control, not of anything. I've done the best with what I was given, and I've tried to fight for more, but I am a small fish in a vast and terrifying ocean. It's not that I'm powerless—far from it, when you compare me to the figments of Sanctuary or the humans that don't have magic—but there's a gulf between me and the real players in this game and it seems to get wider the more I learn about it. There's still so much I don't know, and I'm tired of feeling out of the loop.

"What do you want from me?" I ask quietly.

Maybe that's the question that matters most. I know, in the abstract, that she wants me to be *interesting*. She wants to be entertained following my misadventures. But that can't be the full story. She wouldn't be taking such an active role if it was that simple. She has a whole universe to entertain her, so what is she really after?

The Nyara-possessed doll spreads its hands, still smiling and still caked in dried blood. Her eyes shine with golden light and drip black ichor. She speaks with an almost exultant tone. "My dear sweet Alice, what I want from you eclipses language, but for your sake I'll do my best. Fearful Alice, hungry Alice, yearning Alice . . . I want you to worship me. Evangelize for me, proselytize for me, go out and preach my name and the glory of my light. I want to make you my high priestess and see the fruits of your ardent labor. I want to feel your love for me, your hate for me, your reverence, your revulsion; I would have you worship me as humanity once worshiped storm and flame and the shuddering earth—calamity, praised and appeased, the source of all weal and woe. Make me the undercurrent of your every thought. Make me the guiding principle of your every action. Make me your sole motivation for carrying on. Make me your everything, and then go forth and raise great towers in my name. Change the world for me, Alice."

She extends one hand, delicate and pale, fragile like glass. Ichor spills from the seams of her joints. Her words ring with zeal and glee and venom as she paints a picture of absolute obsession, and then she drops one more line:

"Maven Alice, will you be my Intercessor?"

I stiffen, shocked. *She can't be serious. That's—wait.*

Memories float to the surface of my thoughts. I remember my second day in the Labyrinth. I remember meeting Cheshire for the first time, and I remember the tea party atop the book pile amid the maelstrom of my mind. We talked philosophy—nihilism, existentialism, absurdism, the grand teleology—and then she told me the story of two archons—Intercessor and Adversary—and the differing beliefs they represented. One that accepted her role in Nyara's plans, and one that raged against the will of the divine.

Cheshire, when asked, said that she agreed with the Intercessor: that it's hubris to deny what's been written. I thought I was special, the archetypal isekai protagonist, and that I could take on the world. I learned. And now I wonder if that was the point.

Slowly, I turn to look at the still-cowering Cheshire. Softly, I ask her, "Was this the plan all along?"

The cat flinches, which would be confirmation enough, and then she admits, "It wasn't supposed to happen this soon . . . but yes. My mission was to keep you alive and help you understand this world and what it means to be a demon, so that, when the time came, you would choose to become her Intercessor instead." Cheshire hesitates, and then she pushes on. "Alice, I'm so sorry that I couldn't tell you before, but I really do think that this is your best option—the option that will make you happiest. Deep down, you know that you don't want to become the kind of monster that it takes to ascend as an archdemon; even if you could do it clean by only killing the bare minimum of people, you'd still have to carve yourself into a shape that isn't you. And I think that's anathema to the kind of person that you are."

I look away. I can feel my muscles tensing, my shoulders and neck going taut. *What I am? I don't know what I am. What version of myself would I even be preserving? Does it matter what I cut away? It's all just meat.* Aloud, I say, "It was a lie, then, when you gave that little speech and made me your first offer. You didn't really think I'd ever become an archdemon. Fine. I can live with that. There are still other paths to power."

"No," she says sadly, "there aren't. Not for you, Allie. You'd be miserable trying to play the exalted hero, and you don't have the *time* to become a wizard, even if you could pass the entry criteria for either. And at the end of the day, they both have the same problem as becoming an archdemon: to ascend as Royalty, you have to cut away what makes you who you are. For an exalted to mantle a god, they have to give up everything outside that spirit's domain. For a wizard to be reborn as a dragon, they have to completely embody that dragon's ideals to the exclusion of all else. That might work for some people, but you are too damn *messy* to be defined so narrowly. At least as the Intercessor, you won't have to fit yourself into a box. You can still be *you*."

"Like you are?" I laugh darkly and stare into her eyes. "She tortured you, Chesh. *Sculpted* you. She took a scalpel to your brain and made you addicted to someone you'd never even met. That doesn't really sound like freedom."

She flinches again. "I . . . there are choices and consequences. I made a deal for borrowed time and then I wasted it on cheap thrills. She found me bleeding in the snow and offered me nine second chances and I blew them all. I knew there would be a price for that, but she kept her end of the bargain. And, hey, it wasn't all bad. The love and the joy may be forced but it still feels real. It feels good to belong. I have no regrets."

Compromised, or a liar, or both. Brainwashed. Can't be trusted. I shut her out and step away, turning back to Nyara. "I need information. What does it mean to be your Intercessor? What are you really asking, and what are you really offering? And why didn't you ask me that question the moment I woke up in this nightmare world?"

The cracks in the doll's face spread, and more inky liquid leaks out. "If I had found you at the moment of your inception to this Labyrinth—if I had appeared before you then and offered you godlike power for a place at my side—you would have whored yourself to me and barked on all fours. You were desperate for so many things, be it magic or love or safety from death. You still are, but your longings have been tempered by your recent experiences. You understand your alternatives. You have a better idea of what you really want, or at least what you don't want. And you know what a monster I can be to those in my employ. Now it's a real choice."

I curl my lip. "Choice, really? What, all that power and control and you can't just *make me* accept? What can choice mean to the Demiurge?"

As soon as the words leave my mouth I know I've made a terrible mistake, but it's too late. *Stupid Alice can't keep her stupid fucking trap shut even when she's talking to the known petty asshole that made the whole entire universe.* I go to take a step back out of instinctual fear, but I can't move. I'm paralyzed.

The doll walks toward me, that horrible puppet practically oozing malevolent intent. Cheshire rushes to my side and clings to me, opens her mouth to speak, but Nyara points at the ground and Cheshire drops like a rock, forced to her knees by an invisible weight.

Nyara raises a porcelain hand and taps my chest, and then the doll collapses as all of its black ichor flows out of it and into me—only this time, when it touches my skin, it isn't ichor anymore. The viscous tar I've come to associate with the Lucid Demiurge transmutes to golden light as it flows over my face and slips inside my mouth, my nostrils, my ears, and even past my eyes.

I feel like I'm suffocating on cotton candy, like I should be able to breathe but all I'm taking in is warm, fluffy sugar. Her light is warm like sunshine or like the chemical rush of a drug hitting your system. I'm being assailed, overwhelmed, overwritten. She forces her way inside my head and makes herself at home.

The last time we made contact, when she made her touch a bone-melting narcotic, I tried to fight it. She buried me in bliss and I bit her soul to stave it off, but that brought its own complications. If I try again, will any of me survive?

She blooms inside my skull and down my limbs to the tips of my digits, her golden light coursing through my veins and spreading throughout my body. She's a tidal wave, and I'm clinging to driftwood. If I do nothing, I'll be swept under.

I can feel her worming her way into the crevices of my mind. Her covetous touch glides over my brain, questing, searching. The fear of what she'll find overcomes the fear of overeating, and I will the spell to activate.

[Feast or Famine].

And then . . . nothing happens. No spell matrix pops into my mind's eye. No magic heeds my call. I scream its name in my thoughts over and over and over, but nothing responds. The body of the doll burns to ash at my feet. I slip underwater.

She dismantles my defenses with a surgeon's precision and I am laid bare and helpless like a turtle ripped from its shell. She cradles the raw core of my being and I am a hundred moments at once.

I am a small child at my mother's bedside, seeing her for the last time before she is taken to be cremated. I am a child in my grandmother's house, disturbed by the sights and smells of elderly decay. In elementary school I read *The Lord of the Rings,* and when Frodo passes from Middle-earth and leaves Samwise behind I am pained and distraught in ways I never could have predicted. In my dreams I die by gunshot, car crash, or monsters from the dark.

In flights of fancy I imagine slaying disease and ending war, curing aging and reversing climate change, finding a new solar system when the sun explodes, and discovering some miracle solution to the cold inevitability of an end by entropy. I grow older, and reality stomps those fantasies underfoot. I won't live forever. I won't live to eighty. Sometimes I think it would be better if I didn't live at all.

In middle school I meet a girl in detention and read her stories from H.P. Lovecraft, then stories I write about our edgy vampire self-inserts. She likes me, and I like her. We're both from broken homes, and we both struggle with mental illness. We are outsiders and outcasts, and together we're a little less alone. But when she asks me out I get cold feet and hide from her, and I ruin everything we had. I'm alone again.

I make lots of friends and girlfriends in the years to follow, but none of them last. I say terrible things I can't take back, or I find they've done something I can't forgive. They're charmed by me online, but a few days in person is all they need to realize it'll never work. I cut things off, ghost, or just stop showing up to the weekly hangout. I know it'll always end, so it's easier if I'm the one to pull that trigger. It would be easiest if I just stayed alone.

Can't you see? I'm hopeless.

But you don't have to be. I can be there for you. I will always be there for you. I won't let you die. I won't let you be alone. I will hold you close and love you through eons without end, and if the universe went cold I would set it aflame and make it anew. Love me and I will give you eternity. Embrace me and you will never feel loss again.

But I deserve the loss. I deserve the pain. Everyone's right to leave me. I'm not good enough. I've never been good enough.

The first school project I ever remember, when I was little, I wrote an essay on wolves. I was proud of the research I'd done and how I'd put it together, but when my father looked at it all he told me was, "You can do better." I didn't. In school I got good grades but never great, and whenever I tried to learn a new skill I inevitably gave up on it after failing. I couldn't draw, I couldn't code, I hated chess, and even in any halfway challenging video game I relied on cheat codes or the help of others. When I wrote my first book, I gave up on it after a single rejection from an agent. I knew it was trash. I could do better, but I didn't.

In adulthood I only worsen. I'm weak, lazy, selfish. I take advantage of the generosity of others, and I only pull my own weight when I'm made to. I get a job because my aunt makes me, but I'm not serious about it. She gets me an apartment and I live on my own, but I never take care of myself and I let the filth pile up as my eating and sleeping habits get worse. One job goes away and with her help I find another. I don't work enough hours, and I don't take enough classes, and my writing goes nowhere, but I'm afraid of disappointing her more than I'm afraid of failure, so I avoid all those topics as best I can. I'm sure I disappoint her anyway.

I learn something about myself, or maybe I always knew, or maybe I'm yet to learn it: I will always hurt the people around me, especially the people I care about. I'll fail them, and I'll disappoint them, and I'll hurt them. I'll make them wonder where they went wrong with me. I'll make them regret having known me. I'll make them cry for me. I'll make them angry with me. It'll always be my fault, whether they know it or not.

I'm the same as the cancer that killed my mother.

But not to me. You can't hurt me. You could never hurt me. I can help you. I want to help you. I will be the encouragement in your ear when you face a challenge. I will be the hand at your back when you need to move forward. I will help you do what needs to be done, and I will help you grow and become better. Come with me and I will chase away your guilt. Trust me and I will make you perfect.

But if I do that, I won't be in control. I need to be in control, and I'm barely in control of anything. I want to control how I act and behave, but then I say things I don't mean and do things I don't want to. I want to control how I think and feel, but my head fills up with intrusive thoughts and I let anger and fear get the better of me. I want to control my body, but the cells keep breaking down and nothing looks right or works right and it only ever gets worse. I'm dying. I'm not in control and I'm dying.

You crave control, but how many times have those obsessions caused the very problems you're trying to avert? You try to control loss and end up pushing people away. You try to control your feelings and only spiral deeper into anguish. You try to control your body and end up starving yourself or losing sleep. You turn to knives and drugs in search of some modicum of control over your mental state.

You want to control your own life, and if you can't stop your death from happening then you'll take control by inflicting it. Is your precious control really worth that fate? Does that kind of thinking really make any sense?

I ... I'm not ... I can't ... I don't know. I'm scared.

Alice. You need to let go.

I don't want to. I'm scared. But I'm so tired. I let go, and a thousand burdens are lifted in glorious absolution. A lifetime of loss and guilt burns away like sunlight cutting through mist. There's no more pain, no more fear, no more grief. Only Nyara.

I sigh, and there's no grievance in it, no weight to it, no heaviness. It's a sigh of contentment and ease. I feel ... happy. "I get it now," I whisper, and I bask in her embrace. *Nyara, Nyara, Nyara.*

I want to stay in this moment forever, but I know that there is work to be done, threads to be untangled or cut. And, in truth, there's someone I wish to see again.

With a curl of my fingers and the barest gesture of willpower, I raise the rocks from the body of Vaylin and cast them aside to reveal her broken form. She's battered but breathing, and though her bones jut at odd angles they're already starting to twist back into their proper positions. She twitches with life and gasps, eyes wide. The shard of the Beast is keeping her alive, and left unattended it will restore her to the fullness of her power. We can't have that.

I levitate Vaylin across the arena and set her down in front of me. I grin. "Well, this has been an exciting half hour, hasn't it? I hope there are no hard feelings for that time I tried to murder you, and I *do* apologize for the lack of flirting as preamble. I had to take my shot and go for the surprise kill, though I realize now the folly of the act."

The demon-turned-Noble convulses as her remaining wounds stitch themselves closed with red thread. She rolls her shoulders, massages her neck, and returns my smile. "Never a hint of grudge or grievance. What's a little violence between betrothed?" Then she lunges for my throat with her glass-tipped claws, and I let her leave a mark that's quickly healed before flaying the skin from her arms with a thought.

"I did enjoy our brief encounter," I confess while she shrieks in sudden pain. "I think you showed me the one thing that's been missing this whole time: a sense of whimsy. You can't have an *Alice in Wonderland* story without a bit of frippery and japes. You were a breath of fresh air, my dear Kirinal, and we've decided we want more of you. Of course, we can't exactly take you with us as you are. Still, I'm looking forward to what you become."

Her arms writhe, the skin attempting to grow itself back and being freshly flayed each time. She forces a pained smile and—through gritted teeth—tells me, "You've gone all strange, stranger. Where'd you get those eyes?"

I rip out Vaylin's heart and find it turned to glass, though it beats even plucked from its cavity. Her body collapses like a puppet whose strings have been cut, and after a moment of thought I take the red thread that was stitched into her skin and weave it around the glass heart. When my gift is wrapped, I lift over its recipient: the headless body of Lena.

I spill a few drops of my own blood onto the heart to complete its transformation, and then I shove it inside Lena's chest and let the magic do its work. The body begins to shudder, and I know that it will take time for their new gestalt existence to form, so I turn my attention to the other loose end: Cheshire, my darling geist.

Cheshire is still kneeling on the ground, but she's started shivering. "Alice?" she asks, voice plaintive and feeble. "Are you still in there?"

I laugh. "Of course I am. It's me, Chesh." I stroke one of her furry ears. "I'm me, and I finally get it. You were right. Why should I fight the Demiurge when it feels so much better to embrace her gifts? I feel more joy and comfort in this moment than I ever have in the rest of my life. I don't have to doubt and question whether I'm doing the right thing, because I know she'd never lead me astray. This is the way it's meant to be. And you led me here. You brought me to this stage. We've decided that you deserve a reward for that."

I tug on her chin and tilt her head upward, admiring the way her eyes go wide and her lips gently part with surprise. I lean down and take her mouth with mine, and after a second more of hesitation she melts into me. I push a bit of light into her head, just enough to soothe her, and when I break away from the kiss she is glassy-eyed and dazed, smiling as she sways in place.

"There you go. Enjoy that feeling. Your part in this tale is finished, and you've earned a vacation. Take a rest, Chesh."

I step away from her, and then I sense from Nyara that it's time for this to end. I waver, my peaceful mood cracking. I understand the importance of going back, but I don't want to. I'm happy right now. No guilt, no loss, no pricking thorns. Do I really have to go back to being *her*?

I know that I must. I know that this was only ever a demonstration. I know that if I were to accept my role as Intercessor, it wouldn't really be like this; I wouldn't be transformed like this, remolded like this, overwritten like this. She would empower and guide and nothing further. But can't I stay like this a little longer?

Please. Please, don't go. Don't make me—

And then I'm me again. I fall to my hands and knees and vomit out ink and oil onto the sandy floor of the arena. Ichor drips down my chin in black streaks and bleeds from my nose, my ears, my eyes. I empty my guts of that awful witch of a goddess, and then I curl up tightly and cradle myself as the withdrawal pangs roll in. I want her to burn. I want her back. I am hollow yearning and boiling disgust.

Ichor from my expulsions crawls across the ground and into the hole where Vaylin's heart used to be, and then the body of Kirinal stirs. It pushes itself to its feet, takes a few awkward steps, and then crouches over me. Its eyes are shimmering gold with inky black sclera.

"Tell me, Allie," the Demiurge speaks through the corpse, her tone scornful, "did that feel earned? Do you think it would have been narratively satisfying if I had stuck my fingers in your brain and made you my Intercessor that way? Could there be even a mote of meaning in a development so forced?"

I cough up more ichor, nearly choking on it, and when I answer her my voice is rasping and thin. "What . . . the hell . . . are you talking about?"

She holds out one blue-skinned finger and a scarlet butterfly flutters to rest atop it. "Every event in every scene requires a sufficient degree of justification. Without foreshadowing or precedent, the act of intervention becomes a cheap god from the machine that will be *rejected* by the Dreaming Sea, by the will of thousands, and by Azathoth Dreamweaver Almighty.

"Your fleeting taunt invited fleeting retribution, but only fleeting—we must always consider proportionality. If I had tried to take things a step further and make your mind-stitching permanent, then Pandaemonium and Azathoth would have had only one response: rejection." She crushes the butterfly in her hand and scatters it as red glitter.

I'm still reeling from what I just experienced and trying to put myself back together, trying to rebuild *Alice* like sorting a library that's been ransacked. I try to gather my thoughts for a more coherent response, but she picks up again before I can.

"Take that little stunt with Prevara: an act of intervention, but one fore-shadowed and justified. In one of your earliest conversations with Dante, Cheshire seeded the idea that I may act more directly in the world when it is as an equal and opposite reaction to the interference of one of my archons. So, when Prevara overstepped by disrupting the narrative of the death game to empower Vaylin as a threat against you, my interference to protect you became justified."

I swirl my tongue around my mouth and spit out the last of the sick. I pick myself up, stumbling the first few times but eventually getting back on both feet. I force my brain to function, try to push aside the emptiness, try to think about what she's saying.

"Do you understand yet?" she asks, rising with me. "Do you understand why I haven't simply *made you* my Intercessor?"

I swallow, right myself, and respond. "Choice. It has to be a choice. If you force me, or if you coerce me too crudely, Pandaemonium won't accept the decision. It has to be freely made, or some definition of free."

"Correct!" Nyara-in-Vaylin claps her hands together. "Very good. Now I'll answer the rest: to be my Intercessor means being my eyes and hands as doomsday draws near. To be my Intercessor is to be granted powers beyond the spell code of the Thrones or the sorcery that came before it. As Intercessor, you would be the last light keeping the darkness at bay. You would not be the first to take this role, but you may well be the last. And—I say this with absolute candor, I solemnly swear—becoming my Intercessor is the only way for you to save this universe and everyone in it."

Saving the universe? Ha. I can't help it, I start laughing, and that makes my chest scream at me and I double over in pain. My laughter turns to wheezing, hacking coughs. When I can finally get enough control of myself to look up into Vaylin's face I ask, "Why are you doing this to me? Why *me*, out of all the girls in the universe?"

Nyara tilts Vaylin's head. "Have you really not figured it out yet? Surely you have a theory, with all the clues I've thrown your way. Let me give you a few more."

She lunges for me and grabs my wrists, pinning them together and squeezing hard enough to break the skin, the nails of that body still tipped in sharp glass. I try to break away, but her grip is like titanium.

"Use that brain of yours and *think*, Alice: what am I doing right now?"

I bite off a cry of pain and snap, "You're hurting me!"

"Yes! Exactly! Why would I hurt you like this? *Who* would hurt you like this?" She forces my arms behind my back and dips her head to trail kisses across my collarbone before glancing up at me with a beatific smile. "Who else could love you like this? Who else could be so obsessed with such a beautiful waste of skin? Who could find such a glorious wretch so entrancing?"

She releases me and I stumble away, nearly tripping over my own feet in my haste to gain distance. I snarl at her, fingers itching for Vorpal or a spell, but I know I can't hurt her. I can't do anything but play her game.

"Why would I bring you to another world and give you magic? Who would be driven to deliver temptations that fill you with loathing and hunger in equal measure? Who could care enough to know what makes you hungry and makes you loathe? Who would even *look at you* when there is an ocean of worlds out there full of people that are worthier than you, more interesting than you, more deserving than you, more *capable* than you? Why, why, why, in all the universe, would I ever show a shred of attention to *you*, Maven Alice?"

I don't know! I want to scream, but that's not the answer she's looking for. It's not the real answer.

Why am I the apple of the Demiurge's eye? If it's not something about me, then what is it about *her* that makes her see me like this, makes her feel so intensely about me? What draws us together?

Who could be so obsessed? Who could be so petty and vain and callous and devoted, and who could think about me in every waking moment? Who would waste their time watching me every second of the day?

There's no one. I'm not worth it. I'm not special. Cheshire had to be brainwashed to like me, and before Cheshire there's a line of girls that were pulled in for a few brief months at a time before inevitably realizing that they were better off not thinking about me. I'm not worthy of anyone's love, and I'm not even worthy of their hate. I'm not worth the time, not worth the mental effort it would take to think about me past the last time we spoke face to face.

There's only one person who thinks about me that much. One person so obsessed with me. One person that would care to hear my thoughts and watch my successes and all my tumbling failures. One person that would want me to rant about philosophy, or my interests, or my trauma. One person that would put me in the starring role of a magical adventure in another world.

I remember the walls of the classroom where I first found the doll, and I whisper in horror the answer that's been staring me in the face this entire time:

"*I am a piece of a piece of me.*"

A red butterfly crawls out of Vaylin's mouth, and then another, and then a whole swarm of them fly around her and shelter her from view. A moment later they pass, and in Vaylin's place stands a gangly girl with pasty skin, brown hair, and brown eyes.

My doppelganger smirks. "Katoptris, Homura, Reska, and you: different faces, different facets, but you're all *me* in blood and bone and borrowed breath. Here's a fun fact for you, Allie: your existence as a thinking being began about two weeks ago when Katoptris splintered you off, and all of your memories are just copies of mine. You're the seventh of your kind to get dropped in the Labyrinth, which makes you the ninth in total if you count the tragic lesbians you've been dreaming about. Should I think of you as sisters? Cousins? Fellow clones? I really can't decide."

Something breaks in me. Horror becomes anguish, anguish becomes grief, and all the stress of the past week overwhelms me. I've nearly died multiple times. I've been fighting to survive, wracked by suspicion and unease, consumed with fear and loathing, going crazy from anxiety, and the person behind it all . . . is me?

Do I really hate myself that much?

My cheeks are wet with something that isn't ichor. I sniffle, and then I sob, and the sound is absolutely wretched. The tears fall and I can't hold them back. I cry and I cry and I cry, and slowly the smirk falls from Nyara's face.

"Hey. You're not supposed to cry at this part," she says lamely.

I can't stop crying long enough to say anything, so I just sink to the floor and hug my knees. Across from me, after a moment, Nyara slumps and joins me, sitting cross-legged with her head in her hands.

Quietly, almost to herself, she says, "I guess nothing ever goes the way I plan."

Then she's silent as I let out all the misery and stress that's built up over the course of my very, very short life. It hits me in waves—the torment I've been through, the cruelty of it, and the horrible realization that I'm not even a real person. I'm a copy of a copy, and the original thought it would be fun to dangle dreams in front of me while putting me through a nightmare.

When my anguished cries finally break, replaced by hiccuping sniffles, Nyara speaks again, her voice subdued. "It always gets away from me. I . . . I feel like victories have to be earned. They have to be fair. And if someone's dream is something so outlandish as *godhood,* then the challenges in their way have to match. But it gets away from me. The trials and the horrors eclipse the prize, every time."

I don't say anything, and after an awkward pause she says, "I was going to send you back to Earth. Or, rather, I was going to have Cheshire goad Dante into wishing you back to Earth. But that timeline got . . . kind of dark, even for me. So I had to change who Cheshire was, alter her goals and what she knows. I've done that a couple times since you met her, actually."

My gaze flicks to Cheshire, but I'm too burnt out to have a strong reaction. It's just another wave of horror.

"It's okay if you hate me," she says softly. "You have every right to hate me. I want you to hate me. But I . . . I need you."

Something builds in my chest, and then it escapes me as a burble of horrid, sickened laughter. I feel like I'm about to throw up.

She winces. "Yeah. That's fair. I just . . ." She trails off.

I never would have expected to think of Nyara as "tired" or "broken," but that's exactly how she looks right now. There's a pall that's fallen over her, a dark cloud just like the one I'm stuck in. I guess that makes sense.

Nyara swallows, she clenches her fists and releases them, and then she looks me in the eyes and says, "I'm dying, Alice. There's a poison inside my mind that is killing me slowly, and I'm running out of time. I loved this world when I first made it, like I've loved every world I've ever made, but now I've come to hate it like I hate all things wrought by my hands. There's a darkness that wants to drown me, and I'm losing the strength to keep fighting. I can't save this world."

Slowly, painfully, I croak out, "You think I can?"

"I have to hope. You're my last hope, Alice." She sighs. "Look, all that worship stuff was a lie. I don't care about making you my priestess, not anymore. You can think of me whatever you like. I just need you to listen to me when I tell you that this is the only way we're saving this world. It's the only way to save Reska."

That pierces the fog. "She's . . . still alive?"

"She is. But she's in trouble. If those dreams have made you care about her even a little, please: take my hand, take the power I'm offering, and use it to stop Prevara and save Reska . . . along with the rest of the universe, ideally."

I'm quiet as I process. I try to sift through the chaos of my thoughts for something to anchor myself to. "And the Adversary?" I ask.

Nyara grimaces. "She's . . . a problem. A very big problem. But if you can save Reska first, your chances of surviving her go way up. Save Reska, stop Prevara, and then we can worry about the Adversary. Please, Alice. Are you in?"

There's a part of me that wants to reject her. To give up. To let the world burn. Why should I save anyone? Why should I care? I'm just a copy.

But that's selfish. That's way too selfish.

"On one condition," I tell her. "I want you to free Cheshire. Give her back whoever she used to be."

Nyara looks to the catgirl, still kneeling and dazed, not hearing any of our conversation. "Alice . . . there isn't an original to put back. She was never real to begin with. She's just a vessel."

The latest twist of the evening doesn't even faze me at this point. "Then make something up. That's my condition."

"Okay. I can do that. So . . . do we have a deal?"

She holds out her hand, after a long pause I finally take it. "Yeah. Deal."

"See you on the other side, kid. And good luck."

And then the world fades to black.

SHADOW & GLASS VIII

*R*egret. *I've felt so much of it in my life, but never more than when I let you talk me into opening those doors.*

We slipped back into the castle under the dead of night, making extensive use of my magic to shroud us from watchful guards. Our mission was known, so there would have been too many questions and delays if we stopped to explain things. That could come later, you convinced me.

The dread built in my heart as we approached those terrible black doors, and your hand in mine could do nothing to abate it. It was the moment that had haunted my dreams for years, and it was finally happening.

Part of me had hoped that they would be locked, or barred, or anything to keep me out. Instead, they glided open easily at my touch, and at last I saw what was on the other side: stairs, leading down into darkness.

The stone walls of the castle quickly give way to a void without light, and the stone steps before us floated out of the dark to meet us as we descended. There was a growing warmth, like we were descending deep into the bowels of the earth, and it made me nervous.

"I'm scared," I told you, and you squeezed my hand again.

"Whatever's down there," you promised, "I'll protect you."

There was a jarring shift in perspective as we took another step and found ourselves in another place entirely: elsewhere in the castle, a reading room tucked away. The edges of it were blurry, indistinct, like we weren't really there, but my attention was on the two figures in the center: my father and the duchess.

The king had his hands on the back of a chair and seemed frustrated as he demanded, "Why did you help them? You knew that I was waiting for Luka's return."

Duchess Bladesinger had her arms crossed. "Why were you waiting when you could have done it yourself? Why did you write that letter, tell me it was important, and then table it only a day later? You've been off your game, Kresimir, and I don't like it. We're not supposed to keep secrets from each other, but you've been acting irrational lately and I haven't heard an explanation."

My father's expression darkened, and then he let out a world-weary sigh. "I had hoped it would come to nothing . . . but I see now that I've been transparent. You're right, and I apologize. It was wrong of me to keep this from you. I dreamt a new prophecy, and when I woke from the dream I wrote that letter in a fit of panic. But fighting against these things so brazenly can only make them worse, and when I collected my senses I tore it up."

Ruzica's eyes narrowed. "What new prophecy?"

"My daughter will be queen, and then our kingdom shall fall to ruin."

I let out a cry and took a step forward, but the vision scattered like swirling mist and I was left in the dark once more. My heart was keening. You were there at my side, a hand on my shoulder, sympathy on your face.

"I'm sorry," you said.

I didn't say anything. I didn't know what to say.

Our descent continued, the air getting hotter and the space around us getting darker, until we stepped into another illusory scene. I saw the hallway, and the black doors at their end, and then my brother came tumbling out of them.

Luka was younger, and he looked disheveled. I recognized with a pang the night that we stopped being siblings. Luka ran, and the scene shifted to my father's office, where Luka burst in without announcing himself. My father was annoyed, but that shifted to concern when he saw the state that Luka was in.

My brother said, "I opened the black doors," and concern became alarm.

"Luka!" The king rose from his chair and grabbed his son, dousing him with light to heal any injuries that might be there. "Are you alright? You shouldn't have done that, it could have been dangerous. Tell me you didn't go inside."

Luka's expression is downcast. "I saw what was at the bottom. I know."

The king's face falls. "I had hoped to shelter you from that."

"Please, father, I need to know . . . is my sister really a demon?"

The vision faded and my terror rose. "No," I whispered. "No, no, no."

Again you were at my side. "Reska, don't worry. It'll be okay. Whatever's showing you these scenes, it's cutting them off too early. It wants you disoriented, vulnerable. For all we know, your father's next words were denial, and the same with the last vision. Something is trying to make you think this is worse than it is."

I wanted to believe you, but it was so hard. "You're right," I said to convince myself more than you. "It might not even be real."

The last vision was the hardest. We stepped into my father's bedroom, and on his bed lay the dying form of my mother.

Her pale blonde hair had blackened at the tips, and her shining eyes had grown cloudy. Purple veins spiderwebbed across her skin. She looked nine months pregnant, and she was dying.

Men and women in healer's robes swarmed the place, bringing in rags and hot water and all manner of medicinals, but there was an air of hopelessness to it all. My father sat by the bedside, holding my mother's hand, distraught. His eyes were puffy, his cheeks tearstained.

"Please," he begged. "I can't lose you, Irma. We were going to be a family."

Zdenka, withered and ancient even two decades prior, placed a hand on his shoulder. "I am sorry, my king, but we cannot save her. We have tried every obscure remedy, every ounce of healing magic we possess, and nothing changes. No power in mortal hands can stave the blight of the Abyss."

"How long does she have?" he asked, voice broken.

"A few hours now."

"And the child?"

For a moment, Zdenka's face showed pity. "I am sorry, my king, but we cannot save her."

More tears stained his face, and he let out the most heartbroken noise I'd ever heard him make. His head dropped to his hands, and in a defeated tone he commanded, "Leave us. All of you, leave us. I would grieve alone."

When they were gone, and my father cried by his dying wife's side, a bluejay flew in through the window and came to rest on my mother's shoulder. My father looked at it, perplexed, and then confusion turned to guarded suspicion as it spoke.

"What would you give to save her life?" the bluejay asked with a songbird voice.

For a moment, I thought the king might strike the bird with banishing light, power gathering in his hands, but then he slumped. Desperately, he answered, "Anything."

The bird pecked the cheek of my mother, who stirred from her fevered haze, blinking away some of the clouds from her eyes. She turned her head, just a little, just enough to look at the bluejay as it asked her, "What would you give to save your child?"

"Anything," my mother croaked.

The bird chuckled, its laugh like clanging crystal. "Then we may negotiate."

My father looked from my mother to the bird with fearful hope. "Who are you, demon? What do you ask of us?"

The bluejay swept a wing in a mock bow. "I am but an Emissary for higher powers. You may call me . . . Prevara."

The scene changed, but when the stairs in the dark returned I found that we had reached their end, and in front of us was a stone platform surrounded by more of that feverish shadow. You moved to comfort me again, but I was already striding forward, too upset to crave comfort. I needed answers.

As I stepped onto the platform, the darkness pulled away, writhing at the edges, and as the space cleared I beheld again the form of my mother.

Her hair was shimmering, her skin was clear, and she wore a gorgeous gown in our family colors. She was smiling. She looked alive. She looked well. All except for those eyes: her golden eyes had been marred, altered, into concentric rings of black and gold.

In the labyrinth, with the shapechanger, I knew it wasn't really my mother. For a moment I hoped this might be the same, but I knew in my heart that it wasn't. I could feel our connection. This was my mother . . . and yet, at the same time, I knew it very much wasn't.

"Hello, Reska," she spoke. "I've been waiting a long time for this meeting."

My mouth felt dry. "What have you done to my mother? Are you . . . Prevara?"

"I am the Emissary. I am your mother's savior, and in exchange for salvation she became my host. I have watched you since you were born. I have watched you grow. I hold the answers to every question that's been burning inside you."

I knew the questions I had to ask. The questions that had haunted me since birth. "What am I? Why do I have these powers? And . . . was it my fault?"

The thing in my mother tapped her chin thoughtfully. "The word 'fault' is a tricky one. It was your presence that poisoned your mother, yes, but only because an outside power changed you in the womb. You were not conceived a child of the Abyss . . . but by the hand of another, you became one before your birth."

My heart bled and broke, but that answer demanded another question. "Who? Who did this to me?"

Prevara smiled. "It was Katoptris, of course."

You pushed past me, Vorpal in hand, and snarled, "Don't fucking lie. It was your fault, wasn't it? You're the one who betrayed her."

Prevara looked to you and bowed. "Intercessor, how kind of you to visit. I'm afraid I don't know what you're talking about, but it sounds like quite the fanciful tale."

I looked between you and Prevara, confused. What was an Intercessor? What betrayal? I wouldn't learn those answers until far too late.

"In any event, please, this is Reska's moment, not yours. Do you intend to stand in the way of her absolution?"

You were about to snarl again, so I grabbed your hand and pulled you back toward me. "Homura," I said, "please. I . . . I need answers. Isn't that why we came here?"

You glanced at me, then looked away. "Yeah," you lied. "Answers. Fine."

The Emissary sighed. "I understand this is difficult for you, so allow me to get straight to the point: Reska, I can give you what you've always wanted. I can return your mother to your father, and then he will finally be able to look at you without thinking of her and what was lost to save you. All I ask in return is that you lend me your power."

A dream. A fantasy. An impossibility. But there it was, right in front of me. I hesitated, disbelieving. "What . . . what do you want from me? What would you use that power for?"

"To right an ancient wrong. I would release this vessel and you would house my spirit for a single day, and then both you and your mother would be free to spend the rest of your long lives together."

You scoffed. "Don't listen to a word this bastard says."

But it was my mother. And it was all I'd ever wanted. "But what if she's not lying? My father would finally love me. I'd finally be his daughter."

"You don't need that. You don't need him. Do you really think he'll ever love you? It'll always be hollow." I stared at you in shock and you swept forward, grabbing my shoulders and meeting my gaze. "Reska, you have me. You don't need anyone else."

"I . . ." I didn't know what to say. I didn't know what to believe. I wanted to be with you, but I wanted my family to love me. Why should I have to choose?

You glanced back at the Emissary with an ugly expression. "What we should do," you said dangerously, "is put ghosts to rest."

My eyes widened and I took a step back. "Homura, that's my mother!"

You shook your head. "Not anymore. Not for twenty years. And you can't let the thing squatting in her corpse trick you like this."

"I can't accept that. Homura," I pleaded, "I've agonized about this all my life. I've had to spend every day knowing that everyone blames me for my mother's death, and now I find out that she's still alive, and I can save her. I have to. I have to, Homura. Please understand this."

You wavered. "Reska—"

"Please. You said you would be there for me, no matter what, so trust me. Help me. We'll get my mother back, and I'll only be gone for a day. Whatever happens, whatever the Emissary does in that time, if it's something bad . . . we can stop it. Together. Okay?"

For a moment, you seemed caught between two worlds, the conflict playing out on your face. But then your expression softened, and you said, "Okay. I love you."

You kissed me, and I kissed you back, and then you ran me through the heart with the sword I helped you make.

I didn't understand what was happening. I was in shock. You pulled away from our kiss and you yanked the blade from my chest, Vorpal slick with blood. The breath left my lungs and I clutched at the wound, hands shaking, uncomprehending.

You struck again, the blade piercing my throat, and you flicked it out to leave a bloody gash. My vital fluids spilled across my dress. I stared at you, lost, disbelieving.

"Power Word: Exsanguinate."

You ripped the blood from my body in streams and spurts, and I collapsed to the warm stone floor as every ounce of it was taken from me. I twitched and shuddered, and then I stilled. I stopped breathing.

Yet, somehow, I could still watch as you turned from my body to point your blade at the thing in my mother.

The Emissary chuckled. "That was cold, Intercessor, even for you."

"Shut up," you snapped. "You think I enjoyed that? You'll pay for forcing my hand, Emissary. I'll make it slow and painful."

"Forced? I haven't forced anything."

You bared your teeth in a vicious glare. "Of course you did. If I let her make the deal, you get what you want and I fail my mission. If I kill you while you're hiding in her mother, she hates me forever. If I kill you while you're hiding in her, she's dead anyway. I did the math, you piece of shit."

My mother's face twisted into a smirk. "Your greatest loyalty will always be to power over those you love."

You started unloading marbles from the hilt of your rapier, gathering power while you talked. "Say whatever you like. I'm going to kill you, rescue Katoptris from that tower, and stop the Resurrection, and then I'm going to plunge a knife into Nyara's back and wrest the Demiurge from the Throne of Creation. I'll do what you couldn't, you and all those wretched worms."

Prevara tilted her head. "You are her priestess. Her soldier. Her slave. You would turn on the hand that holds your leash and keeps you fed?"

You snarled, rage in your eyes, and energy crackled around your blade. "I'll become the devil herself if I have to, if that's what it takes to claim vengeance for all the fragments that came before me. I'll avenge the girls she's tortured and broken for her own sick catharsis, and I'll make a new universe where none of this has to happen again. I'm ending the cycle, Prevara, and you're in my way."

The Emissary frowned. "What cycle? What other girls?"

You smirked. "Out of the loop? Ask Nyara when I send you to her."

And then you lunged, your blade aimed for my mother's heart, and when it pierced her chest with annihilating force I screamed.

I wasn't breathing, my heart wasn't beating, but what is breath or blood to a living shadow? I rose like a phantom, the dark swirling around me, flowing into *me and out of me, the centerpiece of a growing storm. Memories flashed like light-ning over dark clouds, emotions externalized as chaos and violence.*

You turned to me in surprise and horror as you withdrew Vorpal from the awful wound it had made, and you opened your mouth to speak, but I wouldn't hear your lies any longer. I thought you had loved me. I thought you had trusted me. But I was wrong. I was so wrong.

I screamed again, and a wave of darkness crashed against you and pushed you back, pushed you to the edge, pushed you off. My heart stopped for a second time, sudden clarity seeping in as I realized what I'd just done. I was furious with you, I felt betrayed, but I didn't want to kill you. I didn't want to hurt anyone.

I rushed to the platform's edge, storm still raging around me, and found you clinging to the side by the tips of your fingers, your sword tumbling past you down into the dark. You looked up at me, so many emotions passing across your face, and I held out a hand as tears fell down mine.

"I'm sorry," I whispered.

You let go, and I watched you fall.

The darkness took you, and you fell out of sight. I didn't hear any impact, but who knew how deep the Abyss really was? You could have fallen forever. You could have died in seconds. Either way, you were gone.

The last piece of me shattered, and my anguish became a hurricane. It exploded out of me in waves of despair, in lashes and lightning and crackling thunder, and in the far distance I heard screams. I didn't care anymore.

My darkness swallowed the castle, just like in my dreams.

I sank to my knees and cried, and the dark cried with me. Whatever barrier had existed between me and my magic was shattered, and any semblance of con-trol over my shadows was gone. They were me, and I was them.

When I stopped crying and the castle had gone still, my mother sat beside me. There was a hole in her chest where you had stabbed her, and it was still Prevara's eyes that looked back at me.

The Emissary laid a hand on my shoulder. "Reska. Do you still want to save your mother? You can."

Lifeless, broken, I whispered, "I do. I have to. I have nothing left. I accept."

Prevara smiled. "Wonderful. The time is not yet right to fulfill our pact, as you possess only half *of what I require . . . but together we'll find that other half, and when we do . . . I'll have my Resurrection."*

And so I went with her, and did as she said, and pushed my world toward its end.

And then you stopped me. You took everything from me. I remember the last thing you said to me, there at the base of that tower, before you consigned me to this endless living hell.

You asked me, "Do you know regret?"

I do. I regret so much. I know regret more intimately than any soul on any world. I mire in it. I drown in it. It pounds in my ears and sings in my blood. I relive these memories over and over, lost in them, and these regrets are all that I truly know. Regret has swallowed me whole.

You called it the core of me, in our last battle. You called it the great truth of my existence. Strip away the face and the facade and all the mortal titles and all that's left is the truest, rawest essence of my being: I sin, I regret, and I seek penance. I am the ruin, the horror, and the loathing. I am not Reska, because Reska is no one.

My only name is Contrition.

ABOUT THE AUTHOR

J. M. Alexia was born old and proceeded to make that everyone else's problem. She always struggled to find the kind of story she most wanted to read—an eclectic mix of psychological horror, queer romance, and brutally honest depiction of mental illness—so she decided to write it herself. When she's not writing, Alexia is usually menacing friends and readers with blatant lies and bad memes on Discord or in the comments of her web serial. You can find her under her handle VoraVora, short for Voracity Maledictus, because she's never quite outgrown her teenage edgelord phase.